To Be Continued

To Be Continued

BOOK ONE

GRACE WOODS

PURPLE INK
LLC

SHERIDAN, WY

To Be Continued

Copyright © 2023 by Grace Woods and Purple Ink LLC
All rights reserved under International and Pan-American Copyright Conventions.

Published by

PURPLE INK LLC

1309 Coffeen Ave.
Sheridan, WY 82801

Library of Congress   2023909821
ISBN 979-8-9884133-0-1 (print)
ISBN 979-8-9884133-1-8 (ebook)

Author's Note:

Welcome to *To Be Continued*, a racy and inspiring trio of books. It's so exciting to share them with you. Just a heads up, in this love story there are mentions of sexual assault and gun violence, and there's an accidental injury. There's also chemistry so hot the periodic table blushes.

You're in for a joy ride.

I T'S TIME TO MAKE A *difference.*
Ashley Barris walked into the dimly lit high school classroom where she taught, radiant with purpose. It didn't matter the walls were stained, the tables carved, the chairs breaking down. She loved this room where magic happened, where
young people learned to overcome problems using chemistry—
and there were big problems to overcome. The morning news
had her galvanized.

Out of habit, she looked at the poster on the wall across from
her desk. *Think like a proton, stay positive.*

She twisted her long honey-brown hair into a low, messy
knot, fixed it with a pencil, then walked to the closet where she
kept her white lab coat. After covering up her cream blouse and
blue pencil skirt, she caught her reflection in the small magnetic
mirror inside the door. She was no knockout, but she liked what
she saw. Brown eyes. Clear skin. A woman who worked hard to
do her best. *Hence the bags under my eyes.*

"You can sleep in tomorrow," she promised her reflection.
"But today, make it fun, make it matter."

She walked to the closet marked *Dangerous Chemicals* and
began her first-period prep. Just as she finished, students crashed
into the room, a human wall of backslapping and screeching.

This was her smallest class, twenty-five kids. And today, the last day before spring break, their usual racket had magnified.

She cleared her throat, then said in a voice only slightly louder than the hubbub, "Why do chemists like *nitrates*? Pete?"

Pete shrugged. Ashley waited as the class settled. "Because they're cheaper than *day rates*."

"Ohhh," the class groaned. Ashley flashed them a lopsided smile.

"Today, a change in the syllabus," she announced. "Based on yesterday's events in the Gulf of Mexico, we're going to simulate an oil spill. We'll determine which sorbents best absorb oil from fresh and salt water, and we'll see just how easy or not it is to 'clean' an oil spill."

Especially when it's three and a half million gallons.

She'd already left a message at her senator's office this morning suggesting new legislation for oil companies. But teaching these kids was her long game.

As usual, half her students looked bored already, but the other half—Ashley saw in them curiosity and passion that mirrored her own.

Like a proton, Ashley.

She stood taller and began talking them through the lab.

———

Eight, nine, ten, eleven, twelve. Ashley smiled to herself as she got to the top step of the wide stairwell in the bookstore. She'd guessed twelve steps, and it gave her a small hit of pleasure to be right.

She browsed the new staff favorites, then walked to the back wall, set her armful of books on top of a freestanding shelf, and knelt to find this month's book club selection. There, on the bottom: *The Path to Love.* It was an older self-help/psychology book by Deepak Chopra, but one of the women in her club insisted some members needed its wisdom.

Like me.

Ashley's path to romantic love seemed mostly made of obstacles. There was a reason books were her favorite dates. They didn't drink too much, didn't spend her money, didn't cheat on her.

One copy left. Still kneeling, she read the back cover, then scanned the chapters, feeling skeptical until her eyes rested on lines that sang true:

> *energies that make us act out of anger, fear, insecurity and doubt...are like an old, dark house we return to whenever things get too hard to handle.*

She deflated with self-recognition. *Do I really want to hide in an old, dark house? Guess I'll read the book.* She felt a tingling, as if butterflies were landing on her bare arms. Unnerved, she moved to stand and was surprised to find two strong legs in tight jeans beside her. She let her gaze travel up the thick, muscled thighs to the trim waist. Up the dark gray Henley to the strong jaw, the smooth, full lips. At last, her eyes met the man's eyes, twin windows of midday sky.

Well, hello.

A rogue smile curled up his cheek, as if he were keeping a delicious secret. Her lungs tightened, apparently forgetting what to do after the inhale.

What was it about this man? Something beyond the lustrous loose curls of raven hair, beyond his olive-skinned face, his eyes sparkling with amusement. He had pure sexual allure. A predatory confidence. And something else...a total lack of arrogance. Her stomach felt as if a star had just exploded inside it and the light was trying to escape through her fingertips.

To her dismay, she watched his smile grow, as if he were amused that she was checking him out.

Oh my god, I did just check him out. An embarrassed blush began in her chest and quickly bloomed up her neck.

"Excuse me." His voice was like black coffee with sugar—strong, warm, smooth. "Didn't mean to startle you."

He made a move to be closer to her. She stiffened. *What is he—?* Then she realized, almost disappointed, he wasn't getting close to *her* but to the low shelf beside her. She watched as he scanned the spines. Something in her told her to stand, but a louder voice overrode the impulse, and she stayed where she was, almost hypnotized, pretending she was looking at the book in her hand.

"Oh," said the man, noticing the book Ashley was holding. "That's the book I'm here for, too."

He was going to read *The Path to Love*? Not the title she would have expected a thirty-something professional alpha-looking man to read. "I would've pegged you for John C. Maxwell or Tom Clancy."

Why did I say that?

"I see." Somehow, the dark velvet in his voice turned the two syllables into a full-blown erotic sonnet. As if with his words alone, he could undo the buttons of her blouse.

"I, um, I got the last copy."

What? I never "um."

Ashley looked at the empty space on the shelf, then back to the man. She fought the urge to hand the book to him. *He probably expects me to give it to him, like I'm some pushover—*

"I'll just have to order a copy, then," he said, rising. "That's all right. I'm not in a hurry. I hear it's a long path."

Ashley narrowed her eyes in confusion.

"A long path to love," he clarified. He extended his hand to help her up. "Hand?" Ashley couldn't help but notice how he *moved*—graceful, totally at home in his body.

"Thanks, I've got it." She drew in a steadying breath, then rose on her own, grateful she was wearing flats. Something about this man made her feel off-balance. Standing, he was eight or nine inches taller than she was, probably just over six feet. She caught herself studying how his ribbed shirt hugged the strong planes of his chest. Her breath frayed, turning thready and shallow. *What is this man doing to me?* She stood taller and straightened her skirt.

"So," the man drawled, looking into Ashley's eyes, "read me a passage? Something to inspire me until my book comes in?"

Ashley wondered if he was teasing her, but his expression was sincere.

"Um, okay." She scanned the book, cleared her throat for effect, then read aloud:

> *Every time you are tempted to react in the same old way, ask if you want to be a prisoner of the past or a pioneer of the future.*

"I know which one I'd rather be."

"Mr. Pioneer, I presume?"

The man angled his head gently and nodded.

"Me, too. I'm just not sure reading this book will make much of a difference."

"You know what they say." His eyes danced with mischief. "If you fail, it's not the book's fault. You can only blame your *shelf*."

"Ooh," Ashley moaned. "For a pun like that, I'm going to have to *Dewey decimate* you."

The man faked a crumple, as if she had punched him in the gut, his eyes never leaving hers. Then he rose to full height, and Ashley shuddered as warmth sizzled down her spine.

For a moment, they stared at each other, a giddy ebullience blossoming between them, a fragile connection built out of bad pun comradery, the thrill of finding another book lover—and something else. Something sensual and mysterious. It felt so good Ashley almost overrode the warning bells clanging in her pulse. But the bells were there for a reason. Her mouth felt dry. She should walk away now. Mr. Wrong always met her wearing a Mr. Right suit to start. She added *The Path to Love* to her stack of books and moved to pick them all up.

"Considering I already know you have fine taste in books, mind if I ask what else you're reading?"

Ashley thought a moment about her selections and felt a bit self-conscious, but what did it matter? She'd never see him again. "Ah, sure." The man took a step closer, and he fanned out her books.

"*The Peru Reader*," he read, pulling it off the top. "*Divorce Recovery*." He nodded. "*The Headache Healer's Handbook* and *The Chronology of Water*."

Ashley summed up in her head what her books said about her—a divorced traveler in her early thirties who gets migraines and loves reading about other people's messed-up lives.

"Do you read them sequentially?" he asked. "Or all at once?"

What an interesting question. "All at once. I like the way the books speak to each other through me."

"Like a symphony," he agreed. "The way all those instruments, so different from each other, make incredible, soaring music when played together."

"Yeah." Ashley nodded, oddly mesmerized by the way this man thought, how he articulated her experience. A pleasant heat rose in her. She didn't try to tamp it down.

"How about you, Mr. Pioneer," she teased, her words coming out breathier than she meant them to. "I showed you mine. Show me yours?" The flirty question was out before she could stop it, and she bit her tongue too late.

Why am I acting like this? She reprimanded herself even as she leaned closer to him to see his book selections. As she breathed in his faint masculine smell—*mmm, citrus, amber, musk*—a sweet giddiness shimmied in her belly. She felt an urge to touch his arm, then stopped herself.

He rotated the books, showing off each cover with a Vanna White flourish of his hands. Ashley read the titles aloud. "*Why Do I Do That? Understanding Our Actions, Understanding Our Past* and *Zero Hour.*" She looked up at his dancing eyes. The bottom book had Tom Clancy's name in bright orange letters across the top.

"Guess I'm not as unpredictable as I thought." The corners of his mouth tilted up, and Ashley longed to press her lips to that smile, to taste his delight. *What the hell, Ashley?* Her pulse quickened, and her heart knocked hard against her chest. She felt the urge to run, but as she gathered her books, she found moving away from him impossible.

What would it feel like to whisper my fingers across that cheekbone?

"Hey." His smile shined through in his eyes as he extended his hand toward hers. "I'm Luke."

Ashley stepped toward him again to slip her hand into his, and she had the feeling that if she succumbed to his gravitational pull, she'd never manage the escape velocity to get back out. "Ashley," she replied, willing her voice to be strong and professional.

She was proud of her handshake: grip firm, pump twice, look the other person in the eye. Her mother had made her practice until she got it right. *If you're going to get ahead, Ashley, you need to make a good impression. You need to shake hands like a confident woman.*

When Ashley's palm met Luke's, she nearly jumped. *Like a match to benzene.* Her skin burned as Luke held her hand a few seconds longer than he should have. Or was it that *she* held *his* hand too long?

Despite the feeling she might combust, it almost hurt to pull her hand away. If her hand had been in charge, it would have continued to explore him to see what other reactions were possible—would have traced up his arm to explore the calculus of his muscled shoulders, traveled up to his cheek to study the angle of his jaw, slipped behind his neck to analyze the sine waves of his sleek hair. She returned her hand beneath her books, as if to keep it in check.

"Ashley," he repeated, tasting her name as if it were fine wine on his tongue and he was admiring its finish and undertones. "I was just going for a cup of coffee downstairs. Join me?"

Ashley shifted a bit, then looked at her watch as if considering his offer. It was just before five. She did, in fact, have time for coffee before meeting her friend for a drink at six. What should she do? Her body was suddenly hyperaware of everything—the chatter of women a couple of rows over, Luke's strong forearms exposed beneath his rolled-up sleeves, how her own skin felt suddenly too tight for her chest.

"Oh, no. Thank you." *Why are you saying no?*

"What, did my self-help book scare you away?"

More like I want to lunge at you.

Ashley hesitated. "We all need a helping hand, Luke." She said his name purposefully, cementing it in her memory. As if she could forget it. "It's just that I've made other plans."

And because you scare me. You're too charming. Too funny. Too handsome. Too sincere. Too clever.

No. Luke didn't scare her. Her reaction to him did.

He lifted his shoulder in a playful shrug. "Sometimes other plans get in the way of our lives."

Was that an admonishment? A regret in the making? A lesson in philosophy? Encouragement to change her mind about coffee? But Luke's tone didn't seem to express anything but genuine disappointment.

"Maybe we could meet another time?" She could almost taste the dark honey in his voice.

"I'm going to be gone for a while," Ashley hedged.

"I see." He nodded, a curious look in his eye. Ashley imagined women didn't turn him down often. "I can wait."

"Well, I'll be gone a really long time."

"Will your number work when you return from wherever you're going?"

Ashley bit her lip and said nothing.

"Okay, I understand. You don't want to give me your number. Too bad for me."

"Nice to meet you, Luke." She willed an air of self-control into her voice. "Sorry about taking the only *Path to Love*." Then she blushed a little, realizing what she'd said.

"Maybe there's more than one path to get to the same place." Luke grinned, openly teasing her. "I *am* slightly wounded, but I believe in collaborating with fate. Don't worry about me. Clancy and I will have fun hanging out for the next few nights. I'll be all right."

Is he making that up? Surely someone that attractive didn't spend his nights curled on the couch with a book.

"Nice to meet you. Ashley." The way he said her name threw her off-balance, as if Houston had just had its first earthquake. He smiled and turned toward the staircase.

Ashley didn't even try to take her eyes off him as he walked away. His gait was smooth, his posture straight. He had an economic grace—as if he always landed on his feet—and he was just so *male.*

What is your deal, Ashley? Her mouth was slightly open, her chest was pounding, and she was panting. Every textbook cliché about falling for someone was physically manifesting in her body.

And you just told him goodbye.

What was it he said? *I believe in collaborating with fate?* Who said stuff like that? She leaned against the bookcase and let it hold her up. That five-minute interlude had exhausted her. And supercharged her. She replayed it in her mind. His lively eyes. His hypnotic scent. The sense he kept his power in check. What would it be like to kiss him? Would he be tender? His lips were so full, so generous. She imagined him touching them to her lips, like a sojourner just arriving at a shrine, then pulling her into a crushing embrace. She imagined his hands kneading into her back, his fingers fanning out over the place her wings would be. Would he gaze at her while kissing her the way he'd gazed at her while they spoke, as if she were the only thing in the universe that mattered in that moment? Or would his eyes close as he focused on the warmth and wetness of her mouth?

Her body was buzzing, aching with want. How long had it been since she'd kissed someone? A year? More. But it wasn't just his body she was remembering and the fantasy of a kiss; it was the growing feeling, even after his departure, that he had *seen* her. He'd asked her out.

And you, Ashley Barris, you retreated into the old, dark house of fear and said no.

"Here's the star teacher." John Truman rose from a table by the window in one of their favorite Mexican restaurants. They hugged, and he pulled out her chair. "Hope your day was less stressful than mine. These kids!"

He crossed his eyes and grimaced, but Ashley knew he cared about "these kids" as much as she did, and she loved that about him. Other single teachers whispered in the lounge about his square jaw, racy blond hair. But it was John's lighthearted goodness that drew Ashley in—his laughing brown eyes, his sincere, goofy smile. And most of all, she loved that beneath his tough principal act, John was a softie who would do anything for students.

Ashley shrugged. "The day before spring break is always high-energy."

"Yeah, well, I spent the day with kids high in *other* ways."

"Oh, John." She shook her head. "No wonder you were so keen to go out."

Sueño was casual, so John stood out in his charcoal suit and loosened tie. Ashley supposed she stood out with her attire, too. They were alike that way—though John sported Italian designers and she wore TJ Maxx, they both liked to dress professionally for school. She wondered again how a principal managed to buy such fine threads. He didn't live high—made his own PB&Js for lunch and lived in a modest neighborhood. He did, however, drive a newer Porsche. Said it was a gift for doing someone a "grand favor."

The waitress arrived with margaritas, frozen for her, on the rocks for him, both with chili salt. Ashley shot John a quizzical look. He held up his hands innocently. "I figured you'd like the same as usual."

Of course, he knew what she liked. They went out every month or so—always platonic, though sometimes Ashley wondered if she were prettier or had a better figure, whether John might see her as more than a friend. They were both early thirties, both single, and sometimes she thought they might have chemistry.

Regardless, she was grateful he hadn't asked her out. He was wonderful, but she wasn't interested in a relationship, especially not with someone at school. And she liked having a male friend—it was unusual for her to trust men, but she trusted John.

"I like the way you think, Mr. Truman." Ashley lifted her glass. "To vacation."

"To vacation," he echoed, clinking his glass to hers. "Remind me of your plans?"

"Oh! I'm going to Telluride with my book club. In a private plane!"

"Really?" He leaned in with a giant smile. "Tell me about it."

"My friend Jamila and her husband have a house there with enough beds to sleep all eight of us and a private plane, too—can you imagine? I've barely even ridden on a plane. My usual vacation is driving to my aunt's house in west Texas."

"Telluride sounds great! But"—he gave her a quizzical look—"you're *skiing*?"

"I mean, the rest of the women are skiing, but John, you know I've barely even seen snow before." Every time she thought about it, she felt like a little girl on Christmas Eve. "Mostly, I just want to put my hands in it. And eat it. And make a snowman. I even bought mittens. And a hat. And boots." *And blew my budget.*

"Meg's in your book club, right? Is she going, too?" He referred to an English teacher at their school, one of Ashley's close friends.

"Yeah, she'll ski. Meanwhile, I'll focus on happy hour."

"Just don't go falling for a snowboarder and moving to the mountains. We need you here."

"You know I'd never leave our school, John, not even for a snowboarder. But—" She took a steeling breath. "—I hear rumors about budget cuts. Should I be worried?"

"So, it's true." His face drained of humor. "There's a huge deficit for next year—and this will mean, among other things, a reduction in staff."

Ashley's chest tightened. *I can't lose my job. How would I pay my bills?*

"Letters go out early June. You're one of our best teachers, Ashley, and there'd be a mutiny if you left, but you *are* newer, and, well, you're right to be concerned."

"Reducing staff." A bitter tone crept into her voice. "It's hard enough with classes of almost thirty. What now, classes of sixty? Does anyone out there care about these kids and their education?"

Concern clouded John's face, too. "No one feels good about what's happening, Ashley."

Ashley slumped in her chair. "I love my students, John. I love teaching. As hard as it is, as little as it pays, it's my calling."

"I know." His tone was sympathetic. "And the fact you had other more lucrative options after grad school and still chose to teach…" She shrugged, but he pressed on. "Your passion for helping kids is something I deeply respect about you."

Whatever buzz Ashley felt from the margarita was gone. She was numb, as if some piece of her had torn and raveled.

"Look, Ashley. We don't know anything yet. There's nothing to be done now."

Oh yes there is. First-mover advantage. "I should start sending out my resume tomorrow."

"Don't panic. I'll do what I can to help."

"I appreciate that, John, but I need to be sure I have work. It's how I am." She took a deep breath. "In fact, I already have another possibility in place."

"That's Ashley doing what Ashley does, staying ahead of the game."

"Excuse me," said one of the women at the table next to them, thrusting her phone at John. "Would you mind taking our picture?"

While John clicked some pics, Ashley found her mind wandering again to Luke. She held her fingers to her nose, wondering if any of his scent managed to linger there. *Nothing.* Her lower belly clenched when she thought of his heart-shaped chin, his strong uncalloused hands holding hers. How his whole face lit up when he laughed. His expressive eyes, his soft, deep voice, the explosive chemistry, his wit. *Some get hot for pecs. I get hot for puns.* Well, pecs, too. And the way his jeans fit over his thighs. And how he clutched his books as if they were precious. She could imagine—

"Ashley?" John's voice loudened. "Ashley?"

"Sorry." She felt as if she'd been caught reading a romance book behind *American Scientist.* "What are you doing for break, John?"

As John outlined his plans, she nodded and hmmed, but her mind was a few blocks away from their little table. She was sitting on the floor in the bookstore, thinking about a pioneer and repeatedly beating herself up for not saying yes to coffee, for not giving him her number, for sticking with her *other plans.*

CHAPTER 2

"YOU CAN UNBUCKLE YOUR seat belts and relax, ladies," the captain crooned over the loudspeaker in a strong Southern drawl. "We're going to have a smooth trip to Telluride. Scheduled flight time is two hours and forty-eight minutes. Enjoy the flight."

"Break out the bubbly!" shouted Jamila. She waved to the stewardess. "Stacy? Pull out the champagne and San Pellegrino, please."

The stewardess distributed crystal flutes amongst the eight members of the book club. Ashley and Meg relaxed together in the third row in generous cream-colored seats, same hue as the walls and carpet.

Jamila stood in the aisle and raised her glass. "To my besties and a great time in the mountains."

"To my sisters and the best book club ever," Claire added.

"And to a much-needed vacation," Meg chimed in. They raised glasses and clinked with the women beside them.

Ashley loved these women. Claire was the lead graphic designer for a marketing firm. Aziza had narrowly escaped with her life from the Sudanese civil war. Jamila was a historic preservation architect in the wards. Sarah left her legal career to be a stay-at-home mom. Abigail was a city council member. Lola was a horticulturalist. And Meg taught English at Ashley's school.

Though diverse, they connected through reading and intimate discussions that went far beyond books. In the last three years, they had shared the deaths of Aziza's husband. Sarah's miscarriage. Ashley's sordid divorce. *Tragedy brings people closer together.* She sighed, sinking deeper into the posh seat, looking out the oval window at a clear blue sky as far as she could see. *And so does pleasure.*

Ashley had decided not to talk with Meg about layoffs until after the break. She had polished her resume yesterday and researched new positions. But this was vacation, and she wasn't going to bring the stink of consolidations into this once-in-a-lifetime luxury vacation.

Still, she couldn't shake the feeling something was missing. It was familiar by now—she'd had this feeling for two days. *Since you said goodbye to Mr. Pioneer, idiot.* She tried to stop thinking of his hands, how they held her after their handshake.

How would they feel cradling her face, tracing her lower lip? How would his fingertips feel brushing across her chest, petal soft, her nipples straining to meet them, his palms on her waist pulling her closer to him, his body somehow both silk and steel. Clearly, what was *missing* was the chance to see him again, to discover if the real man could match her fantasies.

Ashley sighed, took a sip of champagne. *Forget him.* But for the whole airplane ride, she didn't.

"A fireplace in the kitchen?" Ashley walked through Jamila's house in amazement. It was something between a log cabin and a palace. The scale was massive—the vaulted ceilings were thirty feet high. The living room alone was three times the size of Ashley's apartment. Still, the main room felt warm, welcoming, and cozy, with huge sofas piled with pillows and oversized chairs.

But the home's grandeur couldn't compare to what Ashley saw through the floor-to-ceiling windows—the rugged San Juan Mountains rising above vast white mesas. No snow clung to the sheer gray cliffs, but the ridgelines and couloirs looked like an endless snowy playground. For the first time in her life, Ashley wished she had a clue what to do with skis.

"Soup's ready," called Jamila, inviting the ladies to join her at a big round table. Eight large bowls of steaming soup awaited them, along with two loaves of bread Jamila's housekeeper had baked.

Lunch tasted as good as it smelled. The texture of warm bread took Ashley back to her childhood when her neighbor Tica taught her to make *pan huaro*, a round, tall Peruvian roll. Surrounded by laughter and bright chatter, Ashley couldn't remember when she'd been this content.

"I mean, really, men should be able to carry purses, too," Sarah was saying. "What do they do with their stuff?"

Jamila scoffed. "Can you really picture my Terrance, a six-foot-four semi-pro rugby player and shark of a lawyer, toting a *purse*?"

"Even a man his size would be teased till his ego was ant-sized," Meg agreed.

"That's why," Sarah proposed, "there should be a set day when all men start carrying their purses at once."

"International Man Bag Day?" Jamila choked on her water.

Claire, who had been scribbling in her pocket notebook under the table, held up an image for everyone to look at: a sketch of a purse with a long strap and a single flap shaped like a giant penis. "Made in distressed cowboy leather, of course, to show scuffing from adventures and, er, rough handling." She giggled. "Actual size is six inches, but advertising says eight."

The room erupted in laughter. "And here comes Mr. Man Bag himself," Jamila hooted. "Right on time." The enormous front door swung open. Surprised, Ashley twisted in her chair to face the door and saw Terrance walk in.

"You've all met Terrance, right, gals?"

Terrance walked to his wife and kissed her cheek. "Here's the hardworking birthday girl."

"Gals, I forgot to mention Terrance is here with his colleagues, staying next door. They have their own place and their own plans. This is *totally* a women's weekend, but I thought we could all meet up tomorrow for après-ski."

Terrance smiled apologetically at the book club. "Sorry to interrupt, gals. I'll just be a minute. I came to grab a few things, and, of course, I wanted an excuse to see this beauty." He put his arm around Jamila and pulled her close.

Ashley was happy for her friend, but she noticed the pang of envy that gnashed in her gut. She took a bite of soup, aware she was trying to feed a craving that had nothing to do with hunger.

"Hey, Terrance," said another voice from the door, "could you grab me a…oh, Jamila. I don't mean to crash your ladies' event. Just need to grab something."

That voice. Ashley's spoon was still in her mouth, her body leaning forward over her bowl. She wanted to turn, but she was immobilized.

"How have you been, Jamila?" said the man, his voice nearing.

"Great."

Ashley stared sidelong as the man from the bookstore walked up to Jamila to hug her. *Luke.*

Breathe, she reminded herself. Her heartbeat was erratic, almost audible. *Thump. Thumpity. Thumpity.* She tried to swallow her soup without choking. She turned from him to keep herself from staring, not yet ready for him to see her. *Is this happening?*

Luke. Here in Telluride. In Jamila's house.

Could he have known she was here? *No. That doesn't make sense.*

The rest of the room blurred as she returned her focus to Luke—his fitted black snow pants hugging his legs, his trim waist covered with at least three layers of ski clothes, his strong shoulders. *Oh god.* Ashley bit her lip. *His face.* High cheekbones. Strong jaw. Hair the color of midnight. He'd been clean-shaven in the bookstore, but now his two-day stubble made him look both more rugged and more sophisticated. As her limbs froze, a warmth sharpened between her legs. She blushed, thinking of the ways he'd touched her last night in her thoughts.

"Delicious," Meg whispered in her ear. "Damn."

Ashley felt a surge of possessiveness rise in her, and she didn't take her eyes off Luke as she nodded an affirmation to her friend. *Luke is here.* The world was giving her a second chance. But would he?

"So, this is the infamous book club," he said, turning to face the table. "I'm Luke."

"I'm Aziza," said the woman to Jamila's left. Luke smiled at her, warm and authentic.

"I'm Sarah." Ashley followed Luke's gaze to her friend's face.

"Claire."

"Hi, Claire."

One more seat. *This is it*, Ashley thought. She would know by his face if she still had a chance.

"Hi, Luke, I'm Meg," said her friend, her voice sultry. Ashley almost growled. Luke's expression stayed congenial, and he turned to Ashley.

"I'm—"

"Ashley." And there it was. The same dark honey she remembered in his voice. It sent flutters through her whole body. She tried to read his expression, but she couldn't. "What a *nice* surprise." He held her brown eyes in his blue ones. *God, those eyes.*

More intense than she remembered. They sparkled with something akin to amusement, as if he was in on some kind of grand cosmic joke. He flashed her a triumphant smile before turning to greet Abigail on Ashley's left. Out of the corner of her eye, she caught Jamila staring at her with a sly cat air.

Ashley couldn't focus on anything being said around her; she heard only voices within. *What a nice surprise, he said. And he remembered my name.*

Her whole body was clamoring, soaring with adrenaline-edged desire. Was he feeling it, too, this surge of amazement, this swell of outrageous luck? Could he sense it, too, this wild chemistry?

Then reality set in. It had been a brief interaction in a bookstore. All this star-crossed stuff was her own fabrication. In two short days, she'd elevated him from man to god. She'd turned a five-minute exchange into a passionate affair. Even if he *were* interested in her, she had no business with a man like him. He was way too handsome for her. Not to mention, Ashley Barris was officially not interested in a relationship. Not with Luke, not with anyone.

Jamila caught Ashley's eye, and Ashley interpreted the message in her dark brown eyes. *How about a fling?*

Ashley flashed her a look that said, *Shut up.*

Every inch of her skin was tingling. *Stop it,* she told her body, but it went right on with its quivering, its excitement, its thrill.

She was a mess. She desperately wanted to run away. She equally desperately wanted to run into his arms, those arms that had dominated her imagination for two days straight. She felt queasy, supercharged, and breathless. Though she hadn't wanted his eyes to leave her, now she was terrified for when he would look at her again. What could they possibly say to each other?

She didn't wonder for long. Luke said something to the whole group about it being a pleasure, then rounded the table to stand beside her. Ashley felt the heat of his body; she also felt the eyes of all seven women searching her, curiosity steeping in the air. Then Claire made some joke about man bags, and they were all laughing again.

Relieved by the distraction, Ashley mumbled a quiet "excuse me" and rose to stand beside Luke.

God, that smell again. Citrus, dark tea, musk. And underneath his cologne, the man was a pheromone factory. Every cell in Ashley's body vibrated with longing. Was she responding to the man himself? Or the daydreams she'd had about him? In truth, she knew nothing about the musculature of his back, the heat of his lips raining kisses on her neck, but her imagination disagreed. She'd gone there over and over, and kissing was only the beginning. Could Luke sense her arousal? She walked beside him, thrilled to be close to him, even as the back of her mind started tapping out a distress signal.

They walked a few feet from the table and stood near the window, away from the ears of Ashley's friends. For a moment, they said nothing, just looked at each other. Ashley tried to be stoic, but she knew her face was an ever-open page. His face, on the other hand, was enigmatic. Whatever surprise she'd seen earlier had been replaced with an almost serene expression.

"I'm glad the universe didn't take your no for an answer." His voice was resonant, warm, rich, teasing.

"Perhaps I should learn to believe in collaborating."

"With fate?" He filled in the phrase he'd left her with in the bookstore. His lips curved up into the most magnificent smile. He looked pleased she'd remembered what he'd said.

Ashley nodded, uncharacteristically dumbstruck.

"Meeting you here, Ashley, is the perfect example of why I believe in collaborating with fate. When I run into a brick wall, fate has its way of finding a secret passage."

"Sooooo." Ashley hung on the word, not sure what came next. "What exactly *are* you doing here? I mean, obviously you know Jamila and Terrance, but—"

"Terrance and I work together," Luke explained, "and a bunch of our team members are here for a retreat of sorts. Because Jamila had their house booked for this week, we're using my sister's vacation home next door."

So, Luke was staying next door. How could things be rigged so astonishingly in her favor? Just this morning, finding him seemed impossible. Now, they were neighbors, at least for a day or two. Ashley teetered between elation and terror. She'd fallen for a dream man before. It had ended in a nightmare.

"I've been thinking about you." His eyes dared her to admit the same.

Ashley's breath hitched. Her attraction to him alarmed her. She took a half step back. He took a half step forward.

"Ashley, I get the feeling I'm scaring you." He softened his shoulders. "That's the last thing I want to do. But I *do* want to take advantage of this chance to get to know you. I know you're here with your friends, but maybe we could find time to talk. Are you skiing tomorrow?"

"Oh, no. No skiing for me. I'll be curled up with a book on that burgundy couch over there."

"The conditions are great..."

"Luke." She shifted on her feet. "I don't ski. I came to relax and hang out with my friends."

"Well, you're in the right place at the right time to learn something new. The weather tomorrow should be clear and warm. Perfect for a first-timer to get on skis." He chuckled at the doubtful look on her face. "Skiing is like flying, Ashley, like getting wings, only they're on your feet."

The enthusiasm in his voice was genuine, and Ashley almost wished she could go, but there were many reasons she was saying no to him again.

She shrugged. "I don't have any gear."

"Let me outfit you. You're about my sister's size, and I know she won't mind if I lend you her ski stuff. I'll bring it over in the morning."

"Why are you so—"

"Ashley would *love* to take you up on that offer," said Jamila, walking up behind Ashley and putting her arm around her. "I offered to let her use my stuff, but it would be too big for her."

Ashley scowled at her friend, causing Jamila to laugh. How could Jamila be so sure she wanted to ski with Luke when she wasn't so sure herself?

"Then it's settled," Luke said. "I have to work in the morning, so you'll miss the first lifts, but I can be over by ten. I'll bring my sister's transferrable ski pass, too."

"Thanks, Luke," said Jamila. "That'll be great." She gave Ashley a squeeze, as if everything were settled, and slipped off toward the kitchen.

"But," Ashley blurted, "I don't know *how* to ski." The last thing she wanted was to be an incapable klutz in front of this man.

"That's what lessons are for. Don't worry, I'll get you set up in the morning with gear *and* an instructor."

Oh. So, we won't be skiing together? Then why was he offering to help her out?

"That's my Luke," said a woman's voice. Ashley watched as a pale, well-manicured woman's hand appeared on Luke's shoulder, then slipped possessively around his waist. "Always taking care of other people."

"Hello, Savannah," Luke said casually. "About ready to go?"

Ashley stared at the ravishing woman who had just wrapped herself around Luke. She was an inch or so shorter than Ashley, with long, silky blonde hair, wide blue doe eyes, and a bee-stung lower lip that pouted even though she was smiling. Her all-white ski outfit hugged her curves and showed off her slender waist. Ashley immediately envied her—not the clothes, not the body, not the flawless face, but the fact she had her arm around Luke.

"Aren't you going to introduce us?" The woman's voice was surprisingly friendly.

"Of course. Savannah, this is Ashley. Ashley, Savannah."

Ashley extended her hand. "Nice to meet you, Savannah."

"Are you here with the book club?"

"I am." Staring at Savannah's hand as she curled it again around Luke's bicep, Ashley felt as if she had just fallen off a cliff, a cliff she hadn't known she was standing on. Of course, Luke was with another woman. Of course, it would be someone as confident and attractive as he was. Of course, the world was not rigged in her favor. Luke was just another handsome man who enjoyed playing with his own magnetism, fishing just to see what he could catch.

Or was he? Had he really done anything out of line? He'd asked her for coffee. He'd offered to let her borrow his sister's clothes. He said he'd thought about their conversation. It was all pretty innocent. No lines had been crossed—except in her imaginings.

"What's the book this month?" Savannah asked. Without waiting for Ashley's answer, she turned to Luke and said, "Luke, I think Terrance got lost. Why don't you go find him so we can get up on the slopes already?"

Luke broke away from Savannah, smiled at Ashley, and walked in the direction where Terrance had disappeared five minutes ago. Meanwhile, Ashley turned to Savannah, noting how guilt had crept in. She would never knowingly flirt with another woman's man. *I'm sorry*, she thought to the other woman.

"We're reading *The Map of Salt and Stars*," Ashley said. Savannah had read it already, and as the two made small talk about the book, Ashley was nodding and mm-hmming, but she was a million miles away. A door had just slammed in her heart.

"Now, where are those boys?" Savannah glanced at her watch. A rose-gold Rolex. Diamonds on each hour glittered in a circle around the face. She thought of her mother, who wore a twenty-dollar Casio and was thrilled when she came home from the diner with a hundred bucks in tips. "Time is money. Or in this case, time is fun." Savannah glanced up. "Oh good, here they are."

Luke and Terrance returned with a bottle of medicine for altitude sickness. Savannah explained that another colleague often felt sick when they skied above tree line. "Carl never gets dangerously sick, just feels like shit. Darn oxygen concentration."

"Actually," Ashley said, "the atmospheric oxygen concentration doesn't change at high altitude; it's still about twenty-one percent, same as sea level. It's just that the number of oxygen molecules per breath decreases because the molecules are more dispersed."

Luke, Terrance, and Savannah stared at Ashley.

"I know, it's eerie, right?" said Jamila, coming up beside her husband. "She's like a one-woman think tank."

"Well, *tank* you, Ashley," said Luke with a goofy smile. Ashley shook her head. She felt her pulse quicken at his approval, though she told herself she didn't care what he thought.

Savannah's eyes sharpened at Luke's words, but the look passed so quickly Ashley wondered if she'd seen it.

"*That's* the kind of woman I want as a friend." Savannah raised a brow at her, as if considering options. "Are you on Facebook?" She pulled her phone from a pocket. "What's your last name?"

Ashley rarely spent time on Facebook, and she wasn't sure she wanted to be friends with Savannah if she were dating Luke. It would be too hard to see them together. But for the moment, she didn't want to be rude. And she did kind of like Savannah, despite the envy slowly tearing her heart to bits.

"Barris."

"Ashley Barris," Savannah said with a light Southern drawl as she typed into her phone. Ashley dared a glimpse at Luke. He was still regarding Ashley with something akin to respect.

"Found you." Savannah flashed Ashley a charming smile.

Ashley smiled back, as genuine as she could manage, but the truth was she felt empty, as if a glorious flower that had been blooming inside her had been cut down and trampled.

"Ready to go, trailblazers?" Savannah linked arms with Luke and Terrance, one on each side. The threesome headed for the door.

Luke twisted his head and smiled at Ashley. "See you at ten," he mouthed.

Ashley nodded, but every part of her was shaking no.

CHAPTER 3

ASHLEY FINISHED READING page six of her book. For the sixth time. She set the book on the table beside her and curled into the plush cushions on the couch. Had she ever felt anything as soft as the pillow she'd just tucked under one arm? She snuggled in deeper under a golden chenille throw and let the winter sun warm her through the window.

The rest of the women had left to ski almost two hours ago, eager for first tracks. They would meet at four for après-ski in the Great Room at The Peaks. In the meantime, Ashley relished her time alone. *Five, six, seven...*she counted exposed rustic roofbeams. *Stop counting, Ashley.*

Drowsy, she let her eyes close. It wasn't as if she'd slept much last night. She had obsessively replayed the moment when Luke's eyes had first met hers across the table, how his face had lit up— and she hadn't just imagined it. Meg couldn't stop talking about it last night. "That blonde is history. 'Lukey' was obviously hot for *you.*"

But Ashley couldn't muster the same cavalier attitude about significant others. If Luke was taken, she was hands off. Hell, she should be hands off, *anyway.* The last thing she needed was another chance at heartbreak. It had been two years since her divorce. She'd dated in the meantime, but she'd built thick walls around her heart for good reason. She hoped someday those walls would come down, but if anyone were going to play wrecking ball, she didn't want it to be another cheater.

"How do you know he's a cheater?" Meg had goaded her last night.

"You saw him and Savannah," Ashley said. "They were clearly together, and he was borderline flirting with me. Nope."

And then at dinner, Ashley had undergone lots of playful questions from the whole club, though she'd explained there was nothing more to tell than a brief meeting at a bookstore. For as loud as Meg was about it, Jamila, who actually knew the man, had been notably quiet. *Is she hiding something?*

Despite her own pep talks on cultivating disinterest, Ashley reclined in the morning sun and imagined what Luke would be like in bed. Domineering? His voice firm, his blue eyes piercing? Would his kisses leave her lips swollen? Or would he be excruciatingly tender and teasing, his soft lips traveling like warm sunlight across her body until she begged him to bite her, to give her more?

She skipped through different scenarios. Like what if Luke walked into her bedroom here in Jamila's house, his finger on his lips signaling her to be quiet. She'd be already naked beneath the covers, and he would slowly, slowly pull down the sheet to reveal every shivering inch of her. Desire bloomed in her like a whole field of red poppies, the petals fluttering through her bloodstream. She imagined him peeling off his long-sleeved shirt in a leisurely striptease, imagined the cut muscles she was sure he was hiding beneath his Henley. And then he was beside her, the denim of his jeans rough against her naked legs, his long fingers trailing along her body, dancing over her belly, traveling the curved topography of her breasts. She imagined him inhaling her scent as he dragged the tip of his nose along her jawline, his low groan making her shiver, imagined the hungry part of his lips, his blue eyes glittering as he—

"Ashley?" Luke walked through the living room door. Shit! Was it ten? Part of her believed he wouldn't show. Another part of her dreaded he'd show up *with Savannah*. No matter how much she rationalized it, it hurt to see him with another woman.

But here he was, walking in the door, alone, with two giant canvas bags exploding with parkas and fleece. Ashley jumped up from the couch, her cheeks red with embarrassment as if he could tell what she'd just been thinking.

"Ready to play?"

So ready I'm dripping. "Thanks, Luke." She looked in the bags. "I definitely wasn't planning to ski, but"—she took a deep breath—"I'm looking forward to trying something new."

"That moment you changed your mind, you changed your destiny." He flashed her an enigmatic smile, and then he pulled out several pairs of snow pants and jackets, neck gaiters, gloves, goggles, and a helmet. "Something here should work. Elaine is not the queen of fashion, but she has Texas blood and likes to stay warm." Luke unfurled a pair of black ski pants. "Here, try these."

"Sure your sister won't mind?"

Luke laughed. "Ashley, my sister would do *anything* for her little brother. She spoils me like crazy."

Huh. Ashley tried not to be self-conscious as she pulled the snow pants over her black tights. But she was. She could feel his eyes on her as she balanced on one foot, then the other. She was afraid to look up.

"Perfect," she announced.

"Good. Try this."

Ashley smiled to herself as she slipped into a bright blue ski jacket, thinking how much she would rather Luke were *undressing* her than dressing her. *It's okay. It's just a fantasy.* Somehow knowing he had a girlfriend made him safer. If her fantasies stayed fantasies, her real heart couldn't get hurt.

"Thanks, Luke. This fits great, too."

"Now all you need are skis, boots, and poles from the rental shop, and I lined up an instructor this morning—he'll meet us on the slopes."

"Luke." Ashley stood a little straighter to counteract the embarrassment she felt creeping in. "Look, thank you for getting everything set up for me, but I—" She hesitated before blurting, "I can't afford this."

Luke set down the bags he had just picked up, focusing all his attention on Ashley.

"Ashley." His voice was warm. "Please, let *me* do this. I am sorry I didn't make that clear." She opened her mouth to argue, and he cut her off. "I'm excited to introduce you to skiing. Think of it like me opening a car door for you. A small gesture." As Ashley shook her head, he repeated, "Please."

The way he said "please" moved her. Not macho or pleading or manipulative. It was earnest.

"Okay," Ashley assented, surprising herself. Something about Luke made her want to break her rules—like not letting men pay for her. To her surprise, instead of feeling guilty, she felt relief.

"Thank you." Luke beamed. "Let's go."

"Don't worry, Mr. D," said Dan, the ski instructor. "I'll take great care of Ms. Barris."

Ashley, Dan, and Luke stood on their skis at the base of the ski area. Ashley felt both clumsy and eager.

"Thanks, Dan," said Luke. "Do your magic so she falls in love with skiing."

"Oh, I'll be falling all right."

"And getting back up." In his helmet and ski goggles, Luke looked like an alpine deity with only his smile exposed. "A tip—it's easier to get back up if you fall uphill." At Ashley's grimace, he added, "You're in fine hands. Dan's the best, and he'll help you return all the gear. I'll see you this afternoon at The Peaks, right?"

"Yeah, see you there." Ashley aimed for nonchalance.

"Ashley, I want to give you my number. In case you need to reach me."

"That's thoughtful, thanks."

After their goodbyes, Luke skied away. Ashley admired his grace as he skated to the chairlift. Some part of her heart felt as if it were skiing away with him. The last hour had been so fun and, for her, so charged. He'd been kind, generous, jovial, and encouraging. Even though he wasn't available, she could feel both her curiosity about him and her desire growing.

"Luke," she called after him, wanting to see his smile once more. He turned around. "Thank you."

He gave her a salute and skied away.

"Ready?" said Dan.

Ashley felt a rush of exhilaration. "For anything." She almost believed her own words.

By the time the bellman at The Peaks opened the front doors for Ashley, she was exhausted, exhilarated, and excited to tell Luke about her adventure.

Adventure might be pushing it. She'd fallen at least two dozen times, and small packs of four-year-old children had skied circles around her. But by the end of her lesson, she had made linked turns down the bunny hill. She had even felt the flying sensation Luke had promised—a whole minute of adrenaline-driven bliss—before she caught an edge and fell again.

But here she was, slightly bruised, elated with the thrill of trying something new, and high on gratitude for the man who made it possible.

Ashley scanned the Great Room: impressive fireplace at one end, a whole wall of floor-to-ceiling windows, and clusters of oversized club chairs and couches. The crowd was so cosmopolitan and international it felt like a James Bond movie set. Finally, she located her friends by the windows.

Luke stood out—tall, handsome, almost exotic, but there was something else about him. Ashley continued to watch him, wondering about his charisma. Even when he wasn't speaking, he commanded the conversation. How? Watching, she realized his secret. He engaged one hundred fifty percent. He listened intently, with his whole body. It made him a magnet. Ashley felt her energy rev. She knew how good it felt to be the object of his attention, and she felt a little like an addict, wanting another hit.

All day, she had looked forward to this moment, being in his presence again. Then she saw Savannah lean closer into him, her laughter carrying across the room. Ashley hated the crack of resentment that split through her chest.

Determined not to let her good mood deflate, she walked toward the group, forcing brightness into her body. Jamila saw her and waved her over.

"You're fifteen minutes late," Jamila chided, laughing.

Ashley looked at her watch. "Eighteen minutes late."

Jamila shook her head. "I can always count on you for precision. How was your ski day, friend?"

"It was fun." Ashley took the glass of tempranillo Jamila handed her.

Jamila raised her glass. "Here's to your first day on skis!"

As they clinked glasses, Ashley caught Luke's eye. He gave her a wide smile and raised his glass toward her, though he was too far away to clink. Ashley did the same, thrilled to have his attention, but then he was turning to the man on his right again, nodding and laughing. Meg was there, too, standing a little too close to a very attractive man. They were all laughing now, and Ashley wished she were in their circle.

If she walked eight steps, she could join them. But in her mind, the scene was supposed to go differently. Luke was supposed to come over and give her all his attention the way he had this morning. She wanted him to ask her how her day had gone. She wanted that same yummy feeling of connection she'd felt before he'd skied away, as if he really saw her.

Don't act like a petulant kid. She turned back toward Jamila and Claire and tried to focus on their talk of skiing.

"Hey, Ashley, bottom's up." Jamila pantomimed a chug. "The rest of us had a pretty good head start on you, and we're all ready to relax back at the house."

"Sure, I'm ready." Luckily, Jamila had poured her a light serving. She took a couple of large sips of wine and felt the buzz go immediately to her head. *Altitude.* But the wine gave her enough courage to approach Luke before leaving.

"Hey!" His eyes lit up when he saw her. "How was your first day on skis, Ashley?"

"It was a great experience. Thank you, Luke." She wanted to say more, but Meg was there, tugging on her arm.

"Come on, Ash." Meg cocked her head toward the door. "Car's waiting."

Ashley gave Luke a parting smile and walked away. Her legs were tired. Her heart was tired. She had no idea when she'd see him again.

"There she is," said Terrance. "Ashley, come sit with us."

Ashley was walking downstairs from her room. She'd gone up after dinner to have a few moments alone. As much as she

loved the book club members, she wasn't used to this much socializing. And it was a bit of a surprise to see Terrance had come
over, and, from the look of it, the rest of his crew had come, too.
Ashley's heart leapt up, hoping for a glimpse of Luke.

And there he was, sitting across from Terrance, right next to
the empty space where Terrance was gesturing she should sit.

"Hi, Terrance. Hi, Luke." She took the empty seat next to
Luke. The couch was small, and she found herself sitting quite
close to the one person she most wanted to be close to—and far
away from. For a moment, she let herself sink into the feeling of
being beside him. She could feel his heat, could smell the good,
male scent of him, could almost touch his muscled quads with
her own leg.

"Hi, Ashley." Luke leaned back and rested his arm on the
back of the couch behind her, not quite touching her skin. Still,
she felt cradled by him. She tried to not imagine how it would
feel to be truly enveloped by him, the weight of him crushing onto her, her legs parting for him, his hands pinning her
shoulders.

"Right, Ashley?" Terrance was saying.

"Oh, sorry. Ask me again?"

"I was just saying the stars are so much sharper here than in
Houston. Less light pollution, right?"

Ashley shrugged. "Yeah, that and less atmosphere to distort
our view."

"Then I'm surprised we can see stars here at all," Luke said,
grinning at Ashley. "Because you, Ms. Science, are so *bright.*"

Ashley twisted in the seat to give Luke a playful punch in
his side, but the jovial gesture shocked her with its electricity. Touching Luke, even in jest, took her breath away. Was it
obvious?

Luke leaned forward to pick up his drink, bringing their
bodies momentarily closer. *Oh, the warmth of him.* Ashley

yielded to his radiance. When he leaned back again, her body felt almost bereft, and she fought the urge to nestle closer.

"So," Terrance said, "tell us about day one on the slopes."

Ashley smiled. She'd been hoping for this chance to share her skiing experience with Luke, to convey her gratitude for the chance to try something exciting and new.

"Well, by the end of the day, I could feel an internal rhythm—"

"Yes!" Luke's eyes sparkled. "Tell me about—"

"Lukey! Hey, Lukey," called Savannah, swinging through the front door, staggering drunk. "Let'sh get in the hot tub!"

Luke stood and faced her. "Savannah." His voice sounded resigned.

"Oh, no," she slurred. "Lukey ish all sherioush. Why are you sho sherioush, Lukey?" She put on an exaggerated pout, then stumbled toward him, her body swaying, barely able to stand. She grabbed for his hand but missed, tottered, and ended up on the ground.

Terrance gave Luke a look, a cross between pity and indignation, as Luke bent over to help Savannah rise. But Savannah had now sprawled on the floor, apparently happy to be there. She stared up at Luke with big eyes.

"Let'sh go play in the shnow, Lukey!"

"You are going to bed." Luke's tone was grim. Instead of letting him help her up, Savannah now tugged on his hand, trying to pull him to the floor.

"Savannah, let's make this easy, okay?" His voice was gentle, as if speaking to a petulant child. He pulled his hand away.

"Can't catch me!" Savannah rolled away and hit a table. The lamp on it teetered but didn't fall.

"Okay, Savannah. Let's go." Luke easily swept Savannah up into his arms and carried her toward the door.

"Oh, Lukey, you're sho shtrong." Savannah hung rag doll limp in his arms. "You're sho shtrong and sho pretty. Sho shweet."

Luke turned to face Ashley and Terrance, still seated on the couches. "Excuse me."

As the door shut, Ashley heard Savannah say, "Yesh, Lukey. Take me to bed."

And they were gone. The whole room had hushed to watch the spectacle, and when the door clicked closed, the party burst into chaos again.

Terrance flashed Ashley a wry smile. "I've always said Luke's MBA from Wharton really stands for 'Must Be an Angel.' How does he handle the unexpected so well?"

Jamila came over to confer with Terrance about a house matter, and Ashley sat alone on the couch. She didn't even try to subdue her disappointment. She hated Savannah for stealing her special moment with Luke, for being the woman he picked up and carried to bed. And what was up with her being so drunk? Luke deserved someone better. She hated herself for being interested in a man who was taken. In fact, she hated herself for being interested in anyone at all.

Why had she let Luke in? *Because he's mesmerizing?* There had been that sweet click in the bookstore. Something in her had turned on and *stayed* on. She thrived in his presence. The connection went beyond intellect, beyond strength, beyond sexual chemistry. He nourished her; being with him made her feel more herself.

And he belonged to someone else.

———

Ashley woke long after the sun had slipped into her room. She was, not surprisingly, sore. She rolled over and looked at the phone. After eight? Four missed texts from yesterday. All from Luke.

Luke: You nearby?

Luke: Wanted to hear more about skiing today

Her heart raced, despite her intentions to ignore her attraction to him.

Luke: Do you turn into a pumpkin BEFORE midnight?

Why was he texting her so much last night?

Luke: Let's ski together tomorrow

What was this all about? After taking Savannah to bed, he'd sent all four of these texts? That didn't make sense. Ashley saw he hadn't left any voice messages.

Ashley: ???

Within seconds, the phone rang. *Luke.*

"Hello?"

"Good morning, sunshine." God, that voice. Better than coffee. She was awake now. "Where did you go last night?"

To get off by myself while thinking of your beautiful, round ass. "I was sore from skiing—well, more like sore from falling—so I went to bed."

"How do you feel this morning?"

Like I wish I could stop thinking about you. "Um, sore. But nothing serious."

"Sounds right for the day after your first ski lesson." Luke laughed. "Hey, sorry I had to leave so abruptly. As you noticed, altitude, alcohol, and dehydration really got to Savannah. I had to help her, but I came back to talk to you after I got her situated. I wanted to hear more about your day." He paused. "And more about you."

He's flirting. I'm not making it up. He's flirting. Though she couldn't blame him after Savannah's antics last night, she resolved not to encourage him in any way. "The lesson was great, Luke, thanks." She forced her voice to be a little flat. An awkward silence followed.

"So, I was hoping you would join me for a few hours on the mountain today. Unless you're planning on skiing with the gals."

Was he inviting her out? Something didn't sit right with her about that.

"No, I'm going to explore Telluride today." That was true.

"Town itself is about six blocks long," he joked. "It won't take long to see the whole thing. Come, ski half a day with me this afternoon. I'll ski with the guys for the morning."

As if sensing her imminent refusal, he added, "Don't tell me now. Text me later. I'll make it fun. Promise."

"Okay." *No way.*

"Okay, Ashley. Talk later." God, she loved the way he said her name—as if the syllables grew petals while they hung in the air.

"Bye, Luke." Once he'd hung up, she added, "I need to stay far, far away from you."

On a whim, Ashley looked up Savannah's Facebook page. There, at the top, was a selfie of Savannah and Luke. He wasn't tagged, but he was laughing while looking at Savannah, and Savannah was staring into the camera, oozing self-confidence.

Savannah: On my way to London after a faaaabulous time in Telluride.

Oh, so that's it. He thought he could play now that Savannah was gone. *I won't be a convenient toy.* As much as she wanted to kiss him, to feel his tongue licking up her thigh, to feel him deep inside of her, as much as she wanted to feed this increasing hunger, she was even more determined to protect herself.

I thought he had more integrity, but I've been wrong about men before. She hated that she was wrong again. Luke *was* a playboy after all.

She stared at the photo. Luke's face was so open, so striking, so handsome. Even his picture caused a sweet clenching at her core.

"Aaaaagh!" Ashley shouted, desperately trying to release unwanted energy. "Aaaagh!"

She needed to find a local bookstore and a hiking trail. She needed to take care of her heart.

—————

By the time she emerged from her hike up Bear Creek, Ashley felt transformed—as if she were a small note in a grand score. The effort of hiking in deep snow had invigorated her. And the vastness of the mountains surrounding the valley had filled her with a shimmering spaciousness.

Not that she'd forgotten Luke. Quite the opposite. She'd thought of him ninety-five percent of the hike, but she felt more ease with herself, more at peace with the fact that people don't always get what they want, and more held by the beauty of the world.

She'd powered off her phone while hiking, but turning it back on, she saw she'd missed six calls from her student and mentee Emilia, no messages.

What could be so urgent? Emilia had left home two years ago at age fifteen and now lived at the Lift House, a foster home shelter for teens where Ashley volunteered. She'd been mentoring Emilia for two years already. It was unlike her to call repeatedly.

Ashley texted Jamila that she would meet the gals that afternoon for après-ski at the Cosmo. She texted Luke a quick "sorry." It almost felt good to have the strength to tell him no. Then she found a rock near the trailhead where she could sit and chat with Emilia.

"Ashley?" said the trembling young voice before bursting into tears.

"I'm here, Emilia." Ashley waited for the sobs to subside.

"I need help," Emilia whimpered. "And you're the only person I trust."

Emilia had grown up with an abusive father and a drunk mother unable to stand up for Emilia or for herself. She turned to drugs at a young age, and though she'd been clean for over a year, Ashley knew it was a struggle.

"I don't want to use again, but I do."

"You've been making such great choices for yourself, Emilia," Ashley encouraged. "You can keep doing that."

By the end of the call, they'd reviewed all the ways Emilia knew to help herself, and they agreed to check in every day until Ashley returned to Houston.

"You can do it, Emilia," she said, still cheering the girl even after they'd hung up the phone. Despite the emotional drain, Ashley thrived on helping Emilia. Though she'd never struggled with addiction, she saw so much of herself in the girl. Ashley, too, had grown up financially poor in a rough ward with loitering addicts and drunks. Street fights. Occasional shootings. Unlike Emilia, she had a wise, loving mother who'd raised her and her younger sister, Jewel. And she'd had a godsend of a neighbor, Tica, who had taken her under her wing while her mother was working three jobs.

It was Tica who had fostered Ashley's desire to become a teacher. Now Ashley got to do the same for Emilia, who wanted to teach art. Ashley loved feeling like a middle link in a lineage of women supporting other women's dreams around education.

Thank god for good women and good books. And with that thought, she headed to the town's bookstore, a charming shop on the main street. She spent the rest of the afternoon browsing books, reading and chatting with the friendly cashier.

They happened to have a copy of Chopra's *The Path to Love*. Ashley purchased it for Luke as a thank-you gift for the ski lesson, hoping he hadn't already picked up the one he'd ordered.

Being in the bookstore reminded her of their meeting, of course. She kept half expecting Luke to show up. Hell, she *wished* he would show up. She *wished* for a lot more than that. For his lips to brush warm kisses across her naked shoulders, for his strong hands to massage up her inner thighs until her back was arching and she was begging for his touch, for his tongue to—

Stop. He's taken.

Usually, a bookstore was her happy place. Now it was a trigger, sparking her longing for him all over again. The man was like crack. She felt an empathic twinge for Emilia's plight.

You've been making good choices, Ashley. Keep doing that.

───────

"Who wants bubbles?" Jamila held her hand high in the air.

Seven more women raised their hands. Jamila hailed the waiter. "We'd like the Taittinger 'Brut La Francaise.'"

"I've never understood why the French chose the word *brut* for their champagne," said Claire. "Sure, it means 'dry,' but it also means 'plug-ugly.' And 'gross.'"

"Only you would think about that, Claire," Meg joked with her.

For an hour, the friends teased and toasted before rising to go to dinner at Jamila's. A few of Ashley's friends went off to the powder room, but she still had half a glass of champagne, so Ashley stood beside the fireplace, sipping, delaying putting on her coat.

"Hey, sweetheart," said a husky voice behind her. "Don't leave with your friends. Let's have a drink together." Ashley turned to face a rugged-looking man with blond hair and dark eyes. His face was tanned with a big white smile.

Ashley felt her habitual "no" rising, but maybe it was the champagne, or maybe it was a misplaced longing for Luke, or maybe it was her sister's voice in her head saying, "Come on, Ash, you've got to date again sometime." She would leave with the gals, but first, she would flirt.

"What did you have in mind?"

"Well—" He stepped closer. But Ashley couldn't focus on what he said next because Meg was behind him, making faces at Ashley, mouthing something, gesturing with her hands.

"Excuse me," Ashley said to the blond man.

"You're here," said Luke's deep voice behind her. Meg smiled coyly, clearly enjoying the unfolding scene.

Luke draped his arm possessively around Ashley's shoulders. "I've missed you, darling. Haven't seen you all day."

Darling?

The blond man puffed up his chest a bit, like a cock ready for a standoff.

Beside Ashley, Luke exuded confidence and control. "My girlfriend's beautiful, isn't she?" Meg's eyes widened in shock.

What the hell?

In a split second, Ashley decided. *I'm playing.*

"Hi, *darling.*" She caressed Luke's cheek with the backs of her fingers. He'd obviously shaved after skiing, and the intimate touch made her burn to touch him more. "What took you so long? Get caught up practicing with the band?"

Luke didn't miss a beat. "Yeah, sound check went long. But it's going to be a great show." Luke pulled Ashley a little closer.

Sweet heaven, it felt good to be in his arms. *It's just a game, right?*

Luke grinned at the blond stranger. "Hey, man, you coming to see us at the Opera House later tonight?"

Blondie took a step back. "Uh, no, man. But have a good night. Nice to meet you," he muttered toward Ashley as he walked away.

"So...*boyfriend.*" Ashley turned to face Luke, deciding to keep up the game. "I can't wait for the show tonight." She played with the collar of his coat, then took another sip of champagne.

"Let's get out of here," he murmured in her ear. "I want to take you somewhere."

That was exactly what Ashley wanted, too, but the game stopped here. "What just happened there, *boyfriend*? Did you think I needed saving?"

"Yes." His tone was solemn. "I came to rescue you. From—" He paused. "—blonds." He broke into a grin.

"Blonds?"

"Sure. From the blond who walked into the bar. *You'd think he would have seen it.*"

"Oooh." Ashley quickly returned his serve in the pun-a-thon. "You got me *hair* and square."

Luke hung his head and groaned, but his smile lingered. "C'mon, Ashley. Really, let's get out of here."

"But *boyfriend*, I need to finish my champagne. It's nicer than anything I drink back home." She held the flute under her nose for a whiff.

"What is it?"

"Try a sip? It's Plug-Ugly Taittinger."

"Ah, the brut. *Oui*, I'll have a sip." He took one. Then another. Then the last sip. "Now you're ready to go."

Ashley gave him a playful pout.

"Oh, girlfriend, don't sulk. There's more champagne where that came from."

"Spoiling my fun and then finishing my drink. Hmph," Ashley teased. She liked this brazen game they were playing, and she was tipsy and horny enough to give herself over to it. "You're not much of a boyfriend."

"We'll see about that." His gaze lingered on her lips as if thinking of catching them between his teeth, and it made her breath catch. "Let's go. Where's your coat?"

"But the gals—"

"I'll deliver you to your friends soon. In the meantime, I've arranged for your own private sky chariot, *girlfriend*." His voice dropped so low and husky on the last word she felt it vibrate through her core.

"I see." She raised one eyebrow. "Sounds lovely, *boyfriend*." What kind of trouble was she getting herself into? And why couldn't she seem to care?

Luke's face softened, his tone evened. "I'll get you back to Jamila's soon, promise." Then, as if reading her hesitation, he added, "Ashley. You're safe with me. Let's go. I won't even bring the band. Say yes."

Ashley had the strange feeling she was signing some kind of contract by saying yes.

"Yes." She grabbed her coat. "Let's go."

<hr />

The gondola that returned them to Mountain Village was just across the street from the Cosmo bar, but Luke suggested they walk around the block first. "To clear our minds," he said.

Ashley's mind was anything but clear, especially when Luke reached out to hold her hand.

"Luke." She cleared her throat. "That was fun back there, but I'm not your girlfriend. Savannah seems nice, though."

"Savannah?" Luke stopped walking to look at her. "What do you...oh! I see why you might have thought that. She's not my girlfriend."

"But last night, you carried her off to bed."

"Savannah needed help. I held her hair while she puked in the snow, then I took her to her room. Then I returned hoping to see *you*."

"But—" Ashley recalled how intimately Savannah had put her arm around Luke the first time she met her.

"Ashley. Savannah and I used to date." He brushed an imaginary hair away from Ashley's cheek. "It's been over two years since it ended. We've known each other since we were kids, so we have a lot of history. But there's no romantic interest. We're friends and colleagues."

"I see." She kept her voice steady as the implication of Luke's statement settled on her like fine snow. A simultaneous thrill and fear raced through her chest, each determined to win. Luke was available! And in her heart, she knew she was available, too. Available to explore whatever was possible with this intelligent, thoughtful man who had entered her heart so easily. From the first encounter at the bookstore to his friendship with Terrance and Jamila to his generosity with the ski lesson, everything about Luke pulled her in. Now that she knew he was single, she didn't want to play it safe with Luke. And *that* terrified her.

"Savannah and I work together, and she joined us here for the planning session. She's been heading up the London office, but she's returning to Houston later this month."

"What's your work?"

"It's complicated." Luke waved a hand. "I'd love to explain another time, but for now, I want to get away from it."

For the rest of the walk, they commented on Victorian houses and the quiet streets so different from Houston. But beneath the easy banter, Ashley experienced a riot of emotions. She was wildly attracted to Luke, felt certain he desired her, too. Luke was sexy. Smart. Big-hearted.

Too good to be true. And yet...

She wanted to throw her arms around him, to kiss him in the middle of the sidewalk, to appease the unsatisfied charge of her wanting. Whatever hesitations she had about relationships were, for the moment, obliterated. Her body and heart were both one resounding *yes*. By the time they returned to the gondola, Ashley's whole nervous system was aflame.

The attendant helped them into their own private gondola car. "Good night," he said as he closed the gondola doors. And then they were alone together.

Ashley sat on the bench beside Luke, facing the mountain, fighting the urge to lean into him. She was highly aware of his body, his heat, the electric charge leaping between them. She felt the inner pulse, the convulsing of longing.

Please, kiss me.

All around them, the snowy mountains reflected the light of the sun just set, and the peaks blazed the most glorious pink. Ashley drew in her breath.

"I've never seen anything like it," she whispered.

"Alpenglow."

In tacit agreement, the two sat in content silence, cradled by rose light as they glided toward the ridgeline in their private bubble. The only sound was the rise and fall of their breaths, the hum of the gondola as it moved on the cable, and the internal pounding of Ashley's heart.

The longer the silence lasted, the more holy it became, almost more intimate than a kiss. At first, reeling with an uncontainable elation, Ashley began counting her breaths to stabilize herself, to stay safe, and then she consciously chose to follow the reeling, to let herself spiral into growing delight. *This is my life.* She, Ashley, was riding above the ground in a rose-drenched world with a wildly desirable, intelligent man who somehow unloosed all her yearnings. She noticed their breaths had linked. Had he done that? Instead of counting the breaths, she focused on the sound of their joining, exquisitely aware of the smallest nuances of inhale and exhale. It was surprisingly intimate.

When the gondola car finally arrived at the station, Ashley and Luke emerged into the world of noise and people. She longed to reenter that glorious cocoon-like state with him. As if he, too, felt the same impulse, Luke, who was walking right behind her, leaned his head down toward hers and hummed a gentle tune in her ear. He held her shoulders from behind and slowly swayed with her, pulling her into a spontaneous slow dance, the rest of the world melting away. Beneath his touch, she became hum, vibration, resonance. She lost all sense of anything but Luke. *Luke. Luke.* Together, they were nucleus. They were molten core. They were a minor chord searching for resolution. Her fear began to crumble; the sharp creases of her crumpled heart began to soften and unfold.

And then he pulled away.

"C'mon. I promised to get you back to the gals."

Shit. She'd forgotten the gals.

Chapter 4

When Ashley walked into Jamila's house, it smelled of garlic, cumin, and ginger. Jamila's chef had prepared an Indian feast and was setting the colorful dishes buffet-style on the kitchen bar.

"Hey, Ash," Jamila shouted from the kitchen, "just in time! I'll grab you a drink."

Ashley curled into the couch next to Abigail and Lola, and they wove her into their conversation about the latest Cormac McCarthy novel, how bleak it was and his curious punctuation choices. Ashley was grateful to slide into the familiar comfort of her friends. Her emotional equilibrium was off, and she was grateful for this stability.

Dinner was delicious, but while eating, Ashley realized Meg wasn't with them.

"She's downstairs with the sexy director she met last night at The Peaks, Terrance's friend." Sarah giggled. "They're, um, playing pool."

"Nice euphemism," teased Claire.

"Well, they *are* downstairs, and I think there's probably a stick involved," said Sarah, assiduously studying her nails.

Dinner conversation leapt from skiing to raising kids to who deserved the Pulitzer Prize. Ashley joined in and laughed and teased with her friends, but in the back of her mind, she was replaying the gondola ride. The ephemeral pink. The joining of their breaths. The sacred quiet. It was a rare person who could share an elegant silence. And then there was her body's response when Luke had touched her shoulders and hummed in her ear. Just thinking about it conjured the same trembling sensation.

When she and Luke had said goodbye, that had been it. When would she see him again? What was this between them? Could he be as wonderful as he seemed? She promised herself to be vigilant. She couldn't afford to miss clues about his character.

"Well, friends, I'm ready for bed." Aziza stood.

"What?" Sarah pouted. "I thought we were having a pajama party!"

"I'm exhausted," Aziza said. "I'm not so young as you, my dear."

"I'm done in, too," said Abigail. And one by one, the rest of the gals admitted to hoping for an early night.

Still wound up from her interaction with Luke, Ashley stepped on her bedroom balcony. She grabbed a blanket from her bed and wrapped herself in it, then walked into the cold, clear night. The naked sky dazzled her—as if the night had unzipped its long black dress and millions of stars had slipped out.

No skyscrapers. No streetlights. No sirens. She stared through the constellations into the dark and let herself be filled with wonder, immensity, peace. And then she heard a cough. She looked left. Standing in the dark on the neighboring balcony was Luke.

"I didn't want to bother you." He projected his voice across the snow-filled yards. "But I really wanted to bother you."

She was bothered all right. In all the right ways. She felt an irrational happiness. "Hi, Luke," she half shouted back.

"Nice to meet you here in the field of infinite possibility." He gestured to the sky.

"You say that to all the girls."

"Gotta stick with what works." She heard the smile in his voice. "You're so far away over there."

"About forty-nine feet."

"That's forty-eight feet too many for a good conversation. I've got some extra room on my balcony. Join me?"

I'll climb right into your bed, boyfriend. She shouldn't go over. Should she?

While her brain deliberated, her body made its decision and was walking her into her room for her shoes. She grabbed the book she'd bought him, then slipped out the back door of Jamila's house, leaving it unlocked. She followed the short snow-packed path to Luke's house.

Luke was there at the open door, wrapped in a red plaid blanket, a big smile on his face.

"Here." He held out a matching blanket to Ashley. "Let's go see some stars."

"Here." She handed him the book.

"Ashley, thank you." He stared at the cover, then fixed his eyes on her. "I was looking for *The Path to Love*. And you remembered." His voice carried surprise and delight and pleasure.

"Maybe you'll read me a passage, Mr. Pioneer."

"I'd like that. But first—"

He set the book down on the entrance table, and Ashley followed Luke through the house to an office and then out to the balcony where she'd seen him. There were two wooden Adirondack chairs, side by side. They settled in.

"So." He looked up. "If you could pick a star to wish on, what dream would you make come true?"

You pushing me up against the side of the house with your lips warm on my neck. "Um, you go first."

"Being here is a dream," he said, sincere as night. "Right here. Right now. Different realities weaving together. Yeah, this is really good."

Ashley agreed. This *was* really good. She tried not to think of all the ways it could improve, but they flooded her anyway. *You could wrap me up in that blanket with you.*

"You?" He turned to look at her.

Ashley was glad the night hid her blush. He was all philosophical, and her dreams were in the gutter.

"I'm guessing"—he tapped his fingers on the armchair—"it has something to do with Peru."

"What? How—"

"You showed me your stack of books at the bookstore."

"Wow, Pioneer. You have a good memory."

"For things I care about, I do."

His words sank in. God, he knew just the right things to say to make her feel seen, to make her want him even more. And god, he looked good in the starlight.

"Yes. Peru. I have a lifelong passion to teach there. It's a promise I made to someone long ago, a promise to help a small village in the mountains, a promise I look forward to keeping."

"You have a passion for teaching," he reflected, leaning in. She could feel him encouraging her to say more about Peru, but she was trying to not think about it much in case that dream didn't come true. Plus, right now, the only passion she was feeling was for him. She imagined slipping her hands up his thighs to feel if he were as turned on as she was. She inhaled sharply and kept herself focused on the discussion at hand.

"I've always loved teaching. I have a dream about helping *a lot* of kids."

"In Peru?"

"There, too, in person. But I mean virtually, worldwide. Starting in Houston."

"Really? Tell me about it."

Sensing genuine interest, she tamed her lust and continued. "I'm a public school teacher, and Luke, our institutions are failing our students. Good kids who love to study are falling through the cracks."

He nodded, all his attention on her words. God, it was unnerving to try to talk to him about this while she was so turned on.

"And kids who need extra encouragement to study are *really* falling through the cracks. My dream is to create a free online STEAM program for high school students who need extra encouragement and supportive mentoring."

"STEAM. Science, technology, engineering, art, and math, right?"

"Right!" She was impressed he knew the acronym. "Of course, free STEAM programs already exist online, but I want to make a highly interactive program, customized for kids who find STEAM intimidating. We'd teach them at a slower pace, make the learning more relaxed, take the frustration out of it, make it more fun."

"You've given this a lot of thought," Luke said. "How are students guided?"

"Teachers interact live in small group settings that match students by ability. Each group also has a high-achieving volunteer student who gets extra school credit for helping bridge the teacher and students in the groups."

"Good thinking." It was such a turn-on to have him be so interested in her ideas.

"I have a beta site that shows the model works." She forced her voice to be even. "Not that my primary aim is improving test scores, but we need a metric, and the kids in the beta are substantially improving their scores. And…our retention rate is way above industry standard."

"You really care about this."

"A lot."

"You're familiar with the other online STEAM programs, I suppose. Do you have a strategy for setting yourself apart?"

"Setting ourselves apart. Right. Clearly, STEAM is critical training for the future. In two decades, NASA says we'll have people living on the moon. Elon Musk is planning a colony on Mars. But as we teach this stuff, I can't help but think we're missing something. We added the arts, but something else is missing."

"Put your finger on that missing piece, Ashley, and you'll have yourself a winner of a program." He stared into the sky, then lifted his gaze to her. "I manage a foundation. We allocate large sums of money for nonprofits needing early-stage seed capital—in fact, we *need* to give money away. We're always looking for great, innovative education programs. If you set your organization apart, this would be exactly the kind of program we donate to."

Ashley was stunned. Seed capital for early-stage opportunities? That was exactly what she needed. Exactly what every other potential funder had turned down, all of them saying she needed to get it up and running before they'd look at it. Most potential donors didn't even respond to the proposals she'd sent. And here, wrapped in a plaid blanket, was her angel investor.

"Wow, Luke." This was not the turn she had anticipated for this evening.

Talk about the stars aligning. This is it! I need to come up with the angle for him to say yes.

Ashley felt dizzy with elation, excitement. Her dream to make a difference in the world had a chance! Or was the dizziness from wanting to throw her body onto his, her longing to have his hands everywhere, his mouth claiming hers? Could all her dreams really be answered in one savagely dazzling package? She wanted him more than ever. If there were brakes to slow down the feverish racing in her body, she couldn't find them.

"Thanks," she said at last. "I'll give it some serious thought."

"Not too serious, I hope. The best ideas come from play. In fact, let's play together tomorrow. Ski with me?"

"Luke. I got pretty bruised up last time."

"It happens. When it comes to skiing injuries, it's all *down-hill* from there."

She laughed despite herself. "Your puns are *snow* bad."

"Yet you play along. Let's ski tomorrow, Ashley. What do you say?"

"Hey, Luke, you coming or what?" came a man's voice from the office. "Game is starting two minutes ago."

"Just a minute, Carl. I'll be right there." Luke turned to Ashley, his shoulders lowering in apology. "I forgot about the house poker game tonight. And I'm the host. Guess the sight of a beautiful woman in the starlight does that to a man."

He's going off to play poker? That was *not* how Ashley had envisioned the rest of this night going. She must have looked disappointed because Luke's face softened in the loveliest way, as if her obvious longing to spend more time with him pleased him.

"Here." He offered his hand. "Help you up?"

She took his palm, craving the charge she knew would be there when they touched, but she was not prepared when the energy of their contact leapt from her hand to the back of her neck to the hollow of her stomach—an instantaneous synaptic rush.

He didn't let her hand go, nor did she try to reclaim it. He led her off the balcony, through the house, down the stairs, into the starlight, across the snow, and to Jamila's back door. She longed for the path to be longer.

"Tomorrow at ten?" He squeezed her hand goodbye.

"Yes."

And she was alone.

Ashley breathed deeply. The sun glinted brightly on the slopes, but the spring wind was cool and bit her cheeks.

"Here." Luke skied closer to her. "Let me help."

He tugged on the zipper of her parka. "If you don't zip it up all the way," Luke was saying, "the ride up the chairlift today will be miserable." He zipped slowly, as if he, too, was intoxicated by their closeness.

Despite the crowd at the base of the lift, she had the urge to reach up and pull him into her, to kiss him the way she'd dreamed of kissing him all night, her lips insistent, ravenous. How was it they had yet not kissed? Not for lack of opportunity—the gondola, the balcony, the back door. God knew she was willing. More than willing. *Kiss me now.*

He was such a gentleman, maybe too much? Though she loved the way he was caring for her now and appreciated he wasn't the kind of man who just wanted quick access into her pants, the longer he was tender, the more savage her fantasies became.

Last night, alone in her bed, she'd imagined pushing him down to the bed and straddling him, pressing her hands to his naked chest, running her fingernails through the short dark hair she imagined she'd find there. Imagined him rolling her over to top her, knitting his fingers through hers, pinning her to the mattress, plundering her mouth in a searing kiss. Imagined him pulling her dark nipples into the warmth of his mouth, how she would spread her legs for him, inviting his hard cock to push into her wetness, an inch, another inch, another inch. How deep would he penetrate? Imagined writhing beneath him, coiling around him, their pelvises grinding, their bare stomachs sliding. And though it was her own greedy fingers that brought her to climax, it was his name she sighed when she came. Again, and again.

Yeah. She hadn't gotten a lot of sleep.

"What are you thinking about?" His hands reached the top of her jacket.

Your face buried between my legs. She silently rubbed her fantasy all over him.

Luke looked right into her eyes and held them while he let the back of his bare fingers travel slowly along the side of her chin, trailing the caress back and forth. The raw intimacy of the touch made her tremble, and she felt the sweetest tightening in her core, her body demanding more.

Then again, going slow has its advantages. She was loving every minute of this lengthy seduction, astonished that his simplest touch could stoke in her such ferocious arousal.

"I was thinking how lucky I feel." She hadn't meant to say it, but the words spilled out. Perhaps the rush of everything going right at once was too much. This dreamy man wanted to spend time with her. And beyond the mind-blowing good looks that made every woman who walked by them stare, Luke was a better listener than many of her friends. He believed in her project. He believed in *her.*

"Let's make sure that luck continues," he murmured.

The ski day passed in a beautiful blur. Ashley fell repeatedly, and Luke, a graceful, expert skier, stayed close to her, encouraging her, praising her efforts, making her laugh. She loved it best when he skied in front of her, and she watched his round ass and thighs as they flexed into the turns. Someone that comfortable in his body just had to be amazing in bed—such animal grace. Such control. Such virility.

Once, skiing near the edge of the run, Ashley saw a candy wrapper in the snow and, in her efforts to pick it up, crashed and ejected from both skis, her poles flying out of her hands.

"That's what we call a yard sale." Luke chuckled, gathering her equipment as she sat up and dusted snow off her body. "What happened?" He offered her his hand to get up.

Ashley pointed at the wrapper, five feet away. "You were cleaning up?" He raised an eyebrow.

Ashley nodded. "I'm not great at stopping yet."

As she worked on clicking into her bindings, Luke skied over to the wrapper and put it in his pocket. "I'll play on your team."

"I'm voting you MVP, Luke."

His smile then was so undefended, so full of delight that he'd pleased her, that Ashley almost fell again. Instead, she blushed, knowing the cold would hide it. Luke not only made her horny, but he made her feel beautiful. Even powerful.

"*Mademoiselle*," he said in a pronounced French accent, donning an overly dashing expression. "*Je cherche à te plaire*. I aim to please."

Ashley shook her head and laughed. She felt so free. *This is a man I could fall in love with*. And instead of running the other way, she was skiing toward him as fast as she could.

Tonight, she thought as she made turns behind him. *Tonight, I will meet him under the stars again. Tonight, I want that kiss. I want that tongue. I want those hips, that fine butt*. She was glad she had stayed on the pill, despite her lack of recent sexual activity. Truth was, she liked the control of knowing when her cycle would be. But now, she was grateful for the protection it offered her. Surely, he would have condoms, too. *Time to ramp up the flirting*. She wanted to send a message loud and clear: She wanted him. Tonight.

As they rode the chairlift, she sat closer to him, their thighs touching through layers of snow pants. She was about to nestle into his shoulder when Luke commented on her need to pick up errant trash.

"I care about the Earth. Every little act counts."

And then it hit her.

"E. A." Enthusiasm bubbled up in her.

"What?" Luke turned to her.

"Environmental Activism. E. A. We add that to STEAM and make STEAMEA. We directly link our program to the planet's health. We don't just teach students the lessons; we teach them what's really at stake—the survival of life as we know it. We give them an urgent reason to learn."

Luke nodded contemplatively.

"No one else has created an in-depth, hands-on STEAM program with a global ecological focus. We can help shape the generation that will make the real changes needed to support the world. Eventually, we can bring kids from different continents together. We can help create the heroes our planet needs."

"STEAMEA." Luke nodded. "I like your idea. In fact, I *love* this idea. Practical. Unique."

Ashley sat taller as she watched her excitement take root in him. *This is your chance, Barris. Be brave. Make the ask.* "Luke, you mentioned your foundation yesterday. And I want to be clear. I don't need someone to ride in on a white horse and be my hero, but I do need help getting my nonprofit running. Is this the kind of project your foundation would support?"

"Highly likely. It would be a privilege to have our name associated with a program such as this. In fact, I think you'll have people beating down your door to get in. I can already think of three people who would rally to help you launch this. *You* are the MVP now."

Ashley couldn't believe her ears. Luke was not only talking about funding her program himself, but he also had ideas for additional funding? Excitement exploded in her. She'd fostered this dream since she was Emilia's age, longing to affect large-scale positive change for other high school students. And now, marrying her passion for teaching STEAM with her passion for the environment—how had she not thought of it for her online program before?

"Luke." She searched his face. "You mean it?" It was more of a statement than a question. She knew he meant it. His earnestness was one of his most endearing traits.

"Oh, I mean it."

Then gravity hit her hard. She had asked him to commit to a major monetary undertaking, something that not only fulfilled a dream but would give her a job next year when her teaching contract almost certainly would not be renewed. He had said highly likely—almost a yes.

And now, her desire for him, which moments ago felt like a gift, now felt like a problem. The person who was willing to support her nonprofit was the same person she wanted to seduce. She couldn't have both. That was the perfect way to mess *everything* up.

Wait. Was he using the lure of money to get her into bed—an empty promise for a night full of sex? *No.* She'd given plenty of signs she was a willing partner *before* this offer, and he had yet to even try to *kiss* her. The commitment to help fund her project felt sincere. *It would be a privilege to have our name associated with a program such as this.*

Ashley was suddenly terrified of making a mistake. No matter how sexy Luke was, no matter how much she wanted him, what would happen if they had a fling and it didn't work out? Would that jeopardize the funding? He hadn't signed any dotted lines yet, but he seemed to be the first viable investor for her program.

Make this work, Ashley.

For the rest of the ski day, Ashley and Luke continued to evolve STEAMEA. He was a wonderful sounding board. He had a businessman's acumen, and on the chairlift rides, he praised her ideas and shrewdly helped her develop them to entice other donors. They talked about creating a board and rolling the program out in stages. Her respect for him grew by the minute. She could tell his respect for her had grown, too.

The more they talked business, the more she tried to tame her lust for Luke. A doomed effort. His every move turned her on. The tides of his laughter made her knees weak. The way he happily sang beneath his breath while skiing made her heart ache, such a pure expression of joy. Everything about this man made her want to beg him to make love to her. But she wouldn't. She knew now she *absolutely wouldn't*. He was the answer to *all* her dreams, both romantic and career. And those two things were oil and water.

⁓

"Then after the hot tub, he rolled me in the snow," said Meg at dinner, telling everyone about her exploits with the director. "My whole body tingled like crazy! He called it a 'sugar cookie' because the snow stuck like granulated sugar to my skin."

"It's like porn meets that Dutch athlete who says the cold is so good for you," said Abigail.

"And then, when I was chattering, he dunked me in the hot tub again and wrapped me in a giant towel, and we went inside where he, um, warmed me up from the inside."

"Holy shit, Meg," Sarah gasped. "You and that director had sex more times this week than I've had in the six months since my daughter was born."

"Most creative sex of my life," Meg replied. "I'd never be so loose in Houston in case I run into a parent or student. I think I need to vacation more often."

"Josh needs some lessons from your director," Abigail said. "We've never made *sugar cookies* or had sex on a pool table."

"What about you, Ash," Meg cajoled. "You've been spending lots of time with Luke. What's up?"

"Nothing to tell."

"Oh, come on," encouraged Lola. "He's gorgeous. I've been dying to ask you, but I didn't want to pry. And since Meg brought it up—"

"Really, nothing to tell. We had a great time skiing today."

"Bullshit," coughed Meg. Ashley gave her friend a kick under the table. "Sorry," Meg mouthed.

"Ladies." Jamila clapped her hands twice. "I have a bit of a surprise. I didn't want to tell you until it was confirmed, but we got into Dunton Hot Springs on a cancellation, and we'll go first thing tomorrow."

"Ooh, sounds yummy," Abigail said. "My body could use a day of soaking after skiing all those bumps!"

"Day *and night* of soaking." Jamila did a shimmy. "We're going to stay in a luxury ghost town."

"What?" exclaimed all the women in near unison.

"Yeah, restored miners' cabins clustered in a circle around a saloon and dance hall. I've been dreaming of this for years, and Terrance is giving it to us for my birthday! Plus, massages for everyone!"

Though Ashley joined in the loud chorus of cheers, she was thinking of how she and Luke had made plans to meet for a late brunch tomorrow before he returned to Houston. And tonight, he was hosting an event for his colleagues, so she wouldn't see him again this trip. Her heart sagged.

After dinner, she snuck up to her room to text Emilia she would be out of cell range for the next day. Emilia texted back right away that she was safe at Lift House.

Next, she texted Luke.

Ashley: Leaving for a ghost town tomorrow early. Have to cancel brunch, sorry

She waited for the little floating bubbles to appear on her screen that meant he was responding. Nothing. The sinking feeling in her stomach had less to do with missing him tomorrow and more to do with feeling as if she was missing out with him for good.

Hours later, he responded.

Luke: Soon as you are back in Houston, let's meet to
talk STEAMEA

So, they had a date. Thank god. How quickly she'd become accustomed to seeing him every day. It would be hard not to see him—she already hated the emptiness inside her where he was not. And it would be hell to see him and not flirt.

She couldn't wait.

CHAPTER 5

"TO A GREAT TRIP AND A fabulous hostess!" Lola raised her champagne flute. The women clinked glasses and leaned back in the posh airplane seats to return to Houston.

Ashley sat in the front with Jamila. "Thanks," she said. "You and Terrance made all this possible, and it was wonderful."

"Thank *you*, Ashley. That was the best trip I've had in years. Nothing like being with friends."

Ashley felt a little guilty—though the time at Dunton had been over-the-top luxurious and the female bonding at Jamila's house had been soul-nourishing, the most memorable part of her trip had been connecting with a heart-stoppingly sexy man now poised to help make her online program a reality. She was high on potential thinking about STEAMEA and positively *soaring* with giddy tremblings and fantasy-driven flutterings every time she thought of Luke, which was *all* the time.

As if sensing her thoughts, Jamila amended her comment. "Nothing like being with friends old *and new*. I didn't want to bring it up in front of everyone, but you did seem to enchant the hottest, most eligible bachelor under forty in all of Houston."

"Luke?"

"I thought you might not know."

"Know what?"

"Luke is heir to the Dalton oil dynasty. His great-grandfather founded Dalton Oil."

"He's Luke *Dalton*?" Her stomach twisted. Terrance was a lawyer, so she'd just assumed that the other folks in the group he was with in Telluride were all—

"Luke Dalton."

"No." A sour taste rose in her throat.

"Terrance is general counsel for Dalton. Luke's dad is CEO, chairman of the board, and president, and Luke's next in line. Vice president. He's a billionaire."

"Who's made a fortune at the expense of the planet! Why didn't you tell me? You knew I would care."

"Honey." Jamila touched Ashley's arm. "I knew I'd never seen anything like the look on your face when you first saw Luke walk into the house. I've known you a long time. And I've been hoping for two years to see you fall in love again."

"You should have told me."

"*And*," Jamila spoke so quietly Ashley barely heard what she said next, "I saw the way Luke looked at *you*."

Ashley sighed. "But Jamila. I *protest* Dalton Oil and petition them to regulate their oil-drilling practices—among other things. You remember how angry I was when they were pursuing drilling in the Arctic. Thank god *that* fell through." Jamila raised an eyebrow, and with that small gesture, Ashley realized something important about Jamila's husband—and perhaps Jamila, too.

"Wait. All this time I've told you about my protesting, you never said anything about Terrance working for Dalton Oil."

"I know. Just because I'm married to him doesn't mean I can't support you in your efforts. In fact, I really believe in what you do on behalf of the environment."

Interesting. Ashley nodded, taking in the new information about her friend.

"Well. Thanks. That says a lot about you. But I could never..." She let her voice trail off, worried she might offend her friend by saying *she* would never date a man who drilled in the Arctic.

"Honey." Jamila's voice was soothing. "Listen closely to your nevers. They are like little invitations to get tested by the world."

"Well, it doesn't matter anyway. Luke and I are just friends."

"Not what I saw."

"But that's the truth." Ashley's voice was stern. She leaned back in her seat and stared out the window.

Dalton Oil? This changed everything. Not only could she not fall for someone in the oil industry, but she also didn't want to take their dirty money for her program, either. Was that why Luke was so eager to fund her program? Guilt? Some way to pretend to balance all the damage his company wrought while in the meantime creating more damage?

"Ashley, I've known Luke Dalton a long time. He's as good as they come, as close to a fairy-tale prince as I have ever seen. He's got looks. Power. Charm. Only thing missing is a castle, but from what I've heard, his penthouse is pretty darn nice."

"I'm not looking for a prince."

"But you found one. Look. I didn't say anything about his work, Ashley, because I didn't want you to let your ideals get in the way of your heart."

Ashley stared out the window. She was pissed. At Jamila. At Luke. At everything.

"Hey. The other thing I wanted to tell you is—well, I've never seen him like this before. I have this feeling you might be the person he needs."

"Whose side are you on?"

Jamila raised her flute. "Chicks before dicks, always."

Ashley smiled and took a deep breath. "Look. Something's going on with me and Luke, but it's not what you think. And now I'm second-guessing that, too."

"I'm here to talk anytime you want."

But Ashley didn't want to talk about it anymore.

The Monday after a break was never easy. The kids' energy was chaotic. So was Ashley's.

She'd spent all day Sunday trying to reconcile taking money from Dalton Oil. After making a pros and cons list, she had mostly concluded it was better to have the company spend its profits teaching kids how to save the Earth than on anything else. Still, the source of the funds made her uneasy.

Then there was the fact she could not stop fantasizing about Luke. Last night, she'd dreamed of her legs draped over his shoulders, his tongue skillfully licking her, his teeth nipping, his lips traveling. She'd thought of how his cock would stretch her, would hit that perfect spot inside her that made her forget language, how their bodies would crash together like two ocean waves that on contact become one body of water.

"Ms. Barris?" One of her students was raising his hand. "I need to leave early for track."

Five minutes left in the day.

"Sure, Antonio. And everyone, tomorrow is lab day. We'll use lemonade to study molarity." *Because when life gives you lemons—*

She started packing her things. Pulling her phone from her desk, she noticed on the home screen there was a voicemail. *From Luke.* Her heart skipped. Damn her rule about no phones during class.

Five minutes lasted five thousand years. What did the oil exec have to say? *Would he want to meet?* Her body panted, *Yes.*

Her brain said, *Bad idea*. In unison, they seemed to say, *Maybe he'll invite me to his office?* Yeah, she knew where Dalton Oil's main office was—she'd protested there many times. *Oh, the irony.*

As her libido and conscience wrestled inside her—pulling out moves like a half Nelson slam and a double-knee arm breaker—Ashley wandered the room, checking in with the student pairs. By the time the bell rang, she was exhausted.

She sat in her chair and stared at her phone. She'd been hoping he would call. *Libido: So, I can hear his voice and see him again. Conscience: So I can turn him down.*

What a bundle of contradictions she was. Vilifying him in her mind, starving for him with her body.

Too bad a phone message can't transmit his addictive scent.

Stop it.

At last, she pressed Play.

"Hi, Ashley." Even the way he said her name turned her on. Confident, masculine, warm. She felt her chest tighten, her breath quicken, as if he were beside her. "It's Luke. I've been thinking about our talks about STEAMEA. I'm totally committed to finding ways to make this happen. This week's busy. Can you meet Friday night? Dinner? Seven? At Infinity Tower. The concierge will send you up. Call or text and let me know. I'm looking forward to it."

Who conducts business meetings on a Friday night? And that building was in a super-swanky part of town. Was there a restaurant there?

She did a quick Google Maps search. No restaurant in the Infinity, just residential. So, he was inviting her to *his* place? For a business meeting?

And maybe something more.

Stop it.

Ashley pressed her hand to her heart and felt it straining against her chest. *You will never have an intimate relationship with this man.* She summoned a surge of anger about the nature of his work.

Oil driller. Polluter. Defiler. She pictured a brown pelican, its feathers covered in oil, struggling in the sludgy surf. She considered children with asthma that came from inhaling sulfur dioxide from refineries.

And then another voice snuck in. *Of course you will go. This is the chance you have always wanted! To meet with a top oil executive—not with a protest sign, not on the phone, not in an editorial showdown, but face-to-face!* And Luke was a reasonable, thoughtful man. She knew this from all their interactions so far. She could talk with him directly about transitioning his company toward cleaner energy sources.

Ashley shook her head, excited by this new framing. This was an incredible opportunity! Clearly, Luke was open to having discussions about environmental activism—he was enthusiastic about STEAMEA. The way to create real change was at the top, and now she had an in with the *vice president*!

Sit tall, she told herself, a little mantra she'd used for years to help herself find confidence in difficult situations. She straightened in her chair, took a few deep breaths, forced a professional smile onto her face, and hit Call Back. The phone went straight to voicemail.

"Hi, this is Luke—"

Just the tone of his voice made everything steel in her soften and liquesce. She forced her voice to be steady, formal even.

"Hi, Luke. Thanks so much for your call. I'm looking forward to talking with you about STEAMEA. I have new thoughts I'm excited to share with you. Friday is fine. Seven. See you then."

She hung up and let out a huge rush of breath. How could she wait until Friday? And how was she going to be professional all night in his presence when she could barely make it through a phone message without melting? The latest oil disaster hadn't been in the ocean. It had been in her heart. And what a mess it was.

"Step in," said the uniformed concierge, guiding Ashley into the sleek steel elevator. "Mr. Dalton is expecting you. Forty-first floor."

The elegant destination elevator had only two buttons on the inside—one for help, the other for the lobby. The concierge had pressed the button for Luke's apartment from behind his desk.

"Thank you." Ashley drifted in, feeling as if she'd entered a foreign country where she didn't know the customs. Was she supposed to tip the concierge? She'd wondered the same thing about the valet. There was no information about how much it cost to park in Luke's building, but from the building's modern exterior and luxurious interior, she'd guessed it might cost most of her weekly lunch budget. She was relieved to discover she didn't need to pay. But should she tip?

She panicked a bit as the elevator rose. She realized having buttons of her own to push gave her an illusion of control, even if she didn't push them. Not having anything to push filled her with unease. Without a row of buttons on the wall to count, she counted her own toe taps—*One. Two. Three.*

Guard up, Barris. This man was already under her skin. *Don't let him deeper in.*

When the door opened, she gasped. She'd arrived in a spacious, elegant room with no furniture, just a skylight, and astonishing art on the walls—*a Miró?* Ashley turned right, drawn to examine the modern painting. As she stepped forward, she saw around the corner the penthouse opened into a palatial room with cathedral ceilings, floor-to-ceiling windows, and an uninterrupted view of the Houston skyline. The huge living room and its modern couches and tables seemed to float in the sky.

"Right on time." Luke appeared beside her, his smile welcoming and warm. "Welcome."

Damn, you are one handsome man. Dressed in a pale blue Henley and jeans, he looked like a men's cologne model—the dark silk of his hair, the small glimpse of his chest where the top button of his shirt was undone. *Two. Three. Four.* Ashley counted buttons, longing to unfasten them. And he smelled, *mmm,* like Luke.

Shit. She was already undone, and the night had just started. She had promised herself no flirting, no sex. Too much was on the line.

But wouldn't it be wonderful to get him undressed and inside you?

Stop!

Luke gave her an amused look.

"Hi, Luke," she mustered. "Wow. I'm amazed. What a beautiful place to live."

Looking past him, she saw the dining table with half a dozen flickering cream candles. *Is he seducing me? Where does he think this will go?* Ashley realized she had been sending mixed messages, and she couldn't blame him for thinking she might want to be seduced. She was going to have to find a firm and gentle way to set the record straight.

"Luke," she began, straightening. "I'm so glad you invited me over to talk about STEAMEA—"

"And do I ever have a surprise for you." His smile reached into his eyes. "Come in." He gestured toward the table at the far end of the room. "Wine? White or red?"

"White, please." She felt as if she'd walked into an architecture magazine at the doctor's office. At a sleek bar near the table,

Luke poured two glasses of wine. Meanwhile, Ashley noticed a first course already set on the table—and three settings. *Three?*

"Luke! How are you?" said a woman's voice from the entrance. A very attractive woman walked toward them. Brunette, she looked to be in her fifties. With her silk ruffled shirt and pants that flowed and flared, she looked as if she'd stepped out of a fashion magazine. *Who is this?*

Luke gave the woman a brief hug, and Ashley immediately realized Luke had *not* hugged her when she had arrived. She felt bereft. "Welcome, Laura." Luke held out his hand to welcome her in. "You look great."

"Just another day in the glamorous world of investment banking." Her laughter was light and self-deprecating. Ashley liked her immediately. "And this must be Ashley. Hello." She extended her hand.

Nice shake. "Hello. I'm Ashley. Ashley Barris."

"Laura Barnes. I'm so excited to meet you and talk about your vision for helping students. I've known Luke forever." She smiled toward him. "When he recommends someone, I take notice."

"It's nice to meet you."

"You're a teacher, yes?" Ashley nodded. "My mom was a teacher. Not an easy job."

Immediately, Ashley could tell this was a woman who enjoyed helping other women. She flashed a quick look at Luke, thanking him with her eyes. He beamed at her. Here was a man who knew how to open doors. All the anxiety Ashley had felt dissolved into gratitude. This man was a constant surprise.

"Come, Laura, Ashley, let's sit down." Luke handed each woman a glass of wine, then led them to the long, elegant table.

The three made easy small talk over salad, and by the time the chef served the main course, they had moved into talk of mission statements, core business models, and securing grants.

Luke disappeared into the kitchen and returned with an elegant tray. "For dessert, apple pie *and* truffles from Telluride." Both women oohed and aahed. "Here, try a truffle," he said, holding an assortment out for Ashley.

"Chocolate is not my favorite, but I'd love a slice of pie."

Laura eyed her curiously. "Not your favorite? That's okay. I still trust you. But me? I would wither without chocolate." She bit into a triangular confection. "Mmm."

Later, Luke offered the women coffee, tea, or an after-dinner drink, but Laura declined and stood to make her goodbyes. Ashley stood, too. She didn't trust herself to be alone with Luke.

Was that a look of disappointment on Luke's face? If so, he covered it up immediately, replacing it with appreciation.

Ashley smiled at her new allies. "What a wonderful night, Luke, Laura. This evening is a dream come true for me. Thank you for everything."

"Thank *you*, Ashley." Luke took a step closer to her, and she fought the urge to step closer to him, too. "Your great idea is about to make the world a much better place to be a kid."

She flushed at his praise.

"Speaking of kids, I'd better hurry along." Laura grimaced. "Who knows what my teenagers are up to!"

Luke walked them to the elevator and gave them each a brief, platonic hug that set off in Ashley the most torturous ache. She desperately wanted to stay in his arms, to be pulled into the hard planes of his body.

As she and Laura stepped into the elevator, Ashley's last picture of Luke was his blue eyes flashing as the doors slid shut. Inside, she felt fluttery and flustered. Ashley took a mental photo of the feeling. She knew it would need to disappear, but at the moment, she wanted to live inside that delicious rush forever.

Back in her car, Ashley ran through the night's conversations as she drove toward her small apartment. That was *not* how she expected the night would go. Shaking her head, she grappled with her competing desires to shriek in excitement and moan in frustration. *What a night!* Luke was a consummate gentleman, never overstepping his bounds. A valiant knight, intelligently championing her cause. A freaking Adonis with a statuesque body that, even fully clothed, made her swoon.

And did you forget he's an oil man, polluter, contaminator? Did you consider how he paid for that penthouse in the sky?

It had not been the night to talk with him about clean, sustainable energy, but after their discussion, she felt increasingly certain he would respond well when that conversation occurred. He was entrenched in fossil fuels because that was the legacy he was born into. But with the right information, Luke would understand the importance of using renewable sources. The time for that conversation would come. And in the meantime, she was building trust with him.

Her phone rang through Bluetooth. *Luke.*

"Hello?"

"Ashley!" His delighted voice surrounding her made her want to pull a U-turn and rush back to him. "That was phenomenal! You're a natural leader. Your program outline was perfect. I have such confidence in you."

He was gushing. Ashley felt shy in the face of such lavish approval.

"You weren't kidding when you said you had an amazing surprise, Luke."

"I hope you don't mind I didn't tell you first. I wasn't sure Laura could make it, and I didn't want to promise something I couldn't deliver. But I knew you were prepared to meet her—the way you had pitched me in Telluride was so perfect."

"Sometimes there's a blessing in not knowing to be nervous," she admitted. Though it was a lie. She'd been nervous all week thinking about seeing him again.

"You are one special lady."

"Luke, thank you. But I'm the one who should thank *you*." Though she could tell he was speaking from the heart, she was increasingly uncomfortable with the praise. Heat rose in her chest, her neck.

"I'm not going to stop." His voice exuded enthusiasm. "I am going to make a few more phone calls that sing your praises, and we are going to *build* this nonprofit. Laura just called from her car, and she is *in*. So, next steps: in a week and a half, I want you to do a presentation for five to ten people, prospective board members. Is that enough time to prepare?"

Absofuckinglutely! "I think that would work just fine." This was all progressing so fast. In fact, if anything, Luke seemed on a hell-bent mission to get her organization on its feet.

"Good." His tone made it sound as if finding new board members was a done deal. "I'm off to Europe tomorrow for a week, but when I'm back, this will get my full attention."

"Thanks, Luke." She struggled to comprehend how the world had put just the right person in her path to build her a dream team. "I can't believe what a big help you are getting this started."

"Just call me Mr. Pioneer. Oh, and we'll need another educator on the board, too, preferably an administrator. Can you find that person?"

John. "I've got it."

"I'll be in touch in a week. And Ashley."

"Yes?"

"You're amazing."

It wasn't until after she got home Ashley remembered to be guarded.

CHAPTER 6

"WAIT A MINUTE," MEG said to Ashley. They were standing in the teachers' lounge after school got out on Wednesday. "Did the history teacher just ultra wink at you?"

"It's a game we play, Meg."

"That particular wink might have sprained his eyelid. And I think it was directly linked to his crotch. Are you going to put the man out of his misery? He's hot for you."

Ashley shook her head.

"Because you're still hot for Mr. Telluride." Meg watched her friend for a reaction.

Ashley blushed.

"Ahhh, you are."

"Shut up, Meg."

"Are your panties all up in a twist since you found out he's an oil guy?"

"Meg. Keep my panties out of this. And Luke and I are just friends. And we're going to stay that way."

"So, let *me* sit on his face!"

I will scratch out your eyes. "Ha ha."

"For a chemistry teacher, Ashley, you sure do seem to be oblivious about your own chemistry. I could smell the pheromones across the room when you two were together."

"Meg. You can't *smell* pheromones. And no. There's nothing more going on. And no, you can't sit on his face."

Ashley was a little shocked by her own possessiveness. And how transparent she was.

"Whatever you say. But that man is *hot*, and if you're not going to take advantage of that body, I want a shot at him."

Meg's words lit a fire in her. *Jealousy.* That's what that feeling was. *Damn.* Ashley couldn't remember the last time she felt it. And it burned.

———

"Doesn't it feel good, Emilia?" said Ashley into the car's Bluetooth. "You worked hard for that grade, and it paid off."

Emilia had not only chosen to stay clean, but she'd also recommitted herself to her schoolwork. Since the most recent crisis, Ashley had met with her twice at the Lift House for their usual Thursday afternoons at four. With only minimal guidance from Ashley, Emilia had just received an A- on her history paper.

"Thanks, Ashley. Have a good Friday night with your mom."

Ashley was just pulling onto her mom's street. "Talk soon."

As always, Ashley felt a mix of gratitude, comfort, and apprehension the closer she got to her mother's home. The city had started to pay attention to this neighborhood, thank goodness. In addition to the drunks, dealers, and folks prowling for trouble, there were families here like hers. Men and women struggling to put food on the table and give a good quality of life to their children.

At last, she pulled up to her mother's one-story house. It looked like most of the other houses around it—its cream paint was peeling, the roof needed repair, the metal screen door looked weathered and tired, and the yard out front grew more weeds than grass. There were no sidewalks in the neighborhood. *It couldn't be more different than where I was* last *Friday night.*

Ashley made a mental note that this summer, she needed to round up a crew to repaint her mom's house. She wished her mother would move, but her mom always said the same thing. "Why should I waste money on rent when this home is paid for?"

"Hi, Mom." Ashley let herself in with her own keys, stepping directly into the small living room. "Smells like barley minestrone!"

"Only the best for my girl," her mom sang out, coming from the kitchen to hug her daughter. "It's so good to see you, Ashling. More beautiful every day, inside and out."

Ashley smiled at her mother's nickname for her—a blend of *Ashley* and *darling*. "I brought you a pie, Mom."

"That you made? Peach? My favorite. When do you find the time? You do more in a day than I do in a week. I wonder if I ever had as much energy as you."

"Um, yeah, Mom. You held down three jobs and raised two daughters? That was monumental. No wonder you're tired!"

"I *did* do that." Her mom chuckled, rightfully proud of herself. "Though I wish I could have spent more time with you girls. I was proud of my work, but I was gone so much…"

Ashley stroked her mother's salt-and-pepper hair. "You are the best mom in the world. I learned to fly because I saw you fly."

"Well, I may not have a high school diploma, but I did raise two amazing young women."

While Ashley's mom took the pie to the kitchen, Ashley surveyed the small clean house. It was full of trinkets and photos of her and her sister and many shelves of books. All the furniture was the same since she was born—all the furniture except, of course, the couch and its blue sofa cover. Mom had gotten a new one after that horrific night.

Ashley shook free of the memory and turned to her mom in the kitchen. "What can I do to help?"

"You can tell me what's new in your life."

"So much, Mom!" Ashley told her about the trip to Telluride, meeting Luke, the dinner with Laura, and the upcoming meeting with potential board members. She didn't mention Luke's money came from oil. Her mom often accused her of being too judgmental—throwing out the baby with the bathwater—and she didn't want to go there now. Ashley also neglected to mention how *attracted* she was to Luke.

"That's wonderful about STEAMEA, sweetie, but what if you get that job in Peru? Could you do both?"

"That's the blessing of an organization that's primarily online. We can have virtual meetings."

"The world has changed so much. I don't understand half of what people are talking about these days. Still, I think you might want to mention to this Luke feller that you might be teaching on the other side of the world come August."

"Not yet. That job is a long shot anyway, Mom."

"But how could that little Peruvian school not say yes to you? Who could possibly be a better choice for helping those kids learn their potential?"

"I really want that job, Mom. I want to honor Tica—I want to help the children in her hometown the way that she helped me and Jewel. I want to go eat *pan huaro* like she used to make. And hear her songs and see her mountains." *And I want to help Tica's soul find peace by bringing her ashes to her birthplace.* That was a promise she had made Tica, but somehow, it felt too intimate to say out loud.

"What a blessing Tica was in your life. May she rest in peace." Her mom made the sign of the cross. Ashley felt her phone buzz in her pocket. *Luke!* Ashley chastised her heart for leaping up like an excited puppy. *Keep it professional, Barris.*

Luke: Eight people confirmed for STEAMEA pitch! Thursday, 5:30, Laura's office. She will text the address. Can't wait!

"Good news? You're smiling big."

"Mom, it's going to happen. A board meeting is happening! Thursday." Once again, Luke was coming through for her. Was there anything hotter than a man who believed in you?

Ashley's mom reached out to stroke her cheek. "I always knew you were born to change the world, Ashling." Ashley covered her mother's soft hand with her own, remembering how rough her mom's hands had been when she cleaned houses ten hours a day.

"Thanks, Mom."

As they ate minestrone, Ashley couldn't help but think about where she would be five days from now. Her pulse leapt when she thought of seeing Luke again. *Down, girl*, she told her heart, but all night, it leapt up, eager and quick.

"Pour you some more?" Jewel didn't wait for an answer and filled her older sister's glass with sangria from the pitcher she ordered. For almost three years, the sisters had met at different restaurants every second and fourth Tuesday of the month—Ashley considered it an investment in her mental health.

In many ways, the sisters were opposites. Jewel, twenty-eight, was reckless, treated dating like a sport, and preferred to invest in a good time instead of a career. But their love for each other and their mother was fierce. "Now that you've taken the edge off," Jewel said, "tell me why you're having a hard time with the funding stream for your project."

Ashley sipped the sweet, fruity wine and sighed. Aside from her initial conversation with Jamila, Ashley hadn't spoken of Luke's profession with anyone else. *It may be a dirty secret, but you can't keep it from yourself.* So tonight, she'd told Jewel.

"I think it's *perfect* for an environmentalist's project to benefit from an oil man's money," Jewel said, handing her sister the glass of sangria. "If you shake oil and water long enough, they mix just fine. You just have to keep on shaking."

Though her sister's comment was well-intentioned, it made Ashley queasy. What she had been able to rationalize in her mind sounded worse when Jewel laid it out. The truth: oil and water didn't mix. It was foolish to pretend.

Ashley's phone rang. "It's Luke." She stared at his name on the screen. She was furious at herself for the elation that effervesced in her when she saw his name.

"Answer it, dodo!"

Ashley fumbled with the phone, aware her sister was watching her intently. "Hello, Luke?"

"Ashley." Two syllables were all it took for him to launch a full-on seduction—part growl, part purr, part steel, part caramel. "I'm so glad you picked up. I'm just back from Europe, and despite the fact I have a company to run and a dozen departments to check on, I've been thinking about tomorrow's meeting all week. I'd love to go over a strategy for presenting STEAMEA with the group I rallied. You free?"

"Um, when?"

"Now?"

"Aren't you exhausted?"

"You're not wrong," he chuckled. "But this project keeps coming to the forefront of my thoughts, so I'm honoring it. And *then* I'll catch up with all my departments. Sleep's a long way away. So...can you meet now?"

Ashley felt her pulse skyrocket. It was a slightly different tone than she'd heard from him before—the voice of a man used to getting what he wanted. "He wants to meet," she mouthed to her sister, pointing at the phone. Jewel shooed her, both hands flapping like wings.

"Ashley?"

"Um, yes. I can meet you."

"Great. I'm at Alexander's Bistro."

"I'll be there in ten."

"Wonderful."

Jewel's eyes were devious and piercing. "Wow. Well, it's about time."

"Shut up, Jewel."

"I *won't* shut up. I want to talk about how your voice got all husky and sexy kitten-ish and you started blushing before you even answered the call. Your whole body changed—like you were about to start dry humping your phone."

"It's business."

"Don't lie to me. Now I know why you're having such a *hard* time with the funding." Her eyes flashed devilishly. "You obviously didn't tell me everything about the oil man."

Ashley relented. "Okay. So, he's smart. And kind. And handsome. But we need to stay friends."

"Friends who fuck?"

"Friends who run a nonprofit together."

"How old?"

"Thirty-six."

"Four years older is perfect for you." Jewel rubbed her hands together in mischievous glee. "Ha! My sister, the scientist, is part of a grand experiment. She's mixing oil and water and business and pleasure all in the same beaker. Stir it up, baby."

"I'm glad someone is enjoying this. But Jewel, I'm *agitated*. One minute, I'm so freaking excited, and the next, I feel so guilty. I don't know if I should run away or jump right in. I feel like my standards are being tested. A couple years ago, when I spent half my monthly budget on protesting signs and ads to save the Arctic, that was to get *Dalton Oil* to clean up their messes. And you know who that was on the phone? Luke *Dalton*."

Jewel's eyes sparkled. "Enemies to lovers. My favorite trope."

"Look. No one else has ever given a damn about my business proposal, and Luke was genuinely enthusiastic."

"I see. Oil man covers up guilt from oil spills by investing in wholesome community projects. Makes a mess in one spot, cleans it up in another."

Ashley slumped.

Jewel continued. "His guilt evaporates, and yours grows. But—" She took a sip of sangria and smiled wickedly. "—none of this should stop you from sleeping with him. Think of it as separate beakers. One experiment at a time."

A chemistry experiment was right. Instead of a beaker, it was a business. The materials being tested together were lust. Delight. Altruism. Fantasy. Desire. And *guilt*. Like a true chemical reaction, it was producing heat. Lots of heat. That meant, whether she liked it or not, she was becoming something new.

STEAMEA was becoming a reality. But was the cost her integrity?

Luke rose from the small table in the bar area the moment Ashley entered. She almost stopped breathing when she saw him. He wore a fitted, soft gray suit that hugged his masculine frame and showed off his athletic build. A pale pink shirt. A pale pink silk tie. He looked every bit the powerful dynast he was.

But it was Luke's face that slayed her—so open, so warm, so appreciative of her. It wasn't that he leered. It was just the way he looked at her made her feel so…so woman. It made it hard to reconcile that he was the face of dirty money.

Damn you, body, get a grip.

Part of her wanted to confront him tonight about her concerns with Dalton Oil, but she had promised herself to steer clear of his work and focus on STEAMEA. The nature of their relationship was far too tenuous for her to offend him now. The day would come when they would confront their strongly divergent values.

But not tonight. Tonight, she squashed her unresolved fears, forced them into a small inner black box, and temporarily locked the lid, knowing they would, in true Pandora fashion, demand release and wreak havoc soon enough.

"Ashley," he purred, walking to meet her. He gave her a hug—not an A-frame hug but a full-body hug—and for a moment, she was enveloped in the hard marble of him, her nose steeped in his scent. *Heaven.* She reflexively hugged him back, her hands stiff at first, then relaxing against him. Could he feel her heart pounding against his chest? She didn't want to let go, but she willed her arms to release him.

"Hi, Luke. How was your trip?"

"Very productive. Totally worth the jet lag." He pulled out a seat for her. "A bit of *plug ugly*, perhaps?" He gestured to a bottle of the Taittinger "Brut La Francaise."

"Oh!" Ashley said, both thrilled and concerned. She had already had two glasses of sangria with her pasta dinner. But Luke had obviously bought the champagne with her in mind, and she was rather touched by the thoughtfulness of the act.

"*Oui, monsieur.*" That was about the extent of her French.

"*Ah, ma chère, parle-tu un peu de Français?*"*

"*No, hablo español, señor, pero cuando en Roma—*"** She looked around the bistro as if there were men in togas running around.

Luke laughed, and Ashley watched his eyes light up with pleasure. And maybe something more? Whatever it was, that something more sent a message to her center. Her blood quickened,

---

* Ah, my dear, do you speak a bit of French?
** No, I speak Spanish, sir, but when in Rome—

and she felt an almost painful, delicious spasming between her legs as she imagined him pressing his tongue to the pulse in her neck. She scissored her legs and took a deep breath.

Luke handed her a flute. "To learning." He raised his glass. "And unlearning."

"To learning and unlearning." *And aren't you the perfect teacher.* Ashley raised the glass to her lips, breathing in the sprightly dry scent of the champagne. She sipped. It tasted wonderful.

Luke reached up to loosen his tie, then paused. "Do you mind?" he asked as a true Southern gentleman would.

"Please." She nodded. *Did that come out wrong? Did that come across as "Please, take off your clothes"?* Because that was *exactly* what she was thinking. *Shit.* She was tipsy. *Best behavior, Barris.*

His strong hands worked against the knot to reveal more of his neck. Ashley did her best not to stare at the bronze he exposed there. She forced her eyes to meet his, but that was almost more dangerous. He had a way of looking at her when they spoke that made her feel totally seen. It gave her delicious shivers.

An hour and a bottle of champagne passed in a giddy blur. They spoke about the prospective board members—a lively, dynamic group of Houstonians with a passion for the cause.

She relished the easy comradery, the playful punning, the intoxication of being near him, and the reality of her plans for STEAMEA finding traction. She felt totally relaxed, in her power, and wildly turned on—the combination making her dizzy. She could feel the judgmental walls she'd built around him and the source of his money tumbling down, and the champagne helped her lose her will to reassemble them.

"There will be a lot of questions," he said, speaking of the board meeting. "And I know you're prepared."

"I've never been more ready. I'm on fire." *In so many ways.*

Luke raised his near-empty champagne glass. "To the spud date."

Ashley paused before they clinked. "The what?"

"Oh, sorry. When drilling a new well, the spud date is the day when the main drill bit begins drilling for oil."

"Let's hope it's not one of those spud dates where they drill and drill and drill and leave the toxic waste there without cleaning up the mess."

Hello, Pandora.

An awkward moment followed with both of their glasses raised. A flash of surprise registered in Luke's eyes, but his body remained composed, and his smile stayed constant. He looked at her with curiosity.

"Let me change the metaphor," he said. "Thursday is Chrysalis Day. It will be a great strategic jam session in which the wings for STEAMEA will be forged from imaginal cells. I think I might be even more excited about it than you."

Ashley offered him a weak smile. Despite Luke's celebratory words and deft reframing, her opinionated outburst had decidedly changed the mood. They clinked their glasses and finished the last sips of champagne.

Shit. What am I doing? Ashley felt deeply unsettled. She wanted to castigate him for his business. She wanted to pull him into her arms and not let go. Luke was so genuine, so sweet, and his cash flow came from something so destructive, so devastating. She was confused, and the champagne wasn't helping. *Control yourself.*

"Luke." She looked at her watch. "Thank you for the champagne. Thank you for tonight. I wish I didn't need to go, but it's a school day tomorrow. And I have a big meeting to prepare for the day after."

"I'll take you home."

"It's not on your way," she objected. "I'll just Uber."

"It's what I want."

Ashley liked the way he said it. Ever since Telluride, she'd had a harder time reading his cues. What was their relationship? Clearly, they were becoming partners in business. And she knew *her body* wanted more. But what did Luke want? In Telluride, she'd been so certain that he was attracted to her, and now? Even if she couldn't have him, some part of her still wanted him to want her.

"I'll make sure you get to your door safely. You're tipsy."

"What?" Her voice was playfully defensive. "Tipsy? Me, the new up-and-coming nonprofit executive director?" Ashley moved to stand and felt herself list a little. She looked at him sheepishly and sat back down. "Okay. Maybe a *little* tipsy. It was that ugly brut," she slurred. "He has an unbalancing effect."

"No cham-*pain*, no gain." Luke's grin turned her resolve to resist his charm into diaphanous gauze.

"Ooooh, that was a *pour* joke, Luke." The champagne had control of her tongue now. What else was it going to say?

Luke shook his head, his eyes bright with amusement. "Come on, Ashley. Let's get you home."

"I never thought, all those times I protested outside your building, that I would meet a Dalton, much less that a Dalton would be driving me home."

Luke stood very still, his face unreadable. "Excuse me?"

The dark box was fully open now. Champagne had picked the lock.

"I protested on Main Street a lot a few years ago when y'all had it in motion to drill in the pristine territory in Alaska."

"And what did your sign say?"

"Choose clean energy now."

Luke's expression gave nothing away. "I'm not surprised you're an activist, Ashley. You live up to your acronym—the EA.

I'm just surprised it took you so long to mention something about it to me."

"Now I have."

He leaned back in his chair. "So, what next? What else is on your mind, Ashley?" There was no defensiveness in his tone, more of a real curiosity.

Ashley felt as if she were at the starting line of the one-hundred-meter race. Now that they were talking oil, there were at least twenty miles of topics she wanted to cover. She felt herself sober up and put on her organizer hat.

"Well, in the big picture, I'd love to see Dalton Oil move from fossil fuels to renewable sources of energy."

Luke didn't flinch.

"It's so possible, Luke—a sustainable-energy future. Think of it. Clean water. Right now, seas absorb as much as a quarter of all man-made carbon emissions, and it's causing ocean acidification, and it's imperiling entire food chains."

He nodded, encouraging her to continue.

"And think about the damage made through fracking. Those chemicals—over a thousand of them—don't disappear, Luke; they make their way into our water, our land, our air, into fetuses."

"It sounds like you're judging me." His voice was even.

"You make executive decisions for the company, Luke."

Luke responded with stillness, receiving her words and her energy, giving her the space to continue.

Here she was, facing the oil exec as she had dreamed of doing so many times while out on the street with her sign, and part of her wanted to continue calling him to task, but part of her saw that he was also the generous benefactor of her nonprofit dream. She saw him not only as an opponent but also as a thoughtful, sensitive, kindhearted, caring man. She felt momentarily defused, disarmed.

Ashley felt suddenly exhausted. "Luke, what are we doing?"

Luke looked at her warmly, somehow accommodating her barrage. "We're doing great things together, Ashley."

They both inhaled and exhaled, almost as if it were choreographed. Though the breath was steadying, she had completely lost her equilibrium. She felt stupid.

"Ashley." He stood and held out his hand. "Let me take you home."

———

Luke drove a Chevy Tahoe. *Gas guzzler.* She climbed into the passenger seat while Luke held her door.

"Your chariot, m'lady." He bowed slightly before closing the door. The gesture was so charming it distracted her from her judgment about the car—as usual, she was in a game of tug-of-war between Luke's reprehensible career and wealth and his benevolent and respectable character.

When the radio came on, it was playing "A Thousand Miles" by Vanessa Carlton, and Luke sang along. He had a lovely baritone, perfectly in tune.

Being this close to him in their own private space reminded Ashley of the gondola, and damn if she didn't feel grateful to be together with him in the spotless and shiny gas-guzzling Chevy. For the moment, it was her bubble against the rest of the world—especially the world in which she considered him her opponent. Here, she could listen to her body clamoring for him to be closer and enjoy the easy banter and intimacy of the car ride.

When they pulled up to her apartment, Ashley felt a strange surge of pride. Her place wasn't fancy, but it was *hers.* She'd worked hard for it.

Luke turned off the car engine, and they sat in a charged silence for a few moments, as if they were both toeing the edge of a bluff they weren't sure they should jump off. Ashley reached for the car door handle. "I'll get it." Luke jumped out of the Tahoe. He came around to open her door and offered her his hand to help with the big step down.

"Thank you." Ashley more stumbled than stepped out of the car. *Damn champagne.* "Oh!" She arrived on the sidewalk a little closer to Luke than she'd intended, and he didn't move back to accommodate her misstep. A wild tremor passed through her, a lightning bolt of lust. She inhaled his scent and felt her body tingle in response, barely able to breathe as the rest of the world faded to watercolor and Luke was the only thing in sharp relief.

"Luke." Her voice quivered. As if of their own will, her arms reached up to wrap around his neck, her hands slipping into his thick hair. The curls parted like dark silk between her fingers, just as she imagined they would. The rest of her body urged her fingers on, and they explored the taut cords of his elegant neck, the hard muscles of his shoulders. All the longing of the last several weeks since the bookstore rose like a riptide, carrying her swiftly into currents she didn't have the strength to fight. *Please, I have to kiss you.*

The pure masculine vitality of him drew her in, and she pressed her softness into the hard heat of his body—such tempting erotic terrain. She closed her eyes and stood on tip-toe to reach her lips up toward his, her hands urging his head down toward hers, her mouth opening to receive his tongue, his breath, the warm pressure of his lips.

And firmly, gently, he stepped back, not so much pushing her away as creating space between them.

Ashley could feel her swollen nipples pressing against her shirt, aroused by the brief contact. In fact, it was as if her whole body had opened to receive him, not just her mouth. And now, apart from him, everything, *everything* throbbed like an open wound.

A hot, red flush of embarrassment bloomed in her immediately. She was too raw to do anything but apologize. "Oh. I'm
sorry. I, um, oh, I'm sorry, Luke." She removed her arms from
his shoulders and crossed them in front of her chest in some
primitive, unsuccessful attempt to protect herself. She couldn't
step back because of the truck, and Luke stood between her and
her apartment. Ashley desperately wanted to escape.

Luke smiled at her with tenderness. "It was a wonderful
evening. Thank you." The warmth in his voice almost made the
whole scene worse.

"Thank you, Luke. Um." *Shit.* She exhaled deeply. "See you
at the meeting."

Luke walked back to the driver's side, but Ashley was inside
her apartment before she could hear the engine come to life, hot
tears sliding down her cheeks.

"You idiot," she muttered, chastising herself over and over.
"What have you done?"

———

Entering the lobby of Laura's office building a half hour early,
Ashley did her best to walk tall. She'd chosen a navy blue suit
with a white button-up shirt.

The suit talks, her college teacher used to say. *You need a
look that will get you in the door.* This was a make-it-or-break-it
meeting, the gateway to her dream. She needed to be professional, clear, and competent.

All the things she had not been two nights ago.

It had been hours before she'd finally found a fitful sleep
that night. She kept replaying that horrible moment when she
had thrown her body onto Luke's and he'd rejected her. She
had rubbed her breasts against him and tried to kiss him—and
he'd stepped back. Why had she been so stupid? Of course he
wouldn't kiss her. They were in different leagues. They had a

professional friendship—he was tied to the purse strings for her dream career. She'd let her fantasizing get the better of her. She'd projected her own feelings of desire onto him and assumed he felt the same way. She'd read him all wrong. It hurt. And she was scared. Scared she'd messed up with Luke. She respected him so much. She wanted him to respect and like her, too. He hadn't called her since then. Nor texted. Was he offended? She couldn't afford to offend him. He was now integral to the launch of her program. Dammit. *Damn champagne.*

The other thing that rankled: Ashley couldn't remember another man who had pulled back from a kiss. She was no stranger to abandonment—her father, her first lovers, and symbolically her cheating husband. But no man had ever passed up willing lips.

Does he prefer men?

Did I fuck up everything?

"Ashley!" It was Luke, arriving at the elevator, his usual smiling, confident self. "Ready for the big time?"

Ashley had rehearsed this moment. She forced a smile. "Luke." She extended her hand. "About the other night. I sent a mixed message. Please—"

"Stop." He brushed the air with his hand, as if erasing the whole thing. "Let's go over again who will be here." The elevator opened. He momentarily pressed his hand into the small of her back as they moved forward in unison. The touch elicited an instant forbidden pleasure. Ashley stiffened. Now who was sending mixed messages? At least she didn't seem to have irreconcilably offended him.

Be professional, Barris. Stepping off the elevator into Laura's office, Ashley couldn't ignore the electricity leaping between her and Luke as they walked side by side to the receptionist, but she could redirect it.

"Hello, Luke," said the redheaded receptionist, obviously thrilled to see the handsome businessman walking toward her. She kept her smile genuine as she looked at Ashley. "And you must be Ashley Barris. We're expecting you. Would you like coffee?"

"Please. Black with a hint of sugar."

"None for me, thank you, Jennifer," said Luke. "I'll take Ashley to the boardroom."

The boardroom windows looked out over the other high-rise buildings in downtown Houston. Luke walked to the end of an oblong table and pulled out the chair.

"Your seat, Madam Executive Director." He made a flourish with his hand.

Ashley walked toward him and set down her attaché. "Luke, will you say a few things at the start to welcome people?"

He chuckled and shuddered. Ashley gave him a quizzical look. "I will say a few words, of course, to introduce you and thank people for coming. But I will turn it over to you immediately. I really, *really* don't like public speaking."

Is he just saying that to get me to step up? "Okay. I'll take the lead." *Sit tall.* She flashed him a smile to send a message to her brain, and she felt confidence rise in her. "We've got this."

"Yes, Ashley, we do. *You* do. I believe in you."

A very tall, elegant man walked in. "Alec, welcome. Let me introduce you to Ashley Barris."

For the next two hours, Ashley was an intelligent bonfire, fueled by her passion for teaching, for kids, for science, for sustainability, for grassroots leadership, and for the planet. Whatever sparks of interest already existed in the others, she fanned them into a blaze. She could see it in their faces, hear it in their voices. She went from feeling as if these leaders had something to offer her to knowing she had something winning to offer them and to students everywhere.

And she loved it.

She was glad John was there. His presence calmed her, anchored her. Plus, he had valuable input as to exactly what holes in the system Ashley's program could fill and how it would benefit students, teachers, and ultimately the business world.

And Luke. *Luke.* Twice she saw on his face a look of such admiration that it propelled her to be even more responsive to questions and suggestions, more impassioned, more persuasive, more in her power. It was such a turn-on. God, she loved impressing him. She loved that he loved her brain. And she was glad that the other night's kissing snafu hadn't had disastrous effects on today's meeting. She and Luke were an amazing team. He'd assembled a powerful group, and she was high on the synergistic buzz of great minds. All those years of hard work had prepared her for this moment.

By the time the meeting ended, the mood in the room was grand-slam fantastic. She had commitments for board members and for donations—more donations than she'd dared budget. Elation pulsed through her.

As the last people left, she watched Luke shaking hands with two of his colleagues. Even amongst alpha males, even when he said only a handful of words, Luke was still the inherent leader. He carried himself with *savoir faire*, but he also had a raw power, a primal energy that simmered inside his fine manners and designer suit.

Ashley, Laura, John, and Luke were the last to leave. The foursome stepped together into the elevator. Only then, when the doors had closed and they were alone, did Ashley break her professional demeanor with a loud, exuberant sigh.

"Ashley, you were amazing!" John gushed. He pulled her into his arms and gave her an enormous squeeze. Ashley felt Luke brace beside her.

"Outstanding, Ashley." Luke gave her a polite and approving smile. He sounded sincere, but there was an air of reserve about him. *Strange.* She had caught him sizing up John. *Is he jealous?*

"Great start, Ashley," praised Laura. "You have all the support you need to begin. Now for the real fun."

"To my surprise, *that* was really fun!" Ashley laughed, joy effervescing through her like a Coke and Mentos explosion. "I feel like the richest woman in the world."

"You've worked hard," Luke acknowledged. "And it's paying off. You're going to help so many kids."

"*We're* going to help so many kids," Ashley said to her elevator mates. "I couldn't do it without all of you. Thank you."

Whatever happened now between her and Luke, at least she knew there was wider support for her program. He'd given that to her. *And at least I'll see him eight times this year for board meetings.*

A small familiar knot of sadness and frustration balled in her gut. If only it didn't hurt so much to want what she couldn't have.

CHAPTER 7

THIS TIME WHEN SHE arrived at Luke's penthouse, Ashley was less freaked-out by the valet, the concierge, the buttonless elevator. She was no less agitated, however, by the thought of spending an evening with the handsome man who had set her fantasy life into hyperdrive. At least she knew where things stood.

When the elevator doors opened on the forty-first floor, she took a deep breath and walked toward the kitchen. Luke had said he was cooking tonight, and the apartment smelled of paprika and oregano.

"Ashley!" Luke called from the kitchen. "Welcome. You're like a Swiss watch. Not only are you perfectly punctual, you're just in time for the recipe. Did you bring the olives?"

"Here you go." She set the kalamatas on the counter. The kitchen had everything she would have wanted in a kitchen for herself—an enormous pantry, a six-burner gas stove, every style of knife, and on the stove top, the finest pans. And Luke. He was gorgeous in it—his muscles flexing as he repeatedly lifted the sauté pan to flip its contents in the air. *Mmm.* Ashley wanted *him* for dinner. He was wearing a black-and-white-checked apron from Williams Sonoma. *I wish that was all you were wearing.*

Stop it.

Ashley tossed him a smile and sniffed at the air. "Cajun?"

"Mm-hmm. Your nose *knows*. It's a recipe my Rena used to make me."

"Your Rena?"

"Oh. My nanny, I guess. But she was too much a part of my life, too important, to be called a nanny. I always called her *my Rena*. She's the one who taught me what olives could do to this dish."

Ashley imagined Luke as a little boy. It was surprisingly easy. Though he was roguish and devilishly striking now, he was also so playful she could see him as a young prankster.

"She taught you to cook?"

"Oh, I followed her everywhere. I owe everything to Rena."

"Tell me more."

"Over dinner, sure. There's wine chilling at the bar. Pour us each a glass?"

Ashley walked to the bar and noticed the table set for two. Candlelight. Red roses and white lilies. In some ways, it was the same as when she and Laura had come. Perhaps it looked more romantic now because there were only two settings? She pushed romance out of her head. Her body rebelled and let loose a hundred blue butterflies winging in her stomach at the thought of just the two of them dining by candlelight. *Mercy.*

She found Luke again and handed him his glass. God, he was handsome in an apron. It seemed incongruous—the domestic billionaire—and somehow so right.

"A toast." He raised his glass. "To the lives of all those students who don't know the road that even now is being paved for them."

"To the students."

"And," he quickly added, "to the woman who dreamed of how to make it happen."

Ashley blushed. "And," she added, "to the man who helped make the dream come true. Thank you, Luke. To STEAMEA."

"To STEAMEA."

They sipped the dry white, hints of grapefruit and fresh-cut grass that sang in her mouth. Luke suggested Ashley go out on the balcony while he finished dinner. "Just a few minutes more," he promised.

It thrilled her *he* was the chef tonight, not someone he hired. You could taste the chef's hands in a meal. She could hardly wait.

She walked out the sliding door, already open, and leaned against the corner railing. The sharp-angled towers of Pennzoil Place dominated the skyline in front of her, and behind her, the sun dipped to kiss the horizon. To the east was the neighborhood where Ashley grew up—the place she'd spent thousands of hours studying so she could escape from it. The place her mother still lived.

It was strange to stand in such luxury, feeling high on all that was going right, and look down toward that neighborhood with its empty dirt lots and paths through the weeds, its broken windows and gunshots, its faucets that would never stop dripping.

And somewhere out there, perhaps, was her father, the man who had left when she was four. The man her mother refused to discuss. Where was he? She reached out with her thoughts as if she could sense him, a practice she'd had for at least twenty years, but she never felt a connection, just his absence.

Was he even still alive? Why had he never come back to them? Would she ever meet him? And would he be proud of her now if he could see her here using her tenacity and brains to make her dream come true?

Though she'd long ago given up on finding answers to the questions, they felt no less insistent. Why wouldn't a father want to reach out to his daughters? *Why didn't he want me and Jewel in his life?* She inhaled deeply and felt her shoulders rise and slowly fall.

And then she was aware of Luke behind her. Not that she felt his breath, not that she heard him, more that her nerves were attuned to him, were exquisitely sensitive to all things Luke. And they tingled now, the way strings in a piano resonate at their fundamental frequency when other strings that share an overtone are played.

Luke didn't speak. She didn't dare turn around, afraid the look on her face would give away her desire. For a tenuous moment, they stood in the delicate silence before Luke stepped forward and rested his hand lightly on her hip.

My god. Just the slightest touch and she felt surrounded by him—by his presence, his scent. Her heart thumped with sudden intensity. Desire spiked between her thighs. She felt a small gasp rise, and she swallowed it. *Get it together, Barris.*

It was as if the place he touched was two thousand percent alive and no other part of her body existed. His touch lasted, what, a few seconds? Each second sliced into a million bits, each bit lasting a year, and each year thronged with a million competing emotions.

"Dinner."

Was it just her own longing that had made the touch so intimate? She didn't trust herself to know. If it hadn't been for his rejection the other night, Ashley would have turned around and pulled him into her, but there was no way she was going through that kind of embarrassment again. *Touch is just an electric impulse*, she reminded herself. *Just information moving through your neural infrastructure. Nothing more.*

She followed him in, her body and mind both reeling. "Here." He pulled out her chair.

"Thank you, Luke. Dinner looks and smells amazing."

"At your service." He bowed slightly, his blue eyes not leaving hers.

I wish *you were servicing me.* God, she was wet just like that. Electricity rushed in her veins, and heat surfaced everywhere. *Damn overactive neural circuitry.*

Dinner was a near disaster. They spoke a bit of STEAMEA and his upcoming trip to Geneva for business, but Ashley was so agitated by her own desire, her craving for Luke, and her determination not to crave him that she could hardly take a bite of the etouffee or the red beans and rice. She tried, but her body had gone into survival mode and wouldn't let her eat. Luke's face was a study in concern and disappointment.

"You don't like the meal?"

"It's delicious."

"But you're not eating?"

"I'm sorry, Luke," she apologized, embarrassed. "I love the etouffee; I'm just temporarily not, um, not able to eat." All those butterflies felt as if they were about to emerge through her mouth. And her stomach was a snarl of sexual tension. She tried her best to look dispassionate. "Doggie bag, please?"

Luke stood up, keeping his eyes on her. They were layered with concern, amusement, and something else. Desire? He reached for her hand. She slipped her fingers into his and almost jerked her hand back, shocked by the surge of longing. It was like one live wire touching another. But Luke didn't seem to notice and held her fast. "À *votre service, chère mademoiselle.*"*

"Practicing your French for Geneva?"

"*Mais, oui.*"**

She rose to stand beside him, but Luke did not let go of her hand when she stood. He curled his fingers into hers as if anchoring her to him, and with his other hand, he slowly, tenderly

---

* At your service, dear lady.
** Yes

touched her cheek, drifting his fingertips to her chin and back up to make slow circles around her temple.

"*Ce n'est pas tout ce que je pratique.*"*

"I don't understand." She trembled as he leaned in closer, his scent intoxicating, and she watched his lips approach hers with disbelieving fascination.

"*Comprenez-vous cela?*"** She gasped as he tangled his free hand into her hair, letting it catch behind her neck, where he cradled her head in his palm, angling her face upward to look at him, his eyes intent with rioting desire. "Are you okay with this? I need you to tell me yes."

"Yes," she whispered, her voice a sparkle in the silence between them.

"*Dieu merci,*"*** he growled. Triumph blazed in his eyes, but his head lowered toward hers impossibly slowly until he brushed his soft lips across her temple, her cheek, her jaw, frustratingly tender, and somehow, the tenderness elicited an equal and opposite response in her, an astonishingly fierce, almost brutal desire that surged through her hot and insistent.

Involuntarily, her mouth opened into an O on a ragged inhale, and Luke traced her parted lips with his fingertip, as if they were fragile, holy. So much restraint. A small, strangled cry escaped her throat, a primitive plea for more, and as if that were the sign he'd been waiting for, he groaned and crushed his lips into hers, the wet heat of his mouth claiming her lips in a feverish intensity that matched her own. Like two opposite charges in a storm cloud, both of them shuddered at the lightning they created.

She was more creature than woman, more craving than sense, and she opened to him not only with her mouth but with

---

* That's not all that I'm practicing.
** Do you understand this?
*** Thank god.

her whole being. Their tongues tangled in a wild and silken exploration, and she was desperate for the taste of him, the feel of him, the all of him.

"Ashley," he rasped, pulling briefly away to stare into her eyes, his gaze searching. The air between them rippled with revelation and hunger and whole books of unspoken desire.

Take me now. Please.

His lips hovered above hers for a moment, his fingers curling into the nape of her neck, and his eyes filling with possession and liquid heat. *"Tu es à moi,"** he murmured, and he lowered his mouth again, their kisses obliterating every idea, every memory, every shred of self, and Ashley surrendered to the all-consuming euphoria flooding her limbs, unable to hold anything back.

"Luke," she moaned, her voice thick and tremulous, as he bit at her lower lip, trapping it between his teeth, then sucking away the sharp pain. Instinctively, her legs parted for him, a primal invitation, and Luke stepped between them, grinding his hard length into her softness. *So hard. So good.* She melted into the heat of him, felt her whole body become one resounding yes. She longed to be filled with him, stretched by him, owned by him. Her hips rocked against him, needy and shameless. With greedy hands, she kneaded the hard flesh of his ass, pulling him closer to where she wanted him.

Without breaking their kiss, Luke lifted her into the cradle of his strong arms and floated her across the room. He splayed her out on the couch, lifted his head from the kiss, and sat beside her, his fingers teasing the skin exposed beneath the rising hem of her skirt.

"*Ma belle,* Ashley," he whispered, blue fire in his eyes. "*Je n'arrête pas de penser à toi."***

---

* You are mine.
** My beautiful, Ashley. I can't stop thinking of you.

Though Ashley couldn't understand the French, she could certainly construe the look on his face. "Luke," she whimpered, realizing how completely he had taken charge. She felt caged in by his body, and she liked it. She watched his eyes darken as he slipped a hand up her bare thigh, higher, higher, gliding it under her skirt, his fingers stoking her longing as they came closer to the damp heat of her core. He teased, retreated, teased, retreated. *Touch me, touch me, touch me,* her body clamored.

At last, his fingers trespassed across the soaking lace of her thong, and she gasped as rhythmically, teasingly, he massaged along either side of her clit, igniting the small bundle of nerves without directly touching it, and *oh! Touch me now.* She arched into him, moaning, her hips thrusting and greedy.

"*Oh, mon dieu,*"* he cursed. And slowly, as if it pained him, he drew his hand away, pulling his fingers to his nose, closing his eyes, and breathing in deeply. She, too, could smell the salty perfume of her own arousal.

"Luke?" *Why did you stop?* Whatever hesitation had visited him, she watched as his longing overruled it, and with a tortured groan of surrender, he swung his legs up onto the couch to straddle her, kneeling above her hips, the ridge of his erection visibly straining against his jeans. Heat flared in her, and she trembled as he pinned his hands on either side of her shoulders, surrounding her with his body, his strength. She scratched her nails against his shirt, and he plundered her lips in a rough and hungry kiss that sent lust winging through her.

Oh, the taste of him as they bit and kissed, as he licked and tongued and ravished her mouth. Her body arched and writhed beneath his weight, her hips rising and surging in a desperate attempt to find friction where her body was throbbing. Luke glided over her, sinuous, ravenous, demanding. She moaned

---

* Oh my god.

into his mouth, the low, tortured sound testament to both ultimate bliss and the simultaneous longing for more.

And then, unwanted, some practical part of her started to insist, *What the hell is going on?*

"Luke?" she mumbled between kisses. "Luke?" He paused to hear her, his demeanor immediately changing, as if he sensed the shift inside her. "Luke, I need to ask you something."

Luke lifted himself and shifted his weight, then pulled her up to sit beside him. His expression was hard to read—as if he were exerting great control to not kiss her through her concerns.

"Ashley," he responded at last, his chest still heaving, his lips still glistening. There was some almost imperceptible shift in his demeanor.

"Luke," she began falteringly. "Luke, what's changed since I tried to kiss you last week? When you pushed me away. You didn't even respond. You just...I thought, I thought—"

"Ashley." His eyes softened. His voice was brown velvet. "You were more than tipsy. And for our first kiss, I wanted you to be fully in control. I didn't want you to do something you might later regret. I wanted to be sure it wasn't the champagne making a choice for you."

She looked at him, astonished.

"Wait." His eyes scanned hers, incredulous. "You thought I didn't want to kiss you?"

"That's what I thought."

Luke looked as if he might laugh but then instead exhaled with a low groan, as if he had been containing his desire for so long and could no longer. He stared at her as if there were so much he wanted to say and didn't know where to begin.

That husk she'd built around her scorned heart this past week, she felt it cracking, crumbling. What was left was an incredibly vulnerable, unguarded version of herself that knew nothing of protection, nothing but the terror and thrill of knowing Luke might want her as much as she wanted him, that somehow, as complicated as things were between them, she was being offered the kind of intimacy with him she had stopped believing was possible.

As much as she wanted to keep kissing him now, her brain needed to hear more about where he was coming from. "I've been so confused about you."

Luke chuckled, "It's been confusing for me, too." He adjusted his pants and gave her a sheepish grin. "I'm glad we're talking about this. When I met you again in Telluride, I wanted to support you, to support your dream, to let you know I believe in you and respect you. But then I felt you pulling back. And I understood you couldn't freely kiss someone you felt indebted to. I felt like such an idiot for not seeing it right away."

Ashley stared at him, her eyes wide, astonished. "So…you gathered the board?"

"As fast as I could. Partly to get STEAMEA up and running right away. And partly, selfishly, because I needed you to not feel conflicted about me. I needed to be sure STEAMEA was self-sustaining with you at the helm so you could come to me without feeling obligation, without reservation."

Ashley touched his cheek with her hand, cupping his jaw, relishing the feel of his stubble against her palm. He tenderly set her hand back in her lap and turned to look at her. It was almost as if she were getting a glimpse of Luke in business mode—focused on the task at hand.

"We are in this together, Ashley. This, this—" He waved his hands as if trying to encompass all that "this" might be. "Whatever *this* is, it's fragile. And I don't want to blow it. I am so humbled by you, by how I feel about you. I'm so used to taking immediate action. But with you, I want to be careful."

Ashley's brain and body were both nearing overload. She didn't know which part of her she should listen to first. Her brain was rapidly trying to comprehend the apparent generosity and compassion that drove this man—trying to reconcile it with her judgments against him and his work.

This is a terrible idea, isn't it? Though his foundation was no longer the only funder of STEAMEA, he *was* still on the board. They *were* still business partners. If things went south between them, could he turn against her and poison everything they'd built so far?

Meanwhile, Ashley's body was getting impatient with concerns of her brain. All it wanted was to touch Luke again, to feel his hard cock slipping inside her, filling her.

"What are you thinking?" He caressed her hand with a single finger brushing slowly, gently across her skin.

That I don't want to think anymore. "Luke, I—"

"Say you'll come with me to Geneva."

"What?"

"Say you have some unused sick leave and you can join me in Europe. Say your passport is already current. Say you *want* to come with me. I have some business I'll need to take care of, but then, when that's done, say we can continue this." He kissed her temple. Shivers stippled down her spine. "*Et ça—*."* He kissed the tender skin beneath her chin. "*Et ça—*" And he slowly trailed his fingertips from her cheek to her lips down the center of her chest toward the hollow between her breasts before his fingertips traveled a tender circumference around the outline of one breast. Everywhere he touched became more alive.

Ashley gasped as he lightly strummed his fingers across her hard nipple. "Will I have to speak French?" she asked.

"*Mais bien sûr.*"** He nodded, his expression mischievous.

---

* And this—
** But of course.

"Um, well then—" She ran a finger across his lower lip, "*Croissant*." His eyes darkened, and he bit her finger. She squealed, more out of pleasure and surprise than pain.

She trailed the back of her hand along his strong jawline and whispered, "*Liaison*." Luke's eyes whispered back a litany of dirty promises.

She leaned in until their lips were almost touching. "*Déjà vu*." She ran her tongue over his thick lower lip, and the tip of his tongue flicked toward hers. Then she drew his hand to the gap where her skirt hem met her thighs and rested it there at the edge of the fabric, rucking it up a mere inch. In his ear, she teased, "*Carte blanche*."

She felt him shudder with arousal, and she nibbled on his earlobe until she elicited a moan from his lips. God, she was loving this. She had never had foreplay like *this* before—real play. A seduction that engaged both her body and her imagination.

He whispered in her ear, "*Dites-moi oui*."*

She knew that *oui* meant yes.

"Tell me *yes*, you will come to Geneva," he purred. "*Dites-moi oui*." He pulled back and studied her face for her answer.

Can I? He said he'd be gone for a week. Could she leave school that long? She was allowed ten sick days, and she had only used two for headaches. She had plenty of days to spare, and the year was almost over. *Why not?* Her body insisted. *Why not?* Her brain got on board. She'd already gotten her passport renewed in case the job in Peru came through.

She gazed at him through lowered lashes. "*Oui*," she breathed. "*Oui, monsieur*."**

A swallow rippled down his throat, and he stared at her, arousal intensifying on his face. "*Ma belle*,"*** he groaned as he

---

* Tell me yes.
** Yes, sir.
*** My beautiful.

very slowly leaned her back against the couch again. Her legs fell open, and he climbed between her thighs and deliberately lowered himself to her body.

His thick arousal jutted against her, and she became a writhing, twisting thing, reveling in the weight of him, the animal of his body as he moved against her, pinning her to the couch with deep and leisurely thrusts of his hips, his movements so languid, so intentionally unhurried, it felt as if he was resetting time itself so the night could last forever.

"Yes, Luke," she whimpered, her hands finding the hard planes of his back, and she curled her fingertips into his flesh. But he slowed his movements and stilled his hips. *Don't stop!* With honeyed slowness, he dragged his lips down her throat. She arched her head back, offering him more of her. *More, please, more.*

"Ashley," he moaned as he kissed the long column of her neck, his hands exploring her sides, her hips. *"Je envie de me promener avec toi à travers les villes médiévales, te faire l'amour partout, te faire l'amour si doucement que tue me supplieras de te pénétrer."* *

"Yes," she murmured, "whatever you're saying, yes."

Luke gave her a wicked, playful smile. *"Ah, mon amour, alors c'est parti."* **

Luke let one hand play against the skin exposed by Ashley's V-neck shirt, dipping a finger beneath the fabric, teasing as if he were going to undo the button, then lowered his mouth to suck long and hard on her breast through the fabric.

"Oh," Ashley mewled, thrusting her hands through his hair.

He lifted his mouth, and instantly, she missed the heat. He undid a button on her shirt, then another, exposing the lacy

---

* I want to walk with you through medieval towns. I want to make love to you everywhere. I want to make love to you so slowly you beg for me to enter you.

** Ah, my dear, then it's game on.

outline of her bra, the dark areola showing through the white lace, and he continued to undress her with only his eyes. His gaze seemed to polish her, burnish her with its dark praise. *"Chaque seconde de la journée je ne pense qu'à embrasser tes seins et à comment faire pour que tu sois mienne, et cela dure depuis des semaines."**

Ashley trembled as he licked his lips and pulled back just a bit. *Like a hunter*, she thought, *weapon ready, waiting for the moment he can take the best shot.* And god, did she love being his prey. A sharp tremor pierced her body, and she gasped at its ferocity.

"Tu vois comment ton corps aime quand je te prends doucement."**

Faster. More. Now. "Please?"

He was loving this, tormenting her with slowly titrated pleasure, watching her come undone with anticipation. Ever so slightly, he shifted his hard cock against her damp core, sweet promise of plunder, and she arched into him, becoming desperate.

"I want—" She bit her lip to keep herself from begging. *Or does he want me to beg?* Her mouth opened, but all that came out was a thin bleat.

Luke gave a husky approving laugh and moved dolphin-like against her, watching her reaction to the most minute of his movements. She was breathless, beyond language, beyond consequence. She was feral now, primal. She wanted him. *Now.*

As if in response to her craving, he whispered into her ear, *"Je vais prendre soin de toi, ma belle, mais ça fait longtemps que*

---

* I have thought of kissing your breasts every minute of the day for weeks, thought about how to make you mine.

**See how your body likes it when I take you slow.

je rêve de te voir me regarder de cette manière et je veux juste en profiter."*

She reached up to undo the buttons on Luke's shirt, but he shook his head and raised an eyebrow as if she had been naughty, then took both of her hands into one of his and pinned them on the couch above her head.

She unraveled into a whimper, her whole body entreating him to stop this exquisite torture and just take her.

He tilted his head back, admiring her hunger. *"Oui, maintenant tu es prêt pour moi, je vais prendre soin de toi maintenant."***

"Gah," she shouted, finally undone by the torment, her voice thick with wanting. "Stop teasing, Luke. Shoot me, now."

And he froze. His whole body tensed, arrested above her. "Oh." He exhaled, as if it were painful. His face fixed in a grimace.

"Luke?"

For a moment, they stayed like that, immobile, Luke a statue and Ashley studying him, both of them breathing hard, but the cadence of his inhalations had changed from arousal to, what?

Though her body had just been flooded with heat, it was now almost chilled. Something had set him off. Was it because she'd said to stop? He'd stopped before, too, when she'd asked him to and had gotten all businesslike. But this was different. Something internal.

"Luke?"

When he opened his eyes, they looked clouded, haunted. She gazed up at him with worry. A weak smile came to his face, apologetic, as he realized he was still holding her wrists. He released them and started to move off her.

"I'm sorry."

---

* I will take care of you, beautiful, but I've dreamed so long of seeing you look at me like this I need to savor it.

** Yes, now you're ready for me, I will take you now.

"What happened?"

"I just—I need to step back."

"Did I—"

"Ashley." His voice was tender and filled with, what, remorse? He pulled her up and sat beside her on the couch. "It's not about you."

Unspoken questions filled the air between them. What had changed? How had it gone from erotic to awkward so fast? Though she didn't understand, she wanted so much to soothe him.

"It's okay," she heard herself say. "I'm here."

CHAPTER 8

"O-M-G, ASHLEY." JEWEL PULLED a slinky blue dress from her closet for Ashley to try on. "This one will look *so* good on you in Geneva."

"Jewel, I am *not* wearing that. It's the size of a passport."

"A passport to *love*," Jewel teased. "That's okay. I'll pack it for Cancún." She threw it toward her open suitcase. "How about this one?"

Ashley looked at the next tiny dress. "Oh, please. I'm not wearing it. And *you* shouldn't, either." Ashley rolled over on her sister's bed. "Don't you have anything, you know—"

"Um, boring? Prude? No, I don't. How about this?"

Jewel held up a sleeveless burgundy dress with a plunging neck and a slightly flouncy short skirt. It was beautiful. Elegant. Simple. Sexy.

"Okay," Ashley consented, reaching for the hanger, when she felt her phone buzzing. Though things had been awkward last night when she'd left Luke's apartment, today he'd been texting her all kinds of information about their trip, making Swiss puns, and acting exceptionally normal. Ashley hadn't told Jewel about the strange interaction—it felt too intimate. *What had happened?* In Geneva, perhaps she would ask.

Ashley did, however, tell her sister about the note Luke somehow slipped into her purse before she left that night. On a stiff note card embossed with Luke's initials, he'd handwritten a note in neat, slanted cursive centered on the card:

> A—
>
> *Thank you for saying yes. To be continued.*
>
> —*L*

"Oh sistah," Jewel crooned. "You've got a live one. That man wants to—"

Ashley cut her sister off with a sharp teacherly look she'd perfected with the teenagers in her class, a skill she was proud of. Jewel stuck her tongue out, then lasciviously licked her lips, when Ashley's phone dinged. "He's gotten us a reservation at some restaurant in Geneva with three Michelin stars."

Jewel grabbed the phone from her sister. After a quick search, she reported, "Ashley, this restaurant has a five-month-long waiting list. Damn, the man has taste. And he's typing."

Ashley grabbed the phone back and watched the dancing dots until his message arrived.

Luke: Meet me tonight?

Jewel looked over her shoulder. "Hook, line, and sinker."

Ashley rolled her eyes at her sister.

Ashley: Hanging out with my sister tonight
         Her bday

Jewel grabbed Ashley's phone and typed.

Ashley: And you are invited
         Meet us at La Favorita in an hour

"Jewel!" Ashley shouted.

"It's *my* birthday, sis. And I want to meet the *oil man* who's got my sister all tongue-tied."

Ashley shot her sister a searing look. "Don't call him that."

"But he *is* an oil man."

"Well, he is making changes."

"Wait." Jewel leveled her eyes at her sister. "You think you can change him, don't you?"

Ashley glared at her.

"Wow. You do!"

Ashley sighed.

Jewel put both hands on her head and squeezed, as if her head might fly off if she didn't hold it down. "You didn't even try to deny it." Jewel almost cackled. "Now I get it. I *knew* you wouldn't be able to just let it drop. I should have known—"

"People change, Jewel."

"Are you kidding?"

"He's already on board with my environmental activism program for kids."

"Um, yeah, because he knows that's how to get in your pants."

"No! Because he knows it's *right.*"

"And you think you're going to be able to convince him to stop drilling?"

Ashley said nothing.

"Oh, Jesus, Ashley, really?"

Ashley took a deep breath, trying not to take the bait. "He's a very thoughtful, smart man. He's a good listener. And I think he doesn't know enough yet about the alternatives. He was born into an oil dynasty family, so of *course* he's following in their footsteps. But he could be the one to lead them *all* toward change."

"Do you hear yourself?"

"People change, Jewel."

Jewel threw up her hands. "You're dreaming."

"Who are *you* to judge me?"

"Ashley." Jewel faced her sister. All the playfulness left her voice. "My whole life, you have tried to change *me*. Has it worked?"

"No, I hav—" She stopped. "I have, haven't I?" Jewel nodded.

"Holy shit." Ashley didn't move at all. "Oh, Jewel, I'm sorry."

Jewel shrugged. "It's who you are, Ashley. You don't do it to be mean. You just think you can control things. And people."

Ashley felt as if she'd been punched in the gut. By herself. She didn't like the mirror her sister held up. For a long moment, the two didn't move as Ashley wrestled with demons of self-revelation.

"Hey." Jewel put her arm around her sister. "Come on. It could be a lot worse than having a control freak for a sister. You could've been a crack addict. Or a bully. Or a trombone player."

Ashley gave a half laugh.

"Someone had to be the control freak in our house. I'm just glad it was you so I got to be the fun one."

Ashley punched her sister in the shoulder.

"Come on." Jewel punched her back. "It's my birthday. Let's go dancing. We don't want to keep Mr. Oil Dynasty waiting outside the bar, do we?"

Ashley shook her head. "Luke is going to be so out of place at La Favorita. I don't get the feeling he's hitting the dance halls a lot."

"Then we'll get to see what he's made of, won't we?" Jewel gave Ashley a wink, then grabbed another outfit from her closet and threw it at her sister. "Wear this."

<hr>

"Is this dress legal?" Luke shouted into Ashley's ear. It barely covered her ass, and Ashley was a bit horrified by it, but Jewel had called it her birthday present for Ashley to wear it.

Plus, some part of Ashley was dying to see what a little red dress might do to Luke. He had suggested they wait to have sex until they went to Geneva. *Talk about delayed satisfaction.* She'd agreed. It would be special for their first time, and there was something exquisite in the torture of waiting.

Ashley replayed the scene from the night at his house, how he had instantly switched from so hot to so quiet. What had triggered him? Surely it wasn't because she'd said stop? She remembered how stiff his body had gone, how pained his face. And then, how he'd come back from that wounded place to assure her nothing was wrong. If her saying *stop* had put the brakes on, then tonight, she would make sure he understood her signal was go.

Luke and Ashley were standing beside the bar, margaritas in hand. The bright flare of the salsa band made conversation almost impossible. *Let your body do the talking.*

Ashley smoothed her hands down the dress's fitted front. "You like?" she mouthed.

"Wars could be fought over your legs," he shouted. "You look amazing."

Ashley rolled her eyes, brushing off his compliment. *Doesn't he see all the cellulite?* Still, she liked that he seemed genuine. This stunning man who turned the heads of gorgeous women really did seem attracted to her body. *Incredible.*

She glanced at the dance floor, where Jewel and her new boyfriend, Gabriel, were already dancing. Luke stared, too, as Gabriel spun Jewel repeatedly, their arms opening and closing together, their bodies connecting and retreating in beautiful synchrony.

"Dance?" Ashley shouted.

For a moment, Luke looked positively shy, a look she never dreamed she would see on his face. She liked it. The innocence of it. The authenticity of it. The vulnerability of it. It gave her an extra boost of confidence. This dance floor was one of her favorite playgrounds.

"Come. *Bailar conmigo.*"* She raised one arm, flicked her wrist, and twisted her hips to let him know she meant "dance with me."

"Me?" he mouthed, pointing at his chest.

Ashley nodded. "*Tu. Ahora mismo.*"**

She led him by the hand, her body already moving to the familiar beat. *One, two, three, pause, five, six, seven, pause.* She kept the move simple, and Luke was a quick study. After a few measures, he had the basic gist.

Nice. She nodded and smiled encouragingly as his feet began to mirror hers.

She placed his right hand on her left shoulder blade, put her left hand on his shoulder, then held his other hand with hers.

"Who's leading?" he shouted.

"*Todo tu.*"*** She nodded at him.

For a man who didn't know what he was doing, Luke had enough charisma and natural athleticism to carry off the dance with grace. His eyes never left hers. His body grew increasingly relaxed, and the song, thank god, went on and on and on.

She loved the feel of his hand on her back, the rhythm they found together. She loved how his shoulders dipped, how his hips found a flirtatious rotation, how his waist stayed still. By the time the song was done, they were both glistening with sweat. After clapping for the band, they grabbed their drinks and went out to the back porch for air.

"You're a beautiful dancer, Ashley."

"*Por supuesto, que sí,*"**** she laughed. "I grew up rich with culture and kindness, Luke."

"Soon—" he said.

---

*Dance with me.
**You. Right now.
***All you.
**** Yes, of course.

"Yes?" She looked up at him through thick lashes.

"Soon, I'm going to see what you are barely hiding beneath that dress."

I'll show you now. "Tell me more."

"Soon, I will explore every curve of you with my tongue."

And I will open for you like a tulip. "What else, Luke?"

"Soon, you will come so many times, even you will stop counting."

"What—" she began, then stopped. He knew she liked to count?

"You do like to count things, right?"

"Yes, but how—"

"Lucky guess." He smirked, pleased with himself.

This man knew her from the inside out. It was odd. And hot.

"There you two are!" shouted Jewel, dragging Gabriel behind her. "Get your hot asses out on the dance floor. Birthday girl's orders."

"Well, okay then." Luke ran his finger along the curve of Ashley's hip. "Let's see what new tricks this old dog can learn."

They danced another hour, and Ashley was sure that after what amounted to sixty minutes of Latin foreplay, Luke would come up to her apartment with her when he dropped her off. Why wait for Geneva? But when he opened her door and she stepped out, he gave her the briefest of kisses on her cheek.

"Soon," he said.

But I am so wet for you right now. "In three days," she said.

And yes, she was counting every minute.

———

"Twenty-one hours, six minutes," Ashley said to her cat, Bamba, as she stroked her under the chin. "Then I'll be off to Geneva, and you will be here with Meg. She'll take such good care of you."

The phone rang.

"Hi, Mom!" Ashley didn't even try to restrain her happiness. If she were a lilac bush, she'd be in full fragrant bloom. She couldn't remember ever feeling so alive, so full of excitement. Her bag was packed, her passport was by the door, her sub was lined out on the week's classes, and she'd splurged on a new flirty dress to wear their first night in Geneva—complete with some lavender lingerie. Thanks to Luke, her heart was in sync with the season. It was spring, and everything felt new and possible. Tomorrow morning couldn't come soon enough.

"Mom, you there?"

"Ashley," her mom croaked. "Ashley, honey, can you come? I need—" She began to violently cough.

"You sound terrible. I'll be right there."

Between hacks, her mother croaked out, "Thank you, honey."

Ashley grabbed her keys from the counter and ran toward the door, still talking into the phone. "Talk to me, Mom. What's wrong?" More coughing.

"Mom. Drink some water. Lie down. I'll be there in eighteen minutes."

On the way to her mom's house, Ashley dialed her sister, then remembered Jewel and Gabriel had left yesterday for Cancún. *Shoot.* Better to call after she knew more, anyway.

She pulled up to her mom's house and ran for the door, fumbling for her key. To her surprise, the door was unlocked.

"Mom?" Ashley called into the house.

"Here, Ashling," came the weak voice from her mom's bedroom. Ashley found her on top of the covers in her old nightdress, shivering, her breathing fast and shallow, her skin pale. She fluttered her eyes open for a moment, and Ashley read fear in them. "Thank you," she coughed, "for coming, sweetheart." She coughed more.

Something was very wrong. Ashley's heart skipped, and she willed her voice to be calm. "Mom, you're going to be okay," she said, not believing it. She felt her mom's forehead. Feverish.

"Mm-hmm."

"Mom, how long have you been like this?"

"Couple days," she choked out before violent coughs began shaking her body.

"We're going to the hospital."

"No!" Her mom coughed, shaking her head. "No!"

"Mom, just because you had one bad experience there doesn't mean you don't belong there now."

"No," she whimpered, still coughing.

"Mom." She struggled to keep desperation out of her voice. "I'm taking over."

The rest of the day was spent in waiting rooms and offices, but eventually, Ashley's mother was diagnosed with pneumonia. The doctor wanted to keep her in the hospital, but her mother adamantly refused. Eventually, the doctor relented that she could go home if someone stayed with her for several days to monitor her breathing and be sure her symptoms didn't worsen. "You understand," the doctor warned, "if her pneumonia advances, it can be fatal."

Ashley immediately agreed to the doctor's conditions, understanding what her mother needed. As she nodded yes, she knew exactly what she was saying no to. Geneva.

The timing couldn't be worse, said a voice in her head. But looking at her mother, fragile and needy, Ashley was overwhelmed with gratitude that her mom hadn't waited to call her tomorrow when she would already be on a plane headed across the world and it would have been too late. Ashley forced herself not to imagine what would have happened. *Thank god I'm still here.*

"Mom, it'll be okay." She held her mother's hand. "I'll stay at your place. I'll take care of you."

When her mom didn't argue, Ashley understood just how sick she was.

Luke would understand, too. Wouldn't he? *I'm sorry, Luke. I know I said yes, but—* She looked at her mother, trembling in her chair, and bit her lip. She wanted to go to Geneva. She wanted to be with *Luke*. And there was no question where she needed to be.

CHAPTER 9

ASHLEY ROLLED OVER ON the flowery quilt and buried her face into her childhood pillow.

"Agh!" she screamed.

She knew she was where she belonged: here, in her childhood home, taking care of her mother. But at 9:55 a.m., she couldn't help but imagine how the plane would be just starting to taxi its way out of Texas. Instead of holding her pillow, she would be holding Luke's hand as they took off together toward Europe. And that's not all she imagined she'd be holding as the flight went on.

She tortured herself with thoughts of leaning her head against his strong shoulder, nuzzling in for a nap, sleepy from first-class champagne, and Luke, lazily, discreetly slipping his hand beneath the blanket and sliding his fingers up her short skirt, teasing the soft bud of her clit while he whispered in French.

My god. She'd been so close to having him, so close to discovering if their sex would be as euphoric as she had fantasized.

She imagined how sore she would be from days of straddling and grinding and opening wider and writhing and riding, imagined how satisfied and exhausted she would be after he made her *come so many times, even you will stop being able to count them.* She'd replayed *that* conversation over and over and even now felt the insistent pulse of prurient desire between her legs just thinking of how she *knew* Luke would make good on his promise.

"Ashley." Her mom's voice scratched the air. Her room was across from Ashley and Jewel's old room.

Ashley jumped to her feet. "Right here, Mom." Tucked under the light blankets, her mother's body looked so fragile, so small, not at all the determined woman who raised her. *C'mon, Mom, be strong.*

"Juice?"

"Right away, Mom." She walked toward the kitchen just as someone rapped the door knocker. Ashley looked through the small window beside the door to see a young man holding a giant bouquet of white lilies.

Lilies? That Luke. She smiled and unlocked the door.

"Delivery for Teresa Barris."

Flowers for her mother? Seriously, Luke really was too good to be true. He had been understanding about her missing the trip, of course, and here he was, reaching out so generously.

Ashley tipped the deliveryman and brought the flowers in.

"Who's there?" her mom queried feebly.

"Shhh. Special delivery, Mom." Ashley walked quietly into her mother's room.

Her mother struggled to sit as she saw the armful of flowers. "Oh my goodness," she coughed. "Who is that from?" Ashley set the flowers and juice on the bedside table.

"Let's see, shall we?" Ashley pulled a small card from the greens. "For the very special mother of a very special woman, hoping you feel better soon. Luke Dalton."

"Luke Dalton?" Her mom leaned back into her pillow and lost the fight to keep her eyes open. Her voice was a wheezing whisper. "I think you have a lot to tell me, my dear."

Ashley hadn't told her mother about the trip. She was glad. She didn't want her mom to feel guilty.

"Oh, you know, Mom."

She coughed, but she struggled to speak. "He's the man helping you with your online program, yes?"

"Yes."

"And he's sending your *mom* big bouquets of lilies?" It was the first smile Ashley had seen on her mother's face in two days—and of course, she was smiling. She had always wanted her daughter to fall in love with a man who treated her well and made her happy, the opposite of Ashley's previous marriage.

Ashley sat on her mom's bed. The thick, sweet perfume of lilies filled the room.

"He's nice." Ashley smoothed her mother's gray hair.

Her mom scoffed and stuck out her tongue, an uncharacteristically playful gesture from her hardworking mom.

"I think *someone* is feeling better," Ashley teased.

"I think *someone* has a lot to share with her mom," her mom rattled before starting to cough again.

"Oh, I left that prescription in my car. Be right back." Ashley rushed out to her car on the street and opened the back passenger door, reaching in for the small bag from the pharmacy.

"Real nice ass, bitch. Tha's wha' I'mma talkin' 'bout."

Ashley whipped around to face the lewd voice just a few feet from her car.

"You're one good-lookin' woman," slurred a large middle-aged man, visibly drunk, swaggering down the street.

"Get. The. Fuck. Away. From. Me." Ashley's voice was steel. Her heart pounded fiercely, ready for a fight, despite the fact the man didn't seem to pose any real threat. He was almost too sloshed to stand.

"Gimme some 10:00 a.m. ass, bitch."

"I'm calling the cops." Ashley slammed the car door and strode to the house, leaving the drunk calling after her.

"I don' mean you no harm, baby," he said, his voice scraping in her ears.

Ashley hurled her body into the house, then locked the screen door. Locked all three locks on the front door. Felt panic rise from the soles of her feet to her chest. She leaned against the door as if that way, she could keep out all the memories he brought up.

But there they were, those memories, breaking in, the door of her mind splintering, the sickening scent of old piss and sweat, the sound of screaming, her sister screaming, Ashley's heart bucking wild in her chest.

"Ashling? Honey? You okay?"

Ashley breathed deep. She looked around the empty room.

"Yeah, Mom." She willed her voice to sound normal.

"I heard you shouting, honey."

"It's okay, Mom. Just a drunk on the street."

"But I—"

"It's okay, Mom." Ashley walked into her mom's room with the medicine. She forced her voice to be soothing, though her heart thudded. She looked out the window. "He's gone. I just—" Her voice broke.

Her mother's face looked impossibly sad. "I know, honey," she struggled to say between coughs. "I know."

She did know. Ashley sat on the bed beside her mom. She closed her eyes. She practiced calming herself down with a centering question: What was *really* here in the room? All she could hear was her mother's short breath. All she could smell were lilies.

When the doorbell rang again, it was late afternoon. Ashley had fallen asleep in the chair beside her mother's bed. Her mom was rising to answer the door.

"Mom, stay where you are."

"But—"

"Got it, Mom." Ashley bounded up. She glanced out her mother's window. A black car was parked on the street. She heard the door knocker.

"Coming," she shouted. Through the peephole, she saw a well-dressed man in a suit.

Ashley shouted through the door. "Can I help you?"

"I'm looking for Ms. Ashley Barris." He smiled, his voice pleasant.

She undid the locks and opened the doors.

"That's me," Ashley said, puzzled.

"A gift for you from Mr. Luke Dalton." He offered her a beautiful small red bag with red cord handles. On the side was written "Cartier" in gold.

"Thank you." Ashley signed her name on his clipboard.

"Have a beautiful day, Ms. Barris." He returned to his car, leaving Ashley dumbfounded in the doorway.

What is Luke up to now? she wondered, a smile playing at her lips. She locked the doors and stared at the crimson bag. She couldn't decide if she wanted to tear into the present immediately or savor the mystery.

"Honey." Her mom coughed. "What was that?"

"Delivery. Something from Luke." She appeared in her mom's doorway and swung the bag from its handles like a pendulum.

"Someone has been bitten"—*cough, cough*—"by a love bug."

"Mom," Ashley chided.

"I didn't mean you, honey."

Ashley blushed.

"Well, open it. I'm thinking whatever it is"—she coughed—
"will make me feel a lot better."

"Oh yeah, Mom?"

"You know what they say—you're only as happy as your least
happy child. Your happiness is my happiness. And whatever is
in that bag, I think, is going to be a symbol of your growing happiness." Ashley felt her own happiness growing when her mother got through several sentences without coughing.

"There's a card." Ashley saw a white envelope peeking out of
the bag.

"Well, read it, honey. You don't have to share."

Ashley removed the envelope. She read to herself.

> *Dear Ashley,*
> *I'm counting the hours till I'm with you again.*
> *Count with me?*
>
> *—Luke*

Of course she was already counting. Seven days, two hours,
and forty-some minutes until his plane landed.

She smiled and looked up at her mom, then reached into the
bag to pull out a deep red box. She ran her finger over the gold
lace border.

"Do you have a guess?" asked her mom.

"I don't know. Cartier? Isn't *everything* there expensive?"

"Let's see."

Ashley slowly opened the box to reveal, nestled in black velvet, a stainless-steel watch. The face was round, with four diamonds setting off the quarter hours. Gold framed the face.

"Oh," Ashley exhaled.

"Oh, honey," her mom purred. It's beautiful. Just right for
you."

"Mom, are you kidding?" Ashley said, her voice quiet. "It's all wrong." She shook her head. "Sure, it's beautiful. But it's all wrong." She stared at the watch in her lap.

"Ashley Louise Barris. What are you saying?"

"Mom, this watch must cost thousands of dollars. It could feed so many kids. It could help girls go to school."

"Oh, my dear Ashling. Bless you. Bless your generous soul. See how you long to give to others. It's your gift, your service-oriented heart. Your generous heart." She coughed, and then, once she stopped, she gently touched Ashley's knee. "And Luke clearly has a generous heart, too. He sent flowers to your mother. He is helping you establish a program for students. And he sent you a lovely watch. Something elegant and precise and beautiful—just like you. Why is it you easily accept him being generous to others, but you flinch when he is generous to you?"

Her mother's question rested in the air like a dew-shining web barely moving in the breeze.

Ashley said nothing.

"Ashley, look at me," said her mother, taking both of Ashley's hands. "Of course, my dream is for you to meet your Prince Charming. Someone who cares for you and loves you and makes you feel special. But no one, not a prince or a pauper, will ever make you feel special if you don't let him."

"But Mom—"

"Giving is only half a gift. Receiving is the other. That is not easy for you, I know."

Ashley sighed. She felt some of the fight drain out of her.

"This man is trying to show you, in the way he knows best, that he thinks you are someone wonderful." She coughed through her words, determined to get them out. "If you would rather he gave a donation in your name to the food bank, well, that is something you can teach him. But that may not feel like love to him. At least not yet. You may need to guide him so he understands you. And you, my love, have some work to do to understand him."

Now *that* was an understatement. If only her mother knew just how Luke got the money to buy that watch. There was so much about Luke Dalton that Ashley didn't know how to reconcile.

"Try it on," her mother persuaded.

Ashley lifted the watch from its velvet case and wrapped it around her wrist. It *was* beautiful. "I want you to think about whatever it was that Luke wrote in his note that made you smile so beguilingly and know that *that* is what you are wearing. And you deserve it."

"Thanks, Mom," Ashley said, flushing. "It's complicated. But I'm trying."

Ashley stared at the watch, so out of place on her wrist, and focused on the steady sweep of the second hand. She imagined it was Luke's finger drawing perfect circles on her slender wrist, each circle bringing them closer to being together.

Her pulse instantly quickened. There *was* something Luke had to give her that she was *very* interested in receiving. In fact, now that it had entered her mind, it was all she could think about.

CHAPTER 10

"HI, LUKE," ASHLEY SAID, stepping into her childhood bedroom and closing the door. She opened the curtains on the high window to let in the midnight breeze. "I was hoping you'd call." In fact, she'd stayed up just in case. He'd landed in Europe almost an hour ago. She was still undecided on how to best talk to him about the Cartier watch. Some things were probably best done face-to-face.

"Ashley," Luke rasped. "Yes. I needed your voice." The hunger in his words flew arrow fast to her core. Ashley audibly inhaled. "And that's not all I am needing."

"Luke," she sighed, her arousal spiking in spontaneous crimson bloom. "I—"

Luke groaned. "Ugh. Sorry. Wait. Let me start again. Ashley. How is your mother?"

Ashley's head spun with the quick change in tone. The man had gone from starving to tender in half a nanosecond.

"Well—" She scrambled to catch up with the turn in conversation. "Thank you, Luke, for asking. She's improving. She's sleeping now. In fact, she's sleeping most of the time. It's what her body needs. She should be fine soon."

"Oh good." He exhaled with relief. "I didn't mean to be so one-track-minded when you picked up the phone. I guess I, well, I miss you."

"I miss you, too." It was oddly sweet to hear the confident Luke Dalton somewhat undone. It made him so human. She liked that glimpse of vulnerability. She liked knowing that she had something to do with it. "Thank you for the lilies. They made her feel great."

"I'm glad."

"And Luke, about the watch—"

"Are you wearing it now?"

"I am."

"Where are you?"

"In my old room. Why—"

"What else are you wearing?"

Ashley laughed. "Um, an old pair of jeans and a long-sleeve pink shirt."

"I want to take them off." His voice was instantly gravelly.

"What?"

"Are you alone?"

"Yes."

"Good. Let your hands be my hands. Will you do that for me?"

The confident Luke was back, but Ashley was slightly confused.

"Oh-kay," she acquiesced.

"Say yes."

"Yes," she whispered.

"I want my hands on your naked body now." His voice was erotic and thick. "Put down the phone. Take off only the jeans and shirt. I'll be waiting for you when you're done."

No matter how awkward she felt about his request, Ashley was so turned on by the gruff desire in his voice that she did as he asked, her clothes dropping to the floor.

"Okay," she said, picking up the phone again, the two syllables laced with lust.

"Tell me, Ashley, how are my hands? Are they rough? Or careful?"

"A little rough." She blushed at the admission.

"Good. Tell me what you're wearing now."

"My bra. It's navy. Just a little lace. And a navy thong." She heard his breath hitch. "Oh, and of course, the watch."

"Leave those on for now," he murmured. "Lie on your bed."

How far was this going to go?

"Luke, I—"

"Now." His voice was a braid of longing, vulnerability, and control. "I've been thinking of nothing but touching your body, thinking of all the ways I want to bring you to orgasm, over and over. So, lie on the bed. On your back. And spread your legs."

Ashley could feel a sweet, warm pulsing between her thighs, her body keenly aware of the fact that Luke had *not* been touching her. She arranged herself on her bed as if Luke were right here beside her instead of 5,300 miles away.

"Are you lying down?"

"Mm-hmm."

"Ashley, let me make you feel good."

"Luke," she said, feeling suddenly bold. "Where are *you*?"

"In my hotel room."

"I'll tell you what *I* want." *Is that sultry voice really mine?*

"Mmm. What is that?" He seemed surprised and pleased, his voice eager and low.

"Luke, what are *you* wearing?"

She could hear his grin on the other side of the Atlantic. "A white shirt. Jeans. Black socks."

"Take them off."

A brief pause. "Yes, ma'am." His tone was playful.

She hummed her approval. "And Luke."

"Yes?"

"Use *my* hands."

She heard him chuckle just as a light thud indicated Luke had dropped the phone on the bed.

"Ashley." Even his voice was naked now. Ashley shivered, thinking of the sexual charge racing from Luke in his room in Geneva to her in her childhood room in Texas and back to Geneva again, a loop of rapturous energy fueled by a fiery, demanding force. Part of her wished this were a video call so she could see him, but there was something so sexy about just their voices, and the first time she saw him naked, she didn't want it to be on a screen.

"Put the phone on speaker and set it beside your head on your pillow." He waited as she did. "Now, touch both of your breasts, Ashley. Use both of my hands. Yes, that's it—squeeze them and play with them and claim them. Let me pinch and roll your nipples till they're stiff."

Ashley involuntarily gasped as she did as he asked.

"Are they nice and tight, Ashley? Pinch them again. Hard. Do you like it like that?"

"Yes," she whimpered.

"Wonderful dirty girl."

"Luke?" She felt suddenly shy. Were they going to masturbate over the phone? Here in her childhood bedroom with her mom next door? It felt so wrong. And so hot. *And I couldn't stop if I tried.*

"Now, hook your hands into that navy thong and pull it down, sweetness. Show me your beauty." She did as he asked, her middle finger traveling across the hood of her clit, and her back arched up in immediate response. She was so turned on she thought she could come just listening to his voice.

"Now, slip one of my fingers between your thighs and tell me what I feel."

Ashley dipped her middle finger toward her, *what did he say?* her *beauty*, gliding it through the slickened folds, curling it slightly before pulling the pad back up to flutter against her swollen nub. She had gotten waxed and trimmed in anticipation of their trip, and she was a bit surprised to not feel her usual nest of tight curls.

"Tell me. What do I feel?"

She was too turned on now to be shy. "God, I'm a river for you, Luke," she said, breathy and panting. "I'm so, so wet."

"Lick my finger, Ashley. Slip it in your mouth and suck."

Really? Ashley brought her finger to her tongue, tasting her own sweet darkness. She moaned.

"That's right. Suck those sweet juices off my finger. Now stroke it back inside your beauty. All the way. Make it disappear inside that tight warmth. Now in and out. With my voice, Ashley. In. And out. And deeper. Thrust it deeper."

It felt so good, so different from how she normally touched herself that Ashley could almost believe it *was* Luke's hand touching her, Luke's hand exploring the soft, erogenous regions of her, Luke's hand bringing her to the crest of a tide of pleasure. If she were the ocean, his voice was the moon, tugging her, pulling her, irresistible in her ear.

"Tell me what's happening, Ashley," he groaned. "Are you trembling? Can you smell our sex, Ashley?"

"Yes," she breathed, "yes."

"I want to come with you. Tell me when you're close." His voice was an audible feast, making it even more agonizing that she was the only one here.

"Luke," she gasped. "Do you have my hands on your cock, Luke?" She willed her voice to be strong. "Are you stroking yourself with my hands, Luke? I want to milk your cock, Luke."

Were those words really falling out of her mouth? She could hear him groan on the other side of the phone, and it made her smile, this small power she had over him. God, how she wanted her hands to be touching him now, reveling in his hardness.

It occurred to her she didn't know if he was circumcised or not, didn't know how thick he was, how long. She wanted to know him inside her, wanted him pumping into her, wanted his heft, his shape on her. God, she wanted *him*.

"Luke," she gasped, breathless, her heart racing, her shameless body tensing, wriggling, her whole being focused on her want. "I'm so close."

"Go slower, then, Ashley. Lighter. Let me give it to you."

No. "Slower?"

"Slower."

I can't. "Okay." Her pulse sped, but she willed her body to melt, her fingers barely moving in and out of her sex.

"We're going to get there together."

"Luke," she whimpered as the red song of climax hovered mid-crescendo. She slowed her hand, though every other part of her body screamed *faster, now.*

"It's so good, Ashley, your hands on me."

She could make out the slick sound of his strokes, and it stirred something primal in her, making her moan.

"You want me to let you come, sweetness?"

"Yes."

"Is your beauty quivering with need? So hot and slick and greedy for me?"

"Yes," she whimpered, rocking into her hand.

"Ask for what you want."

"Please, let me come." The words spilled in a desperate rush.

She heard his own rhythm slow down as he rasped, "I'm going to give you everything. Make your beauty shudder all around me."

Luke's words were making her hotter than the touch of her own hand, and she could feel her orgasm about to spill over, rising beyond her ability to stop it. "I'm going to—"

"Come, sweetness."

And with the lightest, merest thrust and curl of her fingers, the pulse between her legs surged through her, shaking her body, devastating her. "Coming, Luke," she panted, her hips bucking, her eyes screwed tight, her neck flung back as pleasure ripped through her. She turned her face into her pillow to moan into the down, her fingers still curled inside her, her palm cupping her mound as if she could hold the pleasure in just a few moments longer.

"Ashley," he moaned her name again and again in shared ecstasy.

Hearing Luke cry her name through the phone like a prayer, Ashley fell even deeper into postorgasmic rapture, deeper into herself, deeper into her body—as if she now knew her body in a new and wildly intimate way, knew it as Luke would know it. She felt bliss-high and pleasure-drunk and joy-dizzy.

"That was crazy," she huffed into the phone, her chest still heaving. "I've never masturbated on the phone with someone before."

"Still haven't."

"What?"

"Those were *my hands* touching you, darlin', not yours. And when I come back to Houston, my hands and my tongue and my cock will continue to indulge you, spoil you, please you."

Ashley completely dissolved. "Mmm" was the only sound she could muster. This man had so much to teach her about pleasure. And she was ready for the next lesson.

CHAPTER 11

WELL, THAT WENT WELL. Ashley leaned back in her chair and thought about the conversation she'd just had with her students about sustainable water use. Knowing that an eight-minute shower uses over twenty gallons of water, they'd come up with creative ways to time a *five*-minute shower, for instance, listening to a five-minute song like Nirvana's "Smells Like Teen Spirit." She felt so strongly about the need for short showers, and today, she had thirty new converts.

"Whoa, nice flowers," whistled John as he walked into Ashley's classroom, nodding at the enormous bouquet that occupied most of Ashley's desk.

The room had emptied out quickly once the final bell rang, and Ashley startled at John's voice.

"Hey, John," she greeted him from the counter in the corner of the room, continuing to prep tomorrow's experiments. "A big bouquet is perfect for a STEM classroom, don't you think?"

John knit his brow.

"STEM. Get it? Flower *stems*? Science, tech, engineering, math?" John forced a small pity laugh. He never really did get her pun humor. Ashley shrugged.

"We missed you last week here at school." John perched on her desk. "How's your mom?"

"Improving, John, thanks for asking, but still weak. I'm heading there as soon as I leave."

"You're taking such good care of her." John's smile was sincere.

"She always took such good care of me. Now it's my turn."

"And who's taking such *good care* of you?" He leaned into the bouquet, smelling the flowers.

"I'm not sure. There was no note."

"Any guesses?"

"Maybe?" *I hope they're from Luke.* He was supposed to come home tonight, but she hadn't heard from him in a couple of days, which seemed odd, considering how much they had texted the first half of the week. But who else would send her such a big bouquet? Her mind clicked. *John?* No. Why would he send her flowers? But it did make sense it was someone in the school. How else would the flowers have arrived in her room without even a name card?

"No one sends flowers to the principal."

"It's not easy being head honcho." Ashley laughed and pulled a white rose from the vase. "Here, have this one."

"Aw, you always cheer me up. Thanks, Ash. And speaking of thank you, thanks for inviting me onto the STEAMEA board. The program's growing so fast."

"I should be thanking *you*. That report you gave last week was spot-on."

"I get so excited about helping kids. And the planet."

"Two things I love about you."

John waved off her compliment. "You say that to all the guys. Hey, you gonna meet up with the rest of us at Hello Bar tonight for a drink?"

"Nah. I've got other plans." *Don't I? Why hasn't Luke texted or called?* "Have a margarita with chili salt for me, will ya?"

Before following John out of the room, Ashley stared at her wrist where the watch wasn't—she'd taken it off two days ago, uncomfortable with its opulence. Was Luke having second thoughts? Was she?

———

The car behind Ashley was honking its horn. *Shit.* The light had turned green, and she was still sitting at the intersection, zoned out, wondering where the night had gone wrong.

She was on her way home after visiting her mom's—fun, but not the night she'd expected. She'd imagined she would pick up a dinner from her freezer at home, drop it off for her mom, then meet Luke at his house for a little, um, reunion. His tongue had promises to keep, after all.

As it was, Luke never contacted her. She hadn't joined her mom in eating because she was still hopeful he'd call. Instead, they'd played a round of Scrabble, her mother's favorite game. Ashley couldn't spell even simple words—a blot in her perfectionist standards for herself. Scrabble was like medicine she didn't really enjoy taking.

Ashley sighed. Why hadn't Luke called? She pulled over to check their text thread again. The last text from Luke two days ago said he was deep in meetings and he'd get in touch with her once he landed in Houston on Monday to make plans for the night. *Be very ready,* he'd written.

She was *very ready* all right. Her lips, her thighs, her hands, her sex. But she hadn't wanted to appear too needy by contacting him when he'd clearly said he would contact her.

But you are *needy, Barris. And you're eager to see him. Text him now.*

In her mind, she could hear the voice of the therapist she'd hired after her divorce when she'd asked him how to have a successful relationship: *Communicate, communicate, communicate.*

Even the best communication wouldn't have helped her marriage. But it might help her now.

Ashley: Hey, just checking to see if you landed

There. Nice and simple. Almost instantly, the phone rang. "Luke!"

"You didn't show." His smooth baritone was deep and seductive and...disappointed.

"Wait, what?"

"I hoped you'd call if you weren't coming, but you didn't."

"I texted just now."

"Did you get flowers at school today?"

"I did! But...they were from you?"

"I guess you must receive a lot of bouquets. Next time, I'll need to make mine bigger so it will stand out."

"There was no card." *Then how had they gotten to her room?*

"Oh." Understanding seeped into his voice. "I told them what to say on the card. So much for my romantic plans. I thought I'd let the flowers do the talking. In the future, when I really want to be sure my message gets through, I'll put my trust in Verizon."

Relief flooded Ashley's body. He *had* tried to contact her—through white roses and blue hydrangea. Damn therapist was right. She should have texted him hours ago.

"Luke, what did the card say?"

He spoke in a deep, playful voice, as if he were dictating the message. "Geneva was no fun without you, period. Meet me tonight at Hayden's, question mark. 6:04 p.m."

"6:04?" Ashley laughed.

"I know how you like precision." God, this man. He really got her. "Plus, it made me happy thinking of you looking at your watch."

Oh. And in some ways, he didn't get her at all.

Ashley glanced at the clock on the dash. *6:27.* Though she wasn't purposefully late, she still felt bad. "I hate missing twenty-three minutes with you. Are you still at Hayden's?"

"It's me and the brut. I was ready to give up on you coming, but the brut told me, *Ne t'inquiète pas, Luke,* don't worry, *peut-être elle pourra te résister, mais jamais à moi.*"*

Though Ashley had no idea what Luke had just said, her body most certainly remembered what had happened the last time he'd spoken to her in French.

"Well, my dear *soufflé,* I'm on my way. I didn't eat dinner because I, well, I had been hoping you would call, so—"

"So, the brut and I will be waiting."

Hayden's was at least fifteen minutes away. Jitters pulsated through her, and she changed her route. It was hard to believe just four minutes ago, she'd felt like a bird with a broken wing, and now she was soaring. *And it's only going to get better after Hayden's... The only thing I really want to eat is at Luke's.*

At the next stoplight, she fumbled in her purse for lip gloss, then checked her reflection in the rearview mirror. She fought the urge to be self-critical and focused on how much her shining lips were looking forward to kissing and being kissed.

The phone rang through the car speakers, interrupting Van Morrison's "Moondance," and the display showed Emilia's name.

"Emilia!" she answered, always happy to hear her mentee's voice.

Sobs. Sniffles. "Ashley?"

"I'm here." Ashley's tone was calm and solid. "Emilia. Are you safe?"

"I want to get high so bad," she sniveled. "I bought a fix. I'm so weak."

"Emilia, are you high right now?"

---

* Don't worry, perhaps she could resist you, Luke, but she could never resist me.

"No."

"Good. You're doing the right thing, making smart choices for yourself by staying clean and calling me."

"Ashley," she moaned, "I need help. Can you come get me? Please? I need—"

Ashley knew how hard it was for Emilia to ask for help.

Though inside her, a voice was pleading, *No, no, no,* the only syllable that came through the phone was "Yes. What is your location, Emilia?" And Ashley turned the car around, her rearview mirror facing the direction her heart longed to go.

Ashley leaned back in her chair and rubbed her temples. The pile of tests to grade was only slightly lower than it had been an hour ago. She was having a terrible time staying focused. Luke had been, not surprisingly, a little distant since she'd let him down twice in one night. His disappointment had made it hard to concentrate for the last four days—that and her incessant fantasy of what would happen when they saw each other next.

Luke was, in fact, literally distant. He'd left the morning after their botched dinner date on another business trip and wasn't going to be back until Saturday. They hadn't made specific plans, just said they would get together then.

Communicate. Communicate.

Before she could talk herself out of it, she'd picked up the phone and dialed Luke. It was not lost on her that his number was just beneath the two senators she kept in her favorites so she could advocate against oil companies. Companies such as Luke's. This man had her knotted up in so many ways. Calling him, she felt a little as if she were cheating on her ideals. But not calling him, she felt as if she were cheating her heart.

"Ashley." Just hearing him say those two syllables made her body shiver, like waves on a moonlit sea.

"Hi, Luke. Hey, are we still on for tomorrow night?"

"Yes, yes, and yes!" His voice radiated enthusiasm. Relief and arousal flooded her—hello, dopamine, nitrogen oxide, and noradrenaline. Was this what it was like for Emilia to get a fix?

"Three yesses?" she asked.

"One for my heart, one for my body, one for my soul. Not necessarily in that order."

Ashley's heart fluttered. "Look, Luke, I'm so sorry about Monday—"

"Yeah, the waiter felt so sorry for me he gave me a free trio of artisan sorbets."

"I want to make up for lost time."

"I think we can arrange that," he drawled, molasses dark and slow. Then he brightened. "Look, I realize many people need you, Ashley. And devotion is a beautiful trait in a human."

How did he do that? Found secret doors in the walls she'd built around her heart and then flung them open. Not knowing what to say, she said nothing.

"You have plans tonight?" he asked.

"Ha, yeah." She glanced at the names on the tests: "It's me, Joaquim, Julio, Randy, Lucia, Grayson…and a rubric. And a green pen." She never corrected in red pen. Too much stigma. Something about green seemed less threatening.

Luke laughed. "Like I said, you support a lot of folks."

"Want to go out to eat on Saturday? Jewel and I found a great new Peruvian place last week."

"Come to my place. I want a very private, quiet moonlit dinner. No other voices, no other eyes."

All she wanted was to be alone with him, but it did seem a tad unfair. "You sure? Seems as if you're always making me dinner."

"Is my cooking all right?" he teased. "Last time, you took a doggie bag."

"Oh, yes, I just meant that—"

"It's my pleasure, Ashley, to cook for you. I love cooking. I love feeding you. Plus"—his voice lowered—"there's something most special on the menu."

Ashley flushed, his implication clear. "Can I bring anything?"

"Um, maybe *don't* bring your phone? I don't think I can take it if you don't show up again."

Ashley laughed. "Deal."

CHAPTER 12

"Mmm." Ashley walked toward the kitchen. From the moment she'd stepped off the elevator, Luke's penthouse smelled of something Southern and strong—onion, paprika, and peppers. She could hear him moving in the kitchen. On the stereo, a solo piano was playing something slow, classical, and vaguely familiar—at once sensual, melancholy, and beautiful. Chopin? "It smells so good in here," she murmured to herself.

She stood a moment in the open room and counted the seconds before Luke emerged. *One. Two. Three. Four. Five.* Luke was barefoot, wearing thigh-hugging jeans, a fitted blue tee, the same apron he'd worn the last time she was here, and a naughty smile. He stood still as marble for a moment. Only his eyes moved, slowly raking over her, appreciating the shape of her, the curves of her, the flesh of her, leaving no question about his intentions for the night. Ashley's breath caught in her throat, and her body shuddered in heated anticipation, signaling to her brain that the body was in charge now. As if he could sense her inner switch flipping, the edge of Luke's lips curled up.

That one small motion released a surge of thrill, a tangled swell of arousal.

He looked feral. Leonine. Predatory. Intoxicating.

"At last—" Luke grinned, his smile irrepressible. "The universe realized that for tonight, *I* am the one on this planet who needs you the most."

Ashley blushed a little, hopelessly turned on by the dark growl in his voice. She took a tentative step toward Luke.

"Have you read *Meditations*?" He nodded to the book on the hall table.

"Marcus Aurelius?" She picked up the book and turned it over, not really looking at it.

"Mm-hmm."

"No." *He wants to talk books? Now?* "Have you?"

"I was just reading it on the plane. Again."

"Again?"

"Oh, I may have learned much of it by heart when I was younger."

"Of course you did."

"That copy I bought for you." He took a few steps closer. "Gregory Hays. My favorite translation."

"Thank you."

He took the book from her hands and set it on the table again. "But then I thought I'd rather show you what it says."

"Oh, really?"

Luke pressed his thumb to her mouth, then slowly traced the curve of her lower lip. "Really."

A delicious shiver raced up and down her spine, a radiance gathering in her throat. "Show me now?"

He stared into her eyes, and she stared back into his, two glittering seas.

"Now." It was a single molten syllable. The pad of his thumb was the only part of his body touching hers, and all her longing focused on that one point of connection as it traveled across her mouth. It was an astonishing intimacy, but she hungered for more, the way a nocturnal flower longs for the darkness that follows the amber dusk. She longed to be fully opened. She longed to be gathered completely into his arms, to feel the full crush of his weight.

"Luke," she whispered against his finger, her desire spiking to meet his. She felt the liquid heat of her own arousal begin to gather between her legs in anticipation.

Luke lowered his lips to her ear and whispered, "*Some of what now exists is already gone.*" Then, with infinite tenderness and control, he brought his hands to cup her face and touched her forehead with his own. The softness in his touch was infused with such reverence Ashley gasped. She had expected, even wanted their coming together to be something rougher, more reckless, something ravaging to meet her wild passion, and his restraint slightly confused her. How was he always so restrained? She wanted to be captured by him, taken by him, ravished and overcome.

Luke pulled back and searched her eyes for assent. Her return gaze was wanton, open, an absolute raw yes.

The dark lust in his eyes made her hold her breath, and for these long seconds separated from his caresses, she was exquisitely aware of how powerful he was, how every inch of her body clamored to belong to him. How was he holding back?

He slowly smoothed one hand down her arm toward her palm, saying, "*Do everything as if it were the last thing you were doing in your life.*" Everywhere he touched, he left a wake of pebbled flesh. Then he kissed each fingertip, saying, "*Concentrate every minute like a Roman...on doing what's in front of you with precise and genuine seriousness, tenderly, willingly...*"

This was the craziest seduction she'd ever experienced—allurement fueled by philosophy. It was heady and sexy, and she loved it. "Do you think Marcus Aurelius has a quote that says, 'Hurry, please'?"

Luke laughed at the urgency in her voice. "I think he would say be very present in every moment. Will you do that with me?" he whispered into her ear, husky and confident. "Tonight, will you meet me as if it were *the last thing* we were doing in our lives? What woman would you be then?"

She heard his words through a rhapsodic haze, not quite knowing how to answer him.

"I know what kind of man I'd be. These last two weeks, I was afraid I wasn't ever going to know your body the way I long to know your body. I want to know what you look like when you're drunk on pleasure and coming on my cock."

Yes. This. More. Now.

His breathing was ragged, uneven. He stepped back to drink in her body with his eyes, moved his gaze like praise across her, taking in her bare arms, her rising and falling chest, her hair spilling dark gold down her long neck. With her eyes, she begged him to go on.

"The longer I went without making love to you, the more I began to think *the world could be gone* before I could touch you like this—" Luke let his fingers glide up the inside of her bare legs and play at the flouncy hem of her green dress. She gasped at the trails of fire left by his fingertips. "Or this," he said seductively, pushing his hands up beneath her dress to roughly massage her inner thighs.

Higher, please, a little higher.

"Ashley." His eyes both pierced and pleaded as he wrapped his strong hands beneath her ass and gripped her there, kneading, pressing his strong fingers gently into her flesh and pulling his thumbs slowly across her hip bones, molding her like clay on its way to becoming a masterpiece. "Sometimes time does run out. Sometimes we don't get another chance. And if it *were* the end of the world tonight, I would spread you out on that white rug and bring you to ecstasy over and over, make every cell in your body shimmer like the Milky Way so you feel wildly alive. *If it isn't ceasing to live that you're afraid of but never beginning to live properly...then you'll be worthy of the world that made you."*

She pressed a hand to his chest, felt his heart race, felt his heat radiate into her palm.

He leaned down, placing his lips close to her ear, his voice hoarse. "There is nothing, *nothing* in the world I want more than this connection with you—to *begin to live* with you." He inhaled as if breathing her in. "Will you do this with me? Live this night as if it were our last?"

Every word he said ignited her further. If he didn't take her now, she might not make it through the night.

"Mmm," she purred from deep in her throat as she pulled his head down to hers, her mouth straining upward to meet his.

"Tell me *yes*. Pretend with me." His voice was ragged, insistent.

"Yes," she hissed.

And the moment the word left her lips, Luke was kissing her with a scorching ferocity that made her blood sing. One muscled arm wrapped around her back to pull her in tight; the other fisted in her loose hair, controlling the angle of her lips as he crushed his mouth onto hers with ruthless intensity—a bruising, needy, brutal kiss. Ashley met his onslaught with equal force, releasing all her dammed-up desire. She teased her tongue between Luke's teeth, and he groaned into her mouth—a sound of hunger and aching so carnal that Ashley's knees lost their will to stand.

Luke laughed with pleasure as her body went slack in his strong embrace. He swooped her body into his arms, carried her to the center of the living room, then laid her gently onto her back in the center of a thick, white fluffy rug, just as he had promised. He sank to the floor and knelt over her as if praying at the altar of her.

Her hips rose to meet him, seeking friction, and he groaned as their bodies connected. Spurred by her response, Luke ground his hips into the triangle between her legs as he plundered the long expanse of her neck with lush kisses. Ashley thrilled in the steel-hard length of his erection pressing into her. *Inside me, now, please.*

But *slower*, she told herself, turned on by the story Luke had wrapped around them. If this were her last night on Earth, if this were her last chance to make love to Luke, *heaven forbid*, then by god, she wanted this night to last. And last. She wanted to delight in every nuance of his body, wanted to know him intimately, profoundly, completely. Wanted to know exactly how to make him shudder and moan, wanted to memorize every look on his face as he lost himself inside her. Wanted him to devour every inch of her, to make her come again and again.

Something in Luke's face told her he knew exactly how she was thinking, and the wicked grin on his face said he was going to deliver on every one of her desires. She sucked in a harsh breath, then realized she was panting—*panting*! Had she ever wanted someone this much?

"I need to taste you," he said hoarsely, staring into her eyes as he moved his body down the length of hers, bringing his face to the bottom of her dress, his tongue beginning a sweet, wet exploration of the tender skin on her inner thigh. "Spread your legs, sweetness, so I can bury my tongue in your beauty."

Luke's explicit language thrilled her. Gone was the gallant and courteous businessman. In his place was a confident, sexual force. Her hips fell open, and he nipped at the flesh of her inner thigh, an exquisite almost pain. Her hands moved to Luke's thick dark hair and massaged into his scalp. His curls flowed like black silk through her fingers.

"Oh, heaven, Luke," she gasped.

"Yes, sweetness, talk to me. Tell me everything you want."
He moved his face closer into the warm core of her, his breath
hot through the barely there purple lace of her thong.

"Take it off," she whispered.

In one swift movement, Luke used both hands to pull her
dress over her head. He stared a moment to appreciate the slender slope of her shoulders, the ripe swells of her breasts, the
naked plane of her midriff, the creamy curves of her legs. "So
beautiful." Hooking his thumbs into the elastic of her thong, he
dragged the dark purple scrap down to her ankles and off, bar-
ing her sex to his hooded eyes.

"Oh, yes," he purred. "Ashley. Your beauty. Your gorgeous,
glistening beauty. So naked, so wet, and so perfect for me."
He gazed at her with need, part predator, part pilgrim, a look
that clipped her breath and sent an arpeggio of shivers playing
across her skin. He parted her legs with his hands. "This," he
whispered as he dipped his head to torment her with short, slow
licks, sampling her, tracing the tenderest flesh with his tongue,
flicking and fluttering and flattening the tip against her swollen
bud. He read her squirms, her moans, adjusting his pace and
pressure, then speared into her like a man obsessed. Ashley's
thighs quivered, and her sex clenched and unclenched, her hips
shamelessly bucking into his face.

Shifting, he dipped his left shoulder under her thigh and
draped her leg over his back. "So perfect here." He blew lightly across her sex, soothing her before diving in again with his
tongue. Ashley stared at Luke's head buried in between her legs
and whimpered, writhed, arched into his assault. His lips, his
tongue, his teeth, they were everything she imagined, and she
lost herself in the reality of him as he feasted on her.

"So. Good," she rasped as the first small waves of orgasm
surged on the shores of her senses. Just when she thought she
had waded into pleasure as deep as she could without the crash

of an orgasm, Luke slipped a finger inside her, then two, pulsing and crooking his fingertips into her slick heat as he winged his tongue across her clit, and she clung to the edge of ecstasy.

"There, yes, there!" He suctioned her bud with deep suckling pulses, and a low, all-consuming groan crescendoed through her as her toes began to curl and her body stiffened. And then she was crying out incoherent praise, soaring, glittering even, as if a tide with the shine of ten thousand diamonds had just been released in her bloodstream. Luke continued to lap at her, surge in her, and her orgasm opened and curled into self-obliterating light. And she was floating, hovering, suspended in space and time, vaguely aware she was making small little sounds, like breath turned into song.

From the ragged edge of her consciousness, she was aware of Luke's tongue as he gently touched it to the exquisitely sensitive flesh, his fingers still warm inside of her, and damn, but even so sated, she wanted his cock inside her now.

"Kiss me." Her fingers mindlessly raked through his hair before attempting to pull him up to her lips. She wanted her mouth on his, wanted to claim him somehow after he had so completely claimed her.

But Luke growled, still intent on pleasing her, and he continued his gentle attentions, slowly increasing the pressure of his tongue, lengthening the stroke of his fingers inside her, and she realized he intended to bring her to orgasm again.

"Too soon," she mumbled, tugging on his shirt, but like a man who'd thirsted too long in the desert, he continued to slake himself at the well of her, his tongue teasing her slick folds, sweeping her cream, greedy for signs of her satisfaction.

He grazed his teeth across the tip of her clit, then nipped, and Ashley gasped as a near-instantaneous second climax crashed through her. She convulsed, the rapid patter of her heartbeats fluttering in her chest, her breath a wild and untamed thing. At last she began melting into a puddle of exhausted bliss, moaning garbled versions of his name.

As her shudders subsided, he slowly pulled his soaking fingers from her heat, wiped his glistening chin on her inner thigh, and pulled himself up to hover above her. He beamed at her, boyishly, playfully, even as he pressed his thick arousal into her thigh.

"Luke," she exhaled, smiling weakly, shaking her head in elation and disbelief. "You're still dressed."

"You. Are. Marvelous," he said. "I knew it would be like this between us. I knew you were everything I could want. So responsive. So beautiful. Here between your legs is my heaven."

Ashley felt drunk on the salty scent of his heated skin, the musk of her own blossomed sex, the sweetness of beeswax candles from somewhere else in the room, and the perfume of his praise. "I want you naked."

"Yes, ma'am," Luke said, one eyebrow raised, his Southern drawl more pronounced, his tone both playful and heated. He rose to kneel beside her. At the same time, they both realized he was still wearing his apron.

"Maybe later, you could wear just the apron?"

Luke's face lit up with the most fantastically naughty smile. "What the lady wants." He removed it. Something in his voice transformed her laughter into a breathy huff. Had she ever smiled so much during sex? But her smile turned feral when he pulled up his shirt to reveal the taut stomach and cut abs she had felt there before.

Ashley let out a long, audible exhale. Luke grinned at her appreciation, continuing to lift his shirt, revealing the planes of his pecs, his strong shoulders, the curve of his biceps. Ashley whispered huskily, "Let me."

She kneeled in front of him and raked her fingernails over the ridges of his lower abs, then dipped her fingers into the waistline of his jeans, delighting as he shuddered beneath her touch. In an instant, he was unbuttoned and unzipped, and her eager hand squeezed his stiff cock through his briefs. *So hard.* Luke chuffed in pleasure, and she stroked him, her hand brushing the damp cotton wet from precum; then, she gripped him tight as her other hand kneaded the firm flesh of his ass.

"Stand," she whispered, her voice needy and breathy.

He kept his eyes on hers as he stood, his jeans hanging off his hips, fly open, his cock straining for release. He slid down his jeans and stepped out of them, and Ashley angled her head back, her eyes daring him to go on. She could feel her sex clenching again, every cell in her aching to see him fully naked before her.

He smiled, knowing damn well what she wanted.

"This?" His thumbs hooked in the waistband of his briefs.

She laughed, low and hungry. "Now."

With grace, he stepped out of his briefs. God, he was beautiful, his cock long and thick, the head dark and swollen with desire. She wanted to feel him spreading her open, pushing into her. *But not yet.* She crawled the short distance to him, aware of his eyes on her hips, and she kneeled before him.

"Ashley?" Luke seemed, what, surprised? Excited? Humbled?

"I've made myself come thinking about this," she admitted, and his groan was carnal and low. She bit her lip, raised her eyes, then took the tip of his cock in her mouth, swirling her tongue around the smooth, rounded head. She lingered at his slit, relishing the faint bitter taste with her tongue. Luke inhaled sharply.

She sucked, purring as she pulled him more deeply into her mouth, knowing he would feel the vibration through his whole body. She wrapped one hand around his shaft at its base and began to pump him, stroking and sucking in a slow, rhythmic dance.

"So good," he guttered, his voice distorted by pleasure.

She increased the suction, hollowing her cheeks, releasing her jaw, and impossibly, she felt him stiffen even more.

"Like that," he praised as she swallowed hard and took him deeper in, her lips sliding over the satiny skin, struggling a little as his head hit the back of her throat. He tried to pull back, but she wouldn't let him, pulling him toward her with one hand on his ass. As she bobbed and sucked, she kept her eyes open, wanting to memorize every response, thrilled as his neck arched back in ecstatic surrender. Part of her wanted to make him come like this, wanted him so undone he was spilling down her throat, but she gave his cock one last tight suck and one last lush lick, then leaned back to look up as he gazed down in awe.

"Luke." Her voice was hoarse. "Show me to your bed."

With apparent ease, he gathered her from the floor, and she wrapped her legs around his back as he walked with her, kissing the whole time they traveled. He lowered her onto the edge of a king-size bed in a candlelit room. His room. It smelled like him. It was spare, just a bed with two tables beside it, two chairs and a table in the corner. A wall of windows revealed the city lit up below. In this moment, she was grateful they'd talked about birth control and safe sex before the trip to Geneva. Though she was on the pill and he'd emailed her an all-clean report, they'd still agreed to use condoms.

Luke walked to a drawer beside the bed, pulled out a strip of condoms, and ripped one open. Ashley took in the dozens of white candles in glass jars that flickered from every shelf and table in the room. "You knew I'd say yes?" She lifted an eyebrow.

"The answer to my prayers." He grinned at her, mischievous, then gently pushed her back onto the bed. He spread her legs into a wide V with his knees, and then he leaned down to position his cock between the furled petals of her slit.

Please, now, now, now.

Slowly, he pressed his crown to her entrance, stretching her delicate inner lips, opening her with his cock. She gasped as he breached her, widened her, his girth almost painful in the most exquisite way. His eyes never left hers as he took her deeper, deeper, impossibly deeper, and she held her breath, as if she'd forgotten how to exhale.

"Ashley," he gritted, his voice charged with wonder. "Ashley, it's so good. Your beauty, you hold me so snug."

Need pulsed through her as she clenched around his shaft, urging him in, her body writhing beneath him. Luke, as if intuiting what she longed for, bent her legs up to her chest, spreading her open to him even more.

"So hot, Ashley," he hissed, looking down at their union. "So. Damn. Hot."

His slow, measured pulses matched his words, each syllable bringing him closer to the end of her, the end of him. He sank down onto his arms to support his weight, and with the new angle, in one final thrust, he buried his cock wholly inside of her, his balls warm against her ass, and there he held still. She surrendered into the fullness, how it both ached and thrilled her. She took in the taut cords of his neck, the sheen of sweat on his chest. Catching her breath, she wrapped her legs tightly around his back, anchoring her feet into his ass, and he drove his hard length into her with long, deliberate lunges. She rhymed his movements with upward thrusts of her own, their bodies two flames becoming one fire.

"Yes. Luke," she mustered, her whole body flaring with pleasure, burning somewhere between greed and satisfaction. There was nothing, nothing in the world now except for her and Luke.

He slipped a breast into his hot mouth and sucked hard, swirling his tongue around the nipple. At her whimper, he chuckled, a deep-throated, thickly erotic sound that did crazy things to her belly, and then he playfully bit her. She cried out in surprise and delight. He dipped his head to pleasure her other breast, and as his thrusting accelerated, Ashley lost herself in a chorus of nonsensical groans and fevered sighs. She clawed her fingers into his back, clutching for something, anything to tether her to this moment, even as her body rushed headlong toward release. *So close, so close.*

"Open your eyes, Ashley," Luke ordered, which was the only way she knew she had closed them. "I want to see you when you come."

Opening her eyes, Ashley gazed into Luke's face, his sweat-damp curls falling in a dark curtain of midnight around his cheeks. She could see he was straining to not come himself. He rocked inside her hard and deep, his gaze intense.

"I'm going to touch your clit now, sweetness." His voice was ragged and rough. "And you are going to come for me."

And just like that, as if his words themselves had massaged her sensitive bud, she felt a tidal wave of pleasure crest, then slam through her, bringing with it bright glinting spasms and surge after surge of sparkling euphoria, as if she were carbon being made into diamond. The world seemed luminescent—everything glowing from within, from without.

"Luke," she cried, forcing her eyes to stay open. It was wildly vulnerable to not hide in this moment of undone ecstasy, but she wanted to give him what he had asked for, this intimate gaze. And as the crashes of pleasure flooded her blood, she stared into his face, marveling at his raw beauty.

"Ashley," he grunted, his voice like shadow, like velvet. He stared back at her, riding her climax, moaning as she fluttered and contracted around his cock. His strokes came faster, harder, insistent.

"Yes," she urged. "Take me. Hard." He groaned as her body softened to receive him, her hips rocking in rhythm with his punishing drives. With one final thrust, he drove deep into her satiny core, the scent of their pleasure thick in the air, and with a strangled cry, his body jerked and braced in his ecstasy. And always, always, his eyes stayed with hers, and she marveled as they transformed from rapture to fulfillment to downy tenderness. "Ashley." He shook his head as if in wonder, then collapsed on her, full weight, his breath escaping in tattered gasps.

Ashley made no attempt to stir beneath him, as if by being still, she could make time stop and let this moment be forever, their bodies joined in exhausted satisfaction. Such peace she felt now with Luke draped on her, such openness. Luke rolled to the side, removed the condom, then stretched his naked body against hers. They lay there side by side, holding hands, staring at the ceiling. Easy silence settled over them like silk.

Luke was the first to speak. "I would torture myself at night with the thought I would never get to touch you..." His voice trailed off, and he rolled onto his side so he might lightly trail his hand across her skin, moving from her hip to the dip of her waist and up to the soft curve of her breast. He gazed into her eyes as he brushed his fingertips back and forth against her nipple. "If the world ended at dawn, I would die the happiest man on the planet."

"It isn't dawn yet," she said with a wicked smile and a suggestive arch of her back.

"You glorious creature." He rolled on top of her and growled in her ear, and she giggled, while all around them, the night steeped into a most beautiful darkness.

Chapter 13

WEARING ONLY THE APRON, Luke looked amazing in the kitchen. Though they'd just spent hours making an erotic time capsule for the end of the world, Ashley was still aroused watching Luke's ass muscles flex as he reheated the dinner they were just now getting around to eating. He gave her a wink as he spooned red jambalaya into a bowl and handed it to her.

"You're really drawn to Southern cooking."

Luke beamed. "It's thanks to my Rena."

"Tell me about her." They moved to sit on the floor in the living room, leaning against the couch, cradling the warm bowls in their hands. To Ashley's disappointment, he covered himself with a blanket.

"She has the strength of a lion, the beauty and fragility of a magnolia, the integrity of a colony of ants."

"Wow."

"She was my savior when I was a boy." Luke looked for a moment as if he were far away, and then his expression shuttered a bit. "She's the reason I'm still here."

"She sounds very special." Ashley hoped he would say more.

"Mmm."

"She's still alive?"

"Mmm. In her eighties now."

"Well, you learned well." Ashley took another bite of the spicy rice dish. "This is so good!"

"I spent a lot of time in the kitchen with Rena. She taught me the holy trinity: onions, bell peppers, and celery. And a few secret tips I promised never to share." Luke's eyes sparkled. "This dish was always one of my favorites. Reminds me of being a kid. How about you? Favorite dish?"

"Enchiladas." Ashley didn't hesitate. "My father's recipe."

"Did you make them with him?"

"Ahhhh. No. Dad left us when I was four." Ashley felt tears rise. *What the hell?*

Luke stopped eating and laid a hand on her knee.

"Funny. I always think I'm over it. And I never am. He left and never came back."

Luke nodded.

"Anyway." Ashley took a deep breath and forced the emotions down. "I found a couple of his recipes in the back of one of Mom's cookbooks when I was ten. One was for Wiley's Famous Enchiladas. I knew Mom would rip up the recipes if she saw them—she'd done it once before when I'd found a recipe in a drawer. She erased my dad from our lives. Did a good job, too. Those recipes were the only hint I ever found in our house that he had lived there with us. They're my only link to my dad, really. So, I took the recipes to my neighbor's house. Tica. She was like my Rena, maybe. She only had sons, so Jewel and I were her *hijas*, her daughters. My own mom was always working, so Jewel and I spent a lot of time at Tica's house. Jewel was always playing with the boys, but I stayed close to Tica."

"Are you still close with her?"

"She died. A couple years ago. Right around the same time I got my divorce. That was a heck of a year."

"So, you were married?"

"Yeah. Two years."

"What happened?"

"I was twenty-eight when I married Mark. Thought I knew something about love. I had a solid job teaching, and I carried both of us financially while he went back to school for an MBA." Ashley shook her head.

"Tell me more," he encouraged.

She closed her eyes and pictured that last night with Mark. "He had just graduated and had a job lined up with a clean-tech magazine. It was his birthday, and I planned a surprise party. All our friends were there. And he came in late. Very late. Drunk. Lipstick on his collar, the whole cliché story."

"Oh."

"Yeah. We all yelled *surprise* when he came in, but I was the one in for the surprise. It was his former professor. Charlotte. They'd been having an affair for months. And right there, in front of everyone, he announced that opportunity was knocking, and it wasn't with me."

"Idiot." Though the word was a curse, Luke's voice was a caress.

She held back telling Luke how ugly it had been. The names he'd called her. The looks of pity and horror on the faces of their friends. The shame. "And I moved on. Only saw him once at the courthouse after that."

"What's something you learned from it?"

"What?"

"Well, you know. The only way I've been able to move on from some of the hardest experiences in my life is by figuring out what I learned from them."

"Okay..." Ashley cocked her head, a little defensive.

"You could get back to me later. Or never?"

"I mean, there's the obvious lesson: *don't trust your heart with men.*" It was supposed to be a joke, but it came out sharp. And neither of them laughed. "Okay. That wasn't funny."

"I understand." Luke's expression was soft, thoughtful.

"I guess I learned I couldn't control other people, but I could take charge of my own actions, my own thoughts. And I guess I learned how important my family is. Mom and Jewel. Friends, too—Meg, who you met in Telluride. She texted me bad jokes every day, trying to make me laugh. And she listened. A lot. She really helped me heal."

"I could tell in Telluride the two of you have a great connection."

"We don't hang out as often as we used to, even though we see each other every day at school, and once a month, we have book club. But when we need each other, the other is right there." Ashley sighed. "Okay, that's enough about me. Have you ever been married?"

"Married, no, but I do have a daughter. A beautiful girl."

Oh! "Does she live in Houston?"

"No. I don't get to see my girl very often. Her mom lives in Boston. But when we do get together..." His voice trailed off, and he chuckled at some memory replaying in his mind. "Well, it's wonderful being a dad."

Ashley could totally picture Luke as a dad, pushing a girl on a swing, taking her out for pancakes, cuddling on the couch with a book—all the things she had longed to do with her own father. Things she'd never gotten to do. The way Luke clearly loved his daughter touched a pale gray emptiness in her.

"How often do you see her?"

"Not often enough. She loves coming to Houston, though, and we stay close on the phone and with video calls."

Ashley chewed her last bite of jambalaya and thought of questions she wanted to ask Luke but wouldn't. Questions about his daughter—what he most wanted to teach her, what she had taught him, what memory had made him smile?

She wanted to ask about the girl's mother, too. In fact, she was surprised at the surge of possessiveness that flooded her. Had he loved her? Why hadn't they married? Had she hurt him?

"So, now that you've restored my faith in my cooking abilities"—he moved her empty bowl to the side—"I have something I want to give you." He flashed her a rascally grin. Luke reached into the apron pocket and pulled out a small, dark wooden elephant, rustically carved. He handed it to Ashley.

"For me?"

Luke nodded.

Ashley laughed. "Huh. There's an elephant in the room."

"Precisely." Luke spread his hands as if pointing to a much larger, invisible elephant.

Ashley looked at him quizzically.

"I'm multi-*tusking*." He waggled his eyebrows. Ashley groaned. "Seriously, I wanted to give you a present from Geneva—I found this in a small antique store. *And* I wanted to encourage a long-overdue conversation between us."

Ashley's heart began beating too strongly. "What do you mean?" She knew darn well what he meant, but she'd been trying to ignore it for so long now that she was resistant to Luke bringing it up. In fact, she had specifically locked away any thoughts of Dalton Oil in a mental box labeled "Do Not Open Tonight."

But here he was, offering her a platform to talk frankly about Dalton Oil. And she was wearing his shirt and smelled of their sex. She felt wholly unprepared for this conversation.

"I know from our work with STEAMEA how important the environment is to you. And I know from your own admission you've been out on the street in front of Dalton Oil with a protest sign. And I know that for a woman who has very strong opinions, you've assiduously avoided talking about this with me."

Ashley stared at Luke, part of her relieved and part of her desperately wishing they could just put Dalton Oil back in its Do Not Open Tonight box.

"Ashley." Luke folded his hands in his lap. "I haven't been this attracted to a woman in a long time. Maybe never. Since the day we met, I've been looking for ways to get closer to you. Relationships don't come easily for me, but I want ours to grow. I know that. And I feel you want the same, too, despite your previous lessons in 'don't trust your heart with men.' Let's put our elephants on the table and acknowledge them."

Ashley sat bone still and, to her frustration, felt tears welling up again. Something about Luke invited her to be much more vulnerable than she wanted to be in this moment. She wanted to find her anger and resentment about the oil industry, Dalton Oil in particular. Hadn't she dreamed of the chance to tell someone in Dalton exactly what she thought about their policies and polluting practices? But for now, she was so moved by Luke's sensitivity and openness she felt disoriented.

Sit tall. This is it—the chance to help him change his mind. He's a smart man, and I know he will hear me.

And the fact that Luke had said that he wanted their relationship to grow? She could almost feel her confidence grow wings—confidence in their relationship and in her ability to help him see the value of turning toward sustainable energies.

And that he'd been so honest about relationships being difficult? Yeah, *that* was an understatement. *But here's to getting us on the same page.*

"Talk to me." Luke took the elephant from her hands and set it on the glass table in front of them. "Ask me any question. The elephant has the best chair in the house. I know the fact that I work for my father's company might be a problem for you. I know my work to provide the world with energy pushes your buttons."

Ashley took a deep breath. "Do you love your job?" *That's your question, Barris?*

"I love making things possible in the world."

"What do you mean?"

"Dalton Oil improves living standards universally."

Okay. Now her picketing hat *was* on. "What about the oil spills that don't get cleaned up? What about the high cancer rates from the chemical plants?" Ashley forced her voice to stay even, though she was becoming more heated by the second. "What about the toxins in the soils from drilling that make their way into drinking water?"

"Yes." Luke nodded. "There's so much not going right. That's why we hire the best scientists. To help solve these problems. We're spending millions of dollars because the answers to those questions can't come soon enough."

Ashley shook her head. "What about that oil spill last month?"

"It was a terrible accident."

"It was a *disaster*."

"Yes. Not just an accident. A disaster. The cleanup is extremely complicated. It's going inconceivably slow. It's so frustrating. All the marine life. All the effects we have yet to know." Luke's face was pinched with dismay.

"And it was due to irresponsible drilling, old equipment, drilling beyond capacity." Ashley's heart was pounding, but she forced her voice to be steady. "It could have been prevented. But it wasn't. And then Dalton couldn't clean it up. Teams were overworked. It was not repaired properly. And how did it all start? The company was too greedy, going for more oil. Turned up the production rate full speed and blew out the valve. Dalton should have let go of the residual. It was greed, Luke."

Luke kept his eyes on her. "The equipment broke. I wish our team could go back and change that decision."

"Hmph." Ashley drew a long breath. "*In the meantime*, Luke, Dalton Oil is a driller and always will be, it seems. You're causing problems faster than you can fix them. And *that* doesn't add up for the Earth."

"Ashley, the way I see it, the company is building solutions. Most of the products in the world need oil to be produced. Most of the world's manufacturing facilities are fueled by oil. There are no perfect answers."

Ashley held her lips in a grim line.

"What did you use for your protest sign, Ashley? A large poster board, I am guessing. And what was it made of?"

"I know. It takes fossil fuels to make the board."

"Yes, it does. And the crayons or markers to color on it. And even if you drove a Prius to the rally, there are seven gallons of oil in each tire, plus another two gallons used in the manufacturing process. Not to mention how much energy and mining goes into making a lithium-ion battery." Luke's tone was soft and factual. "Yeah, Dalton Oil is still drilling. Because *in the meantime,* before we have answers to our energy problems, there's a demand. And oil companies, such as Dalton, are the providers."

Ashley picked up the elephant and let it stand on her raised palm, choosing to look at it instead of Luke.

"Oil companies provide the shampoo that keeps your hair so soft." Luke's voice was husky. "And the pink polish you wear that makes me stare at your nails and imagine you raking them down my back. And the red lipstick you wore at the first board meeting that made me want to push you up against the elevator wall and kiss it all off. You, being conscientious, might have lipstick made of beeswax, but does it come in a plastic tube? Oil companies help provide almost everything, even the clothes you wear that I want to tear off with my teeth—"

Is he really getting me hot talking about petroleum products? Ashley was deeply frustrated with her body. Luke took the elephant from her hand and turned it around to face her.

"*I want to get in your mind,*" he said in a deep voice that was, presumably, the elephant talking. "*What else is bothering you about Luke's work?*"

Luke was being cute, but Ashley felt a flush of purpose. She needed to get him to understand. Right now, she was feeling distracted by their mutual attraction, but she pushed it away. Luke would see things her way—she was sure of it. It might take some time, but he would come around.

"Do you ever make decisions based on what is best for the Earth? That's a bigger picture than what is immediately best for people. If you think of it that way, how would it change your company's decisions to destroy virgin land? How would it change decisions to drill, knowing it could result in an oil spill that will destroy the chain of marine life, destroy the habitat for years? There needs to be more proactive practices, less reactive cleanups."

Luke listened intently.

"For instance, Dalton Oil doesn't have wind and solar programs. We need oil companies to transition to renewable energy sources."

Luke nodded. "Not only, but also."

Ashley gave him a quizzical look. "*Not only* fixing the problems *but also* creating new sources." He gave her a small smile. "*Not only* responsibly using petroleum *but also* expanding into wind and solar. *Not only, but also* was my great-great-grandfather's motto. It applied to his work as a wildcatter, and it applies even more to what must be done about energy now. Eventually, Ashley, your wish will come true. We all know fossil fuels will run out. In my company, conversations are happening about renewable energy."

"Dalton hasn't been sharing anything about that progress."

"Give it time. I know it feels urgent—it *is* urgent. And... there's a ripening process for all things, even for rolling out new energy programs. We want to do it thoughtfully, effectively. Believe me, there are wrong ways to do the right thing."

"A ripeness, huh?" Even if she didn't like what Luke was saying, she sensed the truth in it. Perhaps there was more progress happening than she'd thought. Perhaps she didn't need to do as much convincing as she'd feared. Perhaps Luke was already leading Dalton Oil away from oil.

"A ripeness. True in all things, especially apparent in relationships." He bobbled his head comically. "For instance, there's a lot about me you will come to know."

"Such as—"

"Such as, if all the oil companies went belly up, my backup plan is to become a dessert chef. It's one of my hidden talents. And that's not *irrelephant*."

"Ooh. Your puns—"

Luke's expression went serious. "Look, Ashley, it's important to me we keep talking about this. What you think *matters* to me. I know how dangerous it is to stuff thoughts and feelings, how it eats us up inside. I don't want that for you. Or for us. Your side of the coin, my side of the coin. I want us to realize there is just one coin. And we spend it together."

He held out his hand. Ashley took a deep breath and slipped her hand into his. All her life, she'd been able to see the world as an equation, could see *what to do* as a formula. All her life, she'd been able to use her reasoning skills to solve her problems. But she couldn't find the equation that would explain what was happening with her and this gentle, thoughtful, sexy-as-hell oil magnate who was wreaking havoc on all she thought she knew about herself and the world. And it was driving her crazy.

CHAPTER 14

"COME BACK!"

Ashley woke with a start to the sound of Luke's voice. She hazily remembered where she was—Luke's bedroom, the candles still burning all around them. Luke, naked beside her, was tossing, whimpering.

"Please."

His voice was desperate and deeply pained, his eyes still closed, his body tense and shaking. Who was he talking to in his dream? Another woman? Ashley felt instantly jealous. And protective.

She put her hand on his shoulder and spoke softly into his ear. "It's okay, Luke. You're dreaming. You're okay."

Luke didn't wake, but he stilled beneath her hand, and his breathing evened. Ashley, on the other hand, couldn't fall asleep again. She lay in the candlelit dim and thought about the night before. Luke had followed through with his promise—she *had* lost track of how many times she had come. Obviously, there was chemistry, and Luke was a generous lover who delighted in pleasing her. But there was something else she couldn't quite put her finger on. He had whispered over and over how beautiful she was, how he loved being inside her in these "last moments of the world." It was playful, sexy, a bit odd. *He's not like other men, Barris.* He was unusual. Never what she expected.

Though her body was deeply satisfied, her mind was like a melody being sung slightly out of tune. It kept reminding her of their differences, Luke with his wealth, his oil dynasty. Her, an environmentalist who grew up in the wards. She appreciated he had initiated the talk about their differences, and she smiled in the dark, thinking of the little wooden elephant.

He was thoughtful. Big-hearted. Hot as Houston in July. So why did she feel herself building a wall? Even now in the glow of ecstatic sex, only inches away from his naked body, she could feel herself becoming distant.

Don't have to be Freud to figure that one out. Her father. Her ex-husband. She might as well have the words *abandonment issues* tattooed on her forehead. Of course she wanted to protect herself.

What wound would Luke have tattooed on his forehead? "Don't leave," he said in his nightmare. Did he have abandonment issues, too?

Ashley must have fallen asleep at some point because she woke to Luke's fingers lightly tracing her face, the sun streaming in the floor-to-ceiling windows.

"Good morning, sunshine."

Ashley blinked a few times, her eyes adjusting. She was befuddled. "You seem happy."

"You. Are. In. My. Bed." He continued to trace her features, as if trying to memorize them. "Happy is an understatement." Ashley closed her eyes again and relished the intimate touch as Luke lightly caressed her chin, her ear, her cheekbone, her eyelids, her forehead.

"What happened?" He traced the almost invisible scar line on her temple.

"When I was a girl," she mumbled drowsily. "I tripped and hit a table."

Luke gently massaged the scar. "It's usually covered by your hair. But now that I know of it, this is only one of many places I plan to kiss you this morning," he hummed into her ear, making it tickle slightly. She felt it in her belly, a thrill, a flutter, a clench-ing. "But first, breakfast."

"Is that what I smell?"

Luke gave her a wink.

"You already made breakfast?"

"You looked so beautiful sleeping I couldn't wake you up, but now that breakfast is ready—" Luke stood, and she saw he was wearing only boxers. *Beautiful, that body.* He picked up a big thick white robe from the bed, presumably his, and held it out for Ashley.

"I could get used to this."

"That's what I'm hoping." Luke grinned as Ashley stood, his eyes openly appreciating her nakedness. "Why don't you take your time and come to the kitchen when you're ready."

"Thank you, Luke."

After he left, Ashley took a moment to take in her surround-ings more fully. Luke's room was simple, elegant. No knick-knacks, no photos. Colorful contemporary art on the walls. A meditation cushion in the corner.

His bathroom was the same—spare, elegant, but not ster-ile, simultaneously Zen and down-to-earth. The only thing that took her aback—a split-screen TV playing Bloomberg and CNBC simultaneously. The volume was off, but she could tell it was international oil talk and business news. It agitated her. Ashley hated screens in a house. Hated TV. Hated how people tuned out around screens. And the oil talk felt like an assault.

Deep breath, Barris. This should not surprise you.

On her way to the kitchen, Ashley wandered through an open living space, seeing it for the first time—she hadn't tak-en in any details as Luke had carried her through it. There was a guitar in the corner. Many shelves of books. Comfortable reading chairs. Tables and reading lamps. Here, too, the surfaces were clear of knickknacks, except there was a whole wall of shelves devoted to monkeys—monkeys of glass, clay, beads, cloth, corn husks, stone.

Monkeys? Cute. And surprising. Luke didn't seem the collector type.

And there, on the wall, was another small split-screen TV with the same two stations. Ashley scowled.

"Your coffee, mademoiselle." Luke appeared in the kitchen doorway, holding a white mug.

"Oh, thanks. I like it—"

"Black with a hint of sugar."

"How did you—"

Luke gave her a boyish smile. "*You* are my favorite thing to study. I took note when you asked for it at the first board meeting."

Ashley remembered just how sheepish she had felt that day after her drunken attempt to kiss Luke. And here he'd been observing her, taking notes on how to please her.

"You are wonderful, Luke." Did she just say that? Wasn't it just hours ago in the quiet uncertainty of night that she'd been building invisible walls? Luke and his thoughtfulness kept tearing them down. Ashley felt supremely vulnerable, well aware of just how badly her heart could get hurt. She wanted to protect herself. But somehow, with Luke, she couldn't.

As Luke made himself a second cup of coffee, Ashley poked her head into the pantry. "It's almost the size of my bedroom," she muttered.

"Did someone say bedroom?" Luke walked in to stand behind her and slipped his free arm around her lower waist.

Ashley leaned against his solid chest. It felt good. "Your pantry. It's huge."

"Want to find out how to put the *pant* in *pant*ry?" Luke whispered roughly in her ear. She giggled, and he teased, "I'll show you what else is *huge*." And just like that, she felt a tingling between her legs. Though she was a little sore from last night, the man made her insatiable.

"*Can* we?" she laughed, picking up a can of black beans.

He arched a brow. "Is that how you say yes?"

"Yes." A wicked glimmer in his eyes made her breath catch.

"Oooh, then you're asking for it, Ashley Barris. I hope you are ready to take pity on this starving chef and offer him some delicacies." He nibbled lightly on her ear, then slowly traveled his lips down her neck. Ashley's head lolled to the side, and her breathing hitched. "Ha! See?" he said softly against her ear. "Panting for me already."

"Mm-hmm."

"Naughty girl. I've been working all morning over breakfast, and now you've one-upped me. The only thing I'm interested in eating is you." He bit playfully into her skin. It hurt a little, and she felt a surprising rush of slickness between her legs.

Ashley set her coffee down on the shelf next to the black beans and turned in Luke's arms to face him. She was breathing hard already. "Don't stop now."

"Ah, Chef Barris." He looked into her eyes, touching her only with his voice. "Show me what you have on the menu today."

With a little shrug, the oversized robe fell to reveal her left shoulder. Luke's eyes widened with approval.

"Lovely. An *amuse-bouche*." He dipped his head to explore her exposed skin with his teeth, his eager tongue. Ashley flushed as heat pulsed through her. She inhaled his scent and sighed, shamelessly happy. Luke looked up with hooded eyes. "But I'm a very hungry man. What else do you have for me?"

Slowly, she pulled the top of the robe open to bare the dark pink pearl of one nipple.

"Perfection," Luke murmured. He dropped his head to her breast and sucked hard, meanwhile pressing his hardness into her thigh. Clearly, it was not only his mouth that was hungry. And she wanted to offer him the whole feast.

Her back arched as his hands massaged her ribs, firmly kneading her in synchrony with the hard pulls of his sucking.

Luke licked his lips. "Seconds. Now."

"So hungry," Ashley teased. She tugged on the robe to expose the other side.

"You have no idea how hungry." The thick need in his voice made blood rush to her clit, where it pulsed, a beacon for desire. She ground on him, seeking connection with her mound, her belly, her thighs.

Luke purred, enjoying her eagerness. He sucked and nipped and kissed and bit, and Ashley groaned, weaving her hands through the glory of his hair, tugging and twisting, thrilling in the silken strands as they slipped through her fingers.

Luke lifted his face and stepped back, his gaze carnal.

"Still hungry?" Ashley baited. She swayed slightly, drunk on desire, and Luke put one hand on her hip to lock her firmly against his hardness.

"I was thinking something sweet. Something…warm. Something…" His voice trailed off as he slipped one hand between the flaps of the robe and pressed his palm against her belly, his fingers teasing downward. "Something, perhaps, like—"

Luke sank to his knees in front of her and pulled a step stool close to her leg. He tapped her foot, indicating she should step onto it, which she did. The position effectively opened her, and she felt wanton and unreserved, primal. The look of lust on Luke's face as he gazed at her inner petals made Ashley so hot she leaned back against the shelves for support.

And then his tongue was on her, a long, thick sweep across her soaking entrance, his eyes on hers the whole time. "Even more delicious than last night." His voice was low, full of gravel and honey. Heat blossomed in her chest, her cheeks, and he began moving his tongue in languid circles around her already sensitized clit. Ashley whimpered, sighed, as his stubble grazed her inner thigh.

Luke pulled back and gazed up at her, lascivious. "And now the cream."

Whatever embarrassment she might have felt about his forward comment disappeared as Luke leaned in toward her folds and sucked with long, rhythmic pulls. Ashley rocked herself into his mouth, her movements increasingly frantic, Luke's name spilling from her lips. She felt like a time-lapse film of a rose coming into bloom—growing petals and opening impossibly fast.

And then his tongue was spearing her, plundering, starving, and in a startling rush, she unraveled into orgasm, a molten surge, an explosion of pleasure. She cried out in rapture as his heated tongue continued to press and curl into her, prolonging her undoing, and she rocked into his face, riding the swells of her climax until her whole body relaxed into quivering limpness. She sagged against the pantry shelves, spent.

As her heart rate recalibrated, Luke continued to lick every drop of her arousal, then wiped his glistening face on the robe. He smiled as he stood, his eyes full of satisfaction and lust. "I want an MP3 of all the sweet, sexy sounds you make while I'm eating you. I bet I can come just listening to it."

Ashley draped her arms around his neck and hung from him, their bodies pressed together, swaying slightly.

"Perhaps," she said in a throaty huff, "perhaps that can be arranged."

By the time they got to the pancakes—after round two in the pantry—the short stacks were cold. But they poured the last of the maple syrup on them and warmed them in the microwave.

Ashley watched as Luke threw the empty syrup bottle in the trash. "Where's your recycling?" She picked the bottle out of the trash.

Luke pointed to a lower cupboard.

"Luke, why would you throw glass in the trash?"

Luke looked up, his face unreadable.

"You're an energy man. You understand how recycling glass saves on energy." *And reduces related air pollution by twenty percent and water pollution by fifty percent.* Ashley bit her tongue, resisting the lecture she longed to give.

Luke held her gaze for a moment. "You're right. No excuses. Let me have that, please." He took the bottle and put it in a recycling bin.

"Um, great." Ashley realized she was geared up for a fight. Luke had diffused it by agreeing with her, but now her metaphorical dukes were up.

"Come on," Luke said. "Let's eat our pancakes before they're cold again."

As they left the kitchen, Ashley's eyes hooked on the split-screen TV in the kitchen, and though the sound was off, she could read that they were talking about an EPA report on fracking and water quality. She took a deep breath and forced herself to follow Luke into the dining room.

Everything in her was a jumble. Her body was blissfully exhausted from hours and hours of ecstatic sex, her brain was raring for a fight about fossil fuels, and her heart couldn't decide if it wanted to keep its doors wide open or slam them shut. The lack of sleep wasn't helping.

"Ashley, you seem far away."

"I'm tired," she hedged. "Who are the dogs?" She pointed to a painting. She hadn't seen a single photo in his home, but this painting of two golden Labs had the feel of a family portrait.

Luke gave her a look that said, *I know you're changing the subject, and for now, I'll go along with it.* "Happy and Go Lucky. The two best friends a boy could ever have."

"They were yours?"

"Yeah. Saved my life. Many times. You ever have a dog?"

"No. But I have a cat now, Bamba, and she's a great companion."

"Bamba, like the song?"

"It's short for Huayllabamba, a village in the Sacred Valley in Peru."

"*Why-uh-bam-ba*?" Luke repeated hesitatingly.

"Very good! That's quite close. Most people can't say it that well."

Luke repeated the word again as if getting it to sink in. "What's your fascination with Peru?"

"It's where Tica was from. When I was at her house, she often shared about the village where she grew up and the people there."

"It must be a wonderful place."

"I would love to see the mountains there, the market square, the people dancing in the streets." Ashley closed her eyes, picturing all the colorful images she'd conjured over the years while listening to Tica's tales. "And—" She hesitated. "—there's a sacred chapel there, too, and I promised Tica I would take her ashes there so her soul could rest." That last part was still a little too woo-woo for her to be comfortable talking about, but she had a feeling Luke wouldn't think it was over-the-top at all.

"Is this why you're inspired to teach there?"

She gave him a quizzical look.

"You mentioned it in Telluride."

"I can't believe you remember that."

"I try to remember *everything* about you."

Ashley blushed. "Yeah. In fact, I just applied to teach there. It's a long shot. I've applied before." There was more to that story, but she kept it to herself.

"When would you leave?"

"August."

Luke raised an eyebrow. "What about STEAMEA?"

She took a deep breath. "First, like I said, it's a long shot. But second, if it comes down to it, video conferencing is the new way of the world, and I'll make it work."

"I guess what I was trying not to say was, 'What about me? What about us?' But that doesn't sound very macho, does it?"

Ashley gave a little laugh, delighted by his admission of interest in their future. "I don't think there's anything about your manhood in question."

He gave a happy wiggle of his head. "Peru, huh? I might just have to follow you."

———

Ashley didn't want to leave Luke's apartment. Though she had her own clothes on again, she smelled like him, his earthy, musky scent. And Luke, standing there in his tight-fitting gym clothes, was a massive temptation. But she really had to go. She had a full to-do list. Plus, her system was on overload.

"Remind me again why you're not staying here all day?" he asked, blocking the elevator so she couldn't leave.

"I need to shop for my mother."

"And after that?"

"Do laundry."

"And after that?"

"Follow up on that teaching application in Peru."

"And after that?"

"Go see Mom and grade papers at her house."

"Okay." Luke shrugged. "Can't blame a man for trying to keep a wonderful woman close."

Ashley thought about her week. "Meet on Wednesday night?"

"This week's full, but Friday's open. Perhaps you won't be grading papers then? Rescuing young girls? Picketing my office?"

I'll picket your bedroom if it will change Dalton Oil's drilling practices. "Friday's great."

"Can't wait." He took a big inhale and shook his head, staring at her as if she were too good to be true.

"Oh, Luke." Ashley dug in her purse. "Hey. I don't know how to do this, but...I need to give this back." She handed him the red Cartier box.

Luke's brows knit. He did not hold out his hand to receive it.

"Help me understand." His voice was tight.

"You're so generous. And this gift, it's so thoughtful, but I can't accept it. It's too—"

"Too what?"

"Too...much. I feel uncomfortable wearing it. I can only imagine how much this watch cost, and those resources would be much better spent another way. Feeding, clothing, educating girls."

As understanding dawned, Luke's expression softened. "Ashley—"

She shook her head, anticipating his rebuttal. "If you really want to give me a gift, then please, return this and maybe use the money to feed displaced teenagers? I just can't accept it."

"That is what I love about you. You are so caring. Listen. Keep the watch. *And* I will give a donation to the Lift House for the same amount. Not only, but also, remember?"

"Luke."

"Ashley. Wear it knowing that *you* are the resource. Please. I'll write the check to Lift House today."

Ashley sighed deeply.

"Wear it. And think of it as a symbol of how valuable you are and what a gift your time is to the world. Let it inspire you to do more."

Ashley smiled at his words, even if she still felt awkward receiving the watch. "Okay. Okay. Thank you. Thank you, Luke."

Perhaps it was the vulnerability she felt in accepting the watch that made her want to kiss him again, to be wrapped in his arms, to feel that connection. *Maybe just one more whirl before I go?* she thought. Her fingers played at Luke's waistband, curling in to touch his hot skin, his firm ass, and a greedy rhythm throbbed in her still-swollen sex, but Luke was pulling away.

"You. Are. So. Addictive," he whispered in her ear, then moved to adjust himself in his shorts. "So…" He cleared his throat. "Friday?" He gazed at her intently. "At 7:02?" She laughed and nodded. He raised both eyebrows. At the same time, they both exhaled, trying to summon self-control. Then, shaking their heads like mirror images of each other, they both laughed.

He reached past her to press the button for the elevator. The last thing she saw before the door closed was his inviting blue gaze.

The whole ride down, she giggled, thinking of the surprise she'd left him. Stuffed into the pocket of his robe was her thong. How many days before he found his little purple surprise? And what would he think about then?

CHAPTER 15

J EWEL WAS BITING HER NAILS.

"Uhn, uhn, uhn," Ashley chided, taking Jewel's hand in her own. "Hiding something?" She smiled at her sister. Jewel always bit her nails when she was trying to hide something.

They were sitting in Moshi Moshi, a hip new Japanese restaurant. Jewel had made the reservation for their Tuesday dinner over three weeks ago. She'd been excited to take Ashley here, but now, looking at the menu, Jewel seemed nervous.

"How do you think Mom is doing?" Jewel was stalling.

"You know Mom's getting better. Jewel, what's really going on?"

"Ash, I didn't want to say anything, but that man behind you. Isn't that Luke?"

Instantly giddy, Ashley turned around to look for Luke's dark hair and familiar face, but her joy froze and shattered in an instant when she saw what her sister saw. It *was* Luke, his gorgeous, muscled shoulders filling out a fitted blue shirt, and he was sitting side by side on a bench with a woman. Not just sitting—more like mauling each other with their eyes. Ashley couldn't get more than a profile, but that was enough to tell the woman was beautiful; she had long blonde hair that Luke was brushing from her face. Tan skin. The woman was clearly all over him—couldn't stop gazing into Luke's eyes as if she were searching for something. Ashley knew the feeling—knew just how hypnotic he was. *Damn.*

"I take it I'm right?" Jewel's question was an apology.

"And here I thought—" Just an hour ago, he'd sent her a one-word text, *Purple,* referring, she assumed, to the color of her panties in his pocket. It had been so hot and so playful, and she had felt so special and intimate, and here he was—

"I'm sorry, honey. Look. It's probably just a work meeting. You should go talk to him. Find out who she is."

The woman leaned against Luke's shoulder.

"Ooookay. Not just a work meeting." Jewel made a face.

A sucker punch of disappointment slammed into Ashley's gut. Her heart ran out of the restaurant, screaming, and the rest of her body was about to follow.

Instead, in an act of extreme masochism, she twisted further in her booth to size up the competition. Exactly the stereotype she might have imagined. A black dress, obviously designer, something Ashley could never afford. Elegant. Chic. Shimmery. *Shit.* Ashley looked down at her own button-down shirt, one she'd had since college. She'd felt good about how she looked when she left the house this morning. Now she felt dowdy, almost embarrassed to be her un-chic self.

Luke put his arm around the woman and pulled her close as they looked together at the menu.

"I mean, we never said we weren't dating anyone else," Ashley muttered to her sister, to herself. Obviously, Luke was taking advantage of that. Maybe he had *other* women he was seeing, too, not just this one. Her stomachache worsened. Maybe she and this other woman were just two in the grand pool of women fawning over him. "But Jewel. I thought it was different. I mean, I hoped—"

"Fookin' men." Jewel raised her water glass to Ashley. Ashley was too demolished to even pretend to toast. "Oh, get over it, sis." Jewel scowled. "It's a guy. A primo guy, but just a guy. You got your STEMEA, STEAMEA, or whatever you call it. He's good for something. Plus, you know, even though the sex was 'mind-blowing,' you were already struggling about him being an oil guy."

Ouch. As if Jewel's comment wasn't a knife twist enough, her heart and head began to brawl it out, too.

Head: You can't lose something you never had.

Heart: How are you going to live without him?

Head: The whole thing was your projection.

Heart: Maybe he set up the date a few weeks ago and felt obligated to keep it.

Head: Dream on, honey. Move on.

Heart: You will never get over this.

"Earth to Ashley." Jewel's voice brought her back to Moshi Moshi. "Look. I know this hurts. I know you wanted things to be different. Men are fuckers."

"I just thought—" Whatever joy had been driving her for the last two days was erased. Ashley had promised herself she would never let herself be so vulnerable again. But here she was, hollow, weak, trampled.

"I know, sis, I know." Jewel put her hand on Ashley's.

Ashley took one more look at Luke's back. There was no way she could eat. She closed her eyes, forced the tears back, then looked at Jewel. Her voice was steel. "Let's go."

Jewel: Hey sis.
            How RU?
            Any word from Luke?

Ashley: [photo of massive flower bouquet on her desk at work]

Jewel: ?? Sign of guilt. Any note this time?

Ashley: Suggested my place for dinner Fri

Jewel: Menu: knuckle sandwich

Ashley: He also texted he was really busy

Jewel: With blondes

Ashley: Don't remind me

Jewel: And he sent you flowers the next morning??
After he was all over Miss Young Thang?
And what's up with all the purple flowers?

Ashley: ...

Jewel: Fuck him

Ashley: Yeah

That's exactly what she wanted to do. If only—

If only she could get rid of this terrible feeling that she had lost something incredibly valuable, something she apparently never really had.

~~~~

This is a really bad idea.

Ashley was parked in front of Luke's building. She had a folder full of papers for STEAMEA she planned to drop off. It was a flimsy excuse—there was nothing in the packet he couldn't read online. But Ashley felt desperate to see him, consumed by thoughts of him laughing with another woman who clearly wanted him. And as pissed and sad as she was, she wanted him, wanted another chance to feel the weight of him covering her body. She *really* wanted him. And she hated it.

Look what this man has done to you, Barris. She was an even person, dammit, a level, even person. Efficient. Methodical. Precise. She was a scientist for a reason: she loved rational, well-ordered thought. But this relationship with Luke was an experiment with too many uncontrolled variables. And right now, she felt rash, impulsive, and wildly unsettled. Proof: Going up to Luke's apartment, uninvited. What was she thinking?

Thinking about him having sex with another woman, that's what. Undressing that blonde woman, kissing her neck, touching her breasts the way he touched mine less than a week ago, that's what. Thinking of him slipping his beautiful cock into another woman's body. Shit. Can he really be so cavalier about sex?

Luke had made her feel as if she were in a fairy tale, as if she were the only one, as if she really might love and trust again after her divorce from Mark. Did the fact he was having sex with someone else reduce the connection they'd had? Dilute her importance to him? Sure felt like it.

Hypothesis: If people talk openly about seeing other people, there is a chance for their relationship to work.

That is a bogus hypothesis. Still, right now, it was the only scrap of hope she had. She inhaled deeply and unfastened her safety belt.

This is the wrong thing to do, and I am doing it anyway. She stepped out of the car and gave a fake smile to the valet. *Because I need to see him. This is not the kind of thing to work out in texts or on the phone. I need to know what's going on.*

God, she hated this lack of control.

I haven't lost him yet. She stepped through the lobby. *It's not too late to win him.*

Really? To *win* him? That's what she was thinking? *Win* an oil man?

Let me off this roller coaster.

"Hello, Ms. Barris," said the concierge, his smile warm. It was sweet he remembered her name.

"Hi, Nolan."

"Mr. Dalton says to come up."

She gestured to the phone. "Is that him on the line?"

The efficient concierge nodded.

"Oh-kay."

He extended his hand toward the elevator door. "Have a nice day, Ms. Barris."

The whole ride up, Ashley counted her exhalations. *Five. Six. Seven.* She consciously slowed her breathing down. *Luke wouldn't invite me up if there were another woman there now, would he?*

When the elevator doors opened, Luke was waiting for her, grinning, naked except for a pair of jeans. Ashley gasped and felt her face turn fifteen shades of red.

"What a great surprise!" He stared at her a moment, taking her in, running a hand through his wet hair. She felt uncertain about what to do, a boat adrift, as if she had oars but forgot how to use them.

Luke gestured with his head for her to step out of the elevator. "Come in, Ashley. Perfect timing." The way he said her name was crowded with multiple meanings. A greeting. A possessing. A lavish caress. A curiosity.

Ashley stared at Luke's chest, muscular and chiseled. *The definition of statuesque.* Her eyes dropped to the deep V where his jeans met his waist. God, he was so fit, so strong. She wanted to trace his lines with her tongue.

Embarrassed, she realized she was staring and brought her eyes up to look at his face, where his ocean-blue eyes were clearly amused. His hair, slicked back from his face, hung in soft, full curls behind his ears.

As she stepped forward, he pulled her in for a hug, and she was enveloped in the clean, woodsy scent of his soap and shampoo.

"Mmm." The small moan escaped her before she could tame it, and for that moment in his strong arms against his naked chest, her worries about him and the other woman disappeared.

But when he stepped back and released her, the worries scuttled back in like tiny black spiders. He gave her a hug, not a kiss. *What does that mean?*

"To what do I owe the pleasure?" Luke's eyes raked down Ashley's body, lingering at her chest, where her breasts strained a bit against her blue button-down shirt. She could feel a tingling in the tips as they responded to the touch of his eyes. Oh, the effect this man had on her. Talk about owing pleasure. She wanted so badly to drop to her knees and tug down his jeans and see what her mouth might find there.

She bit her lip. "Um—"

"Everything okay?" Luke's voice was inquisitive, concerned. He raised an eyebrow. "You seem, well, nervous."

You don't know what I saw.

"Maybe it's me?" He flashed a cocky smile and lifted his eyebrows, then looked down at his waist. "You seem to appreciate my *jean*-ious."

She laughed, but her brain couldn't come up with a response. Yeah, she was nervous. Luke, however, didn't look nervous. In fact, he looked happy. Really happy.

Ashley held out the manila folder. "Luke, I just wanted to—"

"Is someone here?" purred a woman's voice. Ashley froze, staring over Luke's shoulder. Wearing only a robe, there she was. The woman from the restaurant. Blonde hair wet and tossed back, her skin glistening. She would be beautiful if it weren't for the snarl on her face, a you-are-not-welcome-here glare.

Ashley's heart sank into her flat-soled shoes. It was one thing to imagine Luke with another woman in his place. It was quite another to witness it.

In the restaurant, Ashley had mostly seen the back of the woman's head, but now she took in the pouty lips, the big eyes, the heart-shaped face, the big diamond studs in her ears. Even wearing a bathrobe, this woman exuded wealth and beauty. It was the way she carried herself, some inner confidence, even aloofness, that came with money. And she was sexy. Gorgeous. Ashley felt a sharp stab of jealousy, married with insufficiency. If this were Luke's taste, she couldn't compete.

"I was just leaving," Ashley mumbled. The other woman flashed a triumphant smile.

"Wait." Luke caught Ashley by the arm. "I want you to meet someone special."

Shit. This wasn't going to go well. She wasn't going to be able to pretend she didn't care about Luke just to make Miss Someone Special feel better about her being here. Ashley wanted to disappear. The other woman didn't seem excited about the introduction, either.

"This is awkward. I'm not even dressed."

The woman walked away, but Luke called her back, then said to Ashley, "We've just gotten back from the gym."

The woman didn't return but stopped in place and faced them.

"In fact..." Luke nodded, raising his eyebrows. "Ashley, maybe you want to join us for dinner." Ashley swallowed. The other woman frowned. Luke was still grinning. Could he really be so oblivious to the invisible daggers the other woman was throwing at Ashley? "You wouldn't mind, would you, Corinna?" The other woman smiled sweetly at Luke the moment he turned around.

Talk about two-faced!

Oblivious, Luke continued. "Corinna, remember the work I'm doing with STEAMEA? This woman is the brains behind the operation, Ashley Barris. And Ashley, this lovely woman who needs to hurry up and get dressed"—he held out his hand to the other woman—"is my daughter, Corinna, visiting for a few days from college out East. This isn't how I was picturing your first meeting, but I really wanted the two of you to meet."

He walked to his daughter and pulled a reluctant Corinna into one arm and beamed. "I'm so proud of my baby."

His *daughter*! Ashley felt a flash flood of relief crash through her. She almost laughed out loud thinking of the tower of assumptions she had built, almost whooped as the assumptions all fell down. *This* was his "little girl"! She did some fast math. He was thirty-six, and if he had a kid around nineteen years old, he would have been about seventeen when she was born. That sounded about right. Huh. No wonder Luke had been busy all week. No wonder he hadn't kissed her when she walked in. No wonder he and the girl were so close at the restaurant.

"But Daddy." Corinna pouted. "It's our last night." She turned her gaze to Ashley. "It's my only time with Daddy. You understand, don't you?"

Her jealousy totally obliterated, Ashley grinned a real grin at the offensive young woman. Adrenaline pumped through her as if she'd just finished a marathon. "Of course." She looked to Luke. "Thanks so much for the offer, but I have other plans for tonight." *Like making sure my place is clean for tomorrow night when you come over. Like shaving my legs. Like going shopping for candles.* "Corinna, it's so nice to meet you."

And though everything about Corinna was unpleasant, darned if she didn't really mean the compliment.

CHAPTER 16

"WELL, OPEN IT, GOOFBALL," Meg prodded.

Ashley had called her friend the minute she'd gotten home from school and saw the email from Global Dynamic Classroom in the inbox. Standing in her kitchen, she hovered her finger above the mouse on her laptop, not ready yet to see what the email said.

"I know, it's just…Meg, I *really* want it. This school in Peru is so much more than a job. It's a promise I want to keep." An image of Tica's smiling face appeared in her mind, bringing the prickle of tears with it. Ashley so wanted to honor the woman who had been her second mother, so wanted to teach and mentor kids in Tica's village the same way Tica had been a mentor for her. "Tica wanted to teach there herself before she moved to the US. She had studied in Cusco and always thought she'd go back to Huayllabamba, but then her husband insisted they come here, and—"

"I know, Ash. You've told me." Meg's voice softened. "I know she was important to you."

"And the timing for this August would be so perfect. I mean, with STEAMEA getting started, I'm not so worried about leaving my job at the school. I mean, I may not even *have* a job anymore after the layoffs."

"So why do I feel like there's a big but?"

"Well—"

"Does this have to do with Luke? Things with you two have really taken off, eh?"

Ashley had been so tight-lipped about Luke, *especially* with her book club friends when they were pressing for more info. But now, torn up about big life choices, it felt good to confide in Meg.

"Yeah. I haven't felt this way about a man in, well, ever. But"—she exhaled—"I don't want to sacrifice my dream. I've wanted to go to Peru and teach for so long, I've seen it as a bridge from my past to my future. And I don't want it tainted with regrets—"

"Well, Ash, first we need to know the facts. Are they inviting you to come? Or not?"

Ashley took a deep breath. Inside this email was her future. And instead of reading it, she was sitting here with leaden fingers and a hole in her stomach, feeling the tug of two mutually exclusive dreams.

"Okay. Okay." Ashley clicked on the email.

"The envelope, please." Meg threw her voice dramatically.

Ashley's eyes scanned the letter.

"No."

"They didn't invite you?"

"No." Ashley slumped onto a stool. "Shit." She felt the full gravity of disappointment, the gut punch of rejection, the crush of a dream lost. Tears filled her eyes instantly. One plopped on the counter, leaving its wet signature.

"Oh, Ashley. That hurts. You may not want to hear this now, but there are other ways to get to *why-uh, why-uh*...to that town in the Andes."

"But *this* was so perfect," Ashley sighed. "Working in a school *right there* in Tica's village. What are the odds? It felt like it was a sign, like it was meant to be. The fact that they teach in both Quechua *and* Spanish after seventh grade and rolled out this new English program, and now they're looking for English/Spanish-speaking teachers to join the staff? It just seemed so right for me."

"Sometimes there's a better plan than our plan."

Ashley flashed back to the moment in the bookstore when she'd first met Luke. What had he said? *Sometimes our plans get in the way of our lives.* Was that what was happening now? She sat on the floor and curled her knees into her. "But I liked my plan."

"Well, Ash, as my life coach always says, 'If it could be any other way, it would be.' Life's got something else in mind for you. And it just might include a gorgeous billionaire with a generous heart."

Ashley felt a surge of relief knowing she wouldn't be leaving Luke in the next few months, even though their relationship was no sure thing.

"You gonna be okay, Ashley? Wanna come over for dinner?"

Should she mention to Meg that Luke would be at her place in just over an hour? "Nah, thanks. Rain check?"

"You're always welcome here, Ash, in any weather."

Ashley closed her laptop and set it beneath some books. Long ago, she'd taught herself to seal up unpleasant feelings, set them aside, and move on. Only this time, she could tell that some of the pain was escaping the closed computer. The fact that her eyes continued to leak was proof.

"So that's how it is," Luke murmured against her lips.

Ashley had heard his steps coming down the hall at 7:01, then had heard him pause outside her apartment for half a minute, motionless until he had knocked at 7:02 precisely. This man really had her number. Punctuality was such a turn-on.

He had entered with flowers in one hand and a heavy bag in the other. *Always reward the behavior you want,* she said to herself. So, the moment she'd shut the door behind him, she'd taken advantage of his arms being full: she pushed him against the closed door, pressed herself against his hard body, stood on her tiptoes, and kissed him in the way she'd been daydreaming all week. Her mouth crashed onto his, her tongue flicking and searching. She felt his erection grow beneath his jeans, and she'd growled, feeling a rush of power.

"You like being in charge, Ashley?" Luke's eyes were dark, narrowed with lust.

"Rrrrrrr," she play-roared like a lioness, but somehow, she spoiled the predatory effect by blushing. In fact, it felt somewhat foreign to "be in charge" with sex, but she did kinda like it.

Luke laughed, delighted, then glanced down to see Bamba, Ashley's long-haired black cat, rubbing up against his leg.

"She has good taste." Ashley smirked. "She ignores most people." She made a small act out of straightening his shirt, smoothing her skirt. "Please, Mr. Dalton. Come in."

Luke looked around Ashley's small but neat apartment, nodding his approval. "It feels good in here."

Though she always kept her place spotless, she'd still made an extra effort to make it shine. *As if Luke cares about finger-prints on the fridge.* Still, cleaning always gave her an illusion of control that she liked. And today, she'd needed it.

Ashley filled a vase with water as Luke laid gifts on her counter. A bottle of red wine. Another of white. A bottle of champagne. And a dozen ivory candles, all shapes, all sizes.

The smile on his face was so boyish, so sweet, so longing to please that it somehow hooked into the earlier tears, and Ashley froze a moment, trying to hold them back. She hated being so vulnerable, and he always brought out that side of her.

"Ashley." Luke's face was immediately concerned. "Everything okay?" He stepped around the counter and moved in to hold her, and she let him. "Hey." She leaned in and sniffled as he put an arm around her and with the other stroked her hair. "Wanna tell me about it?"

His tenderness almost made her want to cry more. She took a deep breath and found herself drunk on the masculine, musky smell of him. It was so weird to be turned on and grieving at the same time. "I'll tell you." She forced brightness into her voice. "But later."

"Would a glass of wine help?"

"Yeah."

Luke set about opening the red and pouring it into the glasses she gave him.

"I'm not going," she blurted.

Luke looked up. "What?"

"Peru. I didn't get the job."

Luke set the glasses down and looked into her eyes. "That was really important to you."

Ashley nodded, tears slipping down her face again. *Ugh.* And Luke touched her cheek with his thumb, wiping each tear, lightly massaging her cheek. When the tears stopped, he handed her a glass and raised his own. "To adjusting."

"Adjusting?"

"Yeah. *Adjust* is one of my favorite words. It comes from the Indo-European root that means 'to join,' the same root as for *yoga* or for *yoke*. It's a word that reminds me to be flexible and to join myself to the moment, to link myself to the world as it is."

Ashley laughed a real laugh and shook her head. "Okay, Webster. *To adjusting* it is."

The wine tasted of black cherry, plum, tobacco, clove. Ashley closed her eyes and let the pinot noir warm her from within.

"And—" Luke lifted his glass again. "A second toast. To this evening together. There is nowhere in the world I'd rather be."

His eyes never left hers as they clinked glasses and sipped again. *Me neither*, Ashley thought. *Maybe not even in Peru.*

"Now…" Luke's voice changed from seduction to business. "I smell the enchiladas in the oven—delicious. You have to tell me, is that—saffron?"

Ashley shook her head. "Wow. You have an amazing nose."

"Saffron is one of my favorites. Earthy and salty. But there's something else different, too, something unusual for Southwest cuisine. It almost smells, mmm, Turkish?"

"Ha! Luke. You are amazing. It's mint."

"So exotic. Your father was creative with his recipes."

"And wait till you taste."

"How long do I have to wait?" Luke sneezed.

"Bless you. Maybe ten more minutes?"

"Good. So, show me around?"

She took him by the hand and led him the few steps to the living room, and he stepped in close to her and nuzzled his nose to her ear, inhaling her scent. It was lusty, playful, a promise of untamed moments to come—just what she needed on this disheartening day.

Her apartment was humble, mostly empty. Her simple furnishings were almost all secondhand or hand-me-downs from friends. A teacher's salary meant she stayed on budget, and Ashley cared more about good food than fancy furniture. Still, her place had clean lines and a simple gray color scheme, and she liked the way it felt, uncluttered and straightforward.

"Is that you and your dad?" Luke asked, pointing to a photograph on the wall. It was a silhouette of a man and a little girl holding hands, walking.

"I like to pretend it is. I got it at a garage sale."

"It's wild how the people we got to spend the least amount of time with can shape us the most." There was a faraway look in Luke's eye, as if he were speaking more about himself than about her. He glanced down at her coffee table. "And this looks beautiful."

Luke lifted the most colorful thing in the room: a photo book of Peru, *Lure of the Rural.*

"I dare you to say the title out loud," Ashley said mischievously.

"*Looo-er of the Roor-ul.*" Luke laughed, setting the book down. "That's funny. It's a tonsil twister."

Ashley couldn't stop giggling. "It feels like you're gargling, right?"

"*Loorr a the Rurrrel.*" He spoke the words close to her ear, his lips not quite touching her skin. It tickled.

"Again," she ordered, amused and aroused.

"Lurrrr ath Rurrrrrl," he whispered against her cheek.

Hopelessly amused, Ashley felt a rush of joy fill her until she thought she couldn't contain it all, and she threw her head back in laughter. Luke stepped in closer to murmur the words against her exposed neck, letting his lips vibrate near her skin. "Lrrrr a rrrrrrrrl." The touch of his breath set off an ambush of desire.

"Luke," she began, her voice almost forming other words, but then they vanished into breathlessness in the way rain sometimes evaporates before reaching the ground. The oven timer beeped. "Oh, shit, I forgot about dinner." Ashley pulled Luke toward the kitchen.

"Smells delicious," Luke said as she set the dish on the counter.

"Needs time to cool." She sidled up to him like a cat and began rubbing one shoulder against his. "What do you think we should do while we're waiting?" She bit her lip provocatively.

"Talk."

"Talk?" She pulled back to look at him. *Seriously?*

"About Peru."

Ashley breathed out a little laugh, part sexual frustration, part gratitude.

"Come on, let's sit down." Luke nodded toward the living room sofa.

They sat side by side. Luke tucked her into his body, curling his arm around her, and for a long time, he just held her there. She leaned into his warmth and breathed him in. She closed her eyes and let herself feel: Feel the disappointment she'd stuffed. Feel the loss of her beloved Tica. Feel the sweetness of being gathered in Luke's arms. Feel the generosity of his attention. She was not a crier, but in that moment, she felt so full of emotions her eyes clouded with unshed tears. *One exhale. Two exhales. Three—* Then, feeling safe, she let the counting stop and focused on the dancing tides of their inhales and exhales, the rhythms unsynchronized, like waves on the shore.

Eventually, Luke slipped them out of the silence into conversation, his words like a skiff to carry her. "What hurts most about not getting the job?"

Ashley took a deep breath. "Rejection hurts, of course. Even though it was a long shot. There are a lot of foreign teachers who want to teach in the Sacred Valley—so there's a lot of competition. Still, I wanted to think *I* was the best for that job. It seemed so clear that this job is custom-made for me. There've been reasons in the past when it didn't work out, reasons I could justify, but this year, I had *convinced* myself that *this year* it was meant to be. That's not like me. I'm so practical." She sighed. "It sounds silly, doesn't it?"

"Not silly. *Hope is the thing with feathers.*"

"Emily Dickinson?"

He chuckled, delighted by her recognition, and his laughter jostled her body against his. She curled in even closer. "Yes. That poem saved me once. I know the power of hope. And it sounds as if that's what this job was giving you—hope to follow through with a dream. It gave you wings you didn't think were available to you."

"You are so anachronistic—I don't know any other thirty-somethings like you."

He shrugged. "Not socializing as a kid gave me lots of time to read. Hope you like what you see."

"You're not so bad." The truth was, she *loved* his willingness to just hold her, ask her about her discouraging news, quote poetry. He made her feel heard and seen, even as she noticed his semi-erect cock in his pants.

Luke always had so much control, she marveled, which was, perhaps, part of what allowed her to feel reckless with him, an emotion largely unfamiliar to her, especially when it came to sex. Now, for instance, all she could think of was his hard-on and how much she wanted him inside her.

"What you're saying makes me think—"

"—that what I need now is a lover, not a therapist." Ashley had intended to sound sexy, but the words came out with a strident edge.

Luke looked a little taken aback, and then he laughed the most playful, seductive laugh.

"Perhaps," he crooned, "you can have both." She felt his chest shudder as his breathing became heavier, and that tremor of arousal in him caused a crescendo in her own.

"What do you mean?"

"I can make you feel better." His voice was low and rich with innuendo. "Will you let me be your *therapist*?"

"My therapist?"

"In this moment, taboos don't exist. Just us. Lie on the couch and let me take care of you." He stood so she could stretch out. "Show me your best patient pose."

"Um, okay." Ashley reclined on the couch, trying to look like the iconic Freudian patient. She felt like giggling, but the look on Luke's face had become intense.

He slowly paced. "Do you believe your therapist has answers that can satisfy you?"

Ashley cleared her throat. "Yes." She stared at his cock, now looking fully erect in his jeans.

"Are you willing to let your therapist try...alternative treatments?"

"Yes." Her assent was husky. She scissored her thighs to give herself the tiniest bit of relief.

Luke stepped closer to the couch.

"Will you let your therapist touch you?" The bundle of nerves at the apex of her legs pulsed like a metronome.

"Yes."

Luke sat on the arm of the couch opposite her head. He lifted one of her bare feet and massaged it, his thumbs pressing hard into her delicate arch. It was heaven, and she closed her eyes for a moment, giving in to the pleasure of it, the magic of his fingers. He lifted the other foot and did the same, kneading and rubbing her soles. *Exquisite.* The whole time he massaged her feet, her desire swelled. Her head lolled back; a small sigh escaped her lips.

Luke stopped, and she opened her eyes to gaze at him. He smiled devilishly. "You respond well to treatment."

Ashley opened her mouth to say something, but nothing came out. She just stared at Luke, curious about what came next. As much as she had relished being in charge when he walked in the door, she was most certainly enjoying Luke taking control right now.

"Will you let your therapist do *anything* to your body?" He ran the back of his hand along her ankle and up her calf, leaving a wake of shivers everywhere he touched.

Right now, please. "Yes."

"Then flip."

Ashley rolled her belly to the cushion.

"Watch me." She turned her head to look over her shoulder and watched his face as, with both hands, he spread her legs open and gazed intently at the flesh where her short skirt rode up. His eyes dilated when he saw the blue thong. Surely, it was soaked. He inhaled his appreciation and exhaled a deep rumble of desire.

Slowly, too slowly, he massaged past her knees, up her thighs, his strong fingers kneading the soft stretches of her skin until he reached the hem. Ashley's hips had their own will, and they arched up to meet him.

"Don't move," he ordered, his voice a quiet caress. "It is very important you remain relaxed. Let your therapist do all the work."

Nothing in Ashley wanted to relax. Every cell was screaming at her to writhe, to tense, to respond. Against her instinct, she agreed. "Yes."

"Good." Luke's gaze followed his hands as they continued their upward journey toward her core. She knew she was slick with anticipation, and she was aching to be touched *now.* God, his fingers were so close.

Please, please hurry. Her hips inadvertently bucked as he slipped his fingers under the edge of her panties. The moment she moved, his hands lifted away from her skin.

"Don't move at all."

"Luke." She gasped.

"Do you trust your therapist to know what you need?"

"Yes." *Just don't stop.*

"Open your eyes." She did, not realizing she had closed them.

Luke rewarded her by grabbing her ass cheeks and massaging them hard, pulling her apart. Ashley gasped but forced her hips to stay in place, trying desperately not to rise to meet his touch.

"Open wider."

She did, and he slipped a hand firmly down the center of her ass to curl it under her. He stroked her through the damp fabric, then stilled his hand.

"Will you let your therapist take advantage of your wetness?"

"God, yes. Please."

Luke rewarded her urgency with a sexy smile she felt in her toes, in her palms, in her molten core. "Oh, I will. Believe me, I will." He gently pulsed his fingers against her swollen folds, making her sigh. "Ms. Barris, you're doing so well."

Ashley's chest rose and fell dramatically as her breath became increasingly ragged and her body became increasingly stirred. She was totally at his mercy. And then Luke's hand stilled.

"Luke?"

His breathing was labored. "I need you to trust me. Intensity is good, but, in this, this, ah, *treatment*, if it gets *too* intense"—his voice lowered—"I think we need a safe word."

She stiffened. "Safe word? You mean like for whipping and spanking?"

Ashley paled, and her heart pounded. He wasn't going to hurt her, was he? Did she have him all wrong? She may have fantasized a time or two about restraints and blindfolds—she'd even liked it when he'd bit her last time—but she was not interested in BDSM, not even with Luke. Luke read her mind.

"No, Ashley." He looked right into her eyes. "I would never mark your skin. *Never.*"

Her body softened in relief.

"But if we take this, ah, therapy too far, I need you to have a way to let me know. Right now, we're creating a fantasy, a fantasy designed to *indulge* you, to bring you ultimate pleasure. But sometimes even pleasure goes too far. And because I am in control right now, I need you to have a way to feel control, too. So, if this fantasy becomes uncomfortable, say *yellow*. I'll back off. If we've gone too far, say *red*."

Ashley nodded, though she still wasn't sure she understood.

"Your body will know only ecstasy, Ashley. It's your mind that might rebel. Though it's also your beautiful mind that will fuel your imagination and lead you to rapture." He trailed a finger down her spine, and she quivered. "Rapture beyond any pleasure you've known before. So, if at any time you are *really* enjoying this treatment, then say *purple*. That is my cue to intensify whatever we're doing."

Ashley nodded, her heart hammering as if she had waded into a strong current thinking it was a puddle.

"What's your safe word?"

"Red."

"What's your pleasure word?"

"Purple."

"Purple," he murmured, his big hand again massaging her upper thigh. Her body responded instantly, grateful he'd begun touching her again. "Now, *that* would be something to aim for. So, where were we, Ms. Barris? I believe we had just discussed the matter of your wetness."

It was crazy, but all this talk of safe words and pleasure words had put her on high alert, which, if anything, had made Ashley even more turned on. Her sex was literally thrumming like a bass string between her legs.

Luke bent over so that his face was hovering just above her sex, and he inhaled deeply. "I can sense your arousal. So, I understand you had an interesting dream. Tell me about it."

Was he serious? Did he want her to talk about her dream of going to Peru while he was sniffing her and rubbing her thighs? Ashley groaned as Luke glided down the zipper on the back of her skirt. She heard the small hitch of each tooth as it loosened, and then in one swift movement, he pulled the skirt and her panties down and off.

"Oh." That was all she could say as his hands rubbed up the back of her legs and neared her core.

"You need to talk to me about this dream, or I'll need to stop touching you. The more you tell me, the more I'll reward you." He paused his hands in the creases below her ass. He pressed his lips just above her tailbone and whispered, "Let me refresh your memory. Our last session, you told me you had a dream of going to Peru."

"Yes," she managed, her voice low and guttural.

"You wanted to go there very badly, didn't you?" She could feel the warmth of his breath as he moved his lips up along her spine without actually touching her skin.

"Yes."

"You were very disappointed to get that email." He unhooked her bra where it impeded the travel of his breath, and she sighed with the release. She started to help him remove her shirt, but his hands left her body. She felt instantly bereft.

"I know it's hard, but you must be completely still, Ms. Barris. You must let what you want come to you. You must trust the world to give you not only what you want but so much more."

She forced her body to still. It felt as if she had electric currents running through her, hooked up to Luke's voice. Plus, she was buzzing from this crazy line of questioning as he seduced her with his hands and mouth.

Once her body stilled, he pulled off her shirt and bra, then moved his hands across her skin as if she were an instrument, a cello, perhaps, and he was learning her shape.

"Oh!" She gasped, forcing her body to stay still. It was so hard to not buck against him, so hard to just lie here and let him touch her. *Sweet, sweet torture.*

And then he began to play her, one hand massaging her breast, the other sliding down her ass to stroke through the dewy slickness that gathered in her silken layers, coaxing an erotic music from her—long, low, tremulous moans. He leaned his mouth close to her ear. "So how long have you been having this dream?" He took the lobe between his teeth and bit it lightly, flicking her flesh with his tongue to wet it, and then he blew softly over her ear. A symphony went off in her core— he was finding every erogenous zone and exploiting it. She whimpered. "How long, Ms. Barris? Since you were a child?" "Yes," she panted. At this moment, her life depended on his touch as much as it needed air to breathe.

"It's devastating to lose a dream," he said as his fingers plunged into her slick channel, curling against her tenderest spot, then slipping back out.

"Oh!" Ashley's chest tightened. Some part of her was aware she was deeply grieving the news about Peru, but her body was so fraught with riotous want she felt frantic for him to keep touching her. She could tell she was close to a shattering orgasm—it hovered just beyond her, like a song she could almost hear.

"You stayed still. So, so good." His voice was thick with his own need. He licked and nipped a hot trail down her neck and kissed his way down her back.

"There are other ways, Ms. Barris, to fulfill a dream. Can you think of any?"

When he reached the curve of her ass, he lifted his head, then thrust his hot, firm tongue into her channel and lapped, and she almost climaxed spontaneously. He raised his head and whispered, "Can you think of any other ways to fulfill a dream besides this trip to Peru? Can you let it go?"

No. As close as she was to orgasm, the question threw her. It was *not* just a trip. *Not* just a job. It was the fulfillment of a promise, a giving back. She'd wanted it so much, and Luke couldn't replace the dream with sex, no matter how good the sex was.

"Yellow," she panted.

"Yes," he said, gently stroking her back, recalibrating the moment. "Yes. That was very good work. You're strong." Ashley felt her whole body surrender to him, so grateful he'd responded to her immediately.

He waited many breaths, calming her with soothing sounds, gentle as a lullaby, before he spoke again. "Dreams are important, Ms. Barris. So important. Perhaps we should talk about how you see your life in the future. You see yourself in Peru?"

"Yes." She relaxed into the moment again and felt her own warm cream almost drip down her leg. Holy shit, Luke had been right. The fantasy was messing with her mind. *And* it was wickedly good foreplay. Her stomach clenched, impatient for him to touch her secret places again.

"Good." The pressure of his hands on her back grew stronger as he worked her muscles.

"You can have your dream," he soothed. "You can have everything you want, Ms. Barris." And then his hands were gone. *What?* And she heard the unzipping of his jeans, the shush of his hands shoving down his pants, the rip of the condom wrapper. *Yes.*

"Do you trust your therapist to give you what you want?" he asked as he half climbed on the couch and rubbed his cock at her entrance, sliding his length along the outside of her silken walls. *Oh, sweet heaven.*

"Yes, Luke, yes."

He stood. "Get on your hands and knees."

Ashley found her balance on the couch, and he smoothed her honey-brown hair to fall over one shoulder so he could see her face. Through half-mast eyes, she marveled at how sexy he was, his thick cock erect. She wanted to touch him so badly, to stroke him, but she kept her hands pressing into the cushions beneath her, positioning herself as he'd asked. "So beautiful," he whispered, trailing his hand from her shoulder down her back to her ass. "So beautiful. And powerful. And strong."

And then he was kneeling behind her, his hands on her waist, his cock poised to push into her slick inner channel. She tilted her hips to let him in. He groaned, and in one long, primitive thrust, he filled her and pulled her hard against him, his cock hot and thick and filling her emptiness, meeting her craving, satisfying her want. It was as if the imaginary soundtrack had gone from Moonlight Sonata to Carmina Burana in an instant.

Ashley's whole body tightened like a bowstring, every muscle clenching, her inner walls clamping down hard on his shaft, and she wailed out in pleasure, a long keening descant of fulfillment.

"*Now* rock into me." Luke slid out and slammed himself into her again and again, his thrusts violent and hard, the most welcome invasion. "Take what you want, Ashley, take what you want." He pumped her faster, pulling out, plunging back in. It was everything she wanted. Ashley mewled. She could hear how wet, how sloppy it was, felt the divine friction as he pulled and pushed, watched the flex of his powerful thighs, felt how swollen her lips had become. "You. Are. The. Dream, Ashley. Take it. Take what you want."

She clamped around his heat and relished the thickness, the stretching, the driving tempo, and her breasts swung in counterpoint as she met each thrust, each lunge, Luke's rhythm, her rhythm, insistent and driving.

"Do you want *this*?"

"Yes," she pleaded, every inch of her taut and aching for release. "Yes, Luke. *Please.*" She didn't care if she was begging. She needed to come.

Luke leaned back slowly, and for a horrible moment, she thought he was going to stop, to make her wait, but no, when he leaned forward again, he had changed the angle of his thrust, slowed the tempo of his stroke, smoothed his tone to tenderness. "Then take it." His strokes were deliberate, precise, unfaltering, perfect. And she pushed against him, taking her pleasure on his cock, again and again, finding just the right spot. "The world is yours," he whispered.

And as if he had given her the key to all pleasure, all possibility, Ashley cried out as her climax overtook her, a soaring, an elation, and she spasmed around his hard length, her heart swelling, her sex rippling in wave after wave of ecstatic red pulsing, her blood wildly chorusing, her whole body trembling in an overwhelming crescendo of feral satisfaction. Surely every neighbor in her building could hear her, and she couldn't care.

For as long as her body convulsed, Luke continued to play her, to untame her, to draw out every last note of her pleasure, and then he, too, was shuddering, moaning her name as his body stiffened and she felt his cock jerking inside her. They both collapsed on the couch, heaving in ragged unison, pulling in air in great gulps. Sweating, panting, messy, and spent, Ashley had never felt so alive, a green fuse lit from within, ready to set the world on fire. She could do anything.

"This has been a very good session, Ms. Barris," Luke whispered in her ear.

Ashley was still fighting for her breath as her body melted into the couch, into him, but she licked her lips and mustered two syllables.

"Purple."

Ashley's body froze, but her heartbeat charged through her in deep panic.

Beside her, Luke slept, his arm draped heavy across her chest, his breathing even. She focused on his face, visible in the moonlight that spilled through her bedroom window. All his features were relaxed, undisturbed.

Maybe she'd dreamed it, the pounding at the door. She felt herself relax.

There it is again. Her breath hitched. Adrenaline flooded her chest, tingled in her palms. A thud. More pounding. Banging. Someone putting their shoulder to the door. *Someone is breaking in!*

Pulse racing, heart pounding, Ashley reached into the drawer beside her, grabbed the loaded Glock 17, and streaked out of bed to the living room. She was ready, goddammit.

"What the—" Luke's sleepy voice floated behind her. "Ashley?"

Ashley positioned herself ten feet from the closed front door, her arms straight in front of her, both hands on the gun's grip, her finger on the trigger, her eyes focused and sharp as she aimed where the intruder would enter. She heard Luke get out of bed and walk to the living room.

"Ashley? What—?"

"Quiet," she hissed, her eyes trained on the door, ready for it to crash open.

Instead, she heard someone stumble in the hall, then fall against the living room wall. Then drunk laughter.

Her whole body exhaled. *No way.* It was her stupid neighbors. She let her arms fall by her sides, instantly drained of energy. *Holy shit.* Adrenaline still pulsed through her, despite the fact she now knew it was a false alarm. Freaking PTSD. Her mouth was dry.

"Okay, Luke, it's okay." She exhaled and moved toward where he stood, the silhouette of his strong naked body filling the bedroom doorway. "We're okay." Waves of relief and disbelief coursed through her, her chest now heaving. Her body was limp. She felt frightened and small and wanted him to hold her.

But Luke backed away into the moonlit dim of the bedroom, his eyes glittering in the dark. "You're holding a gun?"

What's wrong? He sounded breathless, wounded.

"Yeah." She let out an exhausted sigh. "Don't worry, big man. There are drunk kids out there, but I'll protect you."

She stepped closer again, and he backed away, then slumped on the bed, his back to her.

"Luke?"

"Put it down." His voice was barely audible.

"The gun?"

"Goddammit, Ashley," he shouted. "Put it down. Now."

"Okay." Her voice quivered. She walked slowly toward the open drawer beside her pillow.

"Now, Ashley."

She put the gun on the floor where she stood. "It's down." She crawled across the bed toward him and reached to hold him from behind.

"Don't."

"Luke?"

In the dim light, she could see he was shaking.

"It's okay, Luke. No one was breaking in. It was just my drunk neighbors." Though her mind was unnerved by his spooked behavior, she forced her voice to be calm, steady.

"You could have shot someone, Ashley." He began shaking his head, as if trying to force something out of it. "I can't be here."

"It's okay, Luke," she assured him. "It's okay. I know what I'm doing with—"

"It's *not* okay, Ashley. I've gotta—"

In three steps, he left the room, and Ashley remained on the bed, stunned, uncertain how to proceed. She walked, zombie-like, to the living room, where she found him kneeling on the floor, sweeping his hands under the coffee table, searching for his clothes. She saw a sock across the room and brought it to him.

He dressed quickly in the near dark, the only sound his rapid breaths.

Horror raveled through her, and she watched him, unmoving where she stood. She couldn't reconcile this irrational boy-man with the confident, sensual masculine god she'd watched undress in this same spot last night.

She was still so shaken from her own fears about the supposed break-in, and now this? She shivered, feeling like a mouse and everywhere she looked, a trap.

At last dressed, one black sock still missing, Luke left. He never looked back, didn't say a word. Ashley followed him to the doorway, aware of her nakedness but too confused and concerned to care. She stared at his retreating back, then at the empty space where his back had been. *What the hell had just happened?*

It was a long time before she closed the door.

CHAPTER 17

TWO. THREE. FOUR. ASHLEY counted the steps to the Lift
House door. She paused on the stoop before going in
and pulled out her phone. Luke's welcoming blue eyes
and dark curls appeared on the screen as she dialed him again.
Again, the call rang straight to his voicemail. "Hello, this is
Luke—" His voice was warm and self-assured, everything he
hadn't been last night.

She hung up. After the first three calls, she'd stopped leaving
messages. Luke clearly didn't want to talk to her. And what else
could she say beyond what she'd already said? *I'm sorry. Call me.
I'm worried about you.*

She hadn't slept last night after Luke had left around 3:00
a.m. She'd just lain there in the dark, reliving everything. The
banging in the hall. The hammer of her heart. The gun's tex-
tured grip in her hands. Luke's face in the moonlight, frightened
and blank. The scent of cold sweat. His muscled body. His recoil
from her touch. The echo of his *no.* And then he'd *left* her.

"Why did you leave me?" she whispered.

*Because every man you've ever loved has left you. And history
repeats itself.*

She was exhausted now but grateful for somewhere to go this morning, grateful for something to do. She almost turned off her phone, as she usually did. But what if Luke called? She left it on and dropped it in her pocket where she could feel it vibrate, then forced her shoulders back, lifted her chin, and unlocked the door.

The building smelled clean and new, so different from the public school where she worked. Perhaps it was exhaustion that was making her somehow hyperaware of her surroundings. The unchipped paint. The lights all working. The new desks in the small bright classroom where she met the kids to study for the GED.

She looked forward to the questions she knew they would be asking. How many civil wars did America have? How do you find *pi*? These were questions she knew how to answer, unlike every other question that plagued her this morning.

All morning, her phone didn't ring.

———

Ashley jumped. Her phone was ringing. She looked at the clock. 6:00 a.m. on a Sunday? Who was calling? Had she fallen asleep?

She reached for her phone on the bedside table. *Luke Dalton.*

"Luke?" Her voice was drowsy despite her best efforts to speak clearly.

"We need to talk."

"Yeah."

"I need to tell you something."

No shit. "Um, okay."

"Oh, sweetness, it's not okay."

———

Ashley walked through Memorial Park to the intersection where Luke had said to meet. She'd been so relieved to hear from him this morning, but now she was scared. *What was so not okay?*

Was this meeting to tell her it was over? Clearly, things had changed between them. The thought made her sick. Why had she let him into her heart? This last day without him had shown her just how much her life had come to revolve around him. Without him, she felt off course. A planet that had lost its sun. *Why did I set myself up for this kind of pain again?*

Luke was there, just where he'd said, leaning back on a bench, one arm resting over his eyes. Before she got close enough for him to notice her, she paused to take him in. Just two days ago, she'd felt like the luckiest woman in the world. Now, he felt so distant.

Despite the emotionally charged circumstances, Ashley felt her body instinctively respond to him—that same ache that opened in her low gut each time she saw his face, that same flutter in her chest when she thought of his kindness. But as she got closer, she could sense something about Luke was off. His chin was covered in the stubble of a couple of days.

Breathe, Ashley, breathe.

Ashley paused and felt the sun strong on her back. She imagined it charging her inner battery. The scent of cut grass was fresh and bright, and she imagined it filling her with resilience.

Walk tall. She moved slowly toward him, and then she sat on the bench a few feet from him. Eyes still closed, Luke nodded, acknowledging he felt her presence. After a moment, he turned to her and opened his eyes. Oh, those eyes. Blue as ever but turbulent.

What is going on?

Ashley offered him a weak smile, but she didn't say anything, didn't move to be closer.

He attempted a smile back. It didn't reach his eyes.

She wanted him to laugh and say it was all an act. She wanted him to tell her everything between them was okay. She wanted him to pick her up and spin her around and tell her he was sorry he left so abruptly.

Instead, he said, "Let's go."

He nodded toward the woods and began to walk, measuring his steps so she could keep up with him. He gave her a wan smile, but he didn't take her hand—and she was profoundly aware of just how naked her hand felt without his around it.

The walk was solemn, silent, like a ceremony. Wordlessly, they slipped into the shade of the dense woods. The world changed from manicured to untamed.

After a few minutes, they arrived in a grassy clearing ringed with ponderosa pines. The only sounds were a few day crickets, birdsong, their own footsteps.

A large blue blanket was spread out in the sun—he had clearly placed it here earlier. Luke gestured for her to sit. *Interesting.* He sat, too, then lay down on his back and closed his eyes. For long moments, Ashley watched his chest rise and fall, and then she looked away. Her insides were a strange braiding of fear, anger, and hope. She wanted him to reach out for her, to pull her in close. She wanted to reach out for him, to comfort him, but it was clear he was in a private, introspective place. Instead, she ran her palm absently over the top of the grass. She had so many questions, but she waited for Luke to speak.

"It was summer." His eyes were still closed. Luke swallowed. Was he going to cry? Ashley watched the hint of his Adam's apple travel up and back down his throat. He looked so vulnerable lying there on his back.

Like a turtle not sure how it will get right side up again.

"It was hot outside, but the house was cool, and we were playing chase, pretending we were cowboys. Mom told us to be quiet, but we kept shrieking and giggling, running all through the house." He swallowed.

"We raced into my parents' closet. My older brother, Jimmy, was chasing me and Elaine. We were squealing and laughing. And then there was so much blood." Luke's face contorted. "So much blood."

He lay utterly still on the blanket. "I didn't mean to pull the trigger."

Oh my god. All the air left Ashley's lungs.

"We were playing. We were just playing cowboys. And Jimmy…he never got up, Ashley. He—" Luke took a deep breath.

The scene of his memory played out in her head.

"And then my mom was wailing, '*My baby, my baby.*' And Elaine was screaming. And I couldn't get my hand to open. My dad tried to pry the gun from my hands, but my hand wouldn't open."

Luke was silent. He opened his mouth. Closed it again. Breathed.

"It was only an instant, Ashley. I shot him. I was laughing when I shot my brother, Jimmy."

Ashley could hear the breath in Luke's chest as it rose and fell. Rose and fell. She saw the pain that squeezed his every cell.

"He was my best friend."

"Oh, Luke," Ashley whispered. She wanted to touch him so badly, and at last, she let her hand rest on his leg, but he didn't seem aware of the touch. Behind his closed eyes, he was revisioning the scene. Though his body was here, he was not here with her at all.

"I knew Dad had an unloaded gun on his top shelf, and I guess we thought it would make the game more real, more fun. And the stepladder was right there. I don't even remember climbing it. And the next thing I remember is the sharp pain in my shoulder. And Jimmy's face. The scent of smoke." His nose wrinkled. "And his shirt—all that blood." Luke's chest rose and fell. "And Jimmy. His—"

Luke cleared his throat. Ashley felt a hot tear slip down her cheek. And another.

"His eyes were open." His voice broke. "He was twelve. I was ten."

The scraping song of the crickets and locusts was suddenly deafening. *Oh, Luke.*

"The other night, seeing you with the gun in your hands—"

"I understand," she whispered.

"It was just...I can't ..." He took a deep breath. "I can't stop seeing you holding it. I can't..." He shook his head, his eyes still closed. A tear slipped down his temple toward the blanket.

"It was *awful.*" He shuddered. "You were holding a fucking *gun.* You could have *killed* someone."

Ashley imagined what Luke saw in his mind—her naked with the pistol, feet planted in the living room, her arms extended, her eyes focused, her finger on the trigger. *No wonder he freaked out.*

"It all came back, Ashley." He shook his head. "Not that it ever leaves. It's always here." He placed both hands on his chest and abdomen. "The weight of it, the horror of it, the empty place where Jimmy should be. But seeing you with the gun, it all came right back."

Luke opened his eyes and stared straight up at the sky. "I've spent years, shit, *decades,* learning how to move on, how to honor Jimmy, how to deal with his death and the loss and the shame. But sometimes..."

He shuddered. "After seeing you, I relived it. As if it just happened. I saw it all again. I was ten. And Jimmy was there, alive, in front of me. And I told myself, *This time we'll keep laughing. This time, he stays alive.* But I could feel the gun in my hands as if it were real, as real as the gun in your hands. And he's dead, Ashley. He's gone forever."

Ashley didn't move. She didn't speak. Her heart ached for Luke. Whatever walls she had put up to protect herself from the fear of losing him were obliterated, and in its place was a field of compassion. What a thing to carry—the death of a brother, a beloved brother, at his own hand.

And yet now it made sense as to why he was such a philosopher, such a deep thinker, such a deep feeler. After living in hell, he'd had to get wise. His own survival had been at stake.

There was nothing to say. She hoped her silence conveyed empathy, open-heartedness. She had so many questions, but now was the time for receiving whatever part of the story he was able to offer.

"I've never talked about this before with anyone except my family and my therapist. Not even with Terrance. Or Savannah. And it's hard telling you now, but I want you to understand me." He opened his eyes and stared right at her.

She nodded.

"Not like it's a secret," he spat. "God knows it was all over the news back then, though I found out my parents paid a lot of money to keep it pretty quiet. Not that I want to forget; it's just so painful to talk about."

"Luke."

"Not a day goes by when I don't think of Jimmy. Since he died, it's like I've lived two lives at once, his and mine. I try to honor his life every day by living my life the best I can."

A long silence settled between them. "Say something."

"Thank you for telling me."

"If you want to stop seeing me—" His voice hitched.

"What?"

"I would understand if you have doubts about me because—"

"Luke." He was afraid that *she* would leave *him*? Because of a terrible childhood accident? Who would have guessed he was so haunted? "I'm not going anywhere. I'm right here."

He gazed at her, drank her in, as if seeing her for the first time that morning. "Really?"

"Really." Her smile was tender. This was so not how she had thought the morning would go. Relief blossomed in her. "You thought that story would push me away." It was more statement than question.

"That, and—" He paused. "I hurt the person I loved the most in the world."

Ashley nodded, understanding what he was trying to tell her.

"You're afraid of me leaving, but you're also afraid you're going to hurt me."

He gave her a startled look, a look of pure yes, as if he couldn't believe she'd just spoken his truth. "Yes."

"Luke. We all hurt each other. That's what we do. It's part of being human. But we heal each other, too." The truth of her words steeped into her at the same time she said them to him. In that moment, she trusted Luke more than she'd trusted any man. She felt an opening deep inside her, a lightness seeping in.

Finally, she let herself reach toward him, cupping his face in her hand, and he nuzzled his cheek into her palm. But the moment was fragile.

"You have to promise something." His eyes locked on hers.

Anything. "What is it?"

"You have to get rid of the gun."

Ashley stiffened.

He sensed the shift in her. "I can't be in your place with a gun in there. I can't be around it. And the vision of you holding a weapon in your soft hands, your beautiful hands. I can't tell you what it does to me."

Stay calm.

She willed her voice to be compassionate, but her tone was serious as steel. "No."

"No?"

"No, Luke." She felt her walls rising again.

"Help me understand."

So, we're going here. Her chest tightened. "I have a story, too."

"I'd love to hear it." Luke sat up and gave her his full attention.

Ashley took a moment to orient herself. She fought the impulse to shut down. It had been easier to encourage Luke to open up about his story than it was for her to do the same.

"I was nineteen. Jewel was sixteen. We were alone in the house." *How hot that night was.* "Mom was working late at the diner. I was taking a shower and had the radio playing in the bathroom."

Ashley could feel the blood drain from her face; her pulse raced. She hadn't talked about this in years. Luke put his hand on her knee. She was glad for its weight.

"And when I came out of the bathroom, it was too late. When I opened the door, I saw—"

"It's okay."

"I saw this hairy, white butt." She screwed up her face and exhaled loudly as if pushing the memory out. "Jewel had been sleeping on the sofa in her nightgown. He had kicked the door open." *And the frame was splintered.* "And he was holding her down—one hand was over her mouth, and he was grunting, calling her terrible names."

Ashley shook her head, wishing again she could clear the memory of his naked ass flexing as he held her down, saying unspeakable things.

"I screamed, and he pushed himself off her. He was pulling up his pants as he ran back toward the door. Jewel was crying, screaming. And as I ran past the kitchen, I grabbed the cast-iron frying pan, and just before he escaped, I hit him on the head as hard as I could." She remembered the dull *thunk* as the pan connected with his head.

"It stunned him but didn't knock him out, and so he got away."

"Oh, sweetness."

"We went to Tica's house, and she locked us in." Jewel had sat on the floor in a ball, arms wrapped around her knees, rocking back and forth, back and forth. "Tica called 911, but by the time the police arrived, the guy was gone."

"No."

"The cops were there in four minutes, and they picked up a lot of guys, but they never caught him. He went free." The words were bitter in her mouth. "Who knows how many other girls he might have raped." Even after all these years, the anger still came. And the desire to protect. "If I'd had a gun, maybe I could have stopped him. Or I could have slowed him down so the police would have gotten him. And he wouldn't have gone free."

Though Luke didn't move, she felt him retreat a little.

She forced her shoulders down. "So, after that, we got a gun. We all took self-defense classes. Even Mom. And when I got my own place, I got a gun. I *need* a gun to protect myself. Bad shit happens, Luke. And I need to be prepared."

Luke's face was pale. "That's why my father had guns, too."

For a long time, neither of them spoke. Nor did they look at each other. Ashley felt no judgment from him, just great sadness. It rhymed with her own.

"Thank you," he said at last. "Thank you for telling me."

Ashley nodded. She could feel the gratitude in him—as if he appreciated her letting him carry some of her burden. She felt the relief of it, too. What a strange gift, this intimacy. It was terrible to dredge up her horrible memory, terrible to know the pain in Luke's past, and yet she felt the freedom that comes with intense vulnerability. Despite their darknesses, their resistances, there was an undeniable tenderness opening between them now, as if windows in them that had been long shuttered were letting in a soft breeze, a warm light.

"You carry hope with you until it becomes you," he whispered under his breath, staring off through the trees. He was saying it to himself, or perhaps to someone who wasn't there? But the words calmed him.

Luke touched her bare arm with the back of his hand, gently trailing his fingers up and down, featherlight. God, she had missed his touch. She glanced at him, and he nodded his head and widened an arm, inviting her to curl in beside him on the blanket.

Yes. Though the day was getting hot, she molded her body to his, resting her head on his hard chest, the skirt of her blue dress draping across her knees. "Mmm. Luke." He felt so good. The shade they were in was cool and quietening. There was more to be said, but for now, she just wanted to hold him, to be held, to burrow into the shelter of his body. She felt a peace she hadn't felt in years, and it floated in her like a Dorian melody, haunting and unbearably beautiful.

Ashley woke with a start. Her eyes flew open to see Luke's face above her. He was stretched out beside her, pressed up on one elbow, teasing her cheek with a long blade of grass. Her lips slanted in a drowsy smile.

"I guess I fell asleep," she murmured, marveling that she'd felt safe enough with Luke beside her to fall asleep in the woods. That and the fact she'd hardly slept since Thursday.

"Mm-hmm."

"Have you been watching me long?"

"Mm-hmm." She couldn't quite read his eyes, but she could feel the heat in them, as if his imagination had touched her with more than just a blade of grass.

"Did you sleep, too?"

"Mm-hmm. And I dreamed." The words were more purr than language.

"What did you dream?"

"That I had wandered into the woods with a beautiful woman with honey-gold hair. Brown eyes the color of coffee. And a pale blue dress."

"Really?"

His smile was both tender and wicked. Ashley shivered.

"And we wandered in deeper and deeper until we found a small clearing in the trees."

"Tell me more."

"There was a blue blanket there, spread out, and we lay on it together. And she told me a powerful story. I was in awe of her—her courage." His eyes met hers, and the look of devotion she saw there melted her.

"What else happened?" She loved hearing him retell the story of the morning. It was oddly freeing to hear it in third person, as if it hadn't been her own heart squeezed by painful memories.

"I told her I'd gotten us here, but now I was lost." His fingers played in her hair, twirling it absently.

"What did she say?"

"She said, 'Good thing I'm a guide.'"

Ashley laughed. "Are you lost, Luke?" She gazed up at him, her smile mischievous. She could swear his eyes darkened a deeper shade of blue. A ripple of pleasure launched through her.

"Very." He looked around the clearing, feigning confusion. "Very lost," he whispered wickedly. Then he looked directly at Ashley, his face a question and a challenge. "If you were the woman in the dream, what would you do?"

Ashley stared at him, a little bewildered. He was asking her to lead him in a seduction. In the woods. Where anyone could walk by.

If you were the woman in the dream, what would you do? Luke was inviting her to play some kind of game—to be someone not quite herself. Someone who would seduce a man in a public park—not a teacher who carefully guarded her reputation.

Her voice came out husky. "I'd show you where *here* is and make you forget about being anywhere else." *Did I really say those words?*

Luke's eyes smoldered. A lightning storm of desire crackled between them.

"Yes."

And with that one word, the lightning touched down in her, became instantaneous wildfire, burning away whatever parts of her were anxious, unsure. She suddenly didn't give a damn where they were or who might see.

"I'll take care of you," she assured him, her voice astonishingly calm to her own ears.

"I know you will."

And suddenly, Ashley was possessed by a need to please him, to own his body and his pleasure the way he had pleased her and owned her.

"Lie down," she ordered, her voice steel wrapped in silk. Luke's exhale was almost a groan, and it fueled her. She reveled in the sweet red pulse radiating through her bloodstream. She straddled him, then grabbed the hem of his shirt and inched it up to reveal his bare skin.

"Found you," she teased as she traced the dark line of hair that led down to the waistband of his jeans.

"That's all I want." His head fell back, and his eyes drifted closed; she splayed both hands against his chest.

"Open your eyes," she instructed, massaging him, delighting in his muscled flesh. "You have to see where we're going."

He obeyed. She held his gaze as she very slowly leaned over him, the kiss beginning long before their lips met.

"God, Ashley."

The scruff of several days tickled against her lips as she nipped and tongued and bit at his lips. His erection grew beneath her, and she rocked her hips into where it bulged against his jeans, then leaned back and unbuttoned his jeans. She fought the sense of urgency, forcing herself to go slow with the zipper. The sound of the metal teeth provoked an almost Pavlovian response.

She pushed down his pants, then his boxers, and admired his cock as it sprang free of his clothes. *Yes.* She licked her lips. She wanted this even more, perhaps, than he did. She wrapped her hand around his thickness and slid her body down his, slowly, slowly. Her eyes took in every change in his face.

His eyes flared, and he groaned as she flicked her tongue across the plush tip. It thrilled her to see him so vulnerable, so hungry for her mouth, so needing what she longed to give him.

She rooted her hand at his base and slipped the crown into her mouth, then dragged the flat of her tongue down the shaft, all the while holding his gaze.

"So beautiful, god, so beautiful." He groaned.

A rush of lust possessed her, and she opened wide and took him deep, and he cursed and praised and repeated her name as they found their rhythm, her hand stroking, her cheeks suctioning, her head bobbing the length of him. Up and down. His hands tangled in her hair—she loved that feeling—but he didn't push or tug; he let her keep the tempo as she struggled to take his tip into her throat, her eyes watering, her nostrils flaring, her lips curling over his girth in a tight pink O.

"*So good. Yes. Like that.*" His voice strained, and his hips began to piston into the wet heat of her mouth. She could tell he was close. God, she felt like she could come, too, and she brought one of her hands down to touch herself through her dress. She was so turned on—sex in the woods, her taking control, Luke's beautiful cock pumping in and out of her mouth.

Luke was cursing now, his voice louder, his hip movements rougher. He tugged at her hair as if to pull her off before he came in her mouth. Instead, she sucked him in as deep as she could, the back of her throat opening to receive him. He understood immediately what she wanted.

"I'm coming," he cried, cradling her head in place, his fingers firm on her scalp as he pumped once more before the warmth of his cum released in her. His body shuddered magnificently before softening completely, heavy against the blanket, his breath coming in great gulps.

Ashley relaxed her mouth but did not move it, enjoying the creamy, bitter taste. She hummed softly and gazed up to see the most tender awe written on his face. And something else.

He pulled her to his chest and circled her into his arms, and she snuggled into his side.

"Ashley, I—" His voice cracked.

Are those tears in his eyes?

She kissed a tear as it slipped down his temple, tasting the salt on her tongue. She could barely hear the words he whispered into her hair, "With you, I think I love being lost."

CHAPTER 18

"So, you didn't get the job in Peru," Jewel said, wiping teriyaki sauce from her lip, "but you're having fabulous sex with a billionaire who is pussy whipped for you."

"Shhh." Ashley glared at her sister. "The whole restaurant doesn't need to know." Ashley caught the nearby waiter's smirk as he straightened the already pristine table setting at the empty four-top beside them. He had *totally* heard her sister.

"Just sayin', not going to Peru is a bummer, but great sex is a mighty fine consolation prize."

"*Jewel.* Shhh."

Jewel noticed the eavesdropping waiter, too, and flashed him a flirty look before he walked toward the kitchen. "Besides, since Gabriel broke up with me, you're the only one in this family who's getting any. So, spill. I wanna know."

"The sex *is* phenomenal," Ashley whispered, leaning across the table, "and—" Ashley rubbed her forehead and temple with one hand.

"What are you not telling me? Is he kinky? He's not pulling out whips or anything? If he likes that, he picked the wrong sister."

Ashley rolled her eyes and laughed. "Nothing like that."

"Well?"

Ashley sipped her wine. "Have you ever, I mean, what do you think about—"

"For god's sake, Ashley, spit it out."

"What do you know about fantasy? During sex?"

Jewel cocked her head and grinned fiendishly. "You mean like playing pirates and Vikings and shit? Like sexy French maid?"

"Not exactly."

"What do you mean, *exactly*? He wants you to dress up in hooker outfits or something? That sounds kinda fun."

"No, not that."

"Then what? Why are you being so weird?"

"I just don't really understand it myself. I mean, the sex is great—it's *amazing*. But. It's just. It's just that Luke always seems to create different scenarios—well, almost always?"

"I don't get it. Like, give me an example."

"Well, at first, I didn't think anything of it. It was just fun. Like one time"—she blushed with the memory—"he acted as if he were my therapist."

"Oh my god, you sapiosexuals. What's wrong with pirates? And so, you, you just play along?"

"Yeah."

"Okay." Jewel scrunched up her face. "So, the man has a hot body, a hard dick, *and* an active imagination. I don't think that's a problem."

"Yeah. But I think it might be more than that."

"What do you mean?"

"Well, once I started thinking about it, I don't think he's ever even kissed me without somehow setting up a scene. He makes foreplay into a game. Don't you think that's, um, weird?"

"Sounds hot, actually. Look, Ash, everybody's got some kind of kink, don't they? Playing therapist sounds pretty harmless. Better than a guy who wants you to pee on him."

"Jewel!"

"Just sayin."

Ashley shook her head.

"Have you asked him about it?"

"No. I'm just starting to see a pattern. And I guess sex has been so high-voltage and, well, *fun*, I didn't really think about it. The um, scenes, I guess, always kind of rise out of whatever we're doing, but—" She struggled as her heart tried its best to be articulate. "Things are getting more serious between us. And great sex is great, but sex is also about connection, and while we're being intimate, I'm not sure I'm connecting with *Luke*."

"Hmm."

"Do you think he's not attracted to me?"

Jewel scoffed. "Shut up."

"Okay, you're right. I'm just insecure after all I've been through."

"My advice: get over yourself and just appreciate good sex."

"But—"

"Or...you need to talk to him."

"I'm afraid."

"Let's google it."

"What?"

Jewel whipped out her phone. "Hey, Siri. Google *Role. Play. Sex.*"

"Seriously. Lower your voice, and put away your phone."

Instead, Jewel stared at the screen a moment before saying, "*Seriously*, Ash, Listen to this. Wikipedia suggests engaging in fantasy is 'sexually arousing,' and it is a great means for 'overcoming sexual inhibitions.'"

"That's enough."

"And check out this photo of the woman cop in the leather miniskirt putting her high heel into this guy's neck before she beats him."

"I said *enough*, Jewel." *Is that what Luke's into? Did he use fantasies with all his ex-girlfriends, too? Or is it just something about me?*

"I think you oughta go out and get yourself a sexy nurse outfit and some six-inch heels and surprise him when he's back from his work trip this weekend. That's what I would do."

"Everything good over here?" The waiter almost leered, delivering two steaming bowls of soup.

"Things are better than good, huh, Ashley?"

Ashley gave her sister a weak smile, grateful the food had come, eager to change the subject. Jewel clearly thought she was overreacting, and maybe she was. Maybe a little fantasy play was nothing to worry about. But some part of her worried that in their most intimate moments, Luke was rejecting the most real Ashley in favor of a fiction. Even though he'd sent her the sweetest text after their rendezvous in the park: *You so found me.* Somehow, she still felt slightly, well, lost.

Abandonment comes in so many shades. And it hurt.

"Aw, hey, sweet guy."

Ashley had never seen Luke quite so happy as he was on the floor of the dog shelter. He was being joyfully, relentlessly licked by a big husky named Bunny. Though his face was covered in slobber, every inch of him looked relaxed—tender, loving, connected.

"He loves you, Luke."

"He's a good boy, aren't you, Bunny." There was a rich tenderness in his voice, the kind humans have when they speak to beloved animals, and he rubbed Bunny between the ears. The big dog promptly rolled over and offered Luke his belly for scratching.

"So, you come here every week?"

"Yeah, it's my happy place." A small yippy dog named King Kong came over to play, too, and Luke laughed and threw the little guy a ball.

The no-kill shelter was bright and modern, and the animals seemed well loved. She'd been surprised when Luke brought her here. He'd said he had something he wanted to show her. Whatever she had imagined, it wasn't *this*, but what a delight this was. On the way over, he explained he had started the shelter years ago: The Happy Go Lucky Open Door Shelter.

"Those were your dogs," she'd remembered. "Happy and Go Lucky, right?"

Luke had beamed at her for remembering their names.

Now, on the shelter floor, surrounded by happy fur balls, she couldn't help but wonder about Luke's connection with dogs—how they made him somehow *more* himself, not *less*.

"Oh, I love you, Pancake," he baby-talked to a dark brown wiener dog who had quietly curled up on the floor beside him.

I love you. It was shocking how the words affected her. Words she wanted so much to hear herself, words that terrified her. Would she and Luke ever say them to each other?

It was strange to feel so connected to him and so locked out. She'd been replaying how to enter the conversation she knew they needed to have all week. But timing was everything. And this wasn't it.

"Let's take these three for a walk, whaddya say?"

"Sure." Ashley rose to her feet.

"I'll get the leashes."

The May morning was cloudy and cool for Houston, and the dogs were happy to be out. Luke and Ashley walked leisurely through the neighborhood, a content silence settling between them.

"Everyone was judging me," Luke said, soft-spoken.

Ashley wasn't sure where he was coming from, and she waited for him to speak again.

He was looking straight ahead, not at her, but she could tell the words were being tugged from an old wound that might never totally heal. "The reporters were judging me. Even years later, my classmates were judging me—they'd point their fingers and say, 'There's the boy who killed his brother.' They knew I could hear them."

He cleared his throat.

"They blamed me. I blamed me. My mother blamed me, even though she said she didn't. For some time, I tried to blame my father for keeping the gun loaded. But in the end, I was the one who pulled the trigger."

They passed an older woman who stopped to pet the dogs and make small talk. Ashley smiled at her politely but inwardly cursed her, hoping Luke would keep talking after she'd gone.

After a few moments of silence, Luke began again. "Aside from Rena, Happy and Go Lucky were the only ones in my life who didn't treat me differently. They gave me happiness. Comfort. They gave me the strength I needed to recover. And I knew I had to move on, had to honor Jimmy by living the best life I could. The most generous life I could. Otherwise, I should have shot myself, too."

He stopped walking. "Every day, I dedicate my life to Jimmy. I say to myself every morning, *Brother, I live this day for me and for you.*"

He took a deep breath. "And the shelter. There is not a day that goes by when I don't thank those two dogs that saved my life. I wouldn't be alive without them." He reached down to rough up the fur on Bunny's back. "Who knows, these little guys might go out and save someone's life, too. That's why I had to open the shelter."

Ashley felt her throat tighten, the hot sting of tears in her eyes. She took a deep breath and touched his face, running her fingers across his scruff. Her face contorted with pain and hope.

"You're a good man, Luke," she whispered.

"I want to be. Otherwise, what's it all for?"

By the time they got back to the shelter, the sun was hot, and Ashley was sweating, relieved to go back inside. It hadn't been the conversation she'd been planning, but it was an important one. Luke had let her in. And wasn't that what she'd wanted? Wasn't that the most important thing? That he trusted her with his most tender, intimate self? Did it really matter if it had been on a sidewalk instead of in bed?

"Hey." Luke grinned. "What are you doing next Saturday?"

"Grading papers. Like I should be doing now."

"Anything else?"

"Walking Pancake and King Kong and Bunny with you?"

"Gosh, I hope so." He was flirty and happy. The walk with the dogs had done him good. Perhaps the sharing had freed him some, too, from demons that never left him. "We can have another fine day at the *paw-ffice.*"

"Oh, you."

"I'm putting my whole life on *paws* to be with you and these dogs."

"How are you that fast with puns?"

"With you, everything seems *paw-sibble.*"

"Oh my gosh." She shook her head.

"Ashley." Luke turned her by the shoulders so she faced him, his face still lit up with strange pride in his own goofy jokes. "Thank you. Thank you for joining me today. It means the world to me. *You* mean the world to me."

"Oh, Luke." Her heart was pounding. *I love you.* The words formed in her mind, and she felt the possibility they were true begin to bloom in her, but as quick as the realization had flowered, the bloom began to brown at the edges. Yes, things felt so right with him. But she had been fooled before. Already she could feel it, the promise of thorns.

———

"You got this," Luke whispered into her ear as Ashley entered the boardroom. "Just be your powerful, passionate self."

She had a sharp knot in her belly, her clothes felt too tight, and her breathing was shallow. Today, she was addressing the STEAMEA board about fundraising—asking them directly for new contributions and outlining her plan for local and national grants. She hated talking about money.

Do I have this? Me from the wards and these folks from River Oaks? Me in TJ Maxx and these women in Chanel suits? She shook off the comparison. She smiled brightly at the board members as they turned to see her and Luke walk in. They smiled back. *Walk tall. These people are just people like me, people who want to make a difference in the lives of young people and the world.*

"Thank you, everyone, for coming," Ashley said, clearing her mind of anything but the task at hand and taking her place at the head of the table. From the corner of her eye, she saw Luke giving her a thumbs-up and a wink. She took a deep breath and invited the part of her that still felt impoverished to show up at the table. After all, that was part of what had gotten her here.

The meeting went better than expected. She could feel everyone on her side, and instead of feeling defensive when they asked questions, she felt energized. One setback—the board president announced she was leaving the board because her family was moving to Kansas. According to the by-laws, they would elect a new president at the next meeting.

At the end, Ashley announced, "Our last bit of business. When school gets out in a week, we are going to employ a paid intern, a talented young woman who has been part of our beta program: my student and mentee Emilia Sanchez."

There was so much she wanted to tell the board about Emilia—how this internship was a lifeline for her. How she, like Ashley, was learning to rise above difficult circumstances. How it was a step for her becoming a teacher, too.

Instead, she focused on STEAMEA. "Emilia is a good example of how students are falling through the system and why our program is so important. She has not been getting what she needs in education. The math and science books in her classrooms are eight years old. Falling apart. Missing pages. The fact that she's using textbooks at all is outdated. The online programming we offer has changed everything about her access to information, and she is thriving. Also, because she's primarily an artist, the program is allowing her a side-door interest into subjects she's previously avoided."

"Our first poster child!" said a board member.

Ashley cringed and beamed simultaneously. She knew how many kids should be on that poster. There was so much work to do. But this was a start, and she was proud of Emilia's hard work.

"You turn me on when you run a board meeting," Luke whispered in her ear as she graded notebooks at his dining room table. He'd convinced her to come for dinner—*you have to eat, might as well let me cook for you*—even though she had so much work to do for school.

"Luke," she admonished, sensing he had seduction in mind. Meanwhile, she had hours of grading. "Some of us have to work tonight."

He held up both hands as if to show his innocence and walked around to the other side of the table to face her. She kept her head buried in work, but she saw him undo a button. And another.

"I love the passion in your eyes when you're talking to the board." Another button. "As if there's a fire inside you, and all I can think about is how badly I want to be burned."

"Luke—"

"As if I've been shivering in the cold and you are the only source of warmth. It makes me want to crawl across the boardroom table. Like this—" He put a knee up on the table and acted as if he were about to crawl toward her.

"Luke!" she spluttered, laughing as he continued his prowl toward her. "Stop it."

"I don't even care who is watching. One of these days at our meeti—"

"You are incorrigible! How is a woman supposed to get work done?" Ashley looked pointedly at the notebooks for emphasis but then made the mistake of looking directly at him. The feral, lustful look in his eyes caused a stitch of desire to catch in her breath. Luke locked his eyes into hers with the steely look of an indomitable man who would not be deterred. She tilted her head back a bit, exposing her throat to him, and he swore under his breath.

"What you do to me, Ashley." He lifted the rest of his weight onto the table, his strong biceps flexing, and from this position, he stared at her like a last meal.

"Have you no respect for the working woman?" She was partly teasing, but she felt the edge of sincerity slicing into the question.

"It's so cold without you." He feigned a shiver as he crawled across the table to meet her, pushing the notebooks aside. "Ashley. Will you warm me?"

She stood. "Luke, stop." The words came out harsher than she meant them to, but she had so much work to do. No. That wasn't the resistance. As much as her body was begging her to play this new game that he had concocted—she felt the warm flush of arousal—her heart was insisting on clarity.

He stopped.

"Too much?" He grinned.

"Yeah, Luke, too much." She exhaled loudly.

Luke's expression went from playful to concerned. He sat cross-legged on the table.

He took a deep breath. "This is about you needing to work?"

"Yeah," she sighed, looking down.

"This is about *more* than you needing to work?"

"Yeah."

"Okay. What's going on?"

"It's just—" She bit her lip.

"Talk to me."

She felt him pull away a little, though his body stayed stock-still.

"Luke. Whenever we have sex, I've noticed—"

She stalled.

"That we have amazing sex? Off-the-charts sex? That our bodies are brilliant together?"

"Yes, but—"

"Do I please you, Ashley?" His voice was serious.

"God, yes, Luke. Of course. You know." She blushed. Her voice lowered. "You know how much I love our sex."

Relief spread across his face, softened the set of his shoulders. This conversation was harder to have than she thought it would be. And this was the wrong timing. Yet here they were.

"It's just…I've noticed that there's almost always some fantasy involved."

"I thought you enjoyed our, um, play?"

"It's not that I don't *like* it, Luke. I mean, I love it—it's just I don't understand why we don't seem to have sex *without* it. Is it something about me?"

Luke scooched to the edge of the table and sat there, legs dangling. When she didn't move closer, he pulled her in to stand between his legs. He looked at her searchingly. "Ashley. You are perfect, so damn perfect for me."

"Then why are you always weaving stories where things are different?"

Luke let out a long, slow exhale.

"I should have known you'd be the one."

"What?" She was instantly defensive. *The one? What was that supposed to mean?*

"I should have known you wouldn't let me hide. Maybe that's why I wanted you so badly."

"I don't understand."

"No. But you will. I'll tell you."

CHAPTER 19

"FOR THE FIRST HALF OF high school—" Luke cleared his throat. "—I'd never even kissed a girl. I couldn't. I didn't trust myself. I still had to interact with people, of course, in boarding school. But I always thought about how I could *kill* someone with my actions, *by accident*, and I was always afraid I would hurt other people. It was so extreme I couldn't even play contact sports. My therapist had to write a letter excusing me from the school's mandatory basketball and field hockey practices. And over time, my anxiety amplified. I was terrified if I even *touched* someone, I would hurt them."

"Oh, Luke." Ashley sat in the chair and looked up at him on the table. He looked lost as he dragged up the old memories.

"Of course, a teenage boy has, well, physical urges. But I couldn't imagine touching a girl. What if I *hurt* her? I know it doesn't sound rational." He winced.

"It makes sense."

"Oh, Ashley." He chuckled in the wry way people do when they are stubbing their souls on a truth. "I've come a long way. But I am still *terrified* of hurting people, especially the people I love."

Ashley's heart broke open for Luke, and without touching him, she imagined holding him.

"And so, when I was a junior, our English teacher, Mrs. Janson, made us do a play. And I loved it. I loved being someone else. She assigned me to play the 'happy custodian'—I had to dance around with a dry mop and tell jokes." He laughed. "And Ashley, playing someone else that was happy allowed *me* to experience happiness. It was like meeting an old friend. My body remembered what it was to be happy."

Ashley pictured a young Luke on a stage, waltzing with a mop, and she couldn't help but grin back at him.

"I who never smiled. I who barely spoke. I know she did it on purpose to try to help me, that tricky Mrs. Janson." He shook his head. "I don't know how you teachers do it."

"That was inspired on her part."

"Yeah, well, it got me into theater. I auditioned for the next after-school play and got in. And loved it. I loved being, well, not me."

The sincerity in his voice hurt her heart. *Oh, Luke.* He had been through so much.

"And then I got the lead in the play, and I had to kiss a girl. Rebecca. And Ashley, that felt impossible. Imagine, I had avoided touching anyone except my Rena for six years. Thinking about *kissing* someone felt impossible. But my therapist convinced me to try. He told me I was ready. And Mr. Kuhl, the theater director, said we didn't have to actually kiss in rehearsals, not until dress rehearsal and the show."

"So, your first kiss was onstage?"

"Yeah. I was so scared." He shook his head gently. "This fear of hurting people was so deep-seated, Ashley."

She nodded.

"But when I got into that role, well, it was heaven. I loved being someone else, escaping my shame, my fear. And I *loved* kissing Rebecca. Before that play, I had no idea a girl's lips could be that soft. I was so alive in that moment when our lips touched."

"At the dress rehearsal?"

"Yeah. And then I *only* wanted to practice the kissing scene. It was like all the circuitry in my body finally understood what it was for, and my sexuality turned on. And so, after dress rehearsal, I came on to her as Clayton, my character, and I called her Jessie, her character, and she was willing to play along."

"I bet she was."

Luke was quiet. "After that, acting became more than just an after-school activity; it became a lifestyle, and very specifically, a way to engage with girls and meet my, um, physical needs. After Rebecca, I tried 'acting' with other girls. I'd just come up with a fantasy for myself. And I learned pretty fast that not all girls were willing to play along. But some were."

"And so, you've engaged with fantasy with everyone you've ever been with?"

Luke nodded.

"Every single one?"

He nodded again.

"And they all just…go along with it?" *Like I have?* Ashley couldn't quite understand the strange weave of feelings she was having. Jealousy. Confusion. Compassion.

"Yeah."

"So, you've never had sex just as Luke before?"

"I've never initiated sex without imagining I could be someone else."

Ashley blew out a big breath. "But that first time for us—that night when you made me dinner? How was that…"

Luke dropped his head a moment, then looked her in the eyes. "It was less a role I was playing and more a scene we were entering…"

Ashley nodded. "The last night of the world."

"I've never told anyone about any of this before. Well, that's not true. I've talked to a therapist about it. But you're the first woman I have told."

"Not even Savannah? Weren't you with her, like—"

"Two years."

"Two years? And you never talked about it?"

"I think that's part of the reason I broke it off with her. We couldn't talk openly about feelings. It's not all her fault, of course. I was fine with not talking about it if I didn't have to. But some part of me, Ashley, longs for real intimacy, even though it intimidates me. And I realized Savannah would let me hide in my tricks forever."

"You mean you want to have sex without involving a fantasy?"

He shook his head. Then paused. "Yes? No? Someday? I mean, I want to be more open to at least *talking* about the fantasies. Maybe that's a good first step."

"Talk about it, you mean like now? Or—"

"Yeah. So, when I saw the sex therapist, I don't know, maybe eight years ago or so, he told me that needing to engage in fantasy during sex was totally healthy. He didn't even think it had anything to do with my brother. He said all kink behavior kicks in before puberty, and the fact that I was a middle child who felt overlooked and invisible probably had more to do with it than anything else."

"Do you agree with that?"

"I don't know. No? Maybe? But it helped that he didn't judge me. That he didn't think engaging in sexual fantasies was a *problem*. And really, it's not a problem—right? It's a way to explore sexual worlds that are really satisfying for my partner and myself. But—"

"But what?"

"But he did stress it was not okay unless it was consensual."

"And yet you've never told anyone else what's going on."

"Well, my side door is I always ask for verbal permission when I start into a fantasy."

Ashley nodded. "I've noticed that."

Luke took a deep breath. "I'm so glad we're talking about it. In fact"—he closed his eyes, then opened them and looked right into her eyes—"it's a relief."

"What else did the sex therapist tell you?"

"Well, he's the one that suggested the safe words."

"And *purple* for pleasure, too?" Ashley had somehow assumed the word *purple* had been tied to the color of her underwear she'd once left in his robe.

"Yeah, he suggested *purple*, too. And he said that to be really healthy, I should be discussing the fantasy scenes with my partner beforehand. And after. That we should come up with boundaries. Come up with *rules*."

"What do you mean rules?"

"Yeah. I didn't like that word, either. Basically, he meant that the more I co-created the fantasy with my partner, the more it would allow for real intimacy."

Real intimacy. That was what she wanted, right? But was this how she wanted to get there? By coming up with rules? Ashley felt a thick fog roll into her head and settle there.

"He said the only real problem was I wasn't talking about the fantasy with my partner. Before or after."

"I see."

"And so I stopped seeing him. Because I didn't want to talk about it with my partners. But I've *thought* about what he said ever since."

"Why don't you want to talk about it?"

"Because I'm *ashamed*, Ashley." His voice rose a little. "I don't need a therapist to tell me the reason I can't be myself during sex is because *I don't think I am worthy of intimacy.* I know that already. I fucking killed the person I loved the most, and I hate knowing I am capable of really hurting people I care for."

Ashley wanted to assure him that she knew he would never hurt her on purpose, but she knew a handful of words would not touch a wound that deep. Time was what built trust. "Thank you for talking about it with me, Luke." She rested her hand on his jean-clad knee.

"I know it's not *normal*, but…Ashley, our sex is spectacular."

"Yes." Her voice was instantly husky. "You make my body so alive, so, oh, fully aroused. Our sex has so much energy, so much…joy." His upper lip curled up. She forced herself to say the next part. "But I need to know it's *me* you are having sex with. I need to feel like it's real between us."

"It *is* real between us."

"But I need to know it's *you* who wants *me*. Great sex isn't just about orgasms. I want it to be Luke and Ashley. I want Luke, the real Luke, to seduce the real Ashley. And vice versa. With nothing else between us. Can we do that?"

"I don't know, Ashley." He shook his head. "I mean, I've never tried. I've never felt *able* to try."

"Help me understand. You can be yourself right now with me, right? Right? Is this the real Luke?"

"As real as I can be."

"So why can't you be this real, broken Luke with me when we're having sex?"

He was quiet for a long time. "I don't want to make a promise I can't keep." He took a deep breath. "Clearly, this is part of a much bigger process; there's so much we haven't talked about." He closed his eyes. "But look, I eventually taught myself to touch other people—to shake hands. To hug. And part of that—" He cleared his throat. "Part of that, Ashley, is because I am determined to honor my brother's life. I was always the quiet one, the reader, the little philosopher. *Jimmy* was outgoing. *Jimmy* loved to hug and be physical. *Jimmy* loved to be the leader. And so, I have tried to live into who he would have been."

Ashley took his hand. They stared at each other for a long time, not saying anything. Though he was inches away from her, he felt a continent away.

"And part of the reason I learned to touch other people again is because I *like* the touch. So clearly, change is possible. I just haven't had a partner before who made me want to try to change. I am not ready. But someday, I'd like to try."

Ashley took a deep breath. So, Luke *needed* to enter some kind of fantasy to be intimate. She understood. But *she* needed to feel as if he weren't leaving her whenever they had sex. Why was intimacy so hard?

"Look. Luke, this is a lot. I have five more hours of grading to do, and I'm tired and confused, and I think I need to go home."

"Don't go. I'll let you do your work. We don't have to talk anymore tonight. But I need to know you're okay. I'll make you tea."

"Okay." And she stayed. But she gasped as she felt some part of her walk away.

"No." Ashley stared at her computer screen as she ate her oatmeal.

"What is it, sweetness?" Luke came to stand behind her, bringing her coffee. She had barely gotten any sleep last night. The few hours she had lain in bed were spent restless in thought. And she was definitely not ready for *this*.

"We didn't get the grant."

"For STEAMEA?"

"Yeah."

"That's okay. You wrote a lot of grants. It's just one."

"The big one."

"So, it's the big one, but it's just one."

"No. It's going to be all of them. Look at this." She highlight-ed the word "insufficient application" on the screen. "There is a list here of incompletes. They need so much more than what I wrote up. Luke, I did *all* of them wrong." She slumped. "I should have asked for help, but I wanted to think I could do it myself. I'm just so *tired* of needing help. And now I've screwed every-thing up."

"Ashley, it will work out."

"How? And…oh shit! And this means we're not going to get the matching funds from Joe on the board. Oh my god." She plunged her face into her hands. Could she just disappear right now? She felt as if she'd been kicked in the back, in the gut, in the head. And the foot kicking her was her own. "This could be the end of STEAMEA." The private donations they were run-ning on could only take them so far. She felt as if she were falling through the room.

What was she going to do? Not only had she lost all the po-tential grant funding for STEAMEA, but she had also let down Luke. He had believed in her. He'd *invested* in her dream. He had asked his powerful, wealthy friends to believe in her dream. And she had disappointed them all. How would they ever trust her to lead now?

So, this is what it's like to watch a dream die. Luke tried to hold her, but she shrugged away his attempt. Her chest con-stricted, and her heart beat too hard, her breaths too shallow. "Stupid. Proud," she muttered.

"It's okay, Ashley." His voice was chamomile smooth. "We'll work it out. This isn't the end. There are always setbacks before things flourish. It's okay."

She didn't want to be comforted. She'd been an idiot. Why did she think she could do what professional grant writers do?

Damn this day. The last week of school was stressful enough. And now this.

"I need to get to work," she said, standing, not daring to look at Luke. She knew he was hurt by her shutting him out right now, especially after last night. "I'm going to be late."

As she rode down the elevator, her heart plummeted, too.

What am I going to do? Peru wasn't happening. She'd effectively shot her nonprofit in the foot. Luke had opened up to her, and she felt herself pushing him away. At least she still had her day job.

———

Ashley leaned back in her chair and let out a big breath. She stared at the periodic table on the wall. Something so comforting about it—all matter arranged into atomic number, electron configuration, and recurring chemical properties. If only emotions and thoughts could be so neatly arranged.

She had hardly spoken with Luke since the night at his house. He had texted and called her a few times. She'd been half-heartedly responding, sometimes not responding at all. Of course, she'd been crazy busy with end-of-the-year grading and report cards, wrapping things up. But that was just a convenient excuse. Mostly, she just didn't know what to say. So, saying nothing was the easiest thing to do for now.

She felt terrible about not being more present with him—it had been hard for him to open up to her about his sexuality. She knew she was supposed to be more understanding, more accommodating, more loving. But the unforgiving glove of futility was squeezing her heart, and she felt so uncertain. How would she and Luke work out their differences?

And she was so embarrassed about the whole STEAMEA thing, how she'd messed that up. She hadn't written the board yet about the grants, but she had gotten two more rejections.

Two granting decisions left to go, but she already knew what they'd say. She would send the board an update after leaving work today.

At least school was out. The kids' last day was yesterday, and she'd just turned in her grades. And she was spent. Wrung out. Done.

"Ashley?" John was at the door. "Can I come in?"

"Sure, John."

Something was off. He looked like a puppy dog that had just shredded the pillows on the couch.

"Sure is quiet in the halls."

"Yeah."

"Sorry I missed the STEAMEA meeting last week."

"About that," she said, then stopped herself. She just didn't have the energy to tell him about the grants. "Well, nothing. We missed you, too."

"So. I have some bad news."

"What?" Was he leaving the board?

"Here." He handed her an envelope.

"What is this?"

"I'm sorry, Ashley. I talked to everyone I could, tried to pull strings. You're one of the best teachers we have, and this school needs you."

What are you saying? Ashley opened the unsealed envelope.

"I didn't want you to be alone when you found out. I'm sorry."

She scanned the letter. She lost her job? They were laying her off?

"At least STEAMEA's going great, right?" His smile was apologetic. "Your timing starting a new nonprofit was perfect. Now you can give it more time. And with all those grants, you'll even be getting a nice salary."

"Yeah."

She let the letter fall from her hands.

———

"Whoa, slow down," Luke was saying on the other end of the line, but Ashley was a fire hose of enthusiasm.

"Luke, I know what we need to do!"

As soon as John had left her room, Ashley had begun to search online for a new job. She could tell by the suggestions in the search bar that every other laid-off teacher in Houston had been recently doing the same thing.

She hadn't found any leads for science teacher jobs; however, something about her own failure had given her inspiration for STEAMEA. "What if we offer students video games, educational games, in which they use their *failures* to move them forward—we help them to fail *up*. See, I was reading this study about how failure can promote learning through discourse."

"Okay." He was laughing, buoyed along by her enthusiasm.

"And we could create the games based on real environmental disasters. And we set it up for the kids to cooperate to find solutions." Ashley was breathless with excitement. "So, for instance, let's say there's an oil spill."

Luke was silent. She knew she was pressing a button here. But this was her vision, after all.

"And we recreate it virtually. A simulation. It's a five-player game for the five disciplines in STEAMEA, and we have five avatars for the kids to choose, one for each discipline—a scientist, a tech person, an engineer, an artist, and a mathematician. Each avatar has a specific skill set that they can use to solve an environmental problem."

"Okaaay, so it's like an environmentally focused *Jumanji*."

"Sure! Except it's focusing on how to move forward with failure. Each time they fail, they are led to a group discussion on relevant game mechanics with embedded environmental disaster content. It's a way to promote both learning and resilience or what the study is calling productive failure."

"Sounds like a great way to get folks to understand just how tricky it is to clean up an oil spill. It's complicated." Luke's tone was serious.

"Yeah, well, of course, the real solution is that we stop drilling and turn to other energy sources. But in the meantime—"

"In the meantime, your idea for getting kids involved with real problems is a great one." Luke's voice was thoughtful. "And I love that the base goal of the game is learning resilience. It's genius, Ashley. It has incredible potential."

"I know! And I'm certain we could get all kinds of funding for it—*if* I hire someone else to write the grants like I should have done last time." She took a deep breath. "Of course, it will be a computer programming nightmare. And it will take a long time to create. I wish someone would take over *that* part. But *just think* how great it would be for the students…and how relevant it is for the world. And it would set STEAMEA apart from every other program out there."

"I am amazed by you, Ashley, always coming up with fabulous new ideas. Look at you." The pride in his voice was unmistakable. He didn't even know yet that she had lost her job.

"Thanks, Luke." Truth was, she was proud of herself, too. She was going to use setbacks as stepping-stones to rise up. She could feel it kicking into gear, her scrappy, survivor self. And it felt so good, especially after the last few days when she'd buried herself in self-pity. She felt confident that between working for STEAMEA and tutoring, she'd be able to make ends meet—it'd be tight but possible.

"I've missed you," he said.

Something in his tone broke open her heart. No matter how strange things were between them—the oil man and the environmentalist, the rich man and the poor girl, the man who had to engage with fantasy to have sex and the woman who was afraid of being abandoned—yes, no matter how strange things were, there was something powerful, something loving, something real between them. When her world fell apart, Luke was the one she wanted to run to, even if she didn't let herself. And when things were looking up, he was the one she ran to tell. And when she did come running to him, he was there for her, open arms. He was the one who believed in her, believed in her dreams.

"Luke." Her voice wavered a little. "I missed you, too. I'm sorry I've been so unavailable. I've been so overwhelmed, but, well, mostly I've been feeling like a failure."

"I know, Ashley. You've—"

"Can we see each other tonight?"

"I want you with me *every* night. But I've got to go to west Texas tonight, and I can't change this meeting. We could meet tomorrow? Do you want to go out? Or shall I make dinner?"

She hadn't known he was going to be gone tonight. Of course, she'd been cutting him out, and now she felt hurt by her own inattentiveness.

"I love it when you cook for me."

"Done." His smile somehow came through the phone.

"And Luke—" She took a deep breath. "I know you were trying to take a back seat with STEAMEA so I wouldn't feel indebted to you, but, well, you'd be a great president for the board. Will you consider running?"

"Really, Ashley?"

"Really. You're the best at what you do. I may not agree with what your company does, but I know *you* are the best there is at running a company. And I want your leadership skills for STEAMEA."

"I like the idea of us being a team."

"Plus"—Ashley leaned back in her chair—"think of all the good press it will be for Dalton Oil that their vice president is the president of an environmental activism organization for teens. The media will eat it up. And the activists against you will be baffled, too."

"Look at you, looking out for the best interests of Dalton Oil." She could hear his smile through the phone. "You think it might hurt STEAMEA?"

"I think it's a chance to show the world how bridge building is done."

"Ashley Barris, you are one amazing woman." His voice lowered, giving her shivers. "I have something in mind for how we can celebrate tomorrow."

CHAPTER 20

WHEN ASHLEY ARRIVED at Luke's house for dinner, she was nervous and giddy, as if a shimmer of hummingbirds was migrating through her bloodstream. She had a plan she'd been toying with all day. She smiled the whole ride up in the elevator. If Luke wanted to play, well, she was going to play.

Something about losing her job had set her free in the strangest way. She had nothing to lose. And the idea about failing up had reframed her ideas about her and Luke's relationship. How could the thing that felt like a failure to connect become something that brought them together?

She'd spent at least two hours looking at websites about fantasy sex and role play, trying to understand it, trying to find her way into a world she'd never even considered visiting. It was hard to explain the feeling she got as she read through the sites—excitement for sure, and some embarrassment. Curiosity. Fear. Some scenarios felt cheesy: Pirates. French maid. Some of the scenarios she'd read about intrigued her: Criminal interrogation. Erotic masseuse. Others turned her off—no student/teacher fantasies. No rape. And costumes? Wigs? That wasn't really her thing. Maybe not Luke's, either. He'd never suggested it.

Some of the fantasies explored power dynamics—boss and secretary, dominant and submissive. She wasn't sure which side of the power dynamic she'd rather be on. She'd enjoyed it in the park when Luke had guided her to take the lead. She had an adrenaline rush again thinking of how much she'd loved taking control. But then she remembered how hot it was being more submissive, like the "patient" role, and *dang*, it made her cross her legs just thinking about it.

One article asked, *What turns you on in your head?*

She had loved the salsa night with Luke. Could that become a fantasy to explore together? She could be the instructor, rewarding him for getting steps right and...and there it was, the student/teacher fantasy. *Huh.* Maybe she was more open to some things than she thought.

In the end, she settled on something that felt safe and sexy enough to make her nerves fire in anticipation all day.

Luke was waiting for her on the other side of the elevator doors. God, he looked good. His blue shirt had a button undone; his jeans hung low, showing off his V cut. *Mmm.* His sleeves were rolled up, exposing his strong forearms. But it was his blue eyes—glinting, mischievous—and his wide, genuine smile that made her breath hitch. All her reservations from the other day evaporated. *How did I get so lucky?* How was it that this man, this astonishingly handsome, funny, intelligent man, was interested in her?

He pulled her into his arms and held her a moment, as if he could hardly believe his good fortune that she had shown up at his house tonight. In his arms, she felt treasured, safe. He stood back a moment and took her in, his gaze resting on her lips, her chest, her long expanse of bare leg ending in navy heels.

"You look beautiful." He leaned down to kiss her forehead, his lips soft as they pressed into her skin.

Ashley gave him a shrug and a coy smile. She'd tried. It had been difficult to change out of her pajamas today—she'd stayed in them until she'd showered just a couple of hours ago, but now she was glad she'd chosen the crisp white button-up blouse and the short navy skirt. Plus, she wanted to look at least somewhat the part of the role she'd chosen.

"Well, *you* look as if you just stepped out of an ad for men's cologne." She played with his collar, inhaled his faint musk. *God, I love his smell.* His scent prowled through her thoughts like a savage animal, triggering an almost savage response in her.

"I have something for you," he murmured, holding out a flat, black oblong box.

The box was light. *A necklace?* "Thank you." She took the box. "Should I open it now?" Luke nodded.

She pulled on the thick red ribbon, slightly nervous about what was inside. Expensive presents, such as the watch she was wearing now, were not easy for her to accept.

It was scrap of black silk—not quite enough material for a scarf. "A blindfold?" Her heart raced. What did he have in mind?

Luke nodded. "This is part of your surprise. Turn around." His voice was thick and sexy, nuanced by his grin.

This was not how she'd planned the night, and she found herself oddly annoyed. What was he getting at with a blindfold? *What about my plans?*

"You okay?" He sensed her hesitation.

Ashley almost blurted something like, *Aren't we supposed to come up with rules together prior to putting the blindfold on?* Something in Luke's tone stopped her. It was vulnerable. Hurt? Scared? She quickly reassessed. What was the most important thing right now? Her agenda? Or connecting with Luke? *Connecting with Luke*, said her inner referee.

"I'm good." She bit her lip. "I've never, um, played with a blindfold before."

Luke accepted her excuse and chuckled. "Not even to pin the tail on the donkey?"

"Not even."

"Well, then, I think you might really enjoy what happens next." He held out his hand for the blindfold.

The last thing she saw was his lust-darkened eyes. And then it was black.

"Oh. Wow."

Of course, she'd walked through the house in the dark of night, but she was somehow unprepared for what it would feel like to be blindfolded. The silk was thick enough that no light bled through, wide enough that there were no gaps in the edges. She was truly at the mercy of her other senses. And Luke.

"Don't let me get hurt," she whispered. *What kinds of fantasies involve blindfolds?*

"Oh, sweetness, we have nothing but pleasure in store for us tonight," he promised. She felt his finger lightly dust her bottom lip. The effect was immediate. Her sex clenched in exquisite agony as she began imagining what might come next, how he might touch her, how much pleasure she would feel. *Holy shit.* Who knew that losing one sense could so immediately put the others on heightened overdrive?

She was instantly more aware of every sound. The water in the pipes. The brush of Luke's shirt as he moved his arms. The cadence of her own excited breath. Anticipation consumed her and ironically brought her more wholly into the moment. She was aware of the skin on her arms, aroused into goose bumps, felt her nipples bunched and tight, straining against her bra. *Damn, this is hot.*

"Come with me." Luke took her by the hand and guided her with his other hand behind her back. She leaned into the warmth of his body as they walked.

"Oh!" She caught the toe of her shoe on a rug and tripped forward, but Luke held her fast.

"Thank you," she said, breathless.

"Oh, I've got you, Ashley. In so many ways."

She trusted him. *She trusted him.* She had never been more aware of it than now. When was the last time she'd trusted a man completely? Not since that night when her ex had shown up to surprise her at his surprise party.

Ashley could almost not contain all the emotions and sensations flooding her. "Just a moment." She stopped walking, recalibrating. Luke stopped beside her, waiting.

"You good?" The vibration of his voice tickled in her ear.

"Yeah." *And so turned on I can barely put one foot in front of the other.* "I'm good."

They were in the hall, walking to the living room between the kitchen and the bedroom. She could tell. Though she couldn't see the walls, she could somehow feel where they were based on the sound in the room. *Like echolocation.* Luke lifted her chin with one hand and touched his forehead to hers, and she could feel his breath so close to her mouth. Her lips parted in invitation. There was so much tenderness, so much devotion in the almost-touch. It was somehow sexier than a hard, fierce kiss, perhaps because it left her wanting so much more. When he pulled away, her expectant mouth was still open, as if she were a fish trying to breathe out of water and Luke was the sea.

"Please?" She was almost begging!

Luke laughed, the sound low and erotic, expressing pure pleasure. "Oh, there will be more. Later. First, the surprise."

What is this surprise? She squeezed her thighs together, desperate to satisfy the pulsing in her clit. Luke somehow gathered what she was doing and hummed his appreciation for her desire.

"Sweetness, soon. But not yet. Here. Sit." There was so much restraint in him, and it only served to excite her more, make her more desperate. It was surprisingly sexy. He guided her to the edge of the sofa and helped her sit.

She felt the upholstery beneath her bare legs, felt the straightness of her spine as she sat at the edge, felt the fit of her shoes as they shaped her feet, as they pressed into the floor.

"Luke." She felt his weight settle beside her and leaned into him. *Mmm.* He smelled so good. She found his chest with her hands and pressed them against his shirt, clutching at the soft fabric with her fingers. "Luke, whatever the surprise is, I need you to *kiss me*. I need you to kiss me *now.*"

"We will kiss, dear Ashley, but first—"

But first, he had to get her to say yes? She nearly groaned in frustration. Was the blindfold causing all this urgency? She felt the sweet rush of blood to her throbbing sex and agonized as the nerves there involuntarily clenched again and again. My god, this was excruciating. What was he doing? What was his surprise? She couldn't fathom, but two could play at this game. She could force him to move this seduction forward.

She felt for the buttons at the top of her shirt and then, with trembling hands, undid them. *One. Two.*

"Ashley, stop." But Luke's words were contradicted by the desire in his voice.

Ashley smiled. She was going to get what she wanted. She couldn't imagine why he was resisting her, but she had more temptations to offer. She had put on a sexy black lace bra with matching crotchless panties and black lace garters—part of the role she'd prepared. She started to pull up the hem of her skirt and slipped a hand inside to touch herself.

"Ashley, you're completely distracting me."

"Then it's working," she said throatily, slipping her fingers in and out of her drenched channel, thrusting her hand, holding in a moan, feeling equally vulnerable and seductive. She intended to put her fingers to Luke's lips, to make him taste her, so she slipped them out and held them up, listening for his breath so she could locate his mouth.

His mouth found her fingers first, enveloping them in warmth as he suckled them. His groan was erotic and went straight to her core. Ashley felt herself pulsing, pulsing. Just the slightest touch would send her into orgasm. *Touch me, dammit.*

Then Luke pulled back. "Soon, sweetness. God, what you do to me."

His phone rang in his pocket, startling her. And he was answering it? Now?

"Luke Dalton." His voice was all business, but she could hear the rough edge beneath it. "Great. Thanks for coming. See you in a minute."

What?

He hung up. "Ashley. Beautiful Ashley. You are so gorgeous right now, and I am impossibly hard after watching you touch yourself, tasting your cream, and I am desperate to see what you don't have on underneath that skirt. And...now that I know what a blindfold can do to you, and to me, I have lots of ideas that are making me even harder, but we need to straighten up to meet people arriving at my door in one minute."

What the—?

He gently rubbed the outline of her chin, stroking slowly back and forth. "We are definitely going to continue where we left off. But for now, let's take off the blindfold."

"Um, okay?" She gasped slightly as Luke pushed up the silk, her eyes affronted by the natural light in the living room.

Sitting on the coffee table in front of her and Luke was a laptop computer. With a note: *Start me.* She looked to Luke. "A computer?"

Luke reached over to button up Ashley's shirt. "The computer is *part* of the surprise," he rasped in her ear. "Ashley, we don't have much time, but press any key."

"Okay?" Ashley's mind and body and heart were all racing. Someone was coming up, Luke had a surprise for her, and all she wanted was to rip off Luke's clothes and ride him right here on the couch, to plunge his cock deep into her and satisfy this all-consuming hunger for him.

She pressed the space bar. The screen lit up immediately to a program with a green-and-blue window with one word in bold letters: FIXX.

Ashley looked at Luke. He was beaming. "It's a prototype image for your video game, sweetness."

"What? The one I told you about yesterday?"

"I knew you wanted to get the ball rolling."

"*This* is the surprise?"

Luke nodded, his grin huge. Ashley turned her head as she heard the elevator door opening.

"And *that's* the other part of the surprise. I've hired two programmers to come brainstorm with you—the best creative team in town. They were on their way out of town tonight, and they're coming as a favor to me, so I can't really put them off. Otherwise, I'd tell them to get lost so we could attend to other... business."

"Luke! You are amazing!" She threw her arms around him and kissed him full on the lips. "I can't believe—"

"Hello?" a man's voice echoed through the rooms.

"I'll go show them in."

"And I'll, um, I'll be right back."

Luke nodded and gave her a wink as he walked away.

Ashley's mind whirled. Luke had already started on her vision for the STEAMEA game? And he'd hired programmers to come talk with them tonight? And that flare of anger she'd had when she thought the blindfold was part of a fantasy he had concocted without talking to her? *You made all that up, Barris.* She needed to give him more credit. She needed to fall more deeply into that trust she'd been feeling just a few minutes ago.

She stuffed the blindfold between the cushions. Hearing the men's voices approaching, she ran to the bathroom. God, she was so wet, was she going to drip down her leg?

As she washed her hands, she stared at her reflection in the mirror and thought of Luke's warm mouth gliding over her fingers. *You are one lucky woman,* she said to the woman in the mirror.

When she reentered the living room, the men were standing, chatting. Luke looked up at her approvingly. And there was something else in his face—eagerness. Like he just couldn't wait for Ashley to meet these guys and move her dream forward. He looked positively giddy. How could he be such a puppy dog and alpha wolf at the same time?

"Ashley." He held out his hand to invite her closer. "I want to introduce you to Greg and Elijah. I asked them to meet us here today to talk about your ideas for the oil spill game. This is Ms. Ashley Barris, STEAMEA's executive director. And my partner."

My partner. Ashley's heart did a quick skip.

"Nice to meet you, Ms. Barris," said the man on the left. "I'm Greg. This is my business partner, Elijah."

They all shook hands and sat. "Well," she said in her boardroom voice, "this really is a surprise."

"We've heard about your vision, and I think you're going to like some of the ideas we've already brainstormed for how you might implement it." Elijah opened his briefcase.

Her head spun. How were they going to pay the programmers? They didn't get the grants. Unless Luke was planning to pay? No. She couldn't let that happen. They would talk about this later. For now, she had two programmers in front of her, and she was excited to see where her idea might go.

"You are so sneaky, Mr. Dalton," she admonished, swatting his ass with her hand as the elevator doors closed on the programmers.

"You have no idea." He cocked his head.

"Did you call them the instant we hung up yesterday?"

He nodded, proud of himself.

"Amazing. Thank you. I love how they can take my ideas and make them real and gameable." For the next half hour, Ashley and Luke brainstormed ways FIXX would help STEAMEA, both getting more and more excited. Ashley was so stunned, so grateful, so impressed with the steps Luke took to make her initiative a reality.

"And. Now." She put a hand on his leg. "About that blindfold. You are—"

"—doing a great job as president-to-be?"

"Oh, yes you are. But *speaking* of jobs, you aren't the only one who had a surprise for tonight." She went to fetch the big canvas bag she'd left by the elevator and pulled out a black camera bag. Luke's eyes flickered. "I'm on assignment for *Yes, Please* magazine. I'm Ashley." She held out a hand. Luke looked at her, slightly stunned, then took her hand in his. She grinned.

"Nice to meet you, Ashley."

"Thanks for agreeing to have me come to your house tonight."

"Right." His lips curled into a hungry smile that sent sunbeams flaring through Ashley's core.

"I brought the contract for you to sign." She handed him a single sheet of paper. Her breath quickened as he read aloud:

I, Luke Dalton, agree to be a male model. I allow myself to be photographed by Ashley Barris, and for this night, I will accommodate her pleasure and expertise. I will do anything she suggests. I trust all photographs taken this evening will be destroyed before the evening's end.

Luke lifted his gaze to meet hers.

"Define *anything.*"

"It means *anything.*"

"Ashley," he rasped.

He's in. "Of course, the contract is open for negotiation. Anything you want to discuss? Any stipulations or, um, rules?"

He shook his head. His eyes sparked with a dangerous glint. "I'm glad to be in your hands tonight, Ashley."

She gave a cocky shrug of her shoulder and handed him a pen. On the line above his typewritten name, he signed, *Purple.*

Though her heart was pounding, Ashley shook his hand with professional disinterest. Who was this woman she was playing at? Some powerful alter ego that had been hiding in her? Whoever she was, Ashley liked her and was looking forward to getting to know her better.

"Mr. Dalton. I'm glad we have a deal."

CHAPTER 21

"**W**EAR THIS."

Ashley handed Luke a dark purple tie she'd picked up at Marshall's on their sale rack today. Luke's eyes widened.

"Just this?"

"Eventually."

"Eventually." He nodded slowly and laughed, throaty and low, but he did what she asked, slipping the tie into his collar and tying it, watching her all the while. *God, this is fun.* She forced herself to stay nonchalant. *But damn*, he was aroused by this. A surge of adrenaline swirled in her gut and made her tingly. Earlier today, she'd doubted she could really say all the filthy things she'd been planning, but after the brief blindfold experience? She was feeling so down with naughty. She was ready to make him beg.

"So, who exactly is this photoshoot for?"

"We have a target audience of thirty-two-year-old females in Houston, Texas, with cats named Bamba who have read *The Path to Love.*"

"And what do you think they like?"

Thirty-six-year-old men with dark curls who open no-kill shelters for dogs. Ashley didn't speak the answer. Instead, she skimmed her finger over his shoulder and down his chiseled bicep to where his rolled-up shirt revealed muscled forearms. She let her fingers play suggestively against his skin there. She stared into his eyes and slowly swiped her tongue across her upper lip.

Luke inhaled long and deep.

She brought her fingers to draw a tiny circle in the open V where his buttons were undone, then pressed her finger into his chest. "This demographic likes *the best*. That's why we chose you. Come."

She led him to the front room with its big windows and wide view and airy feel.

"Nice place you have."

"Thanks."

"Pretty upscale for a model. You must do well."

"New at it, actually. I could use some tips."

"Don't worry. I know a trick or two about how to make things steamy."

"Oh ho ho." Luke ran both hands through his hair. His eyes lit up with unmasked want. "I'm lucky."

Ashley didn't look, but she could *sense* his hard-on growing in his jeans. She wanted to touch him so badly, wanted him to slip his cock into her right now. She was already so wet, so ready for him, but she was enjoying this teasing too much. She could tell that her taking charge of the fantasy was blowing Luke's mind—especially since she'd been so cool since their conversation. And she full-body loved blowing his mind.

Ashley opened the black bag and pulled out the camera body. "Go pour yourself a glass of whiskey while I'm getting ready. It'll help with the nerves. Pour one for me, too. A double."

"Yes, ma'am." His Southern drawl was pronounced.

Ashley barely knew how to operate this camera she borrowed, but Luke didn't need to know that. It looked very professional. She pulled out one of the long lenses and fit it on, then held it up to her eye. Such an obvious phallic symbol—you didn't need to be an English major to notice that.

Luke arrived with their drinks and handed her one. *Stiff.* She laughed to herself at the pun. The scent of oak and sweet tobacco rose into her nose.

Their eyes locked. "To play." She clinked his glass.

"To play."

The alcohol burned in her mouth and left a hot trail down her throat, and she reveled in the immediate high of it.

"Now, go stand by the table. Take a sip and look at the camera like what you really want to be tasting is what I'm hiding under this skirt."

Luke brought the glass to his lips and looked at her with such raw intensity she almost began to hyperventilate. The room was ripe with lust, and the rapid clicks of the shutter were like audible exclamation points.

"Nice." Her tone was even. "Now undo the tie, leave it on. And unbutton your shirt."

Luke obeyed, creating a thin strip of flesh between the folds of his oxford. Ashley could make out his six-pack in the gap, the ridge of his cock showing in his pants below, and she smiled in approval.

"You must work out, Mr. Dalton."

"I do."

"Our lucky audience." She clicked a few shots. "Unbutton the top of your jeans."

He did. Ashley moved in closer, her camera clicking away.

"Lose the shirt but not the tie."

She watched his muscles flex as he slipped his arms out and dropped the shirt to the floor. God, he was beautiful. And pretending to be a photographer was allowing her to focus on exactly how beautiful he was—athletic chest, narrow hips, muscular arms. Though she couldn't imagine ever tiring of his body, there was something marvelous about slowing it all down, deliberately taking him in, seeing him with new eyes.

"Keep your legs where they are, but turn your torso. Like this."

"Like this?"

"Just a little more. Yes. Hold it there. And look at me as if you're about to rip all the buttons off my shirt and pump your cock between my breasts."

His eyes dropped to her breasts, and again, Luke delivered, his eyes smoldering, a snarl in his lip. *Holy shit.* Her breasts responded eagerly, nipples pushing through her blouse, the peaks so aroused they hurt.

Click. Click. Click.

"Now, ditch the jeans. And your boxers. I'm going to change my lens."

Ashley bent to the black bag to switch out lenses—seemed like the professional thing to do. Plus, she needed a personal breather to cool down. She wanted to drop the camera and take him on the table. *Slow down, girl.* She couldn't help but peek as Luke stripped. She could see his swollen cock straining against his blue boxers, then inhaled sharply as she watched it spring free. Luke stepped out of the clothes, then took his cock in his hand and stroked it once, twice, staring at her ass the whole time.

"Are you staring at my assets, Mr. Dalton?"

She stood to face him, looking up and down his body. He was naked, wearing only the purple tie. She licked her lips slowly, taunting him.

"You did suggest I fuck your breasts."

"No. I said you should *imagine* fucking my breasts. But I see the fantasy is working. It's nice to have a subject with so much to work with. Sometimes I need to offer a little extra, um, incentive."

"Maybe I should go soft," he challenged.

"Oh, no," she backpedaled. "But maybe I can offer you something as a reward if you stay good and hard for me."

"What did you have in mind?"

She let out a soft breath. "Whatever you want."

"You're on."

And just like that, the power tables turned. Ashley realized her bravado had just gotten her in trouble—the kind of trouble she liked. She let the camera click, ten, twenty, ninety times, focusing on Luke's fantastically rock-hard cock. She posed him, prompted him, praised him, but her thoughts had gone to what he might ask for as his reward. *What do I want him to ask?* He was certainly keeping his end of the hard bargain. By the time she had finished with the camera, she was almost sweating with anticipation.

"I think that's a wrap." She set the camera aside. "Nice work, Mr. Dalton. You're the best I've ever worked with."

"Is that so, Ms. Barris?" His tone was predatory. Her sex clenched. "I believe you offered me a reward."

"That I did." She gulped. Holy shit, she was so crazy ready for him.

"On your knees."

"Mr. Dalton."

"On your knees."

"Yes, sir." This was so beyond the script she'd prepared in her mind. She knelt on the white rug beneath her. Luke prowled toward her.

"Show me what's under that blouse."

Ashley blushed.

"It's been keeping me hard all night just thinking of fucking your breasts. I want you to show me."

Ashley's hands trembled as they undid the buttons.

"Take it off. Now." He stroked himself as he watched her, his eyes trained on her bosom. This was animal Luke, carnal Luke, and it was alarmingly intoxicating. She pulled off the white blouse and knelt there in her navy skirt and black lace bra, staring at him brazenly.

"Take off your bra."

"Mr. Dalton."

"Now."

"Yes." Even if she had wanted to disobey him, there was no way her body would let her. She was his. Wholly his. She wanted him to touch her, to take her, to make her completely his.

"Touch yourself," he hissed. "Show me how you rub your breasts to get off."

She brought her hands up and squeezed her breasts together, amplifying her cleavage, pinching her swollen nipples, her whole body convulsing in pleasure at her own touch, at his gaze.

"I think you want me, Ms. Barris."

"Yes," she whimpered.

"What's that?"

"Please give me your cock."

"I like the way you say that." He came closer to her and leaned over to kiss her lips. The tie hung in the space between them. "Take the tie. I want you to put it on over your eyes."

Yes.

"Now. Tie it on." Ashley wondered if a woman could burst from unresolved longing.

She pulled the tie from his neck and threaded it through her fingers, playing with it.

"Now."

"Yes, sir."

She managed to place the tie across her eyes and tied it behind her head. The world went black.

"Good. You look beautiful in my tie, Ms. Barris. I am going to fuck your perfect tits now."

Every inch of her body waited to feel his touch. Every inch of her opened for him. Every inch of her was starving, ravenous for him. She reached out with her senses to find him, but he found her.

His mouth. He must have knelt in front of her because his hot mouth was now closing in on one of her breasts, tugging, nipping, sucking her hard. Her hips rocked as if she had his cock in her already, and she moaned loudly as if her volume were linked to the intensity of her want.

"Oh, Lu—"

He bit her breast hard, and she winced. "Call me Mr. Dalton."

"Yes, Mr. Dalton." She would say anything he wanted her to say as long as he didn't stop now.

"Pull up your skirt. I want to see your beauty."

She felt a glorious cramping in her sex. She pulled up her skirt and heard his groan of appreciation as he took in the black lace and the bare mound it framed.

"Filthy woman. Did you wear those for me?" he demanded.

"Yes."

"Did you want to show me, without having to take those panties off, just how wet your beauty can get?"

"Yes."

"Did you want me to rub my fingers on your clit until you come undone, Ms. Barris?"

She swallowed. "Yes."

"And you want me to pump you with my cock until you can't walk tomorrow."

"Please." Her voice came out hoarse.

"Oh, I will." His thumb ran from her cheekbone to her lips. "I will because it's my pleasure to please you. But first, give me what you told me was mine. I want to fuck those gorgeous tits. Now."

His dirty words touched her everywhere, made her so wet. "Yes." She heard him stand.

"Suck my cock so I'm slippery. Get me good and slick." And she felt his head pressing against the entrance to her mouth. She licked her lips, covered her teeth, and swallowed him in, hollowing her cheeks as she sucked.

She heard his gasp. "So good, Ms. Barris."

He thrust in and out several times, holding her head firmly in place with his hands, leaving no doubt as to who was in charge—deliberate shallow strokes that stopped short of gagging her. Her hands instinctively rose to find his balls, and she gave them a gentle squeeze as she sucked him off.

"You are so beautiful," he moaned. "God, seeing your lips wrapped around my cock and my tie around your eyes, it's so good." And just like that, he pulled out. "Lie on your back."

"In the bag," she said as soon as her mouth was free. She stretched back on the ground as he'd bid her.

"In the bag?"

"A bottle of lube." She hadn't known how she would use it, but now she was glad she'd brought it.

"You're perfect."

She felt him reach across to the bag and heard him rustle inside it for a moment before she heard the click of the top flipping open and the squeezing sound of the bottle. She heard his hands rubbing, then felt them both warm and slippery on her breasts, oiling them, squeezing them together as, once again, he positioned his head beneath her shelf. Then he started to slowly, slowly thrust his cock through her breasts. Up. And down. And up. And down. So long. And hard. And the whole time he plumbed the slippery channel, he was pressing her breasts together, working his thumbs across the swollen nipples, slurring curses and praises under his breath. She imagined what it must look like, his cock slipping in and out, the heat and lust in his eyes as he watched his shaft emerge and disappear in her creamy flesh.

And then he was pulling her up to standing. She wobbled in her shoes, and he steadied her, then reached to her back to unzip her skirt. It dropped in a silken swish to the floor.

Ashley imagined the sight of her standing in her crotchless black panties and black garters, her high blue pumps, the purple tie around her eyes, and her breasts all glistening and reddened from their foreplay. She shivered.

"Are you cold?"

"A little."

And then she was over his shoulder, and he was carrying her across the house, to his room, she suspected. She squealed in delight.

"Luke!"

"I'm going to wrap you up in silk like the perfect gift you are. And then I'm going to—"

"I want you inside me."

He laughed, a deep, throaty, delighted sound. It made her laugh, too, a laugh of sweetest surrender. She had thought she would be the one making him beg her tonight, but here she was again, desperate for his cock in her, strung out on need.

"Yes. I will give you exactly what you want. All. Night. Long."

———

"A woman is a little like a camera, you know," Ashley murmured. Morning light was just appearing through the bedroom window, and Ashley and Luke were lying naked in each other's arms. Ashley felt swirled by a sweet inner delirium.

"Like a camera? What do you mean?"

"Well, the principle is that light enters a dark, enclosed box through a small hole." She let that sink in. "And the image of an object outside the box appears inverted on the wall opposite to the hole."

"And—"

"And when you enter me, through my, um, hole, it's like you bring the whole outside world in and turn my world upside down—in the best way."

"That is the strangest and hottest metaphor, Ashley." He mussed her hair with his fingers. "You are one odd and groovy chick."

"You think I'm odd? I've been *framed.*"

"You're not really going to pun with me now."

"At least until I lose my *focus.*" Ashley giggled. She was so high from the long night of sex. They had laughed and played and pulled the camera back out to take shots of each other on the bed, then looked at all the pictures they'd taken—getting them totally aroused again—before deleting the whole SD card and falling asleep for a few hours.

Was it the lack of sleep that emboldened her? "So, is this a good time to talk about last night, you know, what happened?"

Luke stilled.

"Isn't that what your therapist said we were supposed to do—talk it over?"

"Yeah." He exhaled.

"Luke," she coaxed. "I loved what happened last night, and I am totally willing to enter into fantasies with you. Experiencing pleasure and playing like that *does* bring us together, but I need us to talk about it."

She could feel him breathing into the back of her neck, warm, intimate.

"Okay."

"I guess I don't even know what we're supposed to say."

Luke kissed the back of her head. "Ashley. I don't know what we're supposed to say, either. But I know last night was incredible. No one has ever met me this way. And I was a little nervous, too—I didn't know how it felt when someone else chose the scene. It's always just risen for me out of the moment. But it was amazing. *Amazing. You're* amazing. I didn't know it could be like that."

She rolled over and looked into his eyes. "*You're* amazing, Luke. And I realize how much I love it when you take control. But I really liked telling you what to do, too."

"I liked it, too." He traced her bottom lip with his thumb.

"So maybe we can keep trading it around?"

"Okay." He smiled.

"But for now, I'm going to be in charge. I'm starving from a night of sex. Feed me breakfast, or I'll start making more bad photography puns."

"Uncle," he laughed. "But let's shower first."

"I'm just going to lie here in the sun for a minute—it's so warm. Plus, if I get in the shower with you, I'm afraid I'll attack you, and then we'll be distracted, and I'll never get to eat."

"I think you're *developing* a bad habit, staying in bed like this."

"Ooooh, you're worse than I am." She threw a pillow at him. "Go. Shower. Now."

"Okay, okay."

Nineteen minutes later, Luke was still in the shower, and Ashley was upset.

"Luke." She charged into the bathroom. The stupid televisions with oil talk were on in the corner. It fueled her anger even more.

"Are you joining me after all?" His voice was bright with hope.

"Do you have any idea how much water you're wasting? A six-minute shower is max."

Luke laughed and splashed her. She didn't laugh back.

"I'm serious, Luke. Get out. What a waste. I will take a two-minute shower to make up for you, but this is just irresponsible."

Slowly, it dawned on Luke how serious she was.

"This is a thing for you, huh?"

"This is a thing for *the Earth*, Luke."

He turned off the water and gave her a gentle shake of his head. "Look, Ashley, I'm learning. I'm recycling, right? I'm willing to change. Easy on me this morning." His voice was tender, peace-making.

Ashley softened her face, nodded. "Right. Sorry. Maybe I'm hungrier than I thought. I just can't stand to see resources being wasted. Now, go make me some pancakes." She snapped at him with a towel.

"Yes, ma'am."

Ashley stepped into the steamy shower and turned on the water, her inner clock already timing her. Luke's long shower was a symptom of a much larger problem. Obviously, it had been simmering, and she'd been finding ways to ignore it, letting their other issues—and pleasures—take precedence. But in this moment, she was triggered.

What am I doing here?

Luke's disregard for the environment infuriated her. From his petroleum fuel job to his gas-guzzling car to his thoughtless daily habits. He was a man that did not share her core values.

Yet. Not yet.

Ashley battled with herself as she rinsed off the soap. She had to be patient. As he said, he was changing. *And he is, right?* The more she shared her ideas with him, the more changes he was making in his personal life and in STEAMEA. *And next, in his field. You have the perfect opportunity to change the thinking of the VP of one of the world's largest oil companies. Stay focused, Ashley.*

What was at stake was so much more than one man taking a six-minute shower. She could help him work in the Earth's best interest. As she toweled off, she stuck her tongue out at the screen. A childish gesture. It came with a warning voice. *Do you really think you can change him?*

As she slipped into a robe, her heart and mind scrabbled with each other like kids duking it out on the playground, and she could not imagine how the fight would end.

"What are you doing next Saturday night?" Luke asked as they sat on the couch, eating pancakes.

"Jewel and I have plans to go see a band she's dying to check out."

Luke looked crestfallen. "I should have asked you sooner. I just was too, I don't know, nervous."

"What's up?"

"It's a party. For my parents' fortieth."

"Wow, forty years. That's a long time. You're lucky." Ashley thought of her mother's struggle as a single parent and imagined what it would be like to have parents who had stayed together. What kind of stability and love were possible then? Luke's parents had been through a lot. And they'd made it forty years. *Am I feeling jealous?*

"I was hoping they could meet you."

Oh. Ashley pulled out of her brief pity party to consider that Luke wanted to introduce her to his parents. *Wow.* A flood of conflicting emotions rushed through her. *Embarrassment—* what would Luke's parents think of her, a woman whose mother cleaned toilets in houses like theirs, who worked nights at a diner to make ends meet. Would that sense of disparity between their families ever leave her? *Thrill*—he wanted her to meet his family? He was serious. *Discomfort*—who would be at this party? His parents' friends were probably the entire list of who's who in the Houston oil world. Ashley inwardly winced. She couldn't go to this party. She didn't belong with these people.

"I have an idea." He brushed a stray hair away from her face, tenderness in his touch. "What if you bring Jewel along? There will be a band—maybe not the music she had in mind, but perhaps she'd be open to coming? I really want you at this party."

"Why did it feel like you were hesitant to ask me?"

His eyes met hers so openly. "I didn't want you to say no."

He got it. He understood how hard this would be for her. Something about that awareness made her melt. Despite their differences, this man really understood her. He'd invited programmers over last night, for goodness' sake, to help her meet her dreams. As unsettling as their circumstances were, there was something so authentic, so true about their connection. It was like a photograph that focused on only one thing and blurred everything around it.

"I want you by my side, Ashley. I'm so proud of you. And I want my family to know you."

I want you by my side. A flurry of emotion swirled through her, as if an entire murmuration of starlings were swooping and soaring in her chest.

"Okay," she laughed. "Yes! I'll ask Jewel."

CHAPTER 22

"**A**RE YOU *SHITTING* ME?" Jewel stared into the triple-height marble-and-glass reception hall. "This place is unreal."

"Language." Ashley was annoyed by her sister's crassness, but Jewel was right. The place was unreal. It was hard to take in this kind of wealth. *How many kids could be fed each year with the amount of money they spend on keeping up their lawn?* She didn't want to know. It was a hopeless math. It was hard to not feel judgmental. Ashley had promised herself she'd keep an open mind, but she hadn't quite worked out how she'd do that.

"Right then. Are you *fucking* shitting me?"

Ashley shook her head. She should have known better than to try to censor Jewel. But she wanted to make a good impression, and her sister was a loose cannon.

Deep breath. "You're right, sis. It's another world." Hundreds of hifalutin' people were wandering around the house and the grounds. Women dripping in diamonds. Men who wore their wealth in their posture. *Who throws parties like this?*

"And it's a world I belong in," Jewel said, voicing the exact opposite feeling her sister was having. "And Ash, so do you." She made an hourglass shape with her hands as she looked at her sister. "You are *rocking* that dress—I love the way it shows off your shoulders and back. I can't believe my sister is showing all that skin!"

Ashley felt like a stranger in her own body wearing this dress Luke had bought for her. It was a strapless sheath, deep emerald green, specially fitted for her at Saks. She felt vulnerable without straps, but she also felt elegant and sophisticated, two words that generally didn't describe her. Not that she didn't like this feeling, but it was unusual.

Luke had volunteered to make a donation to the Lift House for twice as much as the dress was worth. That helped ease her conscience, but the opulence of Luke's life still made her uneasy.

"Thanks, Jewel. You look amazing, too." And she did. Jewel always did.

"Gonna get me a mega millionaire tonight."

"Behave."

"Oh, Ashley. You don't get to have all the fun. And speaking of fun—" Jewel's eye caught on a waiter in a tux walking by with a tray of champagne. She grabbed two flutes and handed one to Ashley. "To gorgeous men." She winked and clinked Ashley's glass.

"To gorgeous men." Ashley laughed and shook her head.

"Talking about me?" Luke was standing behind her. He must have followed them in through the front door.

"I was." Ashley turned around and caught her breath. Luke was stunning. In a crisp white shirt and fitted blue jacket, with his dark hair slicked and his full lips and his eyes like lapis lazuli, he was positively mouthwatering.

He raked his eyes over her, noticing everything—her hair styled to the side, her bare shoulders, her naked legs, her simple nude-colored pumps. "You. Look. Beautiful."

Ashley blushed and felt a rush of joy pulse through her. How could his words have such an effect on her? Perhaps because she was so nervous to be here? Perhaps because she so wanted to be beautiful in his eyes.

"And Jewel, you look lovely. Come. I want to introduce you to my parents."

Already? "Okay." Ashley took a large drink of champagne. Luke noticed.

"They will *love* you."

Ashley forced a smile. Somehow, she doubted it.

Luke led them through the crowd to where his parents were holding court in a large reception room. Everything was cream colored—the marble on the floors, the silk rugs, the recessed ceiling. The walls were lined with artwork—as if it were a private Remington museum—and rows of shelves displayed expensive-looking empty vases. Ashley was so nervous she thought she might throw up all over the lovely cream silk pillows. Luke easily navigated the crowd toward his parents.

"Mom, Dad, I want to introduce you to Ashley."

In the moment before they shook hands, Ashley felt like one of the vases on the shelves—an object being appraised for its beauty and value. *A breakable object.*

"Hi, I'm Ashley. Ashley Barris." She held out her hand.

Luke's mother had the poise of the wealthy, but she had the handshake of a dead fish. "Hello, dear, I'm Margaret." Luke's mother spoke with a slight slur, as if she might already be a bit drunk. "I've heard a bit about you. A schoolteacher, right?"

A laid-off schoolteacher. "Yes, I have been for many years." It wasn't a lie.

"Lovely, dear." She smiled in a distant, distracted way, as if she were only partly in the world around her. Despite her inebriation—or because of it?—Margaret seemed warm and compassionate. Ashley immediately both liked her and felt sorry for her.

"And I'm James." Luke's father held out his hand and shook hers. Was she imagining it, or did he hold her hand too long?

James had perfect white teeth that gleamed as if he were in a toothpaste commercial. His gray hair was coiffed, his hands soft and manicured. His smile said he was aware of his own importance.

"My son has good taste." His voice was full of charm, but his eyes were unreadable. This man did not show his cards.

"And this is my sister—" Ashley turned to introduce Jewel, but she wasn't there. "Oh, maybe you'll have a chance to meet my sister later."

"Mom, Dad, I'm going to give Ashley a little tour. Happy anniversary." He gave his mom a kiss, and just like that, the introduction was over. Ashley exhaled a sigh of relief as they walked away. "That wasn't so bad, was it?" Luke raised her hand to his lips and kissed her fingertips. Ashley could feel the curiosity of the other people in the room as they pretended not to notice Luke's actions. He seemed oblivious to anyone but her.

"They seem very nice."

"They are. But now I want you to meet my most favorite person in the world." They came around a corner and ran into two very attractive, hip-looking women. "Oh, Elaine! Darla! There's someone I want you two to meet. This is Ashley."

The shorter woman, almost exactly Ashley's height, looked Ashley right in the eye and held out her hand. "So, this is the woman who's got my brother on an environmental activism board. Girl, I like you already. You know how to shake things up."

"Elaine, nice to meet you." Ashley smiled warmly. She felt an immediate comradery with the spunky woman.

"And this is my partner, Darla. Maybe someday we'll be celebrating *our* fortieth, too, right?" She raised an eyebrow and jabbed Darla in the ribs.

"I'll need a wedding day first, Elaine." The two women were obviously sharing a joke, but Ashley felt somehow included, and they all laughed.

"Hey, thank you for letting me use your winter clothes in Telluride," Ashley said. "I had a lot of fun learning to ski." Luke squeezed her hand.

"No problem. Glad someone got to use them this year. Because *someone's* got me working way too hard at the company." She gave Luke a dramatic withering look. "Because he knows I love him sooo much and would do anything to make him happy." She threw her arm around her brother and gave him a big squeeze and a radiant smile.

Ashley looked at Luke.

"She's our legal counsel with Terrance. Though she *should* have my job."

"Don't even start. It's a party! Now, Ashley, you keep up the good work. I've never seen my brother happier." She gave Ashley a thumbs-up and beamed again at her brother. "Because when the vice president is happy, everybody's happy." She took Darla by the hand and kissed it. "And you and I have a few people yet to see at this party, and I am looking forward to making them very uncomfortable. Nice to meet you, Ashley."

"She's a spark plug!" Ashley said as they continued to walk through the party.

"Understatement of the year. Elaine loves to push buttons. She told Mom she wanted to announce her engagement with Darla tonight at the party. Mom said, 'don't you dare,' and turned cherry red, and Elaine just sat there laughing. She's a master manipulator. She thinks it's fun. Perfect for a lawyer. And here... here's who I wanted you to meet."

Seated in a large, upholstered chair beside a window was a thin, elderly woman wearing a long colorful dress. Her skin was dark bronze, and her short white hair barely showed beneath her turquoise hat. Even from fifteen feet away, she exuded contentment.

"My Rena." Luke bent over to give her a kiss. She set down her water glass.

"Ah, cher." Her voice was shaky with age, but her brown eyes were clear and bright, and her whole body came to life when she saw Luke. "Did you bring her to me?" She had a heavy Southern drawl.

"Yes, I did. This is the woman I've been telling you about." He stepped back. "May I introduce Ashley Barris."

"I'm so pleased to meet you, Rena," Ashley extended her hand. "I've heard so much about you from Luke."

Rena took Ashley's hand in both of her own and held it for a long time, staring deeply into Ashley's face. "Mm-hmm." She nodded. "Mm-hmm. I'm glad to meet you, Ashley. Have a seat."

Ashley sat in the chair beside Rena, and Luke sat on the arm of her chair.

"He's a fine one, Luke. My only boy, you know. I have beautiful girls, but Lukey, he's my boy."

"And you're my Rena." Luke smiled good-naturedly, the same open smile he had at the animal shelter. It melted Ashley's heart.

"Isn't he handsome, though. Hard to believe this is the same boy who couldn't get his nose out of a book. He was a pale and scrawny thing, and now look at him. Strong and tall and charming."

"Okaaay." He blushed genuinely. "And with that, I think it's time for me to go get a drink. You want something, Ashley?"

"I'm better than good." Ashley settled into her chair, eager to hear more stories from Rena.

"I'll be right back." Luke gave her a kiss on her head.

"So, tell me something about you." Ashley turned her body and gave the older woman her full attention.

"Oh, cher, I grew up very poor. I was lucky to find a job here after my own children were raised. People have not always been so good at taking care of each other, but I always felt taken care of here in this house. There were some difficult times, but we got through them together."

"Luke adores you."

"Oh, yes, my boy, Lukey. When they sent him off to boarding school, it broke my heart. I knew I could have helped him here. How I hated to see my little boy suffer. It wasn't his fault."

Ashley nodded, but she didn't want to say anything in case it stopped Rena's memory stream.

"You know, he didn't talk at all for a year after the accident. And who could blame him? The rest of them made enough noise there was no room left for his voice. What with his daddy screaming about the company, and the mother weeping and wailing every night with her wine, and then the girl, my dear Elaine, throwing tantrums the way she did? Thank goodness she didn't succeed when she took all those pills. One family can't take all that loss. Oh, those were difficult times, Ashley. Keeping silent was not the worst way to handle it."

Ashley's head was reeling, taking in all that Rena was saying. "He didn't say a word?"

"No, ma'am. For a whole year. He would just come and sit at the table in the kitchen with me where I was working, and I'd keep the silence with him. We were in it together, yes, we were."

Ashley felt a full-body ache, thinking of Luke shutting down so completely. He'd been through so much pain.

"And then the first words he said were, 'Make it quiet, my Rena. Make it quiet.' Only when he started speaking again, he had a stutter. Took him a long, long time to get out a sentence. This family's been through a lot, but we overcome our tragedies, right, Ashley? We overcome our tragedies."

"Yes." Ashley nodded, letting all that Rena was saying sink in. "Luke was so lucky to have you."

"Oh, cher, I am the lucky one. Been lucky all my life. Why, I have four beautiful children and eight grands, including that beautiful Lisette over there in the corner, who brought me here. I may not have had much money, but I have always been flush with love. Things change, Ashley, even the most terrible things change. And I've lived to see it. You carry hope with you until it becomes you."

You carry hope with you until it becomes you. That's what Luke had said in the park that day they had talked about the shooting and her sister's rape.

"That's a beautiful phrase, Miss Rena."

"It's helped me through many a tragedy. And in the meantime, it's best to laugh as much as we can. I like to think about the time when Mr. and Mrs. Dalton held a fancy campaign party, and little Jimmy dared Lukey to run out into the gardens, not wearing a single stitch." Mirth lit up her face. "The look on his mama's—"

"Okaaay," Luke interrupted. "I see I came back just in time." He gave Ashley's hand a squeeze. "Glad to see you two are getting along, my two favorite women in the world. But I should have known better than to leave the two of you alone. Rena loves to talk and—"

"—your family loves me anyway. Never did try to make me be quiet. But lucky for you, my Luke, I need to make my way to the ladies' room. Otherwise, I'd keep on embarrassing you for an hour. Lord knows you've made me laugh all these years. Lisette, cher," she called. "Come help your grandmother, please."

"It was a pleasure to meet you, Miss Rena."

"I think, my dear, there are no accidents. You are right where you need to be."

Rena's words stayed with Ashley as she and Luke moved through the crowd. She didn't feel as if she was where she needed to be. In fact, quite the opposite. She felt deeply uncomfortable with the wealth, not to mention angered by some of the discussions she was overhearing. In the great room, she saw Gerald Regis, the United States Secretary of Energy, holding court. *Galvanize, galvanize.* She felt the inner call.

She smirked. In her purse was her phone with his number in her "favorites" so she could tell him what she thought needed to be done. Here was the chance to tell him to his face. *On behalf of all the polar bears, the walruses, the seals, the oceans, and the air, I thank you for not continuing to pursue drilling in the Arctic after it was turned down last month.* It was snarky, and she felt her blood start to simmer. It was no thanks to *him* the drilling had been turned down. Quite the opposite. She thought of a few other choice things to say and moved in his direction, but Luke was holding her hand and moving the other way. Just as well. This was not the place to pull out her protest sign. Yet.

"It's my old friend Hugh. I'd love to introduce you."

While Luke spoke with Hugh, she caught a familiar face across the room—Savannah, from Telluride. *Luke's ex.* But that was no reason to not be friendly. At least it was someone she knew. She walked over.

"Hey, Savannah."

Savannah turned, and the smile fell off her face.

"It's Ashley. We met in Telluride."

"I remember. The smart science teacher."

Is that a dig? "How's it going?" Ashley forced a bright smile.

"I've been watching you." The chill in Savannah's words gave Ashley shivers. "You're not very comfortable in this world, are you, Ashley?" She smirked. "I need to see someone." And she was gone.

Ashley stood there for a moment, trying to calm the tsunami about to crash in her chest. *What the hell was that?* She counted people in the room by threes. *Six. Nine. Twelve. Fifteen.*

"It's okay, honey. She can be like that." Ashley startled at Jamila's voice. *Jamila. Thank god.* Of course she and Terrance would be here. Jamila gave her a big hug, bigger than was probably acceptable in *this world*, she thought, but she didn't care, and she hugged her back hard. It felt good to see her friend. "I caught that little show from across the room. She's jealous, Ash. And who could blame her? You're smart, you're kind, and Houston's handsomest bachelor can't take his eyes off you."

"Yeah. Well, she doesn't have to be so weirdly underhanded about it."

"She'll get over it once she hooks a new fish. Come on, tell Luke you and I are going for a little walk around the garden. We have so much to catch up on."

Walking with Jamila was the best possible medicine, and after ten minutes, Ashley felt like her confident self. *Nothing like a friend to remind us of who we are.*

"There you are," Luke said, finding the women in the garden. "Jamila, do you mind? I need a word alone with this lovely woman."

Jamila gave her friend a squeeze.

"Hey, Jamila, will you keep an eye out for Jewel? I haven't seen her since we got here. She might need a little support, too?"

"Sure thing, honey." She gave Ashley a wink and was off.

"So, aren't you the famous *New York Times* book critic?" Luke's expression was impish.

"Why, yes." Ashley nodded, thinking fast. "And you're—"

"—hoping you'll give me a great review for my new book on the art of seduction."

"Really?" A quiver of thrills fluttered through her.

"I'm Luke Dalton. I'd like to give you a preview of chapter nine."

"Mr. Dalton, we're at an anniversary party."

"In every environment, there are opportunities to seduce and be seduced."

Ashley chortled. "You seem rather full of yourself."

"Soon, you'll be full of me, too."

"Huh!" Ashley's mouth dropped open. "Mr. Dalton. You're crass."

"Ms. Barris, you're right."

"What makes you think you could seduce me?"

Luke handed her a small piece of paper folded in half. "Chapter nine, Ms. Barris." And he walked away. Ashley stared at his back, admiring the shape of his shoulders. The way his suit hugged his body made her stomach do gleeful cartwheels. He looked back and caught her watching him, held her gaze a moment, his eyes dancing with invitation, and then he cocked his head and disappeared around a tall hedge.

Cocky bastard. Ashley laughed and shook her head. *He walked away from me.* What did Luke have up his designer sleeve? She opened the note.

> *We shouldn't do this. You shouldn't meet me in the pool house in five minutes. If anyone caught us in there, it would be a disaster. Take off your panties. Stuff them in your purse before you come.*

What. The. Hell. Ashley was torn between laughing and ripping off her panties right here in the middle of the garden and sprinting to the pool house. *Holy lesson in reverse psychology.* She read the note again. He'd even used upright print that didn't look like his normal right-slanted cursive. *That Luke.*

He was right, of course. It *would* be a disaster if someone caught them in the pool house during his parents' anniversary party—it would go down in family history along with his childhood nudity stunt.

Brain: Don't be an idiot.

Body: What's taking you so long?

She took out her phone and texted her sister.

Ashley: You okay?

Jewel: With all these sexy millionaires?

Um, YEAH

Ashley: Behave

Okay then. Ashley walked back into the house to find a bathroom. *We're doing this.*

CHAPTER 23

A SHLEY STEPPED INTO THE pool house and shut the door behind her, her eyes adjusting to the dim.

"You know you shouldn't have come, Ms. Barris, but I am taking your arrival as a yes to my offer to tutor you in how reverse psychology can be a very effective tool when it comes to seduction." She could make out Luke's form in the shadows across the room. A thin slant of light angled across his face.

Her heart was pounding against her chest, blood hammering in her ears. "Tell me why I shouldn't have come. I forget."

"You have your reputation." He slowly walked toward her until their bodies were barely touching. "What would your editor say if she knew you had met me here? Would your readers think our little pool house interlude influenced your favorable review? Hmm?" His breath caressed her skin as his lips moved above her cheek, along her chin, across her lips. And then he turned around, walking a few steps away from her.

Playing hard to get? Two can play that game. She walked in the opposite direction and paused, her back to him, feigning interest in a plastic chair. "What makes you think I'll write something favorable about your book?"

"Because even if I am a devious man you shouldn't trust, you're an honest woman," he whispered.

Ashley scoffed.

"If you aren't interested in learning about how effective chapter nine is, I might just have to find another reviewer to convince." He walked toward the door.

Not a chance you're leaving here. Ashley stepped forward to lightly rest her hand on his wrist. "I'm not sure yet about your offer. Maybe you should give me a small preview."

A wicked joy leapt into his azure eyes. He leaned forward. "That's not a good idea," he rasped in her ear, then lightly bit her lobe.

"Ohhh," Ashley sighed, unable to articulate anything more. Her head tilted back as the sharp pulsing between her legs began to rhyme with her clamorous heartbeat.

"Did you do as I asked?" He kissed a cursive trail up her neck, each touch inspiring a tiny epiphany of longing. "What are you wearing under that emerald dress, Ms. Barris?"

Her breath came in shallow, deckled gasps. "Nothing." Her voice was hoarse, and her head lolled forward until her lips connected with his collarbone. There, she nibbled and kissed along the scalloped ridge, relishing the salty taste of his exposed skin.

"Oh, you shouldn't have come here without that thin layer of protection. What am I to think when I slip my hand up your leg?" he admonished, gruffly slipping a hand beneath her dress. "Oh, no," he groaned as his fingers trailed up the warm skin of her thighs to cup her naked cheeks. A frisson of desire made Ashley tremble. He let his fingers find her slickness and teased her, slowly sliding one finger, then two, in and out of her. "So dirty. You shouldn't let me touch your gorgeous sex like this, Ms. Barris." His voice was low and brusque. His thumb pressed a rhythmic Morse code of desire against her clit.

"Mr. Dalton, I assure you—" She swallowed as a surge of imminent pleasure made her gasp. "I assure you I can remain professional."

"Not if I have anything to do with it," he hissed, and he began an erotic onslaught of kisses—at first gently sucking and licking her lips, then boldly plundering her mouth until they both were breathless, both of them pressing their desperate bodies into each other, his fingers continuing their lyrical exploration of her sex, and her soft flesh urgently clenched around the long digits as they dragged through her slickness.

"Oh, yes, Luke."

"I should go." His fingers stilled.

"No! Don't stop. I'm so close." She was just about to climax. Her whole body trembled with the promise of it.

"I shouldn't," he whispered in her ear. And slowly, he pulled his fingers out.

"No," she whimpered, cupping her hand beneath his, pinning it to her so he couldn't move it away. "Don't you dare stop touching me now."

"There's too much at stake for your reputation." He pushed against her hand as his fingers continued their slow withdrawal. She unsuccessfully tried to stop their retreat.

You want him? Play the game, Ashley. "Are you—are you trying to blackmail me?"

"Hmm. What a novel idea." He stilled his hand, his thumb hovering above her clit but not giving her the friction she craved.

"Tell me." She bit her lip. "Tell me what you want from me."

"I want a five-star review, Ms. Barris."

For a moment, the only things moving in the room were their heaving chests.

Just as she opened her mouth, he added, "And I want your hand in a fist around my cock."

"Yes," she breathed.

"Now."

"Yes." She pressed her right hand against the hard ridge of his erection, palming it, rubbing it, squeezing it through his pants. He rewarded her by pushing his fingers ever so slightly deeper in.

"It would be a terrible idea for you to unzip my pants and stroke me." His voice was dark and promising. He pressed his strong hips into her. "Now."

"Yes," she said, fumbling with his belt, his fastener, his zipper, before plunging her hands into his briefs, pushing them down with his loosened pants, and helping his cock escape. Thank god they'd decided they were monogamous and could now forgo condoms. She wanted to feel him bare inside her, especially knowing it would increase his pleasure, too.

The tip of him glistened with precum, and she involuntarily licked her lips. Deep inside, she was aching for him—wanted to climb him right now and impale herself with him. Instead, she obeyed his command and gently used a finger to swirl the bead of liquid around his swollen head.

"You shouldn't touch me like this," he said against her mouth, his lips barely brushing hers.

"It's a terrible idea," she agreed as she fisted the bare length of him, wildly turned on by how hard he was, how thick. She could feel the blood pulsing in the engorged veins beneath his skin, and her hand found a tempo, a meter ruled by her hunger, the one hand rubbing him up and down, the other hand holding him firmly at his base. She wanted him in her, wanted the tip of him pushing against the end of her. Knowing how good it was going to be triggered almost painful spasms inside her.

"Stop," he whispered as he kissed her and bit her lower lip, his hand now resuming its thrusting and curling, his thumb returning to its delicious rhythm. "You should stop." But even as he said *stop*, his sensual assault on her body was all *go*. Devilishly, he drove his fingers into her, a plot to undo her, to unravel her.

"Oh, yes, I'm stopping," she said as her orgasm revised itself, this time building to an even higher climax. Her knees weakened, her breath quickened, her hand tightened around his thickness.

"Don't. Come," he whispered in her ear, and she tried to obey just as she shattered around his fingers, her cream dripping, her body tensing, every part of her erased save for the brilliant, diamonding place where he was pumping her, milking her, teasing out every last fragment of pleasure, her orgasm unfurling like a sacred scroll only he could write, and she moaned her pleasure into his shoulder to muffle the sound.

Eventually, her moans eased into whimpers, her whole body convulsing for a few more moments. Then she hung from his neck by one hand, her other hand still wrapped around his throbbing cock.

"We should stop now," he said as he slipped his wet fingers from her to cup her sensitive, swollen flesh, as if holding in her pleasure. The musky aroma of her arousal inscribed the air like a poem written in scent instead of ink. Inside her, the unbearable emptiness where his cock should be was throbbing. Once she could support her own weight again, her fingers resumed stroking him.

"I should take away my hand," she whispered into his neck, then lifted one leg to curl it around his hips, trying to press her throbbing flesh closer to his sex.

He moaned.

"I'm going to leave now," she teased, removing her hand.

In one fluid motion, Luke yanked her dress up to her waist, put his hands beneath her ass, and lifted her until she straddled his waist, positioning her right where he wanted her, right where she wanted him. *Yes.* She curled her legs around his ass and slid down until she could feel his head, eager at her entrance, and then in a swift move, he thrust deep inside of her. She was so wet that though he stretched her, he slid right in.

"Yes!" he called out, his head thrown back in ecstasy as he used his hands at her ass to piston her hips into his. "So. Right." Each word was punctuated by a thrust. And each time he pounded into her, an involuntary cry erupted from her throat. She was past being quiet. Past caring who might walk in. Held in Luke's arms in the middle of the room, she felt so safe, so secure, so astonishingly united with him, and she arched her spine and threw back her head, thrilling in the sound of the suction, reveling in the friction, edging toward another orgasm.

"Look at me," he gritted. His eyes were blazing. "I want to see you when you come with my cock in you." She clawed her hands into his back.

His thrusts became more forceful, slamming into her as his desire overtook him, and Ashley bowed against him, letting him in deeper, her eyes locked on his, her inner walls clamping hard around him as he dragged his hard cock out through her folds before surging inside her again.

"You will not come until I tell you to," he ordered. She nodded, trying to hold back the rising orgasm, watching his face as the last vestiges of his own control slipped away. "Do. Not. Come," he gritted out, even as surges of red pleasure scrawled and rewrote her, building, building.

He staggered for the wall where he could pin her against it and increase his leverage, still pumping her as he stepped. Ashley was almost frantic with her desire to come, and she felt the scream of release building in her. She had to come now. She moaned loudly.

"Now, Ashley! Now!" he grunted, slamming into her.

"Yes! Ahh!" she cried out as a searing pain ripped through her back. "Oh!" she shrieked, a terrible red agony spearing her, stealing her breath, shocking her. She whimpered as the pain grew.

Luke, in his ecstasy, mistook her cry for pleasure and continued to drive her into the wall with primal urgency, his own orgasm flooding him as her satiny flesh quivered around him, his head flung back in pleasure. "Ashley!" he shouted. She was wild with pain.

"Stop, Luke! Stop! *Stop!*" She was screaming now. Each bang into the wall intensified the anguish. "Luke! Please! Stop! Red! Red! Red!" Tears streamed down her face, her lips curled back.

"Ashley, what's wrong? What—?" He pulled out of her and gently dropped her to the floor. His face contorted with concern. "Are you okay? What's happening?"

Ashley shuddered and reached for the stabbing sensation between her shoulder blades, about an inch above the back of her dress. Her fingers came back red. "Something. On. The. Wall," she managed.

Luke's face went pale. "Jesus, Ashley. You're bleeding. There's blood everywhere. Oh my god, there's a hook on the wall, a goddamn broken towel hook." Ashley turned to see the small sharp stub of a broken metal hook on the wall. Her blood was smeared on the wall all around it. "Oh my god, Ashley. You're hurting. Your back. What have I done to you? *I hurt you.* Oh my god, what have I done? I'm so sorry, Ashley. I'm so sorry." Luke was bordering on incoherent as he searched for a towel, then pressed the thick cotton against her back to stop the bleeding and soak up the blood. His breathing was coming too quickly.

"It's okay, Luke, it's okay," she said, realizing he might be going into shock. She knew, however, it was not okay. Pain seared through her scapula, and she could tell it was way more serious than a scratch, more like a big gash. But Luke, she realized, was unable to help her in his present state. She needed to calm him down. "I'll be fine, Luke. I'll be fine."

"I hurt you, Ashley," he whispered, quaking. "You're not fine. I hurt you."

"Luke, it was an accident. Come on. Let's sit down on the bench." They stumbled together to the bench nearby and sat, Luke's hand still pressing the towel against her back.

"You need a doctor. And I think I might faint." His voice was thin.

"I'm not leaving you. Put your head between your legs, sweetheart." She was relieved he did as she said. "It's okay, Luke. You're okay. I'm okay."

She lost track of how long they sat there together, the dust suspended in the air, glittering in the low afternoon light. Time froze, as if they were in a snow globe in which the snow never fell. Luke slumped over his knees. She leaned her back against the wall to keep the towel firmly in place, her hands slowly scratching his back the way her mother used to do to her to calm her down. She hummed a little—not an actual song, just a meandering tune meant to comfort.

Her back felt ripped open. Luke was right. She was going to need a doctor. But first, she needed to get some kind of antibiotic cream. Some bandages.

"Luke," she said eventually, keeping her anxiety out of her voice in an attempt to keep him calm. "I need to go take care of this."

When he sat up, his eyes were oddly empty. "Let me see your back."

She leaned forward and let the towel drop. It had stuck to her back, and she winced as it fell away.

Luke slumped as he saw the wound. She thought he might throw up. "It's deep. You need stitches, Ashley. Fuck. Let's get you to urgent care." He jumped up and then had to steady himself on a chest of drawers.

"Easy there, big guy. You're experiencing a mild case of shock." *Stand tall, Ashley.* She was going to have to keep taking control here.

Luke was shaking his head. "I'm so sorry," he whispered under his breath.

"Come on, let's go to the house. I'll ask a party attendant for some antibiotic cream and some big Band-Aids. We both need some water."

"It's going to cause a scene, Ashley, if anyone sees your back."

"Give me your coat, okay? And no one will see."

Luke handed her the coat he'd taken off after he'd entered the pool house and helped her slide into it, but his focus seemed off. Ashley took the towel to the sink, got a corner wet, and washed the blood off the wall. Then she threw the towel in the trash. The last thing Luke's family needed was rumors about a bloodbath in their pool house.

"Do you want to wait here?"

"No. I want to be with you."

She and Luke walked slowly back to the house. The sound of laughter and loud banter affronted them like a brick wall they didn't know how to climb.

"You sit here," she told him, pointing to a lounge chair. There was no way Luke could meet the crowd in this condition. "I'll go in, get a Band-Aid, bring you water, find Jewel, then we'll leave. Okay?" Luke nodded weakly. It reminded her of how he'd been at her house after the gun incident.

On her way to the house, she called Jewel. No answer. She texted.

Ashley: I need to go

No response. *Dammit, Jewel.*

Once inside, Ashley felt herself go into her fix-it mode. She didn't see any attendants, but she saw Luke's mother across the room. *Okay, mother it is.*

"Mrs. Dalton?" she queried as she approached, a smile forced onto her face. Luke's mother turned around, her balance slightly off.

"Oh, Amanda, dear, call me Margaret." Her words slurred. *She's drunk.* "Are you having fun?"

"Yes, ma'am. What a lovely party. I was just coming to say goodbye." No use correcting her about the name. She clearly wouldn't be remembering anything about this evening. And she obviously was in no condition to ask about a first-aid kit.

"Oh, goodbye, dear. Leaving so soon?" She sounded hurt. "We didn't even get to talk. And I don't remember seeing our darling Corinna."

"She had finals for college, Mrs. Dalton, er, Margaret. She was so sorry to miss your celebration." *I can't believe I'm making excuses for the bitchy daughter.*

"Studying. Youth is wasted on the young." Margaret shook her head and laughed at the cliché.

"Goodbye, Margaret."

"Goodbye, Amanda."

Ashley gritted her teeth and walked away. Her back was throbbing, and she wanted to get out of there. *Okay, no bandages. Bathroom. Jewel. Water.* She moved purposefully through the crowd, poking her head into a library-looking room to see if Jewel were in it. Empty.

"Ashley."

Ashley turned to see Luke's father standing behind her.

"Oh, Mr. Dalton." He was blocking the doorway. Alarm bells went off in her head.

"Call me James." He stepped a little closer, as if the room were too loud for casual conversation, and put his lips against her ear. "Are you cold?"

He fingered the lapel of Luke's jacket. "Oh, uh, yeah." *You're too close.*

He straightened the lapel and stared at her lips. "Can I help you find something?"

She stepped back. "No, sir, I'm looking for the restroom."

He stepped into her space again. "I see. Perhaps we could find some time later to, ah, get to know each other better." He brought up a hand to push back his hair, but on the way, his hand brushed her nipple through the jacket. It was the kind of move that could have been an accident, but the look in his eye assured her it was intentional. Repulsion twisted in her gut. *Luke's dad?* How should she handle this? If he were anyone else, she would tell him where to go and shove him out of her way. *Try civility.* She jutted up her chin and stared at him firmly.

"Actually, I need to leave right now." Though her insides were crawling, her tone was steady. And though her words were polite, the translation was clear: *Fuck you.*

"This is goodbye?" He put a hand on her waist and slid it lower, then pulled her closer to him.

Inner alarm bells rang, making her heart flutter quickly. "Don't *touch* me," she bit out. Ashley pulled away, and Luke's dad dug his thumb into her lower hip in an effort to hold her in place. She shoved it away and stepped back, panic rising in her.

"Such a shame." He was smiling. "You've got such a beautiful come-fuck-me look right now."

Fucking pig.

"Goodbye, Mr. Dalton." She pushed past him through the doorway, and he brushed her ass with his fingers as she left, chortling as if the whole interaction had been charming. Her stomach convulsed.

"Goodbye, Ashley." His voice taunted her as she fled.

Could this evening get any worse? Her back was throbbing. Luke was practically catatonic; his mom was a drunk who called her the wrong name, and Luke's father was a vile letch. This was not at all what she'd expected. From the outside, it seemed as if Luke had a perfect family. And where the fuck was Jewel?

Ashley finally found her sister at the bar, getting another glass of champagne.

"Ashley!" Jewel raised her glass to her sister and took a big swig.

"I need to go, Jewel. Now."

"Well, *I'm* not leaving till this party's over."

Ashley exhaled deeply. *Just as well.* She had her hands full enough with Luke. "Text me when you leave."

"Got it."

"And if you don't leave alone, you know the drill. I need his name, contact details, where you're going, the usual."

"Yes, Mom."

Ashley rolled her eyes, gave her sister a fist bump to avoid being hugged, and grabbed a glass of water for Luke. Jewel could take care of herself. Her sister was the least of her problems tonight.

CHAPTER 24

Hi, *you've reached Luke Dalton. Please leave a message.*

"Hi, Luke. It's Ashley. Got your text about not being able to make it for dinner tonight. Yeah. Yesterday was intense. Call me, and we'll, uh, we'll set up something else."

Hi, you've reached Luke Dalton. Please leave a message.

"Um, hey, Luke, it's Ashley. I'm getting the feeling something's really wrong. Thanks for the text you just sent. I was hoping we could talk instead of just texting. My back is fine. Call me soon, okay? I'm worried about you."

Hi, you've reached Luke Dalton. Please leave a message.

"Hey, Luke. So, I saw Jamila at book club tonight. She said Terrance said you didn't come in for work the last two days. I know you're shook up, and I want to talk about it. My back is still fine. Thanks for asking. Call me."

Ashley hung up, blew out a breath, and stared at herself in the bathroom mirror. She was at book club, Aziza's house tonight, and she'd excused herself to try to call Luke. Not that she expected him to answer. She winced at her reflection. She looked like shit.

She'd barely slept the last three nights. Partly because of her back. She'd gone to the urgent care clinic after leaving Luke at his parents' house. He'd wanted to come with her, but she had been firm and told him she was fine, and he really needed to be taking care of himself. It was true. Though she was the one bleeding, at least she had her wits. Taking Luke to the clinic with her would have been a burden. After all that had happened at the party, she wanted to be alone.

Maybe that hadn't been the right call? Had she left him when he needed her? Had she locked him out when he needed in?

The doctor had put in seventeen stitches. And she needed a tetanus booster. Now the wound ached and itched, and the pain served as a constant reminder of how passionate things had been and how suddenly things had changed.

But the wound wasn't the real problem. The real problem was the awful, dull heaviness inside her. She felt so distant from Luke, so unable to help. The weight of it stunned her.

My dear, there are no accidents. You are right where you need to be. Rena's words came back to her. Was she right where she needed to be?

On the other side of the bathroom door, she could hear Jamila and the other gals laughing, but she couldn't imagine joining the conversation. Not that she hadn't loved the book, *The Night Circus* by Erin Morgenstern. In fact, it was her favorite novel they'd read in years. But a line from the book had stamped itself on her thoughts:

> *I couldn't tell the difference between what was real*
> *and what I wanted to be real.*

Cognitive distortion, she thought. Was that what had been happening all along? Had she wanted the relationship with Luke so much that she'd tricked herself into believing it was something it wasn't? Had she pretended their attraction was enough to bridge all their differences?

The party at his parents' had made their different economic and social status come to light. How could someone from near poverty—someone who never threw away a single scrap of food—ever be in a relationship with someone like Luke? They were worlds apart. The amount of food that had probably been thrown away at Luke's parents' party would have been enough to have fed her whole childhood neighborhood—and it had just been thrown in the trash.

She inhaled the scent of the lavender candle Aziza had lit in the bathroom, but the scent didn't calm her. *Of course he dumped me. My father dumped me. My ex, Mark, fucked me over. Men* always *abandon me. Why did I let myself believe in a fairy tale—?*

A knock at the door startled her from her reverie. "Ashley? You in there?" *Meg.*

"I'm here."

"You okay? You've been in there a long time. And you seem off tonight."

"I'm okay."

"No, you're not."

"No, I'm not."

"Let me in."

Ashley sighed and unlocked the door. Meg came in and shut the door behind her.

"Spill."

Ashley put her face in her hands.

"Is it Luke?"

Ashley nodded.

"What is it?"

Ashley shrugged, then winced with the sharp stab of pain in her back triggered by the slight movement.

"This is like having a conversation with a mime. Come on, Ashley. Talk to me."

Ashley gave a faint laugh, despite herself, then sobered. "He canceled our date on Sunday night, and he hasn't returned my calls for three days. Just short informational texts."

"Did something happen?"

"Kind of?"

"Kind of."

Where could she even start? She had kept so much from Meg. She felt a sharp stab of guilt. "I don't know where to begin."

"Look. I am here for you. Always. We lost our jobs together. We've lost our hearts together. We've lost our *minds* together. But you will *never* lose me. Got it? No matter what happens with Mr. Oil Dynasty, I am *always* here for you. I've got your back."

What an apt metaphor. Was there anything so good as a friend? "You're the best, Meg."

"You let me know if you need me to kick his ass."

"We'll take him on together."

Luke: Hey. How's your back?

Ashley: Fine. How are you?

Exactly a week after the party, Ashley walked into the Lift House. She still hadn't heard from Luke except for short texts. She re-read the string as if it would give her new information.

Ashley: Hey, Deepak is going to be featured next week at Houston Books. Want to go?

Luke: Can't

Ashley: Did I do something wrong?

Luke: Just the opposite

Ashley: Help me understand

Luke: It's complicated
        I need some time

And that was it.

Of course it's complicated. But let me in!

Was "I need some time" a gentle way to say, "It's over?" Maybe his father had said something about her to him. *What a creep.*

The lack of communication made it very difficult to move forward. It reminded her of when her cat ran away when she was a girl. She was caught between *grief*—the likely chance that the cat had died—and *hope*—a willingness to believe things could still turn out okay. The not knowing created an unbearable tension that took months to leave her.

That was how it was now with Luke. At times, she was so filled with grief—missing him so deeply. It was as if a skin of grief had taken on the exact shape of her body, but her body was made of lead, and she could barely move. And other times, she was filled with the profound gossamer lightness of hope that he would open to her and let her in and share his pain instead of locking himself away from her, and then they could move forward together and figure out all their differences.

How many times had she replayed that evening in the pool house—the ecstasy, the terrible pain, Luke's face when he'd realized she was hurt, how limp his whole being had gone then. These were powerful demons. Too powerful for them to overcome?

"Hi, Ashley." Emilia was standing in the hallway with a bucket and mop.

"Hi, Emilia. Floor duty this week, eh?" Every week, the residents of Lift House had volunteer chores.

"I actually love it, making things shine."

Ashley's heart swelled for the girl. "Hey, I need you to do some social media polls for STEAMEA so we can fill in the gaps where other programs fall short."

"Sounds great!" Emilia lit up.

Ashley gave the girl a hug. "I think you saved me today, reminding me there can be joy in cleaning up messes." And for a moment, holding her mentee, Ashley felt light, flexible, and elastic, able to bend in the wind. And then, a moment later, she felt herself stiffen again into something brittle and breakable. Something about to crack and fall apart.

The next day, Ashley was in her apartment, preparing for a summer tutoring session the next day. Bamba was curled in her lap. *Thank god for cats.* She thought of how Happy and Go Lucky had saved Luke, and right now, she was getting some essential pet medicine herself.

Is Luke at the shelter today?

She lifted her gaze. Her apartment was ridiculously spotless. She'd scrubbed and dusted and mopped it to kingdom come. If she couldn't have control of her heart, at least she could have a spotless house. She sighed. *Mr. Clean is the only man I can keep.*

With dawning awareness, she realized why it hurt so badly that Luke had stopped talking with her. All the tensions they'd had in their relationship—the gap in economic and social status, their different values about the environment—these were all tensions of circumstance. Despite these differences, she had never doubted that Luke *wanted* to be with her. But now that he was only minimally letting her in…

Her whole life, she had loved solitude, but now, being alone was a prison, a weight, a gaping hole, a loss.

She picked up the phone to call Jewel, but her phone rang. "Hi, Mom."

"Hello, Ashling. How are you doing?"

"Good. How are you?"

"Good. But I had a feeling *you* were having a hard time."

Can all moms do this? "Um, yeah."

"Do you want to talk about it, dear?"

For the next hour, Ashley talked with her mother, telling her everything—well, almost everything. Not about the fantasies. Not about Luke's dad. But about the gun and the party and her back and how Luke had made her feel. And how hurt she was now. And her mother listened.

"Ashling, I have one question. Do you trust him?"

"He doesn't lie or cheat, if that's what you mean. So, I trust him as a person. But I am not so sure I trust our relationship."

"It's a good start. Can you find that trust inside you right now?"

Ashley closed her eyes and visualized what that would even look like. She saw the blanket spread out in Memorial Park, Luke leading her by the hand to the clearing.

"Yeah." Though she said it in a small voice, she could feel the truth of it blooming in her.

"Then trust that Luke knows what he needs. He's done a lot of work on himself. And if he needs space right now to understand himself better, let him have that space to grow. Trust, respect, and patience are the cornerstones of strong relationships. Because, Ashley, you also have things *you* need to do right now. This confusion around Luke is just a circumstance. You need to make peace with yourself at the deepest level—you need to use this time to understand who *you* are. Not Ashley the teacher. Not Ashley the girlfriend. Not Ashley whose house is probably spotless right now. Not any of the labels or habits you might use to think of yourself. Now is the time to lean into what is most essential in you—the you that can never be taken away. And find peace in that."

How did her mom get so sage? Just hearing her mother's words gave Ashley a sense of peace she'd been missing since the pool house. "Oh, Mom."

"The only way out is in, darling. Have patience. You don't know what he's going through. But trust me, love, it is not about you. And with those small daily texts, he's offering you bread-crumbs to follow until you can both arrive home. He has a complicated past, a complicated life, and he's just a man, a man who loves you, whether he knows that yet or not. Now. I want you to stand up and go do something to take care of yourself right now."

"Yes, Mom. Thanks for listening to me so closely. Thanks for knowing *me*. I love you, Mom."

"I love you, too."

Ashley closed her eyes and said thank you out loud. To god? To the universe? To whatever power had given her such a wise and loving mother.

But that thought of gratefulness for her mother bled into its sister thought—her sorrow about her lack of a father. Instead of giving fuel to that old sorrow, she decided to do something productive: make her father's enchiladas. That always made her feel better. And it gave her an idea.

Hi, you've reached Luke Dalton. Please leave a message.

"Hi, Luke, it's Ashley. I know you needed space. I did, too. I've done a lot of thinking. And feeling. And I have something for you I know will help. It helped me. Can you smell it through the voicemail? Mmm. I'm bringing it to you tonight. At six. I hope you'll be there. Otherwise, I'm giving these enchiladas to your concierge, Nolan."

Talking to her mother last night had regrounded her. She *did* trust him, and even more importantly, she trusted *herself* about her feelings toward him. She respected his need to take care of himself and to let her in only when he was ready. Whatever was going on, her mom was right. It wasn't about her; it was an old, deep wound around his brother. Still raw. Surely, the blood in the pool house had stirred up old demons. And she felt like an idiot for taking it so personally.

Still, she was also willing to excuse herself for taking it personally. She was learning how to have a good relationship. And so was he. They were both so broken, and they were teaching each other how to be whole.

I'll drop off the enchiladas and leave. That was her whole plan.

By 5:50, she still hadn't heard from him. No matter. She was going in. And if Nolan got the enchiladas, well, he would probably appreciate them.

"Hi, Nolan," she said as she walked in.

"Ms. Barris. Always good to see you. Let me dial Mr. Dalton."

"Yes." Her voice carried more confidence than she felt.

A moment later: "Go on up."

Ashley's heart banged against her rib cage as the elevator rose. What would he say when he saw her? What would *she* say? She should just bring him the enchiladas and go. *That was the plan. Stick to the plan.*

She tapped her foot and counted the taps. *Nine. Ten. Eleven.* The elevator stopped. That was auspicious. Eleven was the smallest two-digit prime number in the decimal base, and she and Luke *were* an eleven—two equals that came together and then couldn't be divided by anything but themselves.

She stepped into the private lobby when the elevator doors opened. The door to his apartment was open. "Luke?" Her voice rang out in the apartment. He must be here; Nolan had called him. She noticed there were things lying around—drinking glasses, plates. As if he hadn't been straightening. And the floors had little bits of paper and other microtrash that told her the housekeeper hadn't been here for a while.

She found Luke sitting at the dining room table, surrounded by a mess of folders and papers.

She used her most gentle voice. "Hi, Luke."

He looked scruffy. *Oh, Luke. I'm so sorry.*

"Hi, Luke. You look, um—"

"Like I haven't shaved?" His voice was monotone. He smiled at her but didn't get up. "Hi."

"Hi."

An awkward silence wobbled between them.

"You cooked for me." He nodded to the dish in her arms. "That was thoughtful." His voice was polite but not warm.

"I did it for us."

"Your father's enchiladas?"

She nodded.

He opened his mouth as if to say something, then closed it. Then said, "I'm sorry, sweetness."

"I know. You need space. I just wanted to drop them off and see you and let you get back to your, um, space."

"Stay awhile."

You should go, you should go, you should go. "Okay." *Just a couple minutes.*

"Have a seat." He motioned to the chair across from him at the table. She sat.

I miss you, Luke. "How are you doing?"

"I'm a mess."

"You look terrible."

"Thanks for the honesty."

Why haven't you called me? "Are you working from home?"

"I've been going in for half days."

What's going on with us? "Oh."

"I'm not very good company."

I want to stay. "I should go."

"Please stay."

In that moment, Ashley realized she'd been feeling like drift-wood in a river, momentarily eddied but certain she'd soon be flushed away from shore again. And so, when he asked her to stay, she understood just how much she'd needed him to say those words. She needed to feel as if he weren't pushing her away.

Time for straight talk. Sit tall, Ashley. "Luke. What's going on? Can you let me in?"

He sat at the table and stared out the window.

Trust him.

She reached into her purse and pulled out something she'd been carrying with her for over a month. She set the small wooden elephant on the table between them. Luke's eyes flickered in recognition. He gave her a wan smile.

"Let's talk," she said.

"I don't know what to say."

"Tell me why you haven't called."

"Because I couldn't."

"You couldn't?"

"I couldn't, Ashley."

"You—"

"You don't understand." Luke ran both hands through his hair and then pulled them around to hide his face.

"You're *right*. I need you to *help* me understand." Anger rose, and she forced it down.

"I couldn't call you, Ashley. I can't stop remembering all that blood, the look on your face—"

"Luke." She reached out to touch him, and he pulled his arm away.

"I don't know how to be in my own skin, Ashley."

"What do you mean?" She asked the question even though she got it. He meant that he'd hurt his brother, and he carried the pain of that every day. And the thought that he could hurt someone terrified him. But she needed to hear *him* say that.

"I hurt you. No matter how hard I try to protect you and be good to you, I fucking *hurt* you." He dropped his face in his hands.

"I'm fine, Luke."

"Did you need stitches?"

She hesitated. "Yeah."

"How many?"

"A few."

"How many?"

"Seventeen."

"Goddammit." He slammed his fist on the table. It was the first time she'd ever seen him angry—and that anger turned inward now knotted and twisted the features on his face. Every muscle in him flexed and tensed, the cords on his neck popping. And then with a massive inhale and a shudder, he planted his face into his palms and shook his head. "I'm so sorry, Ashley."

Ashley stared at him, shaken, unable to reach for him, unable to speak. *Who is this?* No wonder he hadn't called her. It was a classic case of posttraumatic stress disorder. He was clearly having a physical and psychological stress response triggered by the event in the pool house.

She felt like an idiot. Some part of her knew it as a certainty all along. But some insecure part of her had insisted on making it about some inadequacy in her.

"Luke."

He didn't look up.

"Luke. Listen to me. I'm okay. It was an accident."

"Yes. It was a goddamn *accident*! I hurt the people I love, Ashley. Not because I want to. It's just who I am. I never should have let myself fall for you. I should have known better. I should have been protecting you from me. And instead, I hurt you. You're so good, and I hurt you."

"Luke." She spoke quietly. "You *leaving* me is what hurts. The back is nothing. What hurts most is not being with you. I miss you so much. I know you're suffering. I can't even imagine the pain you've been through. I *know* you don't want to hurt me. So, let me in. Let me *in*."

"What if I hurt you again?" She heard the claws of fear in his voice.

"Hear me. What hurts me *most* is not being with you."

"You haven't given up on me?" He sounded incredulous, even indignant. "Even though I hurt you? Even though I didn't call you?" His voice rose. "Even though I'm a mess?" He held his hands open before him. His voice dropped to a whisper. "Look at me."

"I'm looking at you."

Luke's eyes were twin blue pools of desperation. "What do you see?"

Ashley felt a small seed of truth take root in her, and in the long silence that opened between them, she felt that seed sprout, leaf out, climb, and grow into a vine that twined around her heart and sent out runners toward Luke. It was one thing to fall for a man who was her hero. It was quite another to be in love with a man who shared with her his *whole* self—who, even in his most broken, vulnerable moments, was striving to honor and protect her. She was *in love* with this man, the *whole* man. That's why she was here.

As she grew increasingly sure of her feelings that even now were tendrilling and reaching for him, she watched Luke's expression soften and warm, as if he could sense the experience she was having.

"I see a man who is being transformed. And *I* am being transformed, too, Luke. And transformation is never easy or pretty. Any chemistry teacher can tell you how a substance that undergoes transformation must first be torn apart. But I'm here, Luke, because I believe in *us*. Transforming together." Her words were pregnant with conviction. Ashley reached her hand across the table, palm up in trembling invitation. She took a deep breath in. "A wise woman told me, *You carry hope with you—*"

He opened his mouth, incredulous, and she stopped speaking. He swallowed. "Until it becomes you."

"Until it becomes you," she whispered. "Until it becomes *us*."

"*Us*." He said the word as if tasting it for the first time.

He slid his hand into hers and squeezed it tight. His voice quivered. "Oh, Ashley." His eyes shined with tears, but he didn't look at her. He stared at their hands, joined.

"I am building a bridge to you, Luke." She could feel his sadness, the way it radiated from him throughout the room. "I am not your brother. You are not my father. We are not each other's biggest regrets. You are the man my heart has chosen, and that scares me more than anything I've ever felt. And I am so sure of it."

Luke looked up.

"I know you need space. I'm glad you know what you need. And when you are done with being alone, I am here for you. Let's get beyond this together." Ashley could hardly believe the courage she felt in this moment, how easy it was to both care for him and let him go, how easy to trust that tenderness and respect would return them to each other.

He had never said he loved her. He might not be able to. But he had said *I hurt the ones I love*, and he'd been referring to her in that sad statement, that hopeless story he'd been telling himself for years.

And she couldn't say, even to herself, that she loved him, but she knew it was possible. And for now, that truth was giving her strength beyond what she'd known she was capable of.

"Thank you," Luke said, his words laced with disbelief.

"I'm going home. But lean on me. Anytime. I want that, Luke. Call me anytime. I'm right here."

She gave his hand a squeeze and pulled her hand out, the warmth of their touch still present on her palm.

Luke didn't move. But she could feel a change in him. A gentleness. A calm. A hope.

"Thank you, Ashley."

She pushed the elephant toward him. "Never know when you might need a pachyderm."

The whole ride down to the lobby, Ashley reveled in the peace and hope that radiated through her body like twin suns. She felt illumined, alive. As if anything were possible. Even love.

"Well, look who's here." The elevator doors opened to reveal Savannah, wearing a blue designer suit, her blonde hair framing her beautiful face like a mane. A stack of folders was tucked in her arm. She looked professional. Stunning. Predacious.

"Hi, Savannah." How quickly the twin suns went dim.

"Hi, Ashley." She curled back a lip. Not really a smile. Almost a threat. "Good thing you're leaving. Luke and I have a lot of, ah, work to do." She cocked her head as if directing Ashley to exit the elevator so she could get in. Her smile was dazzling and cold.

Ashley didn't move.

"Everyone at the Daltons' party talked about the little gold digger following him around." She shook her head and closed her eyes, as if reseeing an embarrassing moment. "Pathetic how you're using him to fund your little project."

"You seem intimidated, Savannah." Ashley smiled the most genuine smile she could and strutted out of the elevator. *Take that, bitch. I won't play your fucking games.*

"Intimidated?" Savannah scoffed. "I don't think so. Make no mistake, you're not good enough for him. And after he spits you out, I'll still be here."

It wasn't until Ashley got back into her car that she cried.

CHAPTER 25

LUKE DIDN'T CALL THE next day. Or the next.

Ashley remembered the feeling she'd had at Luke's table, how vigorous, how robust her budding love had felt. But the truth was she'd absorbed the poison in Savannah's taunts. And like any good herbicide, it had strong residual action.

No matter how hard she tried to unhear the toxic words, she still heard them: *He'll tire of you. And after he spits you out, I'll still be here.*

Damn her.

Focus, Ashley. She stared at the proposals she was putting together for STEAMEA, wondering if Luke would come to the next meeting and how she would face him if that were their first interaction after his house. Two weeks ago, they'd been so close—laughing and talking and kissing and playing. And now? Now she worried about what to say when she saw him.

Her phone vibrated on the desk. *Luke!* Her heart galloped in her chest. *Whoa. Take a breath.* She said a little prayer that whatever was coming was a hello and not a goodbye.

Luke: Free tonight?

Of course she was free. She'd been saying no to all evening plans except her dinner with Jewel. Nothing in her had felt like being social since Luke's parents' party.

Ashley: Yes

Luke: Come over?
           I have a surprise

Ashley: What time?

Luke: 6:02?

Ashley: What can I bring?
Luke: Hope

———————

"Mmm. Whoa, Luke. These are *delicious*," Ashley said, taking a second bite of the enchiladas Luke had prepared. "They're better than mine. What did you put in them?"

Luke grinned, pleased with himself. "What will you give me if I tell you?"

"Oh, so that's how we're playing," she teased. She took a sip of wine. Her libido was urging her to make this game sexual— she longed to hold him, to lose herself in his body again—but she was determined to take this reconnecting process slowly, so she countered with a culinary offer. "If you tell me your secret, I'll give you a recipe for blueberry tart—with an ingredient so surprising I bet you can't even spell it. God knows I can't."

"You're on."

She grinned. "So, spill."

"Well, you had mentioned saffron and mint before, so I used both of those. The only special thing I did was caramelize the onions inside the enchiladas."

"That's it," she gushed. "The *onions*. Hauntingly savory and yet—"

"—the kind of sweetness that can only come with time."

Why did she get the feeling he wasn't just talking about onions?

"You're a rap*scallion* for making these better than I can," she teased.

He grinned. "If you've got a recipe, *chive* got a way to make it better."

She kicked him under the table. It felt good to be playful with him. She had missed this so much.

Luke had gone all out for this dinner. It reminded her of the first meal she'd had here alone with him. Red roses. White lilies. Candlelight. An edge of uncertainty.

"Thank you for inviting me, Luke."

"Thank you for coming." They clinked their glasses and said nothing for a while, letting themselves reacclimate to the feeling of being together. They were, at the same time, familiar and shy with each other.

Luke broke the silence. "You were right to come over the other night. That was courageous. And I am grateful."

Ashley set down her fork and gave him her whole attention. *Take that, Savannah.*

He continued. "I want to be with you, Ashley. It's just—I feel so jinxed. Seeing you hurt, seeing you in pain, knowing I caused it—"

"You were innocent." She caught his eyes and held them.

"I still think of him all the time, Ashley. I still see the blood. And when I saw all *your* blood..."

She fought the urge to touch his hand and caressed him tenderly instead with her words. "I hear you." He still had so much pain. Maybe it would never go away.

"You coming over shifted things for me. The feelings you shared. The way you expressed yourself. The woman you are. Ashley, I can't thank you enough. It was the push I needed to be the best version of myself."

"So, what does that look like?"

"Oh, I'll show you." He had the sweetest, most satisfied look on his face. There was something so *real* about it she felt it resonate through her. "In fact, I'd *really* like to share it with you."

After dinner, he took her by the hand. "Come." They walked to a room she hadn't been in before, a small interior room with no windows. It smelled of lavender, sweet and floral, and of sandalwood, warm, exotic. It had an immediate effect on her, both calming and uplifting.

Luke was into aromatherapy? Who knew?

The walls were lined with shelves holding about twenty golden beeswax candles. He lit a few of them as she surveyed the rest of the room: a wood floor with perhaps a dozen cushions of different rich colors. A yoga mat laid out on one side. A low altar in the center of the room, a plum-colored drape over it, and on it were a candle, incense, a wooden mallet, and a variety of copper bowls on a cushion.

Luke finished lighting the candles and turned off the overhead light. It felt good in here, warm and soft and sacred. Silence here seemed generous, honeyed, connective—like a loose-knit blanket that gently covered them both.

Luke gestured for her to sit on one of the cushions, and she did. He sat on a cushion beside her, the altar on his right. He gestured for her to close her eyes. She did.

In the silence, the only sound was the song of her own breath, the subtle tide of inhale, exhale, inhale, exhale. And she became aware that Luke had matched his breathing with hers, such a quiet, unifying gesture. She remembered how he had done that in Telluride, too, in the gondola. She'd been sure then, as now, he was intentionally meeting her in this most simple coupling, a perfect respiratory rhyming, a chaste and yet wildly intimate act.

She couldn't have opened her eyes if she tried. Her lids were heavy—her whole body was heavy, as if she were profoundly aware she was living, breathing clay—the stuff the whole world is made of. She became less sure of her own limits—where her body ended and the floor began, where her head ended and met the infinite air. And she was deeply aware that although they were not touching, she and Luke were very much uniting with each other in this state.

And then the most remarkable sound came from the altar, an ambient ringing that began thin and then opened into such deep resonance it cut through all thinking and embraced her everywhere. And then she became aware the tone was, in fact, two tones—a fundamental tone and an overtone—two waves that were one sound, and they submerged her in tone and washed through her until every part of her body felt renewal, until every cell of her shared its resonance, as if she and Luke were a single instrument being played, and the harmony being made in them was something vitally intrinsic to their mutual being. They had entered a communion, a closeness so pure, so innocent, so real. *So real.*

How long were they joined in that unified space? Ashley lost all sense of time. As if the hands of her impeccable inner clock had melted like a painting by Salvador Dalí. Eventually, the tone resolved into silence, only this silence seemed vaster, richer, purer, more alive, full of infinite potential—or was it that she was now more attuned and available to silence? As if she had somehow relearned how to listen, how to hear.

Once again, she became aware of just how connected she and Luke were through the sound of their breath.

Slowly, slowly, she opened her eyes, and in the glow, she could see Luke, his eyes still closed, his face utterly unguarded and open. God, he was beautiful.

At some point, his eyes opened to meet hers, and they let their eyes converse, transmitting an appreciation for this state of vulnerable wonder and their amazement at sharing it.

For a long time, they sat there meeting each other without words, without touch, with just the essence of their being.

And then Ashley realized her legs were asleep and tingling terribly, and she shifted and winced. Luke nodded with understanding and stood and helped her stand. And again, they stayed in silence, facing each other, holding hands as they looked into each other's eyes, surrounded by the same silence that has been present since before the big bang, the same silence that touched the first leaf and met the first song. This eternal silence had opened every room in their hearts, had permeated them, informed them, joined them. And then, when her leg had passed through the pins and needles stage, Luke guided her from the room.

What was *that?* Only now was she aware that for some long period of time, she hadn't been thinking at all.

They walked wordlessly back to the dining table and sat.

Eventually, she broke the silence, her voice hushed. "So that's what you've been doing?"

"Yeah." He smiled.

"That was amazing."

"Those cushions and singing bowl are old friends—they help bring me back to equilibrium. Instead of reaching out for help, sometimes I need to reach *in*."

She suddenly pictured him taking other women into his meditation room.

"I've never invited anyone else to join me," he said.

"Busted," she laughed. *How did you know?* "That's exactly what I was thinking. It's just that, Luke, that was so intimate, it was almost better than—"

"Yeah." He nodded, his eyes dancing, flirting with the words she didn't say. "But not quite."

She laughed. "Not quite. But I was feeling possessive about you sharing it with someone else."

"Let me show you something else that's been helping me, something else I've never shared—but I will share it with you." He got up and walked to the kitchen and returned with a dark purple box with a lavender bow.

"Chocolate?"

"Not just any chocolate. Dark chocolate truffles from Vosges Haut Chocolat. My secret weapon for making everything better. Here." He opened the box and offered it to her. "I know chocolate isn't your favorite, but these—"

"Not for me." She held up a hand in refusal.

"Okay!" He laughed and set the box down. "Ashley, come with me to Europe."

"What?" She got a fluttery feeling in her stomach.

"Come with me to Europe. I have business for a couple days in London—I need to give a speech at a conference." He grimaced, acknowledging his fear of public speaking. "Let's make a vacation out of it. Let's go to the mountains in Switzerland for a few days. Take the train. Let's explore."

"When?"

"In four days."

"Four days? As in, we leave in ninety-six hours, four days?"

"Yeah." His face was so full of childlike expectancy.

"Really?"

"I don't want to leave you. Come with me."

"For how long?"

"A week. We'll be back before the Fourth of July."

What was holding her back? Tutoring? STEAMEA? Bamba? Polishing her spotless sinks because Luke was away? "Okay!"

"Yes!" He gave a fist pump. "I'll get your ticket tonight." He put out his arms and pretended he was a plane swooping.

God, it was good to be with Luke.

Ashley put a hand on his wrist, loving the feel of his skin. There was, as always, the spark of sensual promise. She ignored it. "Speaking of tickets, I have two for the Lift House Gala." Ashley felt so humbled. He'd invited her to Europe. She was inviting him to the Houston Hilton. "I know it's not international travel, but—"

"I can't wait to go with you. When is it?"

"July 13. Tell me you're not going to be at some chateau in Paris then."

"I'm all yours."

She hoped so. She *really* hoped so.

"Champagne?" Luke handed her a glass in bed. "They were serving it in the dining car." Ashley was just waking in a private room on a luxury train somewhere in Switzerland.

"Isn't it, like, 9:00 a.m.?" She was still upside down from jet lag.

"Does it matter?"

"Nope." Ashley took a sip of the sparkling liquid and leaned back on her pillow. "Thank you."

"Anything for the famous nude in the painting." She blushed, thinking of last night's lovemaking—Luke had touched her body as if he were a painter and she was his model, outlining her shape with his hands, touching her as if she were the most perfect work of art, praising every part of her body. It had been the sweetest torture, holding still in the pose he had given her while he pleasured her again and again. And then she'd turned the tables.

She rolled over to look out the window, mesmerized by the dark sheer mountainsides, the rolling green hills, the sky already deep blue. Everything seemed so new to her, so far from Houston—the little cream-and-pink villages with their churches, the clear rivers, the thick green forests.

How did he even get up? They'd spent most of the night having sex. And in the very early morning, the slight rocking of the train had lulled her into the sweetest, deepest sleep, making it impossible to even think of rising.

"Don't move," Luke said, watching her from the table where he sat. "You look so beautiful. I'm just trying to take a picture in my mind."

"You're just trying to avoid working on your speech."

"That, too."

"Come on—it won't write itself. I know you're avoiding it because you're nervous."

"Maybe."

"I don't get it. You have so much confidence walking into a room. And you loved acting so much. What is it about speaking at a conference that makes you so nervous? How's it so different?"

"When I'm acting, I don't feel as if I'm exposing *myself*."

Ashley pondered his words. "Maybe give the speech as if you're *acting* as the vice president of an oil company."

"It doesn't work. I've tried." He sighed. "I've been working with this a long time, and I guess there's more work to do."

"While you're speaking, you can think of my smiling face?" She shot him a giant, toothy grin.

Luke roared with laughter and stroked her cheek. "Yes, I will think of your beautiful, smiling face." He settled in to work on his speech, and Ashley leaned back, head pressed against the lavish pillows and opulent upholstery.

What was she doing in this fairy tale—this beautiful, luxurious fairy tale complete with a handsome prince?

A ridge of jagged mountains emerged as the train came around a tight curve. She shook her head. *Fairy-tale set, too.*

But if this were a fairy tale, why was she suddenly feeling morose? If she were honest with herself, as amazing as the sex had been last night—playful and racy and erotic and fun—something about it had left her uneasy.

You are the most beautiful woman I've ever seen, he'd growled in appreciation once her clothes were all off, his eyes darkened with unmistakable arousal. And the words had thrilled her, of course, but were they *true*? Did he really think she was the most beautiful woman? Or was it just part of the fantasy? In their most intimate moments, she wanted to *believe* him. She wanted to know what was *real*. She *needed* to know what was real.

Instead of being a famous model, she wanted to be Ashley, the laid-off schoolteacher and nonprofit director. She wanted to make love to Luke, the, what, the oil man? Hmm. No. It wasn't their identities she wanted them to bring to bed—those were just the roles they played on a daily basis.

What she wanted, *really wanted*, was something more like what they had experienced in the meditation room. She wanted sex that obliterated identity and immersed them in the most profound intimacy. The way they had synchronized their breathing that night with the singing bowls, that was how she wanted them to synchronize their hearts. Beyond the union of their bodies, she wanted the union of their *souls*—the way two rivers flow into each other and become one water, that was what she wanted with their sex. That was what she wanted with their relationship.

If he could do it in the meditation room, could he someday do it with sex? Be totally present? Merge with her in that wholly unifying state, beyond what the brain could concoct?

Could she and Luke talk about this without making Luke defensive or ruining the fragile base they'd rebuilt since the gash in her back? By not talking about these feelings, was she eroding the base, anyway?

She stared at the gray-and-blond alpine cliffs, marveling at how sheer they were, then realized she'd been looking at them for five minutes without *seeing* them.

Who needs to be more present now, Ashley? And she promised herself to enjoy where she was, to do her best to accept the man she was with *as he was*, not *as she wished he could be.*

She gazed at Luke across the room, frowning as he worked, and she smiled. He was an amazing man, so admirable, so worthy of love and ecstasy. If only he knew it as surely as she did.

"I can't wait to see the look on your face when you try the mushroom bourguignon." Luke was driving her through the south of Switzerland. They were passing through dense forests, alpine pastures, and the occasional orchard.

Ashley loved these foreign glimpses: endless green fields filled with goats, the cobblestone streets, the fancy trim on the houses. So different from Houston. She felt transported, curious, grateful. Luke was an incredible guide, doing everything he could to create a magical, unforgettable trip. As he said, "I'm specializing in you."

"Here we are." He smiled, stopping the rental car—a fuel-efficient model in her honor—in front of a magnificent chateau-style restaurant built with old white bricks and a red roof that had square turrets rising above the roofline. Luke's excitement was contagious. Ashley beamed back at him.

"And because I'm so sure you'll want to recreate the dish at home, I've arranged for the chef to join us after lunch so you can ask him questions."

Damn, this man is thoughtful.

The instant Ashley stepped out of the car, she felt sick, nauseous. With each inhale, she thought she might suffocate. Her heart raced, and an unreasonable terror filled her.

"Luke," she gasped. "I can't be here."

"What is it, Ashley? What's wrong?"

"We need to go. Get back in the car. Shut the door."

Luke got back in and stared at her, confused and concerned. "Talk to me."

Ashley opened her mouth as if to speak, then closed her eyes and leaned back in her seat, her face pinched with pain.

Luke whipped the car into reverse and sped from the town, calling the restaurant to cancel the special meal. Hot tears fell down her face, but she didn't move to brush them away. She couldn't move.

After about fifteen minutes, Luke pulled over on the side of the road. Nothing but rolling hills and trees as far as the eye could see. She was grateful he hadn't asked her to talk as they drove. Already she was feeling calmer, silly even. She was also feeling guilty about ruining the special afternoon he had planned.

Luke rolled down the windows to let in a breeze and turned off the car, then sat quietly with his hand on her knee. "You okay?"

"I'm okay. I'm sorry. I ruined your beautiful plans."

"I'm worried about you. Can you talk about it?"

Ashley took a deep breath. She felt the breeze on her skin and closed her eyes for a moment. "Remember I told you about Jewel? The attack? About that night when the—" Her voice broke.

Luke nodded.

"We were baking a chocolate cake that night for our mom. And the whole house smelled of chocolate when I came out of the bathroom and saw, you know, Jewel—"

"Say no more."

But she did have to tell him. She wanted him to understand why she'd reacted so strongly to the scent in the town. There must have been a chocolate factory in that town that made the air thickly sweet and acrid with the scent of burnt cocoa. It had smothered her, the horrible memory flooding her as if it were happening in that moment.

"When we came back from Tica's house, after the cops arrived, Jewel was crying and shaking, and the lights of the squad cars flashed off the living room walls, and the whole house smelled of burnt chocolate. The same smell as the air in that town."

"I'm so sorry."

"We threw out the pan."

"I understand." Luke held her hand.

For a long time, they sat in the warm sun with the breeze floating through, until the past became the past again.

CHAPTER 26

ASHLEY ALMOST DIDN'T WANT to leave the hotel suite—it was elegant and warm and intimate. The living room had a fireplace with a walnut mantle. The walls were gold and cream. The bathroom had black marble floors and copper sinks. She wasn't one to care about luxury, but this was *spectacularly* lovely. A bouquet of white lilies and roses was on the living room table, and she had sunken into a soft sofa with a book and a cup of tea.

Why would I ever leave? She snuggled in deeper.

Because London is waiting. And Corinna.

She and Luke had arrived from Switzerland late last night, and already he was off to meetings. He'd arranged for her to go out and explore the town with his daughter, who apparently knew London quite well and had an interview later this week for a summer internship with a fine art gallery. She'd come to the city early to see her dad and look for a flat.

Sure, the first meeting with Corinna in Luke's apartment hadn't gone well, but Ashley was hoping this could be a fresh start. She'd been jealous, albeit unnecessarily, and Corinna had been protective of her time with her dad, but now it would be just the two of them. As much as Ashley enjoyed alone time, this seemed the perfect chance to connect with Luke's daughter. Plus, she could tell Luke was eager for the two of them to connect.

All right then. Ashley got up to find her shoes—which seemed pedestrian and "down at the heel" in this regal room—and searched for her purse. Luke had asked her to buy him a red tie today when she went out. He forgot to pack one, and he'd said something in her ear while she was still dozing about how he left her his credit card on the dressing table to pay for it.

And there was the card with a note beneath it.

> *For the tie—pick one that will bring me good luck. And find something beautiful for you. A dress for the gala in Houston, perhaps? Have fun with Corinna in London. Meet me tonight at the lobby bar around six.*
>
> *xxx,*
>
> *L*

"Have fun with Corinna," she read out loud, nodding. Her chin jutted with determination. "I think I will."

Ashley stared at the card, gold and shiny. What a different world this was. Her credit card had a limit of $5,000. This one could probably buy the whole street they were on.

Some part of her wanted to pick it up and use it. How easy would it be? Just swipe and sign and purchase whatever she wanted. Instead, she slipped the card into his drawer. She'd spend her own money on his tie.

The phone beside the bed rang, startling her. Maybe Luke wishing her a good morning?

"Hello?"

"Oh, Ashley? Hey, it's Corinna."

"Hi, Corinna." Ashley willed a smile onto her face, knowing it would slip into her voice. "I'm so excited to have you as my guide through London today. Thank you so much."

"Oh, yeah," Corinna hedged. "About that. I'm sorry, something's come up, and I can't go with you today."

"I see." Ashley felt a sinking feeling in her stomach. She was a bit surprised at how disappointed she was. *Funny how you find out how much you care about something only when you lose it.* Ashley could have sworn she'd be grateful for the excuse to be alone. "Okay. I'd love to connect with you another time while we're here."

"Yeah, sure!" Corinna said it with the kind of false brightness that usually means, "Probably not."

"Good luck with your, um, plans for the day."

"Thanks."

Only now did Ashley realize she didn't know her way around town. *Walk tall, Barris.* At least all the signs would be in English.

She smiled at herself in the mirror. *Be happy! You're alone in London for the day!* The pep talk mostly worked.

After orienting herself with the concierge, she walked toward the lobby exit, and she saw she'd been spotted. By Savannah. Couldn't she get away from this woman?

"Hi, Ashley," she purred, a lioness ready to pounce.

"Hi, Savannah."

"Is that a Brunello Cucinelli you're wearing?" She fingered Ashley's knit sweater.

"TJ Maxx."

Savannah shrugged. "Of course. It's so thoughtful of you to come to an oil conference."

"It's a first."

"And last, is my guess."

Ashley wanted to walk away, but it was as if her scuffed shoes had grown roots.

Savannah put on a condescending smile and spoke in saccharine tones. "But I will be in this world forever. I understand

Luke's business. I understand his *life*. And *I* understand his family. Speaking of which."

Ashley turned to see Corinna walking up to Savannah.
"Corinna," Savannah cooed, as if she'd not just been speaking in
switchblades. "Darling!"

Corinna was dressed in holey jeans and a slouchy sweat-
shirt—the kind Ashley had seen flipping through *Vogue* at the
dentist—clothes that somehow screamed wealth despite their
grungy nature.

Savannah linked her arm into Corinna's. She flashed Ashley a triumphant smile. "Ashley, have you met Corinna, Luke's
daughter? One of my *favorite* people in the whole world. We've
spent a lot of good times in London together—we're like family."

Something came up. More of a "someone" came up.

"We've met. Hi, Corinna. Nice to see you again." Ashley
reached out to shake her hand, and though Corinna's handshake
was firm, her eyes looked embarrassed. She'd been caught. Ashley felt sorry for her. Almost. "Have fun today, girls. I will."

Ashley spun and walked from the lobby with a confidence
that surprised her. Truth was, Ashley preferred her own company to the company of bitches and spoiled girls who broke
commitments.

Outside, the air was smoggy and gray, despite it being a
summer day. But dang, it was better than the air in that lobby.
Ashley headed down the noisy street with its scent of diesel and
soundtrack of footsteps and chatter, her gait sprightly. She was
ready to find adventure. And a red tie.

Honk. Honk.

Shit! She'd momentarily forgotten which way to look for cars
when crossing the street. Luke had warned her last night that
people drove on the opposite side of the road, and she'd laughed

at him—of course, she knew that. Still, she almost got herself killed. *One. Two. Three.* She counted the expensive-looking awnings that stretched along the street above the exclusive New Bond Street shops.

She walked through an elaborate door into a men's store and was greeted by a handsome and well-dressed salesman. "Can I help you?" His accent was crisp and polite.

"I need a tie. Red."

The shop smelled of expensive cologne—musk and sandalwood—reminding her of Luke's meditation room. It made her want to sit in one of the overstuffed chairs and close her eyes.

"Right here."

Ashley fingered the ties, reveling in the nice fabrics. *The rich can make anything nice.* One tie, though, caught her eye immediately. A berry-ish red with a gray dot pattern that, on much closer inspection, revealed a tiny gray-and-white elephant head inside each dot. She quickly converted the price from pounds to dollars and grimaced. Almost two hundred dollars—her whole budget for buying gifts here in London. But now that she'd seen it, no other tie would do.

She set her shoulders. She wanted *this tie* for him from *her.* She brought it to the counter and handed over her card.

Several hours later, Ashley's feet were tired, and her heart was happy. She'd escaped New Bond Street with its polished streets and extravagant people dressed in extravagant clothes they bought in the extravagant shops—and she'd found more affordable stores where she'd bought small presents for her mom, Jewel, and Meg, plus a little jewelry box for Emilia. But there was one thing more she wanted.

On New Bond Street, she'd gone into Asprey, and while wandering the luxury department store, she'd seen the most exquisite crystal monkey with yellow topaz eyes. *For four hundred dollars.* Out of the question, but it did give her an idea. She had studied Luke's monkey collection at his penthouse and knew he didn't have a crystal one.

So, she'd made it her day's goal to find a crystal monkey she could afford to give him, a special memento of this trip. In fact, she was giddy with the idea, and it had led her into some strange and wonderful shops full of curious trinkets and foreign smells.

And here it was, the perfect little monkey curled in on himself in an egg-shaped form. It was modern and smooth and fit in her palm, and though it wasn't cheap, she felt no guilt as she brought it to the register.

"This is nice," said the saleswoman.

"Please wrap it. It's for the man I care about most in the world."

———

I thought Luke told me to meet him at six?

Ashley arrived at the traditional English lobby bar at five forty-nine to be early, but clearly, the party Luke mentioned had been going strong for some time. The sound of men and women laughing and chatting stopped her like an audible wall, most of them wearing conference lanyards. She'd been so blissfully alone today, and entering the crowd was overwhelming.

She scanned the room and saw Luke standing near the bar, an ornately carved dark wood piece with a bartender in a tux behind it. Luke was surrounded by colleagues, all listening to something he was saying, and standing right beside him—*right beside him*—finding excuses to briefly touch his arm, his shoulder, was Savannah.

A red swell of anger opened in Ashley's chest. *Back off, bitch.*

Ashley stood a moment, considering the best approach, when she felt Luke notice her. He looked up, his eyes brightening, his whole face coming alive, and though he was obviously telling a story to the group of people gathered around him, he held out his arm to her as if willing her to come stand in it. And, as if she were compelled by the magnet of his body, she felt herself pulled right in.

"God, I missed you today," he murmured into her ear, pulling her in tight against him. "Everyone, I want to introduce you to my girlfriend, Ashley Barris, a woman who makes the world a better place." He went around the small circle, offering names. "And of course, you know Savannah."

"Hi, Savannah. We saw each other earlier." Ashley knew the best revenge was the very real smile on her face as Luke held her in his arms.

As the group made small talk, offering suggestions for her itinerary tomorrow, Ashley never once made eye contact with Savannah, though she could feel the other woman's eyes burning through her. No matter. The tighter Luke held her, the more Ashley's anger dissipated until she finally felt compassionate toward Savannah.

Eventually, the group started breaking up for dinner. "Luke," Savannah said, completely ignoring Ashley, "are you joining us for dinner?"

"I have other plans tonight." He held Ashley closer. "Very special other plans."

Ashley didn't even try to hide the flush that blossomed on her cheeks when he whispered discreetly in her ear a few wicked things he planned to do to her. In fact, tonight, she kind of liked showing off that easy blush.

―――――

Ashley felt so sneaky. She'd managed to get into the conference—first through the metal detector, then past the guard checking lanyards. She'd held her bag up to her chest and walked in as if she owned the place.

That shouldn't have been so easy.

For all these years, if she'd known she could slip so effortlessly into an international oil conference, she might have been able to do a significant amount of high-profile protesting. But today, against her better judgment, perhaps, she was here to offer support, not to the oil industry, no, but to one beautiful man who had miraculously managed to open her heart wide. And though they hadn't talked about the specifics of his speech, she knew that today, whatever he was unveiling, he would be articulate and confident.

It had been a magical couple of days here in London. Yesterday, she'd gone on tours that Luke had set up for her—on the double-decker bus, to the British Museum, and this morning, she'd gone to the Science Museum. Luke had heard about a special chemistry exhibit there and had gotten her a ticket.

She knew his speech was supposed to begin at four, and now at six past the hour, the corridors were mostly empty as she looked for the main hall. Bingo. She saw on the marquee "The Future in Oil," Luke Dalton.

The Future in Oil!

Ashley flashed back to the talk at some of the recent board meetings for STEAMEA, how intently he'd listened to her thoughts on the environment. She thought of how he'd mentioned "significant changes" coming in the oil industry. No wonder he'd been so nervous about this talk. If he were going to discuss real change in the future, it would cause major ripples here! She felt a giddiness in her heart, thinking of all the ways he'd transformed in such a short time. She marveled at his courage.

I'm so glad I'm here.

Quietly, she closed the door behind her and tiptoed into the darkness, and there on the stage, above the silhouettes of six-hundred-some heads, she saw Luke in the spotlight at a podium, his familiar voice booming through the room as he began a general welcome and thank-you to the conference leaders.

His red tie. She beamed when she saw it. She was the only one who knew there were at least two elephants in the room. Elephant one: Luke was terrified to be up there. She wondered if knowing she was here would make him more or less nervous. Elephant two: the VP of Dalton Oil was becoming increasingly environmentally minded.

Though Luke was charming, he did seem nervous. His usual, smooth voice had a bit of a hitch in it. In fact, was he…was he stuttering? He was, just a little, and Ashley remembered what Rena had told her about his childhood stutter and how she had helped him move past it. But it seemed likely that in highly stressful situations, it would return. *No wonder Luke doesn't like public speaking.* The realization clicked into place. And of course, he was nervous. Luke, the president of the board for an environmental activism nonprofit, was about to tell this room the real future of oil.

She took a seat behind a tall man, just in case there was any chance Luke could see into the audience. She didn't want to risk throwing him off.

She scanned the stage and saw Energy Secretary Gerald Regis on the panel. Her stomach churned, the way it had when she'd seen him at Luke's parents' party. Luke had to work with lying sleazeballs like this guy, but Luke was so charismatic that apparently *everyone*, even lying sleazeballs, listened to him.

"We have exciting news," Luke was saying, his voice measured and slow, as if he were concentrating on getting each syllable correct. "So, as many of you know, d-drilling in the Arctic has been highly contentious, and plans for exploration and drilling have been dropped d-due to international arguments about these important sites."

There was a collective groan in the crowd. *Wow, these are not my people.*

"B-but now for the good news."

The small stutter made Ashley's heart flood with compassion for her brave oil man. *Come on, Luke, you can get it out. You can do this. Yes, like there are so many other ways to provide energy besides endangering an entire ecosystem.*

"My friends in the renewable sector—"

Yes!

"—and I have been proposing new ways to excavate oil from the Arctic—"

Mm-hmm.

"And we would like to announce we have pulled the permits to begin d-deep drilling—"

A deep shudder of repulsion ran through her.

"—that will offer D-Dalton Oil a semi-exclusive opportunity to access about a billion barrels in the Arctic over the next few years—"

No. The fucker. No! How could he do this?

"—thanks in part to Energy Secretary Gerald Regis." Luke looked very uncomfortable, despite the cheering of the crowd.

Ashley stopped hearing the words he was saying, a sob rising in her, a tide of anger unlike anything she'd felt before. Something stronger than disappointment. Betrayal. *How could he?* How could he do this to *her*? How could he do this to the *planet*? How could this man, who last night kissed her so passionately, who entered her body with his lips and hands and cock, this man who knew such tenderness, such compassion, such benevolence, how could he possibly be the same man now up there talking about raping the Arctic?

Hot tears spilled down her cheeks. *This* was the man she thought she loved? *This man* who was defiling the last great unprotected wilderness, this refuge for endangered species and home to indigenous people whose subsistence lifestyle had existed harmoniously with nature for thousands of years?

"—so many of you are excited about the chance to be involved, and we will be releasing information for bidding opportunities."

Ashley couldn't hear any more. The sound of his voice, that voice that made butterflies come alive in her blood, now sent icy chills down her spine. Bile rose in her throat, and she gagged to keep it down.

Ashley escaped the meeting hall and ran for the women's room, then stood, dry heaving over the toilet, her stomach trying to do what the heart could not. *Get him out. Get him out of me.*

"Madam, are you okay?" came a concerned voice from the stall beside her.

"Yes," Ashley croaked.

No. She was not okay. Nothing was okay.

Ashley couldn't type fast enough. She'd already written to friends at the World Wildlife Foundation, the Ocean Conservancy, and the Alaska Wilderness League to alert them to the news. *Galvanize, galvanize.* They had to come together, and fast. *When they throw fuel on the fire, we put the fire out.* She dashed off a strongly worded email to the governor of Alaska. *You* will *help*, she thought and pressed Send.

She let out a wildlife-refuge-sized sigh. This hotel suite that had brought her so much joy the last few days now felt like ground zero. *This fight about Arctic drilling was supposed to have been put to bed*. And who revived it from the dead? Luke. *Luke!* Just like his father before him.

Ashley put her head in her hands and shook it slowly. The pounding in her head was worse than her migraines—a pain brought on by stress, anger, fear, disgust.

She startled at the ring of the phone. Let it ring. Let it goddamn ring. *I am so not ready for you, and you are so not ready for me.* She blew out a breath so angry she imagined it could singe the desk.

Next step, next step. She called up her mental checklist. A note to Change.org to set up a petition. She opened a new email and began to write.

Five minutes later, she heard the suite door open. "Ashley?" Luke's exuberant greeting rang giddy through the suite.

I so do not want to see you.

"Ashley! There you are! I've been calling you, darlin'. It's our last night in London, and we are going to celebrate." With a lustful, sexy growl, Luke came over to the desk where she sat, her back still turned to him.

Don't you touch me. He nuzzled his face into her hair and slipped his hands under her arms to lift her to him, but she stiffened her whole body and willed it to become lead.

"Ashley? Everything okay?"

He came around to see her face and recoiled a bit at her furious expression. She felt wolverine-ish, willing and eager to take on something much bigger than herself. Her eyes flared.

"Whoa, okay, everything's *not* okay. Talk to me." When she said nothing, he cocked his head, then looked at the screen. "A petition to stop Dalton Oil from drilling in the Arctic," he read out loud. "I see."

He moved back and sat on the couch, composed, watching her.

"I was there, Luke," she spat. "I was there. I snuck into the conference to support you, and I heard what you told that room. I heard what Dalton Oil is preparing to do."

Luke didn't say anything. He studied her carefully, calmly.

"How could you? The Arctic, Luke? Think of all the damage."

"There is more to this story than you know, Ashley."

"You think I care about profit at the cost of life, animals, our air, land, water, our planet!" she hissed.

"Of course, we will take extreme caution, Ashley, and use the most advanced safety technology in the world to minimize those environmental costs." He moved his face to look her in the eye. She watched as a strange emotion passed over his face. As if he were maybe trying to convince not only her but himself. "But the opportunities I thought might excite you are for *research*. This project brings with it opportunities to gather data on the Arctic ecosystem—we'll do studies that actually *aid* in conservation, that add to our present knowledge. We have hired the best scientists in the world to—"

"Don't you dare try to frame drilling for a billion barrels of oil as *scientific discovery*."

"Listen."

"No, *you* listen. You are toying with a carbon bomb that could, no, *will* eventually spray *tons* of carbon dioxide into the atmosphere, will pollute the land and water with chemicals. And the problems with Arctic drilling go *way* beyond the immediate damage done to the habitat teeming with life—the seals, the Arctic fox, the caribou. We are talking about irreversible long-term damage to the whole planet." Her voice was rising, and she knew this was no way to reason with someone, but she was beyond reason. "The only way drilling is even *possible* now in the Arctic is because of climate change—climate change due to carbon emissions from fossil fuels that melt the ice and make the oil reserves more accessible. But accessible at what cost, Luke? At what cost?"

She realized she was clenching her fists and forced her hands to open.

Luke's voice was quiet and regulated. "Even wind and solar have costs, Ashley. Birds die in windmills—that's not perfected, either. With great advancement comes great mistakes. Fossil fuels are still at the heart of the way our society advances, and because we know there are problems with it, we are constantly improving our standards. In the Arctic, there are even new methods to dull the sound in the water so we can protect marine life."

"Don't you dare pretend that you are thinking about the best interests of the animals, Luke." Images of sea otters covered in oil leapt into her mind.

"Ashley, we're committed to positive change, but corporations can't just pivot on a dime into kumbaya."

She reared up. "But you *can* make positive change! Real change, Luke. *You* have the power to turn the tide. Starting *now*."

"I wish it were that simple. And I understand you're upset—"

"Yes, I'm upset! I'm so fucking upset with Dalton Oil. I'm so fucking upset with *you*!" She was screaming now. "I had full confidence in you. I believed you knew better, believed you were becoming more conscious and would act accordingly! I thought you were changing!"

And there it was. *Wow*. She wasn't just angry because of the drilling, the destruction, the damage. She was angry because she had hoped, no, she had *believed she could change him*. She shuddered with how completely she'd fooled herself. *I really thought it was happening. I really thought I changed him.*

She had thought she could lay it all out like a chemical equation: Two reactants, add heat, and *bam*, change. It should have balanced. It should have produced a man who understood the advantages of renewable energy, a man who had the power and authority to turn the industry around, a man who could use his family-owned company to move forward in the best interest of the planet.

But that's not how it worked out.

She *really thought* she could teach him to find the *right answer*. Thought that he, faced with facts, would clearly see how to best proceed in the long-term interest of the Earth. She'd given herself so much credit for opening his eyes to the alternative energy world. *What a crazy idealist joke. Fucking cognitive dissonance.*

Epiphany winged in like a turkey vulture, a big fat black turkey vulture with a scaly red featherless head, and it sat on the fence of her righteousness, rasping and hissing. *Would you change?* it seemed to ask her.

No. There would never be a day she would think Arctic drilling was okay.

Shit. She was the one who'd fucked up. *She* was the one who had assumed his career and his family and his convictions were changeable. Here she was, feeling betrayed by Luke, but really, he was only acting true to his nature. He was like the scorpion who stings—not out of a desire to hurt but because that is what scorpions do.

Of course he was planning to drill in the Arctic. That's what oil men do. He had never pretended he was anything else. She knew all along what his work was. She knew what he'd learned from his father. What an idiot she had been to fall in love with him. What a recipe for pain.

"What was I thinking?" she muttered, holding her head in her hands. The world was spinning. She wanted to lie on the floor.

"Sweetness—"

"Don't call me that." She spoke softly. The man she thought she loved was exactly that...the man she *thought*. He bore only a physical resemblance to the man he actually was.

"Ashley—"

"Don't say anything. There's nothing you can say. I need to be alone."

He stared at her, his face inscrutable.

"Now. I need to be alone *now*. Please."

Luke said nothing for a long time. The silence stretched thin as cellophane until it became brittle, broke.

"Okay." Luke stood. "Space is what you need. I understand. I have needed space before, too." He got up and walked to the door. She heard it open but didn't watch. "We'll work this out, Ashley."

No, we fucking won't.

And he left.

Ashley stayed on the edge of the bed that night. She didn't want to touch him or be touched. But she didn't sleep. And Luke never came back. Not until six minutes before the limo arrived to take them to Heathrow Airport. He packed. She'd packed. They left in the dark.

CHAPTER 27

L UKE PULLED HIS CHEVY UP to Ashley's apartment. He turned the engine off instead of letting it idle. Ashley gave a weak smile. She knew he'd done it to please her. She'd once lectured him how just fifteen minutes of idling released a pound of carbon dioxide into the air.

No wonder I thought he was changing. In small ways, he was. *But not the ways that count the most.*

They had barely spoken on the plane. She'd pretended she was asleep the whole trip. Twice Luke had touched her gently. Twice she'd shrugged off his hand.

Now, sitting in the car, she felt as if they were sitting in a fog—the kind that feels oppressive, thick, unrelenting. It made it hard to move, hard to speak. Just a week ago, when he'd picked her up, she'd felt so alive, so bright. Now she was steeped in sorrow.

At the same time, they both said, "I'm sorry."

"Huh," she laughed feebly.

"Look, Ashley," Luke said. "I know this is about my work. But it feels as if this is about me."

"You don't get it, do you?"

"No."

"You really think you're separate from your work?"

"Yeah, I do. My work has nothing to do with us."

"I don't know how you do that. I'm a teacher, Luke. I'm a teacher through and through, even when I'm not in the classroom. I really thought I could teach *you*. I really thought I could *change* you. But I thought wrong. In the end, I'm the one holding the protest sign, you're the one holding the drill. We're just too different."

"What are you saying?"

"I'm saying goodbye, Luke."

"No," he said. "No. What about everything you said in my apartment about believing in *us*? What about 'Let's get beyond this together.' What about carrying hope with you?"

"My sister once said I am a woman of conviction, not compromise." She dropped her head and rubbed her brow. "I think I've been fooling myself all along. I haven't been falling in love with *you*— I've been falling in love with the version of you I wanted you to be." Luke flinched. "I don't believe it."

"Savannah understands you. She was right. I don't belong with you or your family. But she does. She's probably celebrating Arctic drilling, too."

"Stop, Ashley. I don't want Savannah. I want *you*."

"Maybe the world is testing me, asking me to make a choice. But at least one person needs to stand up for the Earth. And it will always be me."

"You don't have to choose, Ashley. Not only, but also."

Ashley felt her heart breaking.

"I can't fight you and be with you at the same time, Luke."

"Please. Don't do this."

"I need to go." She leaned forward to pick up her purse. "Oh. I forgot. Something for you." She handed him a small present wrapped in turquoise tissue paper.

He held it in his palm, feeling its weight.

"Open it."

He tore the tissue to reveal the small crystal monkey she'd bought in London. Instantly, tears formed in his eyes.

"For your collection. I wanted it to be a happy memory."

Luke looked haunted. Hollow. He stared at the monkey in his hand, then placed his other hand over it, cradling it lightly. He bowed his head.

"My brother's nickname was Monkey."

Her breath stopped. "Oh, Luke. I didn't know."

"I know."

She longed to comfort him, but that didn't feel right. Not comforting him didn't feel right, either.

In this moment of shadow, she couldn't imagine a time in the future when things would ever feel right again.

———

"You look tired. Let me make you some tea, Ashling."

Ashley sat on her mom's sofa, staring at the place her mom had just been sitting, focusing and unfocusing her eyes on a torn spot in the upholstery.

Yeah, that was how she felt. As if she'd been torn and her stuffing was coming out and she had no energy to stuff it back in.

"Here, sweetheart." Her mom handed her a memory from her childhood, her favorite blue mug filled with mint and licorice tea. The sweet and sharp scent smelled familiar, like home. "It's more than jet lag, isn't it?"

Ashley nodded. She'd told herself she was coming over to check on her mom, but it was becoming increasingly clear she wanted her mother to help ease her pain.

"I was sure I could change him, Mom."

"Oh, honey, that's what we women are inclined to want to do. Men typically figure they get what they see, but women, we think we can change men."

"I can't believe I was such an idiot. We are totally incompatible."

"Perhaps."

"What do you mean, *perhaps*? Why are you looking at me like that?"

"Well, you aren't *totally* incompatible. Clearly, there are parts of you that are exceptionally compatible."

Ashley glared at her.

Her mother nodded. "Okay. You're totally incompatible."

Ashley knew what her mother was doing, echoing Ashley's own words. It was a motivational interviewing technique she'd learned herself at an in-service. How did her mom do this stuff intuitively? "Yes! We are *totally* incompatible!"

Her mother nodded. "Totally."

Infuriating. "Okay, not totally incompatible, but—oh, I don't know."

Ashley's mom smiled at her and shook her head. "'I don't know' is probably the truest place to be, Ashley. The most dangerous thought we have is the one we're unable to question."

Ashley sipped her tea, so warm and sweet. She closed her eyes to keep herself from rolling them. Who cared if her mother was right? She didn't want to hear anything now besides, "Having a broken heart sucks."

"Having a broken heart is hard, Ashling."

Did Mom really just say that? Ashley opened her eyes and looked at her mother suspiciously.

Her mom sipped tea and stared off as if wondering how to phrase the next sentence. Finally, she said, "Every relationship requires us to let go of our opinions in some way."

"What happened with you and Dad?"

She felt her mother stiffen beside her. "There are certain deal breakers, Ashley."

Ashley knew better than to ask any more.

"Is Luke an addict?"

"No."

"Does he cheat on you?"

"No."

"Does he physically hurt you?"

"No."

Her mom's face relaxed. "Good. Well, then love is an invitation for us to see beyond our own convictions, to learn to build bridges, to explore how the different values of other people can help us grow."

"He's drilling deep in the Arctic, Mom."

"I know how much you care, my love, for the world. It's almost as much as I care for you. You are strong, darling. You have grown into a wonderful woman with beautiful ideals and a big, generous heart. You can trust your heart."

Ashley nodded.

Her mom added, "Trust it *more* than your head."

Ashley almost scoffed. "Whose side are you on?"

Her mom softened her expression, sipped her tea. "Does he really see you?"

"He does."

"Does he make you a priority?"

"Yeah."

"Does he immerse himself in your life?"

"Yes."

"Does he show you your happiness is important to him?"

"Well, yes? I don't know. I think so? I mean, no. He's drilling in the Arctic."

Her mom's eyes twinkled. "Does he buy flowers for your mother?"

"Is *that* why you're going to bat for him?"

Her mom looked off again, a bit dreamy-eyed, and for a moment, it was the kind of silence that had a fragrance, like rosemary, floral and sharp.

"Once, there was a man, Ashley, not your father, who I believe loved me the way I see Luke loves you. And I made my choices for my reasons." She smiled in a far-off way before returning to the moment and looking straight into Ashley's dazed eyes. Her voice was low and clear. "I can't give you any answers about what to do with Luke, but I can help you ask some important questions."

Mom had a lover? Had she given him up for her and Jewel? As much as she wanted to pry, Ashley knew it would be futile.

"You will be wrestled by your certainties, Ashling. I know it isn't easy. Now, enough. Let's talk about what comes next for your STEAMEA."

And just like that, the world went on spinning.

Ashley's phone buzzed in her pocket. A text: *Protesting Dalton next Tuesday in downtown Houston.*

Ashley nodded to herself. *I'll be there.*

"Hey, Emilia?" Ashley looked up at her mentee. They were meeting at Lift House, going over work Ashley had asked her to do while she'd been in Europe. "There's nothing on this sheet."

Emilia barely looked up. She was slouched, so her hair fell in her face and covered her eyes.

"*Emilia?*"

The girl shrugged.

"You were so excited and said you'd have these tasks finished, and you haven't even started them."

Emilia looked up through dark bangs. "Sorry."

"Anything you want to tell me?"

"No."

"Okay."

"I'll do better, Ashley."

Ashley gave her an encouraging smile. "I know you will. Look, we'll figure it out together and get it done. I'll just go use the restroom first." Ashley stood.

"Thank you." Emilia sounded relieved but still seemed on edge.

"I'll be right back." Ashley walked down the hall and winced at the rapid onset of a strong headache. *Shit.* She turned back around to grab some Advil from her purse.

"What the—?"

Emilia had opened Ashley's billfold and was pulling out two twenties. The girl looked up, horrified.

"What's going on?"

"I'm sorry." Emilia was on the verge of tears, still clutching the twenties.

Ashley's voice was stern. "Sorry is not good enough, friend. You could have asked me for money. But you *stole* it. From *me*, Emilia?"

Emilia put the money on the table.

"What's going on?"

"I'm using."

Ashley sighed. "Oh, friend. You need help."

Emilia didn't say a word; she just stared at Ashley, ashamed, scared.

"It's not worth a criminal record, so I'm not turning you in."

"Don't fire me, Ashley. I need—"

"You need help getting clean. I'm taking you to rehab. We can talk about the job when you get out. I have made mistakes, too, Emilia. They can be our best teachers. And everything you learn now will someday make you a better teacher."

Emilia put her head on the table. She looked spent. Her back shuddered as she silently sobbed.

Ashley put her fingers to her temples and felt the headache's talons start to tear into her. Could anything else go wrong? She felt the impulse to call Luke and tell him about it. *No. Learn from your mistakes, Barris. They are your best teachers.*

Jewel: Where the hell are U?

Ashley: Headache. Home in bed in dark last two days

Jewel: U OK?

Ashley: Better

Jewel: [thumbs-up]

Ashley: Luke is sending links to songs every day

Jewel: ??

Ashley: Whatever It Takes by Lifehouse
           Never Really Over by Katy Perry

Jewel: OMG!!! How long has it been?

Ashley: Almost a week

Jewel: RU going to put him out of his misery?

Ashley: ??

Jewel: Get over it. It's just fossil fuel. Call him

Ashley: No

Jewel: Still taking him to the gala?

Ashley: No

Jewel: How did he react when you told him he's not going?
           Ashley: Didn't tell him yet

Jewel: So who RU taking?

Ashley: You

Jewel: Ha!

Ashley: Please?

Jewel: I have a hot date Saturday
Maybe ask John?

Jewel: He is hot and nice to U

Jewel: Hello??????

Jewel: Jesus, Ash. Get back on the horse

Pretend everything is fine, Ashley instructed herself. She sat at her small kitchen table, drinking coffee. But she was not fine—she felt sick to her stomach. Why was heartbreak so like the flu? Everything ached. Now that shock and anger had run through her system, she was left with sorrow. She wrapped it around her like a quilt. *How could I have fallen so deeply in love with someone so wrong for me?*

She took a sip of coffee and remembered how Luke made coffee for her just the way she liked it. The familiar taste turned bitter in her mouth, and she swallowed hard, tears prickling in her eyes.

She covered her face with her hands as if to block out the world, but there in her private darkness was the image of Luke's face, laughing as they walked Pancake and King Kong and Bunny. Then Luke with tears streaming down his temples after they made love in Memorial Park. Then Luke in his car outside her apartment, the crystal monkey in his hand.

Why did I have to fall in love with you?

Her heart beat dully in her chest, like someone banging on a locked door for hours, wishing that act alone would make the door open.

Jewel was wrong. It wasn't "*just* fossil fuel." *That* kind of thinking was devastating the planet, melting the glaciers, destroying the ozone, killing fish, and infecting the soil and sea with poison. *That* thinking was how a powerful few played loose with the future for everyone. She could not stand by and let it happen.

She looked around her room. Everything was made with fossil fuels—the table, the slippers on her feet, the books on her table, the plastic recycle bin. She was part of the problem, too. But she so desperately wanted to be part of the solution. *Change starts somewhere.*

She found herself staring at the counter, counting the empty spaces where the white candles Luke had given her had been. *One. Two. Three. Four. Five.* She'd put them in a bag by the door, along with other things he'd given her. It was too painful to look at reminders of him.

The irony: she couldn't unsee the candles even in their absence. And she couldn't unlove the man in his absence, either. All her cells had opened to welcome him in—and now he was in her, inseparable, though she was trying to get him out. It was as if they had both been elements in a chemical reaction, and now her makeup was changed, and she could never return to her original elemental state. Self-pity and anguish rose up and consumed her like stubborn flames.

Surely, her heart would heal. Even uranium has a half-life, albeit four and a half billion years.

She took another sip of coffee and choked on it as it slid down. It tasted like unquenchable thirst, like hopelessness.

———

Luke: [link] Jason Mraz: "I Won't Give Up"

Ashley clicked on the link and listened to the song, sighing at its soulful, haunting insistence on possibility. She had to stop listening to these song links he was texting her. There was no use fueling the longing she was trying so hard to douse.

She had already decided the best way to respond to Luke about the songs was to pretend she hadn't received them. But they tugged at her. They reminded her of the man she thought Luke was, the man she wanted him to be—thoughtful, funny, romantic, creative, attentive. The man she just couldn't reconcile with the planet killer she had seen at the oil conference.

Disgusted with herself, she decided to settle some unfinished business.

It took her eighteen minutes and thirty-six attempts to text him a very short message.

Ashley: Hi Luke. Just wanted to be clear I no longer need you to accompany me to the gala

Within seconds, she felt her phone vibrate.

Luke: I wouldn't miss it

She sighed and raked both hands through her hair. The phone vibrated again.

Luke: [link] Mariah Carey: "We Belong Together"

Without hesitating, she deleted the message and felt the small wall she was building around her heart go up another inch. *Enough of this wallowing.* Her head admonished her heart. *Cut this off now. Be clear so you can move on.*

She picked up the phone and typed fast so her heart couldn't find a foothold.

Ashley: I mean it. Plans canceled

———

"Um, hi. John?"

"Ashley! To what do I owe this call?"

"I have to go to a formal gala this weekend for Lift House, and I could go alone, but I have an extra ticket, so I—"

"—thought you'd ask your ex-boss?" he teased.

"Thought I'd ask a friend."

"Why not take Luke?"

"We're, um, having issues."

"Mmm. My luck. When?"

"Saturday."

"When do I pick you up?" She could hear his grin, and her own lip curled up half-heartedly.

"6:10. No later."

"Great. I'll be there at 6:09 so I can knock on the door at just the right second." He was clearly delighting in teasing her about her punctual tendencies.

Ashley knew she was supposed to laugh, but she felt too serious. She managed a lumpy chuckle. "6:10 is good."

"I'm going to start preening now so I can sweep you off your beautiful feet. See you then, Ashley."

"Holy shit, Ashster, what the hell happened here?"

"Give me a break, Jewel."

"No, really, what happened? I've never seen your apartment like this. Even when we were girls, not so much as a pen out of place. And look at this *sty*! Even by *my* standards—" Jewel gestured dramatically.

Unwashed dishes in the sink. Clothes on the floor. Dishes on the table. Unfolded laundry on the couch. Her washing machine was broken, anyway—just like her heart.

"I figured something was up when you canceled our Tuesday night dinner tonight, but this? You are a hurting puppy."

Ashley was embarrassed. She knew she was not doing well. Since saying goodbye to Luke last week, she'd been unable to care about anything. She'd even missed the protest in front of Dalton. She just couldn't get herself to go out.

"Never fear. Super Jewel to the rescue." She produced a white paper shopping bag and set it on the counter. "Come on, sis. You need a little medicine, and I've got what you need. Open it."

"What are you up to?"

"Open it."

Ashley reached into the bag and pulled out a large box. Her eyes widened. "Jewel!" she giggled.

Jewel joined in the laughter. "Thought you might need a little *release* tonight, sister." She pumped her hips. "Soooo, this one is flexible and has an extension for your clit. This one is rock hard with five settings. And this one has a tilt, and it heats up and vibrates."

"Jesus, Jewel." Ashley couldn't stop laughing. It felt so good to laugh. Who else would buy her a bouquet of dildos?

Jewel was clearly delighted with Ashley's response. One by one, she pulled them out of the box and balanced them on the counter, like three stately obelisks. "I think we should name them Luke, Dick, and Harry. Now, you tell me, which one is Luke?"

"Jewel."

"Really, you tell me." She picked up the middle one. "This one is like the hot older guy I'm dating right now. I really like him." She air licked the shaft. "He's got a dick that won't stop rocking, *hard* like this one. And he treats me really well and takes me to nice places. I'm telling you, Ashley. Your problem right now? Too much sexual tension. You need to burn up all that pent-up energy. Have some orgasms." She flopped the dildo in her sister's direction and started shaking it at her. "Get my point?"

"Stop it."

"No, *start* it." Jewel pointed toward the power button on the long five-speed dildo and went to switch it on.

"Jewel, *stop*!" Ashley grabbed the end of the dildo and tugged it to get it out of her sister's hands.

"Ashley, *start*!" Jewel mocked her and tugged back.

"Ohmygod! Stop!" The sisters yanked and pulled on the sex toy in a bizarre and lighthearted tug-of-war, howling with laughter, struggling to pull it from the other's hands until they were snorting and gasping for breath, tears running down their faces.

"*There's* my sister," Jewel chirped at last, relinquishing her hold. "I *knew* you were hiding her in there somewhere—my sister, the woman who won't give up."

Ashley shook her head, a smile stuck on her face like popped bubble gum—nothing she could do to get it off. "Jewel, what would I do without you?"

"Mope, obviously."

"Goofball. I love you so much."

"Damn straight."

CHAPTER 28

S HE CHOSE HARRY. IT FELT good, but every time Ashley closed her eyes, she imagined it was Luke rocking into her. And she'd flutter her eyes open and try to shake his image. Though she found a rhythm, her hips rose more out of habit than passion, and the orgasm kept eluding her. When she finally came, it was like a tiny blue violet instead of an extravagant red poppy. The room was unsettled by its own emptiness, as if its one inhabitant didn't count.

That night, she'd never been more aware that you can't see stars in Houston. What would she have wished for, anyway? Eventually, her eyes closed, and a dreamless sleep came.

Ashley forced herself to go for a walk. It had done her good to get out of her apartment, but letting herself back in, she saw a notice on the kitchen counter.

Right beside the balancing dildos.

She picked up the notice. *Best Appliance Service.*

Oh yeah. The washing machine repair.

Ashley imagined some guy coming in, snickering as he left the note right beside the sex toys. What was he thinking now? *Ew.* Why had she been so lazy? Why didn't she remember he was coming today?

She picked up the brief notice and read it:

We were in your apartment. Washing machine
repair complete.
                        —*Stephanie Sandoval*

Wait, the repairman was a woman? Ashley was so appalled
by her sexist assumption it gave her the giggles. *Stephanie the*
plumber? She laughed until tears were streaming down her face.
Hallelujah for Stephanie the plumber! She laughed till she fell
on the floor, and Bamba climbed on top of her. Stephanie was
probably laughing right now, too, thinking about the apartment with the dildo installation on the counter. The laughter
felt good, as if a week's worth of sorrow was washing away like
caked mud coming off in a hard rain.

She poured herself a glass of wine and went to sit on the
sofa in the living room, pushing her laptop and books to the
side. Of course, the sofa made her think of Luke, the way she'd
kneeled on the cushions and he'd taken her from behind, how
she'd shouted for him, choruses of ecstatic yesses. It was as if her
passionate gasps were tattooed in the air. She missed him. *A lot.*
"Oh, Luke," she sighed. "I wish it could be different." And she
raised her glass toward his apartment downtown. And just like
that, she was crying.

What a roller coaster.

Today, Luke had texted her "Better Together" by Jack John-
son. And though she'd deleted it right away, she'd been singing
scraps of the lighthearted song all afternoon.

She had to hand it to him. He'd found a way to let her know
he was still thinking of her that was sweet but not overly intru-
sive. And as much as she didn't want to receive the love songs,
she realized she did. He hadn't texted the link until late in the
afternoon. And about half an hour before he sent it, when she

thought he wasn't going to send her one today, part of her was downright sad. Pissy even.

Oh, the surge of oxytocin when the text came in! And then she'd deleted it without listening.

She was a contrary disaster. Her heart and head had never been so at odds.

She deleted all photos of him off her phone. Now she regretted it. She wanted to see his face. He couldn't really be as handsome as she remembered.

"Okay," she sighed in surrender. She picked up her laptop and typed *Luke Dalton* into Google Images.

And there he was, staring at her through the screen, with a five-o'clock shadow, full lips, straight nose, and wide, soul-seeking eyes looking right into hers. Damn. She wasn't ready for the physical response, a fluttering in her low belly, a quick intake of breath, the rapid drumroll of her heart. Luke was impossibly *more* handsome than she remembered.

There were professional pictures of him for Dalton's website. A few from galas and ribbon-cutting ceremonies. Several showed him wearing tuxes at events with Savannah. Ashley studied those until the pain was unbearable—examined every detail about how they stood, where their hands were on each other, the looks on their faces. It was torture.

And then, after scrolling through pages and pages of images of Luke, she was drawn to a headline from decades ago: "No Charges in Accidental Shooting that Kills Twelve-Year-Old Boy."

Luke had told her about it, of course, but now, seeing it in a headline, the story came to life again. *That man has been through hell.*

In print, it was just a story, a bad story. *Ten-Year-Old Boy Finds Dad's Gun, Accidentally Shoots Brother. Brother Dies.*

She shuddered. *Poor Luke.*

Ashley looked into the eyes of a more recent picture. She stared at it, thinking of all he had been through.

"I'm sorry, Luke. I'm sorry for everything you've had to endure."

He stared back at her, his expression open, engaged.

She touched his face on the screen. "I wish things were different."

It was the understatement of her life.

Ashley looked at herself one more time in the mirror. For the first time in almost two weeks, she felt pretty. Funny how putting on a dress and makeup and doing her hair helped pick up her mood. Plus, she was genuinely excited about tonight.

Her apartment was almost spotless again. She'd spent the day cleaning and straightening, and the uncluttered countertops and sparkling floors helped her attitude, too.

She'd put on her favorite playlist, "More Cowbell," and was singing along to Howard Jones' "Things Can Only Get Better" when she heard the knock on the door.

Six ten, sharp. She smiled.

"Hi, Ashley, you look beautiful," John said from behind a giant bouquet of flowers.

"You can't even see me," she teased. He lowered the bouquet until his brown eyes appeared over a mound of hydrangea, lilies, and delphiniums, and they raked over her in a slow and sexy appraisal.

"But I wasn't wrong." His tone was seductive and sincere.

Ashley blushed. John looked gorgeous. He had a new hairstyle, a lock of blond hair falling across his forehead. He looked stunning in his tailored tux and black tie. And there was something else about him—a sensual rawness. It made her feel tremulant.

"Um, here. Let's bring in that big bouquet." She stepped aside for him to enter.

John walked in and set the flowers on the kitchen counter. Impulsively, Ashley threw her arms around him and hugged him, surprising them both. She stepped back quickly. "Thank you for the flowers. And for being my date."

"You're welcome." John didn't try to hide his cat-that-ate-the-canary smile.

"Let me, ah, find a vase." The only vase even close to big enough was one from Luke that she had put in a bag by the door to go to the secondhand store. It felt weird pulling it out and using it for a bouquet from John. But she did.

These must have cost a fortune, she thought as she arranged the flowers. A bouquet this size was an extravagant expense for anyone, especially someone with a principal's salary—probably a whole day's work. As she repositioned a hydrangea, she thought she heard John murmur something about lifting up her skirt a bit.

Ashley felt her pulse flutter. It was not at all like John to be so direct. "Excuse me, what?"

"I'm just singing along. *Crash into me.*"

Ashley shot him a quizzical look, then realized Dave Matthews was singing in the background. Feeling slightly off-balance, she found her phone and turned the soundtrack off.

"Okay, big boy," she looked at him sternly. "We're leaving."

What an interesting night this was turning out to be.

CHAPTER 29

"WHAT ARE YOU HUMMING?" John asked.

"Oh, nothing." It was Willie Nelson's version of "You Were Always on My Mind." That had been Luke's text today. She had blocked his number after that, realizing how the daily songs were keeping her hooked into him when what she needed was to let him go. And the irony? Right after she'd blocked him, she'd looked up the song and had been humming it ever since.

"It sounds nice."

"You're the only one who's ever said that, John. It's a well-known fact I can't sing." *Now, stop humming that song, Barris.* But it was true. Luke was on her mind. *Always.*

They stopped in front of a large artistic rendering of a monarch wing. "Give Them Wings" was the theme of the Lift House gala, and the décor included large-scale images of various butterfly wings.

"Smile," prompted the photographer.

"Let's make it like a prom photo," John whispered in Ashley's ear. God knew they'd chaperoned enough proms to know *that* trope. They held each other in a stiff, awkward embrace, making nervous, cheesy smiles for the camera. The photographer guffawed along but then made them take a sincere photo, too, before they walked off to the silent auction room.

As they maneuvered through hundreds of Houston's glitterati dressed in frothy silk and dazzling sequins, Ashley explained she'd donated ten Spanish lessons. When they found her list, four people had already bid on it. Ashley was pleased. She didn't have much money to give the organization, but her time was something she could give.

"*Amo tu gran corazón,*"* John said to her in his fluent Spanish, noting her pleased look. "Hey, let's get a drink and sit down at our table."

Their table was close to the stage. John pulled out Ashley's chair for her to sit. She gave him a big smile and noticed the calming effect it had on her nervous system.

John smiled broadly back. *Mirror reflex,* she thought.

"Ashley," he murmured, leaning closer in.

"John—"

"I need to confess something."

"Okay."

"You remember when that big bouquet came to school for you near the end of the year?"

"Yeah."

"I took the note card."

Ashley stared at him, stunned.

"I took it when I saw the flowers in the office, and I delivered them myself when I knew you were out of the room."

"You—"

He winced. "I'm sorry. I'm not proud of what I did. It was irrational, and I regretted it later. Sort of. It's just...I realized I wanted to be the one sending you flowers."

"Oh!" Ashley blinked and pressed a hand to her lips.

"I hope you're not mad."

"Not mad, John, just, um, surprised."

---

*I love your big heart.

"It surprised me, too. Not the being attracted to you part. That's hardly surprising—you're amazing. But the part about taking the tag—it was out of character."

"It doesn't sound like the John I know."

"It was a wake-up call for me. Look, I don't want to jeopardize our friendship, and I realize my confession might have already done some damage, but I'm hoping it's in service of a greater good. Let's just say that since you asked me to join you tonight, I haven't been able to stop thinking about what it might look like if we were more than friends. Back in May, I tried to not let my thoughts go there before because I knew it wasn't possible, but now that we're not working together, and now that you're not seeing someone else, I wonder what could happen between us, Ashley. And it seemed like honesty is the best place to start."

"First of all, I absolve you, John." She rubbed her thumb on his forehead the way she imagined a priest might do.

"Thank you." He grinned. "I've been feeling guilty for months."

"And second of all, I—"

Ashley couldn't speak. It was as if her thoughts were slogging in slow motion through a marsh. She had to be very careful with her words. John was in a tender place, and so was she. She'd be lying if she said she wasn't attracted to John. He was smart, thoughtful, generous. They shared a passion for education and the environment. He was handsome, they laughed so much together, and she *liked* him. But her heart was so thoroughly rocked right now by Luke she could barely process what he was saying.

"You don't have to say anything now. Take all the space and time you need to think about it. I understand you're in a delicate place, and the last thing I want is to be a rebound when I believe there's a chance for something real, something beautiful, something lasting between us."

"John, I—" Ashley felt the strong presence of someone standing beside her. All the hairs on her neck stood up, tiny needles all pointing to true north.

"Luke!"

John startled when she said the other man's name, and then he looked at Luke with surprise and...competitiveness? *Holy shit.* Ashley had never seen such a look on John's face. Like a boxer in a ring who had just delivered a knockout punch to his opponent. And Luke's face? He looked as if he'd just been told they were amputating both of his legs.

How long had Luke been listening? Judging from his face, long enough to hear about something "real, beautiful, and lasting" between her and John.

"Luke." Ashley rose to shake his hand. *Thank god for formalities.* "What a surprise." *More like a wallop.* Just seeing him, her whole body flared with unreasonable hope. The scent of Luke made her dizzy. And when their hands touched, twin waves of longing and loss surged through her body, battering against the walls of her heart with a crashing *please, please, please.* What did the please even mean? *Please leave? Please take me in your arms?* She ironed her voice into a greeting of casual interest. "What are you doing here?"

"I purchased a table to support your cause. But I see I'm interrupting. Excuse me."

Ashley stared at Luke's retreating back, aware John was watching her. But she couldn't stop herself from watching Luke leave. She could tell from his gait he was wounded. A flood of protectiveness rose in her—the urge to protect his heart *from her.* What a strange feeling. She sank back into her chair and took a sip of her drink, avoiding John's eyes.

"I feel for him," John murmured, putting his hand on her knee. "But I am glad to interpret you are the one who ended it with him, yes? I wondered, of course."

There was an announcement that it was time for gala attendees to be seated.

"Excuse me," she said, touching John lightly on the shoulder. "I need to freshen up quickly." She restrained herself from running and walked slowly to the hall, where she pressed her back against a wall and let it hold her up. She took a few deep breaths, fighting down tears of frustration.

Damn him. Just seeing Luke for a moment brought back an oceanic upswell of emotion, a riptide of longing, a current she could not read or understand or ignore. And after he walked away, it was like standing bereft on a deserted island, terribly alone and starving.

Oh, Luke. With her every cell saying yes to him, it was almost impossible to remember her no. But she flashed on the oil conference stage—the feeling she'd had when she'd seen him there in his red tie, the betrayal she'd felt when he spoke of the drilling, the repulsion when he'd lauded the work with Energy Secretary Regis.

Stand tall.

One. Two. Three. She counted women wearing red as they moved into the dining room.

"I've got this." She stood up straight, shoulders back, chin up. But she didn't believe it. Not for a fifteenth of a second.

"Ladies and gentlemen, a special treat tonight. We are honoring an alumna, and we've asked her to speak so you can hear just how important your donations are and see what kind of a difference they make. Please welcome to the stage one of Lift House's finest success stories, Ashley Barris."

John turned to look at Ashley with surprise, his eyes wide, inquisitive. "You didn't tell me—"

Ashley gave him a shrug, and amidst polite applause, she walked to the podium. She'd been rehearsing this moment in her mind for years. She didn't have notes. This story she knew by heart. She shook the emcee's hand, stepped up to the mic, and took a beat to gaze out at the crowd.

"Sometimes we need help." Her voice was surprisingly calm despite her hammering heart. "Sometimes we find ourselves in a situation where we can't believe life will ever be okay again. Sometimes, in those moments, someone reaches out to help us, and our life is transformed for the better."

Ashley paused and looked around the room. She saw John at their table, beaming at her. She found Luke's dark hair and chiseled silhouette sitting at a table of men in tuxes—colleagues of his? She felt his energy reaching up to her as she stood onstage—pride, curiosity, pain, devotion. Their eyes locked for a moment. She could sense he felt it, too, an almost immediate bridge that spanned between them and dared them to meet each other in the middle. She almost choked. She moved her attention to other faces in the room before going on.

"I'm Ashley Barris, and I am so grateful for this chance to tell you how Lift House saved me from a challenging world. And from myself. This organization gave me tools to go forward, and for the rest of my life, I will be dedicated to finding ways to give back to this incredible nonprofit that has given so much to me and to other young people in Houston."

Ashley had never spoken of her history with Lift House in public before, but she was proud to do so now.

"I grew up in a poor neighborhood in Houston, and though there was violence and crime, I always felt safe at home with my mother and sister. I had wonderful neighbors. But when I was sixteen, a relative moved in with us for a while, and I was no longer safe."

She cleared her throat. "Like many teens who feel scared, I decided to run away."

The huge room was completely silent. Not even the clink of ice in a glass. She closed her eyes for a moment, steadied her breath. "There are over two million homeless youth in this country. I am one of the lucky ones. I didn't need to sell my body for money. I didn't use drugs to escape. I didn't get beat up or raped. Didn't join a gang. Why not? Because when my home became unsafe, I had already heard about Lift House from a friend at school.

"A Lift volunteer, Jacob, had found my friend and some other kids living under a bridge. Jacob offered each of them a blanket and peanut butter sandwiches. He told them about Lift House and urged them to come. Not all of them did, but my friend did. And because she told me about it, I had an exit strategy when my home became unsafe. When I was desperate, Lift House gave me help. When I thought I had no options, Lift House gave me hope." Her breath caught in her throat.

We carry our hope with us until it becomes us. She dared a look at Luke. His eyes glittered in the dim. She felt his full focus on her. She felt as if she were speaking directly to him. "Sometimes we are unable to see we have choices. And so, we run away."

She took a deep breath. "Thanks to Lift House crisis care and their collaboration with local child welfare organizations and legal counsel, I was taken care of. They helped resolve the problems at my home, and I returned to my mother."

She paused as the audience clapped. "While things were being resolved, I lived in short-term housing provided by Lift House and was able to continue school. I had always known my education was my ticket out of poverty. And it was. I got my master's in education. For many years, I taught science in public schools, and now I direct a nonprofit I founded that helps youth not served by conventional classrooms."

The room erupted in spontaneous applause. Ashley saw Luke put his face in his hands. Her chest tightened.

"I've worked as a Lift House volunteer ever since graduating high school. Now, I tutor for the GED, and for over two years, I have mentored a young woman who also wants to be a teacher. Like me when I was her age, she desperately needs someone to believe in her—*especially* when she makes mistakes. Someday, it might be her up here, speaking to this room. Perhaps she will know then what I know now: it is the greatest privilege to give back to this organization that saved my life, that saves so many lives."

Ashley nodded as the room filled with clapping.

"My story could have been so different. I am grateful to the Lift House and to all of you who support it. I am one voice speaking on behalf of many, saying *thank you*. Thank you."

Ashley closed her eyes and bowed her head, and when she looked up again, she could see the whole room standing, cheering. "And now, please welcome Caroline Jones, our executive director." The two women embraced, and Ashley walked down the stairs, returning to her table flushed, relieved, and exhilarated.

"Ashley." John grasped her by both shoulders and pulled her close. "I never knew. You're incredible."

"Thank you." She let him embrace her, then bit her lip and pulled back. She couldn't help herself. Like a sunflower that can't help but turn to the sun, she looked over to see Luke watching them. And he *was* like the sun, brilliant, intense, his gravity pulling her toward him. She wanted to follow her instincts, to run to him, throw her arms around him, kiss him and be kissed by him. She wanted to feel the strong, solid wall of his chest against her cheek, wanted his hands in her hair, on her shoulders, around her waist. She wanted him. So. Much. And the look on his face gutted her. He stood and walked toward the exit.

John followed her gaze. "Let him go, Ashley." His fingers gently turned her face back to his. "Be here," he soothed.

What could she do? She couldn't run after Luke, though every cell in her body screamed at her to do so. Shaken, she turned toward the stage.

Caroline was speaking into the mic now, praising Ashley, and Ashley pretended to listen, but she tuned out until Caroline exclaimed. "We've received an anonymous donation for *one million dollars!*"

What? That donation alone was what they hoped to raise tonight! Ashley whooped and clapped with the rest of the crowd, her eyes sparkling. "I want to hug that person right now."

John smiled at her enthusiasm. "I love seeing you so happy, Ashley."

She returned her attention to Caroline, who was now promoting a new idea for annual gift giving. "This patron suggested a challenge for other donors: instead of buying a luxury item you don't really need, say a new designer gown, consider giving that same value as a donation to Lift House." *Luke. He* did *listen.* She cast a covert look at his empty seat. Tears pricked in her eyes, and she fought them back.

Not only, but also.

The servers brought their dinners as Caroline finished her remarks, but Ashley couldn't eat. She was a jumble of competing emotions.

"What do you think?" John was speaking to her. She had no idea what his question might refer to.

"I'm sorry, John, what were you saying?"

He gave her a wan smile. "I said you don't seem hungry, and perhaps we should go dance instead of sitting here."

"Yes," she agreed quickly, grateful for the chance to *do* something. The rest of the evening passed in a flash. People greeting her, thanking her, congratulating her. A few even offered to further support STEAMEA and handed her their business cards. After another two hours, she was exhausted.

"I know," John suggested as they were dancing. "Let's go back to your place. This has been a big night for you."

"Great idea," she agreed. "On our way out, let's see how the silent auction is going. There are only a few minutes before the bidding stops."

"Sure."

They walked to the table with her Spanish lessons. Last they'd seen, they'd been bid up to $450. The suggested price was $500. Ashley gasped when she saw the last bid.

Five thousand dollars?

There, on the sheet, in familiar cursive, she read the bidder: Luke Dalton. *Holy shit.* She was delighted with the size of the donation, of course, but she felt bought. Then pissed. Then worried. How would she spend ten hours with Luke when just a few moments with him had affected her so? It was hard enough seeing him briefly in a crowded room, much less spending hours with him teaching him Spanish.

"*Artículo popular,*"* John said, obviously bothered. "He's not ready to let you go yet, is he." His eyes darkened.

Ashley sighed. "Why does he have to make this so difficult?" "Oh, Ashley, if you had any inkling of how wonderful you are, you wouldn't be surprised by his actions. He's trying to get you back any way he can. Who could blame him?"

Ashley stared at Luke's name on the sheet as if it could tell her what he was doing and why.

"Come." John offered her his hand. "Let's go home."

---

* Popular item.

By the time John's Porsche pulled up to her apartment, it was nearly midnight. Her thoughts were thoroughly tangled. Luke had come to the event. He'd made an annual donation based on the conversations they'd had. He bought her Spanish lessons. He'd made her whole body more alive with just his presence. This evening had been so difficult. She sighed. There were some feelings so complex they hadn't yet invented a name for them.

And then there was John, charming, kind, supportive, and interested in her? She was so confused about men and her feelings. She wanted nothing more than to be alone.

But she was far from alone. From the corner of her eye, she saw Luke's SUV parked on the street. She could make out his silhouette sitting in the driver's seat. Her poor heart didn't know how to respond. At the same time, she felt it soar up on great wings and fall like a stone off a cliff. *What's he doing here?*

"This is the part where you invite me up," John suggested.

"Oh, John," she demurred, "I'm so tired. Thank you for accompanying me. It was a lovely, lovely night."

"At least let me walk you to your apartment."

"Sure. Please. Of course." He came around and opened her door, and Ashley felt very aware of Luke's eyes watching them.

"M'lady." He offered her his hand and walked her to the building door. She let them in.

When they arrived at her apartment door, Ashley turned to say goodbye, and John immediately put his hands on either side of her, pressing his palms into the door, caging her in. She wasn't alarmed, but she wasn't wanting the kiss she knew was coming, either.

"John." She bit her lip.

"I'd love to kiss you." His face hovered above hers.

His eyes were so dark with longing it did strange things to her belly. But this was not what her heart wanted.

She shook her head, and he stepped back right away. "Okay. No kissing. But I don't want this night to end. What if I come in and we make tea?"

"Good night, John." Ashley was suddenly too exhausted to debate him any longer. "Thank you for a wonderful evening. I need to be alone."

"I understand." He nodded, holding his own hands as if to keep them from grabbing her. "Good night, Ashley. Call me tomorrow?"

"I will."

And with a lilt in his step, he walked away.

Ashley let herself into her apartment and kicked off her shoes, sighing loudly as she rubbed her feet one at a time.

"What a night, Bamba." The cat curled like smoke around her leg.

Without turning on the lights, she walked to the window to see if Luke's SUV was still there.

In the blue light of the streetlamp, she could make out Luke's face staring up into the window. They locked eyes.

"Oh, Luke," she said. A shiver ran through her body, and she put a hand to her heart. "What am I going to do?"

To be continued

Other books by Grace Woods

Grace Woods

Grace Woods is the nom de plume for two female authors brought together by a desire to deliver wildly sensual, unexpected love stories steeped in respect and revelation. They are mentors, mothers, wives, risk takers, businesswomen, avid readers, and lovers of nature. Individually, like the women they write for, they contain multitudes. Together, as Grace Woods, they are a force for telling smart and sexy stories.

For more information, please visit
GraceWoodsRomance.com

Or follow Grace Woods Romance on Facebook,
Instagram and Tik Tok
@gracewoodsromance

Made in the USA
Middletown, DE
27 November 2023

43784852R00229